I0761096

W.E.B. GRIFFIN
DIRECT ACTION

A PRESIDENTIAL AGENT NOVEL

Also by W.E.B. Griffin

HONOR BOUND

HONOR BOUND
BLOOD AND HONOR
SECRET HONOR
DEATH AND HONOR
(and William E. Butterworth IV)
THE HONOR OF SPIES
(and William E. Butterworth IV)
VICTORY AND HONOR
(and William E. Butterworth IV)
EMPIRE AND HONOR
(and William E. Butterworth IV)

BROTHERHOOD OF WAR

THE LIEUTENANTS
THE CAPTAINS
THE MAJORS
THE COLONELS
THE BERETS
THE GENERALS
THE NEW BREED
THE AVIATORS
SPECIAL OPS

THE CORPS

SEMPER FI
CALL TO ARMS
COUNTERATTACK
BATTLEGROUND
LINE OF FIRE
CLOSE COMBAT
BEHIND THE LINES
IN DANGER'S PATH
UNDER FIRE
RETREAT, HELL!

BADGE OF HONOR

MEN IN BLUE
SPECIAL OPERATIONS
THE VICTIM
THE WITNESS
THE ASSASSIN
THE MURDERERS
THE INVESTIGATORS
FINAL JUSTICE
THE TRAFFICKERS
(and William E. Butterworth IV)
THE VIGILANTES
(and William E. Butterworth IV)
THE LAST WITNESS
(and William E. Butterworth IV)
DEADLY ASSETS
(and William E. Butterworth IV)
BROKEN TRUST
(and William E. Butterworth IV)

MEN AT WAR

THE LAST HEROES
THE SECRET WARRIORS
THE SOLDIER SPIES
THE FIGHTING AGENTS
THE SABOTEURS
(and William E. Butterworth IV)
THE DOUBLE AGENTS
(and William E. Butterworth IV)
THE SPYMASTERS
(and William E. Butterworth IV)
THE DEVIL'S WEAPONS
(by Peter Kirsanow)
ZERO OPTION
(by Peter Kirsanow)

PRESIDENTIAL AGENT

BY ORDER OF THE PRESIDENT
THE HOSTAGE
THE HUNTERS
THE SHOOTERS
BLACK OPS
THE OUTLAWS
(and William E. Butterworth IV)
COVERT WARRIORS
(and William E. Butterworth IV)
HAZARDOUS DUTY
(and William E. Butterworth IV)
ROGUE ASSET
(by Andrews and Wilson)

CLANDESTINE OPERATIONS

TOP SECRET
(and William E. Butterworth IV)
THE ASSASSINATION OPTION
(and William E. Butterworth IV)
CURTAIN OF DEATH
(and William E. Butterworth IV)
DEATH AT NUREMBURG
(and William E. Butterworth IV)
THE ENEMY OF MY ENEMY
(and William E. Butterworth IV)

AS WILLIAM E. BUTTERWORTH III

THE HUNTING TRIP

W.E.B. GRIFFIN

DIRECT ACTION

★★★★★ A PRESIDENTIAL AGENT NOVEL ★★★★★

JACK STEWART

G. P. PUTNAM'S SONS
NEW YORK

PUTNAM
— EST. 1838 —
G. P. PUTNAM'S SONS
Publishers Since 1838
An imprint of Penguin Random House LLC
1745 Broadway, New York, NY 10019
penguinrandomhouse.com

LIBRARY OF CONGRESS CATALOGING-IN-PUBLICATION DATA

Names: Stewart, Jack (Novelist) author | Griffin, W. E. B.
Title: W. E. B. Griffin direct action / Jack Stewart.
Other titles: Direct action
Description: New York: G. P. Putnam's Sons, 2025. | Series: A presidential agent novel; 10
Identifiers: LCCN 2025012290 (print) | LCCN 2025012291 (ebook) |
ISBN 9798217046386 (hardcover) | ISBN 9798217046409 (ebook)
Subjects: LCGFT: Thrillers (Fiction) | Fiction | Novels
Classification: LCC PS3619.T4948 W43 2025 (print) | LCC PS3619.T4948 (ebook)
LC record available at https://lccn.loc.gov/2025012290
LC ebook record available at https://lccn.loc.gov/2025012291

Printed in the United States of America
1st Printing

The authorized representative in the EU for product safety and compliance is
Penguin Random House Ireland, Morrison Chambers, 32 Nassau Street,
Dublin D02 YH68, Ireland, https://eu-contact.penguin.ie.

FOR THE LATE

William E. Colby
An OSS Jedburgh First Lieutenant
who became director of the Central Intelligence Agency.

Aaron Bank
An OSS Jedburgh First Lieutenant
who became a colonel and the father of Special Forces.

William R. Corson
A legendary Marine intelligence officer
whom the KGB hated more than any other U.S. intelligence officer—
and not because he wrote the definitive work on them.

René J. Défourneaux
A U.S. Army OSS Second Lieutenant attached to the British SOE
who jumped into occupied France alone and later became
a legendary U.S. Army intelligence officer.

Billy Waugh
A legendary Special Forces Command Sergeant Major who
retired and then went on to hunt down the infamous Carlos the Jackal.
Billy could have terminated Osama bin Laden in the early 1990s
but could not get permission to do so.

FOR THE LIVING

Johnny Reitzel
An Army Special Operations officer who could have terminated
the head terrorist of the seized cruise ship *Achille Lauro*
but could not get permission to do so.

Ralph Peters
An Army intelligence officer
who has written the best analysis of our war against terrorists
and of our enemy that I have ever seen.

AND FOR THE NEW BREED

Marc L
A senior intelligence officer, despite his youth,
who reminds me of Bill Colby more and more each day.

Frank L

A legendary Defense Intelligence Agency officer
who retired and now follows in Billy Waugh's footsteps.

**OUR NATION OWES THESE PATRIOTS
A DEBT BEYOND REPAYMENT.**

I

[ONE]

The Shack on 8th

712 Atlantic Avenue

Virginia Beach, Virginia

1145 29 March 2026

U.S. Army Colonel C.G. Castillo (retired) sat in the driver's seat of the rental Chevrolet Suburban—far more car than he really needed—and looked up through the open sunroof into the clear blue skies overhead. He had made good time on the drive down from Washington, D.C., and was enjoying a few moments of peace in the cool ocean breeze from the top floor of the parking garage.

In truth, he was just dragging his feet. He could have taken a non-stop flight from Ronald Reagan Washington National Airport and already been in Tampa, but instead he elected to make a detour. He had been putting this off for far too long already, and the four-hour drive was just the thing he needed to clear his mind before he said what he came to say.

If he even listens to me.

A flash of gray against the backdrop of blue caught his attention, and he shifted in his seat to sight in on a pair of Navy fighter jets racing low across the beach on their way to Naval Air Station Oceana, two miles away. Even with their throttles pulled back, Castillo still felt their exhaust notes resonating through the SUV and heard more than one car alarm triggered by the jet noise.

It's the sound of freedom, right?

He glanced at his watch, then opened the driver's door and dropped down onto the concrete. Had it been later in the afternoon in the summer, each spot would have probably already been claimed by beachgoers and barhoppers. But before noon on a Sunday in March? He had the place to himself.

Castillo walked to the waist-high wall and leaned over, looking down on the alley separating the garage from The Shack—"an oasis," as its website proclaimed, "smack-dab in the middle of the Virginia Beach oceanfront." Their menu boasted typical mid-Atlantic offerings of salmon, crab cakes, yellowfin tuna, and shrimp. But Castillo hadn't come for seafood or lawn games. He turned away from the wall and headed for the stairs.

His muscles and joints ached, as much from the havoc wreaked on his fifty-seven-year-old body by the four-hour car drive as from all the running and gunning he had done in the Sudan, trying to keep up with a man almost half his age. He had done it. But his body had paid the price.

Then again, Pick was far from an average thirty-year-old. The legacy Marine was a MARSOC Raider and next up to replace Castillo. But, as he had told Marty Fleiss the day before, the kid simply wasn't ready to be the Presidential Agent—yet.

Castillo reached the alley at street level and turned right, making for The Shack's main entrance on Atlantic Avenue. He was there to meet with another kid—one Castillo wasn't sure would even show—but just being there after decades of being absent had to count for something, right?

Out of habit, he pressed his arm against his side and felt for the comforting heft of his full-sized 1911 pistol concealed in a shoulder holster under his travel shirt—thankful that the state of Virginia recognized his Texas resident concealed carry license. But even if that weren't the case, Castillo still had a letter from the President of the United States in his back pocket attesting to the fact that he was "operating on a mission of vital national importance with grave consequences."

Not that he planned on needing it, but he was glad he had it.

I probably should've given the letter back to Marty.

Traffic was sparse on Atlantic Avenue when Castillo exited the alley, but he still caught himself scanning the cars and pedestrians as if he were on the streets of Baghdad or Khartoum. Not the military-heavy region of the Hampton Roads. But living on the front lines of America's war against terror for so long had left a bad taste in his mouth.

Castillo was still half a block from The Shack's main entrance when the well-honed hairs on the back of his neck bristled and brought him up short. Castillo's confident gait halted, and he squinted through rays of late-morning sunlight at two young men standing in an alcove across the street.

Who are these guys?

They had light skin and sandy hair, and appeared to be of Eurasian ethnicity. But that in itself didn't trigger any internal alarms. Still, something about them seemed off. He had almost dismissed it as overworked paranoia—a hangover from his past week spent in the Sudan—but then a gust of cool wind cut through his thin shirt, and his skin broke out in gooseflesh.

Jackets. Why are both men wearing jackets?

Late March wasn't overly warm in Virginia Beach, but it definitely wasn't cold enough to require heavy work coats that were bulging and appeared to be concealing several layers of clothing underneath. Castillo had long since learned to pay attention to the mundane and seemingly inconsequential details when something didn't smell right. And the two men across the street did *not* smell right to Castillo. Not right at all.

See something, say something. That's what they always say, Charley.

Castillo gritted his teeth, looked both ways, then stepped out into the street while slipping his hand through the flap in his loose-fitting shirt, preparing to draw his pistol. Though he didn't relish the idea. No matter what kind of letter he carried in his pocket—or who it was from—it would take a lot more than that to keep him out of jail if bullets started flying and people got hurt. But he couldn't just sit on the sidelines and do nothing.

Recognizing he was succumbing to tunnel vision, Castillo forced himself to widen the aperture on his situational awareness. He scanned along the street in both directions, searching for a law enforcement presence or innocent bystanders who might be caught in a potential crossfire. Looking over his left shoulder—past the entrance to The Shack—he saw a trim, dark-haired young man being led by a large dog on its leash.

Castillo froze.

Max?

He recognized the rough-coated appearance of a Bouvier des Flandres but knew that the grayish-black dog couldn't have been his longtime companion. His Max—the dog that had stood by his side through the worst moments of his life—was buried in a serene patch of land on his family's ranch outside Uvalde, Texas. Not alive and well here in Virginia Beach.

That's not Max. But he sure looks like him.

He glanced up into the eyes of the young man holding Not-Max's leash and saw a flash of recognition there. Then the eyes quickly darkened with something else. Anger? Hurt? Betrayal?

Before Castillo could process the emotion, movement out of the corner of his eye drew his attention back to the pair of young men he had seen standing in the shadows of the beachfront hotel's entrance. All thoughts of a cold beer over lunch at The Shack were forgotten in a blink when they threw open their jackets and revealed M16 assault rifles slung tightly across tactical vests that were adorned with several spare magazines.

Oh, shit!

"Charley!" a man's voice cried out.

Castillo recognized it, but he was already yanking the pistol free from its shoulder holster and presenting it to the first target. There was no time to let disbelief stay his hand, and he pressed back on the trigger as the Novak front sight post settled on center mass.

The handgun barked, but he barely noticed the powerful .45 ACP recoil. He let the trigger reset as the sights settled, then pressed back again and sent another jacketed hollow-point into the gunman.

Even as his target fell backward, Castillo's heart sank when he realized that the sharp staccato of automatic gunfire raking the beachfront appeared to be coming from multiple directions. In the distance, he could hear shrill screams and shouts of alarm echoing over the deep thumping of blood pulsing in his brain. But he tuned it out while shifting his aim to the second gunman. Before his sights had settled, he pressed back on the trigger a third time, already knowing he had rushed his shot.

The man spun and leveled the rifle on Castillo just as he pressed back on the trigger again. But this time, his aim was true. The man's head snapped back and showered the air behind him in red.

Two tangos down.

As he had been trained, Castillo drew his pistol in close to his body and scanned left and right for additional threats. He knew more than one amped-up police officer had reholstered his service weapon too soon after engaging a threat and paid for the mistake with his life. Castillo wasn't about to do the same.

"Charley!" the man's voice cried out again.

Castillo hesitated. From over his shoulder, he heard the stomping of feet of somebody running toward him at full speed, and he spun to see the dog's owner with a stricken look on his face.

"Stay back, Randy! There might be—"

A searing pain slammed into his upper back and spun him around like a dervish, knocking him off balance. He gritted his teeth and pushed the pistol outward with one hand, straining to find the shooter before it was too late.

"Behind you!" Randy yelled.

Disoriented and confused, Castillo pivoted and saw two new shooters, similarly dressed, racing from the hotel. He whipped his pistol up in their direction and squeezed the trigger as fast as he could, hoping for just one of his rushed shots to find its mark. But the dark-clad men continued running at him, spitting fire from their rifles.

Again, something slammed into Castillo, and he staggered. He opened his mouth to shout another warning for Randy to run, but nothing came out. Fear gripped him when he realized he couldn't breathe, and he collapsed to his knees, struggling to keep his pistol pointed up at the shooters. The sound of gunfire was quickly drowned out by the rhythmic beating of his heart and the muffled shouts of men surrounding him.

Castillo toppled forward to the ground and rolled onto his side, looking down the street in disbelief as dozens of dark-clad shooters fired indiscriminately into crowded stores and restaurants. But his vision blurred and his horrific view of what was sure to become a mass casualty event began to dim. He tried lifting his custom 1911 to stay in the fight, but his strength was gone. He was done.

How many died here today?

His eyes closed as the sounds of gunfire and screams faded into silence.

Is this how I'm to be reunited with my Svetlana?

[TWO]

Scott Natatorium

U.S. Naval Academy

Annapolis, Maryland

1230 29 March 2026

United States Marine Captain P.K. McCoy Jr. stood tall with his back to the room, a sly grin hidden underneath his bushy auburn beard. It had been almost ten years since he'd stood there with his classmates—almost in the exact same spot in the coach's office—and added his own bobblehead to the coach's obscenely large and unusual collection. He reached up and flicked miniature Second Lieutenant McCoy's white dress cap and chuckled when his head began to bob.

"Pick!" a voice called out.

He spun and saw Coach Luis Nicolao, a member of the class of 1992, walking into the room with his ruddy complexion and trademark smile plastered on his face.

"Hey, coach."

Luis gestured to a pair of chairs arranged in front of his large oak desk. "Have a seat."

Before miniature Pick's head had stopped bobbing, the real Pick took his seat across from the all-time leading scorer in Academy history and relaxed in the large armchair. "I hope I'm not interrupting anything—"

"Not at all. We're just getting back from spring break and are putting on a clinic this weekend. You know things aren't very busy around here this time of year. Just gearing up for graduation and the next recruiting season."

Pick remembered.

"But I assume you didn't come here just to catch up on the state of Navy water polo."

"Actually, I did."

Luis cocked his head and studied his former protégé. "Uh-huh."

Pick laughed. "Seriously. I was just in the area and thought I'd stop by. Haven't had much time to visit my alma mater since graduating."

The coach ran a hand along his smoothly shaved face and gestured at Pick's exact opposite. "Well, based on your grooming standards, I'm guessing you've either moved on from the Marine Corps or are in some secret squirrel outfit doing high-speed shit."

Pick laughed. "Something like that."

"Seriously, what are you doing now? Married? Kids?"

He knew most of his classmates had already settled down and married their ring dance dates or local girls they had met in Pensacola, San Diego, Norfolk, or wherever else the Navy and Marine Corps had sent them after graduation. But he didn't take offense to the question. He knew the coach viewed his former players like family. "Well . . ."

Luis leaned back in his seat with a sigh. "That long of a story, huh?"

"No, not really. Officially, I'm still in the Marine Corps and based down at Camp Lejeune in North Carolina."

"Officially?"

Pick nodded. "Officially."

"And unofficially?"

Pick stroked his beard. “Now, that story’s a little bit longer and not one I think I’m able to get into.”

“Secret squirrel shit,” Luis repeated. “I knew it.”

I doubt you’d believe me if I told you.

There was no way he could tell his former coach that he had been yanked from his Raider team in Iraq and brought back to the United States to meet with President Natalie Cohen. No way he could even begin to explain how he had been brought in under the tutelage of a former Army aviator and Green Beret—a West Pointer with a Distinguished Flying Cross, no less. And absolutely no way he could divulge to Luis that he had been on the ground in the Sudan the week before, rescuing Secretary of State Frank Malone.

“It doesn’t matter,” Pick said. “I’m thinking about transferring back to my old unit anyway.”

“Which is?”

“MARSOC. Second Marine Raider Battalion.”

Luis craned his neck to look over his shoulder as Moose, his fluffy and charismatic cream-colored Aussiedoodle, plodded into the room and sauntered up to Pick. The coach’s dog was a fixture on the pool deck and as much a part of the Navy water polo team as any of the players were. Pick reached down and scratched behind Moose’s ears.

“Why am I not surprised you became a Raider?”

Pick saw the humor in his coach’s eyes. “Because you know my family?”

Luis leaned forward in his chair. “Yeah, and because you’re part of *our* family, Pick. So, tell me what’s really bothering you.”

Moose nuzzled Pick as if to underscore the coach’s sentiment.

“My entire life, I knew I would grow up to be a Marine.” He looked over his shoulder at the Second Lieutenant Pick bobblehead doll and remembered the pride he felt putting on the Blue-White

Dress uniform for the first time at graduation. "I think my dad gave me a Mameluke sword around the time when most other dads gave their sons baseball bats."

Luis chuckled but didn't say anything.

"And I *love* being a Marine. I love the history. The tradition. I love being part of something bigger than myself." Pick looked around the coach's office. "The way I loved playing for you as a member of this team."

"That's what this brotherhood is all about, Pick," Luis said. "Some of us graduate to become surface warfare officers—"

"Like you."

Luis nodded. "And some of us become submariners or pilots. Some of us even go to BUD/S and become SEALs—"

"And later write books."

Luis ignored him. "And some of us become Marines. But we're all part of the same brotherhood."

Pick had heard this speech before. Most collegiate student-athletes are part of something only for as long as they're playing the game. But those lucky enough to play for a team at one of the service academies are part of something that lasts well beyond their graduation.

"The brotherhood of war," Pick said.

Before the coach could respond, Moose dropped a tennis ball at Pick's feet as if to say, *If you're done feeling sorry for yourself, can we go play catch now?*

But Luis wasn't done. "You know, wearing a uniform doesn't make you who you are. I'd bet that even if you never put on a Marine uniform again, you'd still live by their core values."

Honor, courage, and commitment.

"Are you saying I should get out?"

Luis shook his head, reminding Pick of the bobblehead dolls on the shelf behind him. "What I'm saying is that you need to do what you think is right. As long as you're living by the values you were raised on—the values that were ingrained in you here—you'll always be a Marine."

"Once a Marine, always a Marine," Pick said, echoing the popular sentiment.

"Semper Fi."

[THREE]

The Oval Office

The White House

1600 Pennsylvania Avenue NW

Washington, D.C.

1245 29 March 2026

President Natalie Cohen sat with her back to the *Resolute* desk and stared at the miniature television encased in a golden frame, thus making it inconspicuous among the framed photographs adorning the table. Whenever she found herself alone in the office and free from the prying eyes of the press, she often had the television turned on and tuned to a twenty-four-hour news channel.

Sometimes she listened to pundits debate, just to get a read on how the people were viewing her fledgling presidency. Other times, like now, the television gave her a jump on breaking events before her staff even had the opportunity to brief her. It was ironic—and unfortunate—that her Director of National Intelligence, Marty Fleiss, was there to brief her on a separate matter when the news broke.

"How could this happen, Marty?"

She spun away from the television and looked up at the retired general and former deputy director of the CIA. But he only shook his head in mild disbelief.

"I don't know, Madam President."

She had been in the office for only two months and had already been blindsided by an event that tested her mettle as Commander in Chief. When Secretary of State Frank Malone had been kidnapped while on a diplomatic mission to Egypt, she had been forced to abandon her platform of transparency and bring Charley Castillo back from retirement to serve once more as Presidential Agent.

Cohen calmly folded her hands on top of the oak desk, exhibiting a calmness contrary to how she actually felt. "Marty, you are my Director of National Intelligence."

"Yes, Madam President."

"And we had no inkling that something like this was in the works?"

Instead of answering, Fleiss averted his gaze and looked over her shoulder at the television on the table behind her. She closed her eyes, having already seen enough of the news footage to know that the mass shooting in Virginia Beach wasn't just another act of a deranged individual who had easy access to guns. It wasn't a crime of passion or opportunity, like those that had become all too commonplace on America's streets. Cohen knew it was an act of terrorism—what she was sure would become the deadliest terrorist attack on American soil since September 11, 2001.

"Madam President, every day we assess and evaluate hundreds of threats. But we had no intel whatsoever about a potential attack in Virginia Beach."

And the largest and most capable intelligence community in the world knew nothing about it. Great.

"Where's Castillo?"

Fleiss looked surprised but quickly recovered. "He left here earlier this morning for MacDill Air Force Base in Tampa to begin his next assignment."

Cohen nodded but didn't immediately press for details. She had placed the DNI in charge of Charley Castillo, and she prided herself on letting people manage their resources without her interfering. But sometimes she knew she just needed to take the bull by the horns and steer them in the right direction.

"Don't you think we should put him on this?"

"Madam President, maybe we should allow the FBI to complete their investigation and determine what happened first."

Cohen clenched her jaw, inwardly seething as she attempted yet another round of four-count tactical breathing to calm herself. "I think it's pretty clear what happened, Marty. What's *not clear* is how this could happen right under our noses without anybody catching even a whiff. Not the CIA. Not the DIA. Not the FBI or NSA. Not even Homeland Security, for Christ's sake. Nobody."

"Yes, Madam—"

She cut him off. "I want you to recall Castillo and send him to Virginia Beach to find out if this was a one-off or only the start of something bigger."

When Fleiss didn't answer, she felt her blood pressure tick up a notch until she noticed that the DNI hadn't heard her question because he was focused on the television behind her.

"Marty!"

He gave a little shake of his head to break free from his momentary paralysis, then pointed at the golden-framed television. Cohen felt a chill drop down her spine as she slowly turned to face what she wished she could erase from her mind—a scene that would take years to fade from the nation's collective memory. She turned up the volume and listened to a reporter delivering the most current—and probably inaccurate—information.

". . . authorities have identified him as Carlos Guillermo Castillo, a retired Army Special Forces colonel, who we have confirmed was not licensed to carry a firearm by the Commonwealth of . . ."

"Castillo did this?" Her mouth suddenly became dry.

Fleiss shushed her. "Just listen!"

If she hadn't been so shocked at hearing the reporter mention Castillo by name, she might have taken offense at Marty's uncharacteristic brusqueness. But Cohen's mind was already spiraling at the thought of her Presidential Agent committing such a heinous act, and she almost missed what the journalist said after she continued her report on the attack.

". . . we are being told that Castillo shot and killed three of the attackers before himself being shot multiple times . . ."

"He was shot?" Cohen was embarrassed that she felt relieved.

"Yes . . ."

"What happened?"

But Fleiss ignored her question and pulled out his phone to place a call. "This is Director Fleiss . . . I'm with the President . . . A retired Army officer was shot in Virginia Beach . . . Carlos Castillo . . . I need to know his condition and what hospital he was taken to . . . Yes, immediately . . . Call me back."

"Marty . . ."

He swallowed before answering her. "We're going to get answers, Madam President."

"What are we going to do?"

Cohen turned away from the television and slumped low in her seat. She had felt helpless after hearing the first reports of the terrorist attack. But with her Presidential Agent injured and out of commission, she felt completely lost.

"May I suggest we call in Captain McCoy?"

"Castillo's new Marine partner?"

Fleiss nodded. "Yes, Madam President. You picked him as Charley's successor."

"On General McNab's recommendation," she clarified. "And, if I recall correctly, Castillo believed he wasn't ready to step into the role just yet."

Fleiss looked up at the television again as a subtle reminder. "With all due respect, Madam President, circumstances sometimes prevent us from having the luxury of waiting until we're ready."

Cohen wasn't sure if Fleiss was talking about her ability to lead the country as President or McCoy's ability to serve as Presidential Agent. But maybe they were one and the same. "What do we really know about Pick McCoy?"

II

Summer 2013

[ONE]

Alumni Hall

U.S. Naval Academy

Annapolis, Maryland

0615 27 June 2013

Eighteen-year-old P.K. McCoy Jr. stood in a long line of strangers, looking up at a large Naval Academy crest affixed above the Isherwood Entrance of Alumni Hall. His shaggy auburn hair had already been bleached by the sun, and he wore a lightweight short-sleeved collared shirt tucked into a pair of khaki shorts. As he looked around at the other candidates, he noticed that it seemed to be the preferred uniform of choice.

"Nervous?" a voice asked from behind him.

Pick, as he was known to his friends, turned around and noticed a short girl with long, dark hair and rosy cheeks smiling up at him. "Not really. Are you?"

"I'm terrified," she said, then laughed to hide the slight tremor in her voice.

He smiled back at her. "Actually, me, too."

The girl might have been scared, but she certainly wasn't shy. She thrust her hand out to him. "My name's Hannah. From Savannah."

He shook it. "On purpose?"

The corners of her mouth twitched downward as if to hide her smile. "My mom said they're going to make us memorize everybody else's names and where they're from."

Pick looked behind her at the long line of candidates snaking up the sidewalk along Decatur Road. "All of them?"

This time there was no hiding her smile. "Just the ones in our company. I thought it might make it easier to remember my hometown if I introduced myself like that. What's your name? Where are you from?"

Nope, she's not shy at all.

"Pick McCoy," he said. "Uh, from San Diego."

"It doesn't rhyme."

"No, it doesn't. I'm sorry I don't have an easy way of remembering where I'm from."

The line ahead of them moved, and Hannah gestured for Pick to keep up with the group. "Not many places rhyme with Pick, I don't think."

"I guess not."

"Is that a nickname?"

"Sort of. It's short for Pickering."

Hannah giggled, then quickly wiped her smile off her face. "I'm sorry, I shouldn't have laughed. You're probably named for somebody famous in your family."

"My dad," Pick replied. "I'm a junior."

"Wait, your dad's name is Pickering, too?"

The line moved again, and again Pick shuffled forward a few steps. But he was thankful for Hannah's gregarious personality to keep his mind off what awaited them on the other side of the double doors.

"My grandpa named him after his best friend in the war."

"Which war was that?"

"World War Two," Pick replied. "He was a Marine pilot and flew Wildcats with the Cactus Air Force on Guadalcanal."

"Your grandpa?"

"His friend."

"Was your dad a Marine, too?"

Pick nodded.

"Pilot?"

Again, Pick nodded.

"And you're going to be a Marine pilot, too?"

Pick hesitated, then shook his head.

[TWO]

Pick's eyes glassed over, and he stood with his back against the wall, running his hand across the fresh stubble covering his scalp. Knowing they would shave his head on I-Day wasn't the same as having a barber named Sarge run clippers through his thick hair without regard for his comfort or appearance. His eyes had teared up as much from seeing his auburn locks fall to the ground as from Sarge's rough treatment. Probably more so.

Well, there's no turning back now, Pick.

But that wasn't totally true. He knew he could drop out anytime before his first class in the fall of his junior year and not owe Uncle Sam a nickel. Even if the elder McCoy hadn't made it clear that quitting wasn't an option, Pick had made his choice and wasn't about to return home with his tail tucked between his legs. He smiled at the thought of graduating from the Naval Academy in four years to follow in his father's—and grandfather's—footsteps and become a Marine.

You just have to make it through the summer and take it one day at a—

"Something funny, candidate?"

Pick's smile disappeared. The midshipman speaking to him was dressed in summer whites with two diagonal stripes on his shoulder boards and a red name tag above his right breast pocket. "Uh, no, sir?"

"Is that a question?"

Pick swallowed to buy himself time, scrambling to remember his basic responses. "No, sir."

"Sir, no, sir," the midshipman corrected.

"Sir, no, sir."

"Guess you were just thinking about your girlfriend in a bikini, sunning herself on the beach back home. Is that about right, McCoy?"

The upperclassman couldn't have known he had broken up with his high school sweetheart only the week before and was probably just trying to get a rise out of him to make him break character. Pick bit the inside of his cheek to keep his hot-tempered Irish blood in check. All he needed to do was keep his mouth shut long enough for the detailer to get bored with him and move on to his next victim.

Pick remembered this time to lead with the honorific. "Sir, no, sir."

"McCoy . . ." The detailer scrunched up his face, then snapped his fingers as if something had triggered his memory. "That's it. Not your girlfriend. You were thinking about your cousin."

"Sir, no, sir."

"No? You're not from Kentucky?"

The comment caught Pick off guard. "Uh, no, sir."

"Sir, no, sir," the midshipman corrected again.

"Sir, no, sir."

The upperclassman shrugged, but his strained look of concentration had been replaced with one of humor. "Well, good. The last thing I need is for one of my plebes to be the great-great-grand-something of 'Ole Ran'l' come here to settle an ancient feud on the banks of the Severn."

"Sir, no, sir." It took Pick slightly less time to figure out what the hell the detailer was talking about. "I don't know any Hatfields, either, sir."

The humorous expression vanished, and the midshipman's face contorted with anger. "Did I *fucking* ask if you knew any *fucking* Hatfields, McCoy?"

"Sir, no—"

"All right, listen up, candidates!" The midshipman wheeled away from McCoy and addressed the group assembled in the hallway. "My name is Midshipman Second Class Richardson. You will address me as 'Mr. Richardson' or 'sir.' I have been given the unfortunate task of taking you complete wastes of space and turning you into something that at least resembles a midshipman by the time you take your oath of office at the end of the day. Is that clear?"

"Sir, yes, sir!" the candidates shouted in unison.

"Let's start with the basics. Attention on deck!"

A few candidates recognized the command and shifted in place until approximating the position of attention. Pick immediately brought his heels together, remembering one of the few things his father had taught him about military life.

"Not bad," Richardson said, walking along the line of candidates to inspect their posture.

Each candidate wore a uniform known as "white works," consisting of navy-blue athletic shorts and a white, blue-rimmed T-shirt underneath stark white trousers and a tunic that made Pick feel like the sailor from a Cracker Jack box. A white duty belt with a silver buckle completed the ensemble and was wrapped around his trim waist.

"Anytime you are indoors, you will be uncovered," Richardson said, snatching Pick's blue-rimmed Dixie Cup out of his hand and pressing it against his right thigh with his fingers spread inside. "You will doff your cover upon entering any building and will hold it like this. Is that clear?"

"Sir, yes, sir!" the group answered again, feeling more confident in their responses.

The detailer tossed the cover back to Pick and moved on to the next lesson. "One exception to this rule is when you are standing the watch. For instructional purposes, you may don your covers now."

Pick placed his Dixie Cup on top of his head and made several small adjustments until he thought it wouldn't fall off. Then he dropped his hands to his sides and resumed the position of attention while waiting for the detailer to inspect his handiwork.

Richardson walked along the line and nodded with approval until he came to Pick.

"Jesus *fucking* Christ. You're going to make this a long day for me, McCoy."

Pick kept his eyes fixed straight ahead—in what they called "the boat"—and waited for the detailer to expand on his general criticism of Pick's lackluster performance.

"Candidate McCoy, may I make an adjustment to your cover?"

"Sir, yes, sir," Pick replied.

Richardson squared off in front of Pick and plucked the Dixie Cup from his head and canted it forward. "Place your index and middle fingers together and rest them on the bridge of your nose."

Pick did so and felt Richardson tilt the cover forward until the sweatband rested on his brow, two fingers above his nose.

"This is the correct manner of wearing your cover, McCoy."

"Sir, yes, sir."

Richardson moved on to the next unfortunate soul and Pick swallowed. Not even one day in, and he was already regretting his decision to leave the beaches of sunny San Diego for Bancroft Hall in humid Annapolis.

What have I done?

[THREE]

T-Court

U.S. Naval Academy

Annapolis, Maryland

1830 27 June 2013

Pick held up his right hand and squinted through the brilliance of the sea of white uniforms surrounding him. He and his classmates stood in neat rows in the middle of the large central courtyard and looked up at the Commandant of Midshipmen as he swore them in. It was a stark contrast to the organized chaos of just twelve hours earlier when they had approached the Isherwood Entrance at Alumni Hall, and he could hardly believe what had already taken place. Pick knew that Induction Day was only the first step. But it was a *big* first step.

". . . And that you will well and faithfully discharge the duties of the office on which you are about to enter, so help you God?"

"I DO!" the candidates shouted as one.

It didn't matter that Pick had been born not long after his father's transfer from El Toro to the Marine Corps Air Station in Miramar. It didn't matter that he had attended countless ceremonies and more than a few funerals for his father's fellow Marines. And it didn't matter that he had grown up knowing that one day he would also become a Marine. He still felt a chill roll down his spine as he affirmed his oath and officially took that big first step to realizing his dreams.

Backdropped by a chorus of cheers, Pick and his classmates were dismissed from their formation and broke ranks to meet with friends and family who had come to support them. Everywhere Pick looked, he saw blankets spread out in the grass along Stribling Walk with anxious mothers and proud fathers patiently waiting for their plebes to find them.

But to Pick, it was just a sea of strangers.

"You're still here."

He turned and saw Hannah's smiling face, recognizable despite her short hair. "So are you."

"Come on. I want to introduce you to my mom," Hannah said, taking Pick's hand in hers and pulling him from the redbrick walkway onto the grass toward the Herndon Monument. "Aren't your parents here?"

Pick nodded. "I just haven't found them yet."

"Well, this won't take long."

Pick got the feeling Hannah wasn't used to being told no. And despite the fact he hadn't gotten over Cate—who was going into her senior year at Mira Mesa—he couldn't help but enjoy Hannah holding his hand.

Simmer down, Pick. She's just another plebe.

"Mom!" Hannah yelled, releasing Pick's hand and breaking into a jog while waving at a beautiful older woman with perfectly coiffed dark hair. The woman saw Hannah approaching and beamed, holding both of her toned arms out wide and waiting for her daughter to reach her.

"I am *so proud* of you," the woman said. She wrapped her arms around Hannah and pulled her into a tight hug. For her part, Hannah didn't seem to mind.

"Thanks, Mom." She broke away and gestured at Pick. "This is one of my classmates, Pick from San Diego."

"That doesn't rhyme," her mom said.

"No, ma'am, it doesn't," he said, holding out his hand. "Pick McCoy."

"Paige Rosen," she said, taking his hand and giving it a firm shake while looking over his shoulder. "Where's your family? Are you alone?

They didn't come? Oh, you poor thing! Well, you just have a seat right here and spend your time with us."

Pick opened his mouth several times, but she never gave him the chance to explain that he just hadn't found them yet. "You two could be sisters," Pick said.

"Well, aren't you just the sweetest."

"His parents are here, Mom," Hannah said. "I just dragged him over to meet you."

Mrs. Rosen looked perplexed and gestured at the crowd. "Well, then where are they? Go, sweet boy. They must be anxious to give you a big hug and a kiss."

I doubt that very much.

"It was a pleasure meeting you, ma'am," Pick said.

"Please," she said. "Call me Paige."

Hannah ushered Pick away from their little patch of grass before her mother could waylay him any longer. "I'll see you at formation, Pick from San Diego."

Despite himself, he smiled. "See you there, Hannah from Savannah."

Pick turned away from Hannah and her mother to resume scanning the crowd for his parents. He was starting to regret his decision not to have a personal swearing-in ceremony in Smoke Hall like other plebes with family members who were active, reserve, or retired service members. But he was tired of living in his father's shadow and wanted to avoid drawing even more attention to himself.

After all, he was probably the only plebe whose dad was a fighter ace.

"Junior!"

Pick stopped in his tracks and slowly turned to face his old man.

The elder McCoy had a full head of silver hair styled in his characteristic high-and-tight and stood with his back straight and his arms folded across his chest. He easily stood out as one of the few parents not decked out in Navy blue and gold. And one of the few who wasn't smiling.

"General," he said.

"My boy!" Pick's mom said, pushing aside his father to pull him in for a hug. "We are *so* proud of you! Aren't we, Pick?"

Midshipman McCoy glanced at his father over his mom's shoulder and caught a subtle nod of approval. "Yes, ma'am, we are."

"Thanks, Mom."

"We should've done the private ceremony," the general said.

But his mom came to his defense and turned and swatted at his dad's muscular arm. "Now, we've been over this. He wants to do things his own way."

"Who was that girl you were talking to?" General McCoy asked, changing the subject.

Pick groaned. "Just one of my classmates."

"What's her name?" his mother pressed.

"Hannah Rosen. She's from Savannah, Georgia."

"Hannah from Savannah," the general quipped.

Pick shouldn't have been surprised that his father had just as quickly come up with the same technique for memorizing her name and hometown. His whole life, Pick's father had stressed the importance of being able to instantly recall seemingly mundane details.

"Yes, sir," Pick said.

At last, General McCoy dropped his arms to his sides and smiled, apparently satisfied that his only son was taking the opportunity to well and faithfully live up to their family name. "Your mom and I are proud of you, son."

It was a rare comment of affirmation from the normally stoic retired Marine officer.

"Thank you, sir—"

"McCoy!"

Both men turned at the shout, but their reactions were vastly different. His father broke into a rare but genuine smile, while Pick came to attention.

"Well, if it isn't Jim 'Bull' Hawkins," General McCoy said. "How the hell are ya?"

Pick kept his eyes in the boat as his father pulled the three-star vice admiral in for a hug and slapped him on the back.

"Why didn't you arrange for a private swearing-in ceremony?" the admiral asked.

Pick swallowed.

His father turned to look at him. "Junior didn't want one."

As if the admiral had just noticed Midshipman Fourth Class McCoy for the first time, he turned to look at Pick. "This your boy?"

Remembering the lesson Mr. Richardson had taught them on saluting, Pick quickly brought his right hand up to his brow and saluted. Admiral Hawkins returned the salute.

"Pick, this is Vice Admiral Bull Hawkins," his father said. "He's the Superintendent of the Naval Academy."

Great . . . my dad's friends with the Supe.

"Pleased to meet you, Admiral."

"Are you having a good time, son?"

Pick wasn't sure how to answer that. Of course he wasn't having a good time. He had just been through the longest twelve hours of his life, and he knew it was only going to get worse once they marched up the steps and disappeared inside Bancroft Hall. But he knew a three-star admiral didn't want to hear the truth. "Sir, yes, sir."

The admiral and his father exchanged mirthful glances.

"Well, I doubt that very much. But I appreciate your positive attitude just the same."

General McCoy chuckled at that. "Bull was one of my students in the Phantom before going on to fly the Tomcat. Apparently, he did all right for himself."

"Nothing like your dad," Hawkins said. "He was already a legend by the time I got my wings. I'm sure you can imagine my surprise when I showed up for my first familiarization flight in the F-4 and my instructor was a certified ace with five confirmed kills in Vietnam."

Pick's father had developed a solid reputation in the Navy and Marine Corps fighter community, but he was most respected for his humility. Something most fighter pilots lacked. "I just got lucky," General McCoy said. "Not like Bull here, who went on to be the CO of TOPGUN."

Before the admiral could rebut his father's statement, a lieutenant with a braided gold loop hanging from one shoulder leaned in and whispered something into his ear. The admiral nodded his understanding. "Guess we need to be on our way. It was great seeing you again, Pick."

"You, too, Bull."

The two men shook hands and the easy smile on his father's face disappeared.

"Welcome to the Naval Academy, son," Admiral Hawkins said. "I expect good things from you."

That's what I'm afraid of.

[FOUR]

Bancroft Hall

U.S. Naval Academy

Annapolis, Maryland

1930 27 June 2013

Pick raced up the stairs and into the wide hallway with his eyes fixed on the back of the plebe in front of him. All around, shouts of "Go Navy, sir!" and "Beat Army, sir!" echoed off the walls as his fellow plebes made ninety-degree turns on polished stainless-steel plates set into the floor. He tried mentally mapping his position in the sprawling dormitory, but at best could only figure he was somewhere in the sixth wing and needed to get to his room in fourth.

"Mr. McCoy," a voice called out.

Pick came to a halt at hearing Richardson's voice, and the plebe hot on his heels narrowly avoided a collision by jinking to the side at the last moment. His classmate hesitated for a second, then continued "chopping" down the hall—a movement that fell somewhere between a fast jog and a dead sprint.

"Pleber, halt!" Richardson said, his sights momentarily set on Pick's classmate.

The upperclassman stepped into view, wearing Navy-blue physical training shorts and a bright yellow T-shirt with his class crest on the front. He ambled up to the plebe who had come to a stop in front of Pick.

"Were you just going to leave your classmate behind?"

"Sir, no, sir!"

Richardson's voice rose in volume. "Then where *the fuck* were you going?"

"Sir . . ."

Even though his classmate's intentions clearly had been to leave Pick to face the detailer's wrath on his own, Pick couldn't help but feel sorry for him. They were all in this together and doing the best they could to figure out how to survive the summer with as little pain as possible.

But Richardson had made his point. "Shove off."

The plebe hesitated. "Sir, this midshipman respectfully requests permission to remain with—"

"I said, 'shove off.'"

"Sir, aye, aye, sir."

And just like that, Pick was alone again.

Well, shit.

Richardson watched the plebe disappear around a corner with a half-hearted "Beat Army, sir!" then turned to face Pick.

"Well, if it isn't my favorite plebe, Pickering McCoy."

Pick wasn't sure if the comment warranted one of his five basic responses, so he kept his mouth shut and his eyes in the boat.

"You wouldn't happen to be related to a *General* Pickering McCoy, would you?"

"Sir, yes, sir."

Richardson pursed his lips with apparent satisfaction. "Well, I'll be damned. Your father?"

"Sir, yes, sir."

Robertson hailed another detailer who was walking by and observing the exchange with some amusement. "Hey, Doug, this is General McCoy's kid."

"Who's that?"

Richardson seemed aghast. "Who's General *Pickering* McCoy? The former Deputy Commandant for Aviation? Marine Corps F-4 Phantom pilot and Vietnam fighter ace?"

Doug only shrugged and continued walking.

Richardson looked back at Pick. "Some people just don't care about history."

Again, Pick wasn't sure the comment warranted a response.

"But I've been thinking about the name Pickering . . ."

Uh-oh.

"Ever hear of the Cactus Air Force?" Richardson asked, then smacked his palm against his forehead before Pick could answer. "What am I thinking? *Of course* you've heard of the Cactus Air Force. There's no way the son of the DC Air and fighter ace wouldn't know the history of Marine Corps aviation."

Pick remained silent.

"Am I right?"

"Sir, yes, sir."

"So, now I'm curious . . . Were you named after Malcom Pickering? Marine Corps F4F Wildcat pilot and World War Two fighter ace?"

Shit.

Midshipmen are persons of integrity: They stand for that which is right. They tell the truth and ensure that the truth is known. They do not lie.

But maybe I should.

"Well?" Richardson pressed.

"Sir, yes, sir."

The detailer clapped his hands together like Pick had just told him he'd won the lottery. "I'll be damned. Named for a fighter ace. Son of a fighter ace. McCoy, you probably think you were born for this, don't you?"

Pick *did* think he was born for this, but there was no way he could say so. Richardson obviously thought Pick believed he was some kind of leatherneck nobility who planned on breezing through Annapolis on his way to Pensacola and eventually into the cockpit of a Marine F/A-18 Hornet or F-35 Lightning II Joint Strike Fighter.

"Sir, no, sir."

"No? I think you do. I think that explains why you have a bad attitude." Richardson rubbed his smooth chin as if in deep thought. "But don't worry, McCoy. I'm going to be here every step of the way to make sure you live up to your daddy's expectations and don't sully his good name. It's going to be a long summer, Ace."

Ace?

"Sir, yes, sir."

"Shove off, McCoy."

"Sir, aye, aye, sir."

Pick's mouth had gone dry. This was exactly why he hadn't wanted a private swearing-in ceremony in Smoke Hall. Plebe Summer was hard enough without having the specter of his father's and Malcom Pickering's legacies looming over everything he did. But now the very thing he had wanted to avoid had taken less than a day to come true.

Pick had a sinking feeling as he resumed chopping back to his room in fourth wing.

"I'll be seeing you, Ace!"

III

[ONE]

The Oval Office

The White House

1600 Pennsylvania Avenue NW

Washington, D.C.

1345 29 March 2026

"Ace? His father was an ace?" President Natalie Cohen asked.

Marty Fleiss sat on the sofa across from her. "I'm surprised you didn't know."

"I knew he was a seasoned special operator and came with General McNab's recommendation. That was good enough for me," Cohen said, leaning back to rub her tired eyes. The job was beginning to take its toll on her, and she already felt fatigued—barely two months in. Now she knew why former Presidents always looked like they aged at a much faster clip.

"Captain McCoy's family has a long history of service and sacrifice, not unlike Colonel Castillo's."

Cohen knew Fleiss wasn't referring only to Castillo's father, Jorge, who had been posthumously awarded the Congressional Medal of Honor for his heroics while flying a helicopter in Vietnam. She knew that Castillo was also the descendant of Manuel Martinez and Guillermo de Castillo—both of whom fell in noble battle beside Jim Bowie, William Travis, and Davy Crockett at the Alamo. Not to mention the German soldiers and Hungarian cavalrymen—including several generals—on his mother's side. Military service was in Castillo's blood.

Blood that seemed to also run thick in the McCoy family.

"I'm still not keen on the idea of promoting him to Presidential Agent while Castillo's in the hospital." She paused. "But, like you said, circumstances sometimes prevent us from having the luxury of waiting until we're ready."

"He did prove himself somewhat competent in the Sudan," Fleiss added, trying to make her feel more comfortable. "But it's your decision, Madam President."

Cohen inhaled through her nose and held it for a count of four before letting it out in a rushed exhale. It *was* her decision to make, and she had been there from the very beginning when her predecessor had tasked Matt Hall, the secretary of homeland security, with granting exceptional freedom to his special assistant, Charley Castillo.

There was no question the program ran counter to her platform of transparency. But nor was there a question that sometimes a person of Castillo's character was needed to overcome the cumbersome bureaucracy of the federal government. Charley Castillo had proven that time and time again.

And now it was Pick McCoy's turn.

"Let's bring him in," Cohen said.

"Yes, Madam President."

[TWO]

Scott Natatorium

U.S. Naval Academy

Annapolis, Maryland

1430 29 March 2026

Pick sat in the bleachers at the end of the pool, mindlessly tossing a tennis ball in the air while watching Luis run the current crop of Navy water polo players through a series of drills. In many ways, it felt like only yesterday when he had been in their shoes, suffering through practice after practice when the payoff seemed so far away. The men's collegiate season ran from late summer through the fall and culminated with the national championship in early December, but Luis believed it was never too early to get a jump on preparing his team for the next season.

A shrill whistle drowned out the sounds of splashing.

"Run it again," Luis called out.

Pick watched Moose saunter along the edge of the pool, focused on the players passing the ball back and forth during a drill designed to hone their skills during a six-on-five power play. He wasn't sure who was paying closer attention to the team's ball-handling—Luis or his ever-present Aussiedoodle.

"Hey, coach, who's he?" Pick heard one of the players call out, nodding in his direction.

"How about you mind your own business and slide to the two post like you're supposed to?"

Pick grinned, remembering how the coach had delivered gentle course corrections each time Midshipman McCoy hadn't been doing what he was supposed to do. It was that attention to detail and pursuit of excellence that led to Navy's team being consistently ranked as one of the top programs in the country.

The whistle blew again.

"Actually, bring it in," Luis said, then gestured for Pick to join him.

Pick tossed the tennis ball and watched Moose scamper after it, then popped to his feet and joined the coach at the pool's edge.

"This is Captain Pick McCoy, United States Marines, class of 2017."

"What's with the beard?" one of the midshipmen asked.

"Manners—"

"Thought all Marines had high-and-tights," another said.

Luis blew the whistle again as Moose returned and dropped the ball at Pick's feet. "All right, gents, settle down. Pick is the real deal. Two-time All-American and team captain—"

"Weren't you a three-time All-American, coach?"

Pick shook his head and smiled behind his scraggly beard, then bent over to retrieve the ball and tossed it again across the pool deck. Moose gave chase and Luis gave up trying to control his rowdy team. "They're all yours, Pick."

"Thanks, coach," Pick said.

"You really a Marine?"

"I did say he's a captain, didn't I?"

"Sorry, coach," the offending midshipman said. "You really a Marine, *sir*?"

Pick nodded. "From the Halls of Montezuma."

"So, what's with the long hair and the beard, sir?" another midshipman asked.

"Until recently, I was deployed with a Raider team in northwestern Iraq. We were given relaxed grooming standards while working with local tribal leaders to defeat the Islamic State." Pick paused when he felt his phone vibrating in his pocket. "But now that I'm back stateside, I'll probably have to stop by the barbershop and see Sarge."

"Sarge has been around that long?"

Pick shook his head, trying to remember what it felt like to be a young midshipman who thought ten years ago qualified as ancient history. "He was probably around long before—"

He was interrupted by his phone vibrating again, and he pulled it from his pocket just as Moose returned and dropped the tennis ball once more at his feet.

The White House?

"Will you excuse me?"

Pick stepped over the tennis ball as he moved away from the pool and brought the phone to his ear. "Captain McCoy," he said.

"McCoy, it's Marty Fleiss."

Pick had only recently met Fleiss, but he knew that President Cohen had appointed the Director of National Intelligence to provide oversight on Castillo's Presidential Agent program. But Charley had been perfectly clear where McCoy fit in the hierarchy of their little outfit, so he was more than a little surprised that the DNI was calling him directly.

"Yes, sir. How can I help you?"

A blur of yellow zipped by Pick as one of the midshipmen tossed the tennis ball for Moose to chase. He heard the dog's paws clattering across the tile as he raced after the bouncing object, but Pick was zeroed in on the voice at the other end of the call.

"Where are you right now?"

"I'm in Annapolis, sir."

Pick heard what sounded like a hand move to cover the phone on the other end. But the DNI's voice was still barely audible. "He's in Annapolis . . . No, I don't think so, ma'am." The hand moved. "How soon can you get here?"

"Where? D.C.?" Pick asked.

"The White House," Fleiss responded. "How soon can you get to the White House?"

Moose retrieved the ball and sauntered by Pick on his way to the gaggle of players who were more than happy to cater to the dog's wishes—despite Luis's protests. Pick shifted the phone to his other ear and looked at his Critical Mechanics SOF Mk-1 dive watch.

"I might run into some traffic. Maybe an hour?"

"Start driving," Fleiss said.

"What's going on, sir?"

Fleiss exhaled loudly on the other end as if answering McCoy's question was a burden. "Look, kid, you've been in special operations long enough. Read between the lines. I'll bring you up to speed when you get here."

Pick didn't like the sound of that. "Will Castillo be there?"

"Just come in, and I'll explain everything," Fleiss said, then ended the call.

Pick stood in stunned silence for a beat, listening to the sounds of Moose's paws pattering softly on the pool deck while the Navy water polo team resumed their practice. Only the coach's shrill whistle broke him free from his brooding, and Pick hastened for the exit without bothering to say goodbye.

[THREE]

The White House

1600 Pennsylvania Avenue NW

Washington, D.C.

1545 29 March 2026

Pick was right and had encountered heavy traffic on Route 50 driving in from Annapolis. It was one of the few things he didn't miss about living in the capital's orbit, but he wasn't too worried about being tardy. After all, he had warned the DNI on the phone that it would take him the better part of an hour to get there.

Besides, Castillo was probably already inside, getting spun up while they waited for the rest of the team to arrive. The radio was abuzz with breaking news about a mass shooting in Virginia Beach, but Pick turned it off to avoid being tainted by misinformation. He would learn soon enough if that's why he had been recalled to the White House.

Pick rolled through the E Street checkpoint and came to a stop at the southwest gate of the White House. Like the first time he had visited, two Marine sentries approached the vehicle. But unlike then, McCoy was alone and couldn't rely on Castillo to do all the talking.

"State your business at the White House this afternoon," the first Marine said.

Pick handed the sentry his credentials—a royal-blue-bordered badge with his full name, photograph, and the title SPECIAL ASSISTANT ODNI. "Captain McCoy, here at the request of the President."

The Marine examined the photograph of a clean-shaven version of McCoy and compared it with the long-haired and bearded operator sitting behind the wheel. "Just a moment, sir. Please put your transmission in park while you wait."

Pick did so, then casually glanced in his mirrors at the second sentry, who was conducting a security sweep of the vehicle using an inspection mirror. Before he had finished, the first Marine returned to the open driver's window and handed Pick his credentials.

"Sir, they're expecting you in the Situation Room. Park anywhere that's open, then walk to the south screening building on West Executive Avenue. Your escort will meet you there."

"Thank you, Corporal."

Pick accepted the credentials, then shifted the car into drive and waited for the security barricades to fully retract before driving through. The whole thing was beginning to take on the feeling of déjà vu, and he couldn't help but wish Castillo were there to guide him through the White House's pitfalls and protocols. He was far more comfortable sitting at a ground-level table with Yasim al-Jebouri's Clan of the Jabur tribe.

Pick parked in a spot on State Place NW, climbed out of the sedan, and made for the south screening building at the intersection with West Executive South. Unlike most other visitors to the White House, Pick wasn't dressed in business attire or anything even remotely acceptable for a meeting with the President. But he figured if it was important enough to recall him with such short notice, they would forgive him for wearing jeans and flip-flops.

At least I'm wearing a polo shirt.

As Pick stepped into the screening queue, a distinguished-looking older gentleman with broad shoulders in a blue suit and red tie stepped into his path, blocking his way. "Do you have identification, sir?"

I should have worn actual shoes.

"Yes, sir," Pick replied, unclipping his ID card and handing it to the man.

He studied it for several seconds, comparing the photo with the man standing before him with skepticism, much like how the Marine sentry had. At last, he handed it back. "Captain McCoy, I'm Deputy Director Joel Isaacson, United States Secret Service. Would you come with me, please?"

Pick hesitated for a moment, studying the man's features for any clue as to why he was being sidelined for additional screening before being permitted access to the White House. He tried reasoning that such a task was well beneath the deputy director, but he still felt uneasy.

"What's this about?"

Isaacson's face gave nothing away. "Follow me, please."

Instead of taking him into a side room like Pick had feared, Deputy Director Isaacson personally escorted him through the screening process before exiting the building onto West Executive South. They were moving at a fast clip and halfway to the West Wing before Pick's frustration at being kept in the dark got the better of him and brought him up short.

"Excuse me . . . Joel, was it?"

Isaacson stopped and turned to him with an expressionless mask on his face. "To my friends."

"Okay, then, *Deputy Director* Isaacson," Pick said, emphasizing his title. "As you saw on my credentials, I've been appointed as the special assistant to the Director of National Intelligence, and I'm here at the DNI's request. We can play the formal name game, or we can cut through the bureaucratic bullshit and jump ahead to the part where we start getting along."

Isaacson flexed his jaw muscles. "Look, McCoy, the only reason I came to fetch you is because Charley Castillo is a close personal friend of mine."

Pick looked up and studied the west entrance underneath the iconic white awning. "Is he already here? I'm surprised he didn't come—"

"You don't know?"

"Know what?"

Isaacson's stern expression softened. "I shouldn't say anything—"

"About what? What's going on?"

"Look, I've known Castillo a long time. If you're the guy the President picked to take his place, then I'm sure you're smart enough to understand that I can't give you all the details," Isaacson said.

Pick inhaled through his nose and fought to tamp down his Irish temper. "Can you at least give me enough so that I'm not walking in there blind?"

The deputy director looked around, then reached into his jacket's inside pocket and removed a leather billfold. He thrust it into Pick's hands.

"What's this?"

"Your new credentials," Isaacson said. "Believe it or not, I could have sent somebody else to escort you through screening and into the Situation Room. But I know Charley would have wanted you to have these."

Pick flipped the billfold open and saw two laminated cards with his picture and autograph next to the five-pointed star of the United States Secret Service on one side, and his name and title of SUPERVISORY SPECIAL AGENT on the other. He shook his head in disbelief. "These look real."

"As real as they get. I gave Charley almost the exact same creds twenty years ago."

"Why?"

"Because sometimes they come in handy when you want to travel without having to relinquish your firearm," Isaacson said. "And unless I'm completely off the mark—and I'm usually not—you're about to need them."

Pick studied the credentials again, finding it surreal that the deputy director himself had personally handed him a set of Secret Service credentials while standing outside the entrance to the West Wing of the White House. This was definitely not how he had expected his day to go.

"I don't know what to say," Pick muttered.

"Say you'll put them to good use," the deputy director replied, then held out his hand. "And call me Joel."

Pick shook his hand. "I'll put them to good use, Joel. And you can call me Pick."

[FOUR]

The White House Situation Room

The White House

1600 Pennsylvania Avenue NW

Washington, D.C.

1600 29 March 2026

So much had taken place that Pick found it hard to believe it had been little more than a week since his first visit to the White House. He followed Joel into the West Wing and down a half flight of stairs before turning right into a dead-end hallway, where they were buzzed in. After depositing his cellphone into lead-lined cubbies and receiving a claim ticket from the attendant, Pick proceeded across the hall into the Briefing Room.

"Captain McCoy," DNI Marty Fleiss said, not bothering to stand from his seat in one of the dozen black leather chairs arranged around the rectangular table. "Welcome back. We've got a lot of ground to cover."

Pick pulled out a chair next to the DNI, surprised to discover that Charley wasn't already there as he'd expected. "Are we waiting for the others to join us?"

Fleiss shook his head. "No time for that."

"What am I doing here, sir?"

Without preamble, Fleiss lifted a remote and pointed it at a television mounted on the far wall. The White House logo disappeared and was replaced with what looked like satellite imagery of an oceanfront city. It could have been from anywhere in the world, but it was too green to be one of the usual suspects of the last two dozen years. "Exactly four hours ago, twelve unidentified individuals opened fire at several locations in Virginia Beach, Virginia."

Pick sighed. "So, this is about the shooting."

Fleiss nodded. "At first glance, the shootings appear to be random. But we don't know who's behind it or what their motives are. The FBI is assisting local law enforcement in the investigation."

"How many casualties?" Pick asked.

"As of now, thirty-two killed and just over twice that wounded. Most have been transported to Sentara Virginia Beach General Hospital, but I understand they were nearing capacity and may have transferred several victims to Sentara Leigh in Norfolk. It's a real goat rope down there."

"So, you're thinking this is a terrorist attack," Pick said.

Fleiss nodded again. "The shooters were sterile—without identification—and dressed all in black, armed with U.S.-made M16 rifles. They wore nearly identical chest rigs with several spare magazines and commenced their attacks at almost the exact same time. This was a premeditated and coordinated attack on American soil that caught us all off guard. And President Cohen doesn't like being caught off guard."

Pick had to agree with him. It didn't sound like just another senseless act of violence. But he had to admit his judgment and perception were probably skewed based on his recent experiences in Iraq and the Sudan.

"Where's Castillo?" Pick asked.

"He's at the hospital in Virginia Beach—"

"Great," Pick said, finally understanding why the seasoned Presidential Agent hadn't been waiting for him in the Situation Room. The President had probably ordered him to fly straight there to get boots on the ground as soon as possible before the trail ran cold. "What's he learned so far?"

"I don't think you understand," Fleiss said. "Castillo was there at the time of the attack."

Pick still wasn't getting it. "Okay, so we have firsthand intel on these guys . . ."

Fleiss shifted in his seat and pointed the remote at the television again. The overhead satellite imagery disappeared, and a news broadcast began playing.

"It was a packed conference room here for the press conference at police headquarters this afternoon. The room was filled with local, state, and federal authorities, all with one goal: to find the persons responsible for the deadly attack at the Virginia Beach oceanfront . . ."

Pick leaned forward in his seat as the broadcast shifted from the reporter to B-roll showing various shots and different angles of the expansive crime scene.

"Nearly one hundred people—a third of them killed—were shot while

shopping and dining along a stretch of oceanfront from Rudee Inlet to 22nd Street in the state's deadliest mass shooting since the 2007 attack on the campus of Virginia Tech in Blacksburg."

The broadcast shifted to a uniformed officer standing behind a lectern.

"Eyewitnesses claimed as many as ten to twelve individuals opened fire with automatic assault weapons at a half dozen locations along the oceanfront. This could have been much worse, but they are crediting the actions of a Good Samaritan with saving hundreds of lives."

Pick felt his stomach drop as the broadcast shifted back to the reporter on scene.

"Authorities have identified the Good Samaritan as Carlos Guillermo Castillo, a retired Army Special Forces colonel, who shot and killed three of the attackers before he was shot multiple times . . ."

Pick jumped to his feet. "Castillo was shot?"

"Sit down," Fleiss ordered.

Pick lowered himself back into the chair as the reporter continued. *". . . Castillo was airlifted to Sentara Virginia Beach General Hospital, where he is listed in critical condition—"*

Fleiss pressed a button on the remote and froze the video on an outdated image of a much younger Major Charley Castillo dressed in a green Class A service uniform with a green beret perched on his head. Both men sat in silence for a moment, staring back at the blond-haired and blue-eyed boy who had been the original Presidential Agent.

"How bad is it?" Pick asked, breaking the silence.

Fleiss met his gaze. "We don't know."

"What are my orders?"

Fleiss leaned back in his chair. "If this attack was carried out by a terrorist organization—and we have every reason to think it was—then we were caught with our pants down. Not a single intelligence agency or subordinate organization had any clue that something like this was in the works. And the President wants to make sure nothing like this happens again."

Pick turned back to the image of Castillo on the television and gritted his teeth. He had known the guy for only a week but already felt like they had been teammates for much longer. There was no question Castillo had been hard on him, but that was to be expected. One didn't simply don the mantle of Presidential Agent without first being run through the gauntlet. But that was Castillo's way. Pick would have to do things his way.

The Marine Raider way.

"Until Castillo's out of the hospital and back on his feet, you're the Presidential Agent," Fleiss said. "You're the person the President is relying on to find those responsible and make sure this doesn't happen again. Can you do that?"

"Yes, sir," Pick said.

"You sound confident."

"I am."

Fleiss seemed skeptical. "How can you be so sure?"

"Because I know what it's going to take."

"What?"

Pick didn't hesitate. "Direct Action."

The retired general cocked his head to the side. "What's that?"

"Short strikes and small-scale offensive actions to seize, destroy, capture, recover, or inflict damage in hostile or denied areas," Pick said, reciting verbatim one of the Marine Raiders' core competencies. "But I'll put the emphasis on destroying and damaging."

Fleiss was quiet for a moment before responding. "I want constant updates."

"Yes, sir."

IV

[ONE]

U.S. Coast Guard Air Station Washington

Ronald Reagan Washington National Airport

Arlington, Virginia

1800 29 March 2026

Fleiss had told Pick to leave his rental car while Isaacson arranged for Secret Service transportation from the White House to the Coast Guard air station located on the grounds of the commercial airport five miles away. He barely had enough time to collect his backpack from the rental car and toss the keys to Isaacson before climbing into the Secret Service sedan.

A short while later, the nondescript car rolled through the gate. "Car one arriving with Killer," the agent behind the wheel reported.

Pick bristled at the comment.

Fucking Castillo.

They came to a stop in front of a Coast Guard C-37A—a specially modified version of the Gulfstream V, designed for VIP transport. Standing next to the air stairs was a person Pick hadn't expected to see again quite so soon. Though he had often worked with a Mr. Jones or Mr. Smith during his time in the Raiders, the spook Castillo had brought onto their team took the mystery surrounding his identity to a whole new level. Pick opened the door and stepped out.

"Hey, Junior," Pick said.

"That all you brought?" the spook asked, gesturing to the backpack slung over Pick's shoulder.

"Didn't have time to pack much else."

"Well, come on, then. We're already behind the curve," Junior said, turning to scramble up the steps into the business jet.

Pick reached for the ladder but hesitated when a woman emerged from the cabin and flashed Junior a dirty look. Pick immediately recognized Ani Shaheen, one of Junior's former assets—and brief romantic interest—who had rounded out their team during the recent operation to rescue the secretary of state. Ani's espresso hair was pulled back in a ponytail, and it whipped through the air as she turned to smile down at Pick.

"Well, you guys seem to be getting along," Pick said, glancing up the stairs as Junior disappeared into the cabin.

Ani shook her head. "For now."

"Fair enough," Pick replied. "It's good to see you again."

"You, too."

"What do you know about Castillo? Is he okay?"

She shook her head. "Not much yet, I'm afraid. We'll get the answers we need once we arrive."

He climbed up the air stairs and followed her into the business jet, where he came face-to-face with a very large black man wearing faded blue jeans, loafers, and a dark green polo shirt. "Captain McCoy?"

Pick sized him up, guessing that he was a shade over six feet tall and north of two hundred and twenty pounds. "That's me."

"Richard Miller," the man replied, holding out his hand.

"Call me Pick."

They shook hands. "I go by Dick. Go ahead and take your seat so we can take off and get to Virginia Beach as quickly as possible."

Pick and Dick. Sounds like a bad sitcom.

"Are you coming with us?"

"I'll be your co-pilot today."

Pick studied the man's dress and wondered why he wasn't in a green flight suit like the pilot occupying the left seat was. But if there was one thing he had learned over the last week as Castillo's Presidential Agent under instruction, it was that things weren't always as they seemed.

You're not in the Marine Corps anymore, Toto.

"Pleased to meet you, Dick."

[TWO]

Naval Air Station Oceana

Tomcat Boulevard

Virginia Beach, Virginia

1915 29 March 2026

Less than an hour after taking off from Ronald Reagan Washington National Airport, the Coast Guard C-37A business jet touched down at the naval air station in Virginia Beach. As they taxied to the air operations building, Pick craned his neck to look through his window at a flight line packed with rows of fighter jets. It was an awesome display of American wealth and military might.

Yet neither had done anything to prevent terrorists from killing innocent Americans less than two miles away.

"Somebody's going to pay for this," Pick muttered to himself. He finished lacing his Salomon trail shoes and tossed his flip-flops aside.

But his comment hadn't gone unnoticed, and Junior leaned across the aisle. "We need to find that somebody first, kid."

"That's why we're here," Pick said, ignoring that even after their time in the Sudan, Junior still thought of him as young and inexperienced.

Kid or not, he had promised Director Fleiss that he would find those responsible. And he intended to make good on that promise.

"So, where are we going to start?" Ani asked.

"First, we're going to see Castillo," Pick said, before turning to Junior. "Please tell me you have somebody here to pick us up and take us to the hospital."

The spook only shrugged and gave him a wry smile. But if past experiences were any indicator, Junior had already taken care of everything. Soup to nuts, it didn't matter whether they were in Cairo or Khartoum, Junior was a one-man logistics wizard who took care of everything from transportation to accommodations. Pick wouldn't be surprised if the spook had a long-lost friend or former lover living in Hampton Roads who was on standby to provide assistance.

The jet rolled to a stop, and the three unbuckled and stood from their seats before the pilots had shut the engines down. Seconds later, Dick Miller exited the cockpit and lowered the boarding door, then scampered down the steps. Pick, Junior, and Ani followed.

Not that Pick expected the Navy to roll the red carpet out for the Coast Guard VIP transport, but he was still surprised that nobody was there waiting to greet them. "What now?" Pick asked.

But Junior was already on the move and walking across the tarmac toward the air operations building. Pick glanced at Ani, who shrugged and chased after the spook, then glanced over his shoulder at Dick Miller, who had fallen in behind them and looked to be following them away from the jet.

"I'm not sure how long we're going to be on the ground," Pick said. "But you might want to have the plane gassed up and ready to go at a moment's notice."

Miller grinned. "Oh, I'm not staying with the plane. I'm going with you."

Pick stopped walking. "Excuse me?"

"I'm going with you to the hospital to see Charley."

Pick was really getting tired of being surprised by people who seemed to know more than he did about what was going on. It had started when he was yanked from his Raider team in Iraq, flown to Washington, D.C., and driven to the White House by a surly chauffeur who turned out to be a retired Special Forces colonel by the name of Charley Castillo. And it had continued when the Director of National Intelligence put the burden on him to find the people responsible for the terrorist attack that had put Castillo in the hospital and bring them to justice.

"Who are you?" Pick asked. "Really."

"Charley and I go back a long way," Miller said.

"And you have the qualifications and clearance for this?" Pick asked, though he assumed he must if somebody had allowed Miller to sit at the controls of the Coast Guard Gulfstream and accompany them from the capital to Virginia Beach.

Miller's grin widened. "Did Charley ever tell you how he became the Presidential Agent?"

Guess he knows that much at least.

Pick shook his head.

"When I was a major, the Army loaned me to the Central Intelligence Agency, who assigned me to the embassy in Luanda, Angola, as the station chief under the diplomatic cover of assistant military attaché. I was there because nothing ever happened in Angola, and it was out of the way. Until a Somali terrorist organization, the Holy Legion of Muhammad, stole a Boeing 727 with plans to crash it into the Liberty Bell in Philadelphia."

"Holy shit. I never heard about that," Pick said. "When was this?"

"This was back in 2005. And you never heard about it because the

President tasked Charley with finding the plane before they could carry out the attack."

"I guess he found it," Pick said, thinking that maybe there was more to Charley Castillo than just a grumpy old West Point graduate and retired Special Forces colonel. "But where do you fit in?"

"I gave Charley the classified information that helped him find the plane. And that put me in hot water with the Agency."

"Didn't he have the clearance for it?"

Miller nodded. "Sure, but higher-ups in the Agency didn't want egg on their face. This was right after September 11th, when 'inter-agency cooperation' was all the rage, but that didn't mean those at the top of the bureaucratic food chain still weren't jockeying for political points over their peers in other agencies. I knew the Agency would probably bury my report, so when he showed up in Luanda, I gave it to him."

"Why?"

"Aside from it being the right thing? I owed him. Charley saved my life in Desert Storm."

Pick knew Castillo was a West Pointer, a former helicopter pilot, a Special Forces officer, and the first Presidential Agent. But he was beginning to think he had only half a measure of the man. Miller was painting a picture of Castillo as a loyal friend and dedicated patriot who had no problem breaking the rules or doing whatever it took to accomplish the mission. Maybe he should cut Castillo some slack.

And maybe I should start thinking like him, too.

"Okay, Dick. If you're coming with us, you might as well be on the team. Welcome aboard."

Miller smiled. "I wasn't asking, kid."

Yep. Castillo and Miller are two peas in a pod.

[THREE]

Sentara Virginia Beach General Hospital

1060 First Colonial Road

Virginia Beach, Virginia

1945 29 March 2026

As expected, Junior had made all the necessary arrangements. When Pick and Miller exited the air operations building at the naval air station, the first thing they saw were two black Chevrolet Suburbans idling in the parking lot with drivers behind the wheels of both. The spook and Ani were already in the first Suburban and waiting on them to climb into the second. The moment they did, the mini-caravan sped away.

It had taken less than thirty minutes to reach the hospital, where their drivers deposited them at the entrance to the emergency department. When his Suburban came to a stop, Pick opened the door and jumped out, followed closely by Miller, who had been silent during the drive north from the air station.

"Where to, boss?" Junior asked, after he and Ani climbed out of the lead SUV.

For the first time, Pick realized they were all looking at him to make a decision. He wasn't a stranger to being in command and had been in that position often during his time as a Marine Raider officer. But this was his first time as the de facto leader of this particular band of misfits, and he suddenly felt the added pressure of not letting Charley down.

"Don't worry," Miller said. "I'll handle this."

The former Army officer and onetime Luanda station chief turned on his heel and strode through the automatic double doors as if he owned the place. Pick shrugged at the looks Junior and Ani gave him and followed Miller into the hospital.

It wasn't quite pandemonium inside, but it wasn't far off. Pick suspected the doctors and nurses in the emergency department were more accustomed to dealing with heart attacks, flulike symptoms, and relatively benign conditions on a daily basis. Even on their worst days, they probably saw only victims of car crashes, high-rise fires, or domestic abuse. Despite being employed by the state's largest level-three trauma center, Pick doubted they were prepared or equipped to handle the large influx of gunshot victims.

"Excuse me," Miller said, walking up to a nurse who looked like she was on the fifteenth hour of a twelve-hour shift. "Can you tell me where I can find Colonel Carlos Guillermo Castillo, please?"

"Who's that?" the nurse asked, continuing on her way without even bothering to look at Miller. "We've been a little busy here today."

"He's the one who intervened in the shooting."

The nurse stopped and flashed Miller a compassionate look. "Who are you?"

"I'm his brother."

Pick hadn't thought he could find any humor in the situation. Until he saw the look on the nurse's face.

"His brother," she repeated, her tone making it clear she didn't believe him.

"Yes, ma'am."

"But you're . . ."

"Black?" Miller offered.

She nodded.

Miller turned to Pick. "This lady doesn't believe Charley and I are brothers."

It took effort, but Pick managed to keep a straight face. "Yes, ma'am, they are. Same daddy and everything."

The nurse studied Pick with open skepticism. "Uh-huh. And who are you?"

Pick wasn't sure how to explain his relationship to the retired Green Beret, and he didn't think his identification card proclaiming him as the special assistant to the Director of National Intelligence would suffice. Almost as an afterthought, he removed the credentials Joel had given him.

"Supervisory Special Agent McCoy with the United States Secret Service," Pick said, holding up the credentials for the nurse to examine. He nodded at the others. "And they're with me."

Reluctantly, the nurse gestured for them to follow her through the waiting area and into a private reception room where they could speak without being overheard. "Mr. Castillo was on the first alpha," she said.

"Alpha? What's that?" Ani asked.

"It's a trauma team activation," the nurse replied. "Basically, reserved for the worst injuries, such as GSWs to the neck, chest, or abdomen."

"And he fit that category?" Junior asked.

She nodded. "Multiple GSWs to the chest and back with compromised breathing and low blood pressure. I was one of the nurses who received him and helped stabilize him in the trauma bay. We intubated him and prepped him for surgery before moving him to the OR."

"Is he still in the operating room?" Miller asked.

"No, but he's not out of the woods yet. The first surgery was only to stop the bleeding and stabilize him, because the surgeons needed to move on to the other victims the paramedics brought in."

"So, where can we find him?" Miller asked again.

"We moved him to the ICU," she said. "He's on a breathing machine right now and will probably need several more surgeries in the coming days. I'm afraid if you're hoping to get information from him, you're out of luck. The intensivist is keeping him sedated."

"If it's all the same to you, ma'am," Pick said. "We would still like to see him."

She looked at the motley crew standing in a half-circle around her. "I can't make any promises, but let me see what I can do."

"We would appreciate that," Miller said.

The nurse wheeled away from them and disappeared deeper into the bowels of the emergency department, presumably to gain permission for them to visit the man the news was proclaiming a hero for his intervention in the shooting.

"Sounds like they were busy here today," Ani said.

Junior nodded. "And the last thing they need is all of us crowding them as they keep working to save lives."

"I'm not leaving without seeing him," Miller said.

"Me, either," Pick said. "But I agree. If Castillo's sedated, there's no use in all of us being here. Miller and I will stay while you and Ani go to the oceanfront to poke around. Find a sympathetic police officer who can give you some intel on what happened."

"You know I do this for a living, right?" Junior asked with a wry smile.

Pick didn't answer and instead pulled out his cellphone. "How can I reach you?"

"Call the sneaky one," Junior replied, his smile growing wider.

Ani whipped her head in his direction. "You haven't changed it?"

"Why would I do that?"

Pick's mouth was agape. "What are you talking about?"

“It’s my phone number, boss. 202-763-2591.” When it was clear Pick still didn’t understand, he added, “It spells out ‘sneaky one.’ Get it?”

Pick shook his head. “Whatever you say.”

With a wink, Junior took hold of Ani’s elbow and steered her through the double doors and back into the waiting room. Once they had disappeared, Miller turned to Pick.

“He’s an odd one.”

Pick ignored the comment and returned his focus to the reason they were there. “You don’t think there’s anything we can learn from him, do you?”

Miller shook his head. “Nope. But maybe he needs a fellow Green Beret to give him a swift kick in the ass and motivate him to stop lollygagging and get back on his feet.”

“I’m sure that’s what he needs,” Pick said, just as the nurse returned.

“I can get you in to see him, but I’m afraid it can only be for a few minutes.”

“That’s all we need,” Miller said. “Thank you.”

The nurse turned and led them through the emergency department and into an adjoining hallway that connected them to the intensive care unit. Her Skechers tennis shoes squeaked softly on the polished linoleum, but the sound was drowned out by moans and cries of pain from other victims who were being treated and cared for.

“How many GSW victims did you receive today?” Pick asked.

“More than we ever should,” she replied. “I lost count after the third wave of ambulances arrived.”

McCoy looked at the crowded rooms on either side of the nurses’ station. “How many were there per wave?”

She sighed heavily. “I don’t know. I think we took five in that first wave—Colonel Castillo among them—and prepped the most stable for transport to Norfolk General."

"Why'd you do that?" Miller asked.

"We only had three nurses, three physicians, and two trauma surgeons on call when the first patients came in. We had limited space and manpower to take something like this on, but we sent out a call for help from the neighboring hospitals before we even saw our first patients. That heads-up from law enforcement gave us the time we needed to get ready."

The nurse stopped in front of a closed door.

"Look, I know you guys are only doing your jobs." She turned to face Miller. "And I know you're not really his brother . . ."

Miller looked surprised and flashed her a look that said, *Who, me?*

"But he does have family. His son is with him now."

"His *what*?"

This time, the shock on Miller's face wasn't forced. He pushed past the nurse and lowered his shoulder to the door as he rushed the room. Pick caught the urgency on Miller's face and followed hot on his heels, lifting the front of his shirt to reach for his Sig Sauer P365-XL pistol he carried appendix style in a Kydex holster.

[FOUR]

Pick wasn't sure what they would encounter on the other side of the closed door, but he had performed enough room-clearing operations in Iraq with his Raider team that he felt prepared for just about anything. Still, he felt a little apprehensive about clearing the room with only a washed-up Green Beret backing him up.

They swept into the room and Miller sidestepped left and pivoted right, clearing the entry's blind spots despite not having a weapon. Pick followed a split second later and stepped right while pivoting left, raising the compact pistol and scanning across the top of its tritium front sight post. Within seconds, Pick was certain there were only two other people in the room. And one of them was leaning over an unconscious Castillo.

"Show me your hands," Miller said.

The man hunching over the bed startled but slowly lifted his hands above his head and complied with Miller's command. "Okay. Just be cool."

Once his hands were visible at his sides and reaching for the sky, Miller darted forward, grabbed the back of his collar, and yanked him clear of the hospital bed. He spun him away from Castillo, then wrenched the man's left arm behind his back and pushed him down to the ground.

"Easy," the man said. "I'm not resisting."

Miller dropped a knee onto his back to keep him pinned to the ground while Pick stepped back to cover them and glanced at the monitor above Castillo's head. He gave the vital signs a once-over to make sure Castillo was stable and not suffering from the effects of a poison the man might have injected into him.

"Who are you?" Miller asked.

"His son," the man said, groaning with pain as Miller wrenched his arms upward.

"He doesn't have a son," Miller said. "Want to try again?"

The man turned his head to the side and looked up at Pick. His eyes flashed surprise, but quickly darkened with recognition as Pick felt his stomach drop.

It can't be . . .

"You—"

"What the hell are you doing here?" Pick asked.

Miller whipped his head to look up at him. "You know this guy?"

"Yeah . . ."

"Hey, Killer, how 'bout you tell this guy to get off of me."

Pick felt his face flush as memories from his four years at the Naval Academy flooded his mind. Memories like the Herndon climb, Ring Dance, and graduation were always easy to recall. But some memories were better left forgotten. The fall of his youngster or sophomore year had plenty of those kind.

V

Summer 2014

[ONE]

Bancroft Hall

U.S. Naval Academy

Annapolis, Maryland

1530 19 August 2014

Midshipman Third Class P.K. McCoy Jr. kicked open the door to his three-person room and let one of his two green canvas seabags fall to the floor with a thud. He had waited until the last possible moment to move his things back into Bancroft Hall, which meant he had picked the hottest time of day to lug his meager belongings up four flights of stairs to his room. Still, at least he had one diagonal stripe on his shoulder boards and didn't need to chop through the halls like a plebe anymore.

"Need a hand?"

Pick glanced over at the still figure of his roommate, Javier Santiago, lounging on top of his rack and staring up at the ceiling.

"Nah," Pick said. "I've got this."

"Good, because I wasn't really going to help."

Pick shook his head and lugged his second seabag to the closest vacant rack and set it on the floor before stepping up onto his desk and climbing onto the thin foam mattress. He looked over at the other vacant rack, yet to be occupied by his best friend and other roommate. "Where's Brad?"

Javi shrugged. "Who knows. Haven't seen him yet."

"How long you been here?"

"Long enough to not want to be here anymore."

Javi had spent the better part of his childhood living in one dormitory or another at various boarding schools, and Bancroft Hall was just one more. While Pick had come from a long line of Marines and felt pressured to live up to his family's name, Javi was the descendant of Texas Creoles who had amassed generational wealth while carving out a position of prominence in the new republic.

"What else can we do?" Pick asked.

Javi sat up. "Get out of here and find some trouble to get into for one more night."

"Isn't it a little early to be on restriction?"

"Only if we get caught," Javi said, then rolled over and dropped down from his bed. He tucked his blue-rimmed white T-shirt into his blue Navy athletic shorts, then sat in his chair and slipped on his running shoes.

"Real inconspicuous," Pick said. "Nobody will ever suspect you're a midshipman."

Javi looked up at him and winked. "We're just gonna go for a run."

"A run . . ."

Pick didn't think his roommate really had a run in mind. But they still had several hours before they were required to be back in their company spaces for muster and evening meal formation. The day the Brigade returned to Annapolis from summer training was always chaotic, and most of the juniors and seniors were too busy running the new plebes around to really pay them any attention. Whatever Javi had in mind, he figured this was about as good a chance as they would get.

"Yeah, get your PT gear on," Javi said, lacing up his running shoes. "I've got an idea."

"Why do I get the feeling I'm going to regret this?"

Javi sat up tall and smiled at him. "Because you probably will."

[TWO]

Tecumseh Condominiums

312 Severn Avenue

Annapolis, Maryland

1615 19 August 2014

Pick matched Javi stride for stride as they jogged through downtown Annapolis and crossed Spa Creek into Eastport. Home to the Annapolis city marina, Severn Sailing Association, and Annapolis Maryland Capital Yacht Club, the sleepy suburb of the state capital was full of sailors enjoying their dog days of summer on the water. Even though Javi was a member of the offshore sailing team, Pick knew he had something other than sailing in mind.

"Where are we going?"

"You'll see," his roommate replied, then kicked it into a higher gear as he turned left down Severn Avenue.

Pick might have just come off a two-week summer cruise aboard the Naval Academy's Yard Patrol craft, but he was still in good shape and had no problem keeping up with Javi. The two youngsters ran neck and neck until crossing Fourth Street, when Javi abruptly skidded to a stop and bent over with his hands on his knees.

"Now . . . we can say . . . we went for a run . . . when somebody asks," he said through gasping breaths.

Pick naturally slowed to a walk and rested his hands on his head, standing tall while taking in deep gulps of air and letting his heart rate slow. But Javi apparently didn't want to wait until they had caught their breath before showing Pick why they had abandoned settling into their rooms for an unauthorized jog beyond the Academy's walls.

"I just hope nobody asks."

"Come on," Javi said, leading Pick onto the sidewalk in front of a brick wall and into an alcove next to a sign reading THE TECUMSEH.

"What is this place?"

Javi turned and gave him an uncharacteristically serious look. "You remember that dark-haired girl in Nineteenth Company you thought was cute?"

There was only one girl in their sister company Pick would have described as cute, but he wasn't about to admit it to the least discreet youngster in 4th Battalion.

"You know? Hannah?"

From Savannah.

Pick nodded. "Yeah, of course I remember her. She was the first person I met on I-Day."

Javi opened the door and led Pick into what passed for the building's entrance. "Well, her mom bought a condo here so Hannah could get away from the Yard. Thought maybe this was as good a time as any to break it in."

The condominium complex was split into two separate buildings with units on four floors, divided by an inlet connecting Spa Creek to boat slips and storage for kayaks and other small watercraft. Javi led Pick to the building on the right.

"Okay, but why do *you* have access to it?" Pick asked, though he was certain he wasn't going to like the answer.

Javi's green eyes sparkled with excitement. "Hannah and I started dating over the summer."

Pick felt his stomach drop, even though he had half expected it and didn't really have a right to feel jealous. He might have had a crush on the outgoing brunette since the first time they met, but he hadn't told anybody—least of all her—and had instead focused on school and water polo.

And look how well that turned out for you.

"I'm happy for you, man," Pick said.

Javi eyed him suspiciously. "You sure about that, amigo?"

Pick nodded. "I just didn't take you for a dark-sider."

"So, it's gonna be like that, huh?"

"You're the one who went over to the dark side and started dating another midshipman."

Javi elbowed him in the ribs and led him up the stairs. "Come on, she's waiting for us. You can be the one to tell her that's what you think. She asks about you all the time."

He knew he shouldn't, but the corners of Pick's mouth turned up in a smile as he felt the first flutters in the pit of his stomach.

After climbing four flights of stairs, Pick stood off to the side while Javi knocked on the door. He was surprised that he felt anxious at the prospect of seeing Hannah again. But Pick thought that was probably more due to Javi dropping a bomb on him than it was actually seeing the brunette from Georgia.

They had said their goodbyes earlier in the spring before Pick left for his first block of training, but he would have been lying if he had said he hadn't thought of her over the summer. Standing in front of the door, his nerves started to get the better of him as he heard her footsteps prancing across the hardwood floors on the other side.

Javi shot him a sideways glance. "You good, bro?"

Pick nodded just as the door flew open and Hannah leaped out and landed in Javi's arms. "Baby, I've missed you!"

The couple kissed for several seconds like Pick wasn't even there, before Javi broke away and cleared his throat. "We got company, mi corazón."

Hannah looked surprised when she turned and saw Pick standing off to the side. "Well, hey, Pick from San Diego."

"Hey yourself, Hannah from Savannah."

She released her grip on Javi's neck and took him by the hand to lead him into the condo. "Since my favorite man is here, let's go inside and have ourselves a celebratory cocktail."

Did she just say I'm her favorite man?

No, you idiot, she said Javi was her favorite man. You're just his roommate.

I think she said it.

"Are you sure that's a good idea?" Pick asked, trying to ignore the argument inside his head.

Javi shot him a dirty look. "It's not like we're gonna get wasted, Pick. But I told you I wanted to find some trouble to get into."

"Yeah, but that doesn't mean I want to get into trouble before the semester even begins."

Hannah's eyes lit up as she watched them bantering back and forth, then she released Javi's hand and spun into the kitchen to put an end to the discussion. "What's your poison, boys?"

"What do you got, mi corazón?" Javi asked.

He's really laying it on thick.

As the son of a Marine Corps fighter pilot, Pick wasn't a stranger to alcohol. But his father had always stressed the importance of knowing when it was okay to drink and when it wasn't. More than twelve hours before a brief was okay. Less than two hours from muster and evening meal formation on the day the entire Brigade of Midshipmen returned from summer training was not.

"Nothing for me," Pick said.

Hannah glanced at Pick and gave him an apologetic smile, then turned back to Javi as he sat on a stool at the bar top. "I think my mom left some vodka in the freezer and a few beers in the fridge."

"I'll have a beer," Javi said.

She looked at Pick again. "You sure you don't want anything, Pick from San Diego?"

"No, thanks. I'm good."

"Why do you keep calling him that? How come you never call me Javier from Laredo?"

She turned her back on the boys, opened the refrigerator, and pulled out two bottles of Budweiser. Turning back to them, she twisted the tops off and handed one to Javi. "Because everybody knows where you're from, baby."

"What's that supposed to mean?"

"Just that you're muy guapo," Hannah said, then clinked her bottle against his and lifted it in a simple toast. "Here's to another year together at Canoe U."

"¡Salud!" Javi said, then took another healthy swig.

Pick watched the young couple stare lovingly into each other's eyes for a moment, then turned and crossed the living room for the balcony on the other side looking at the Naval Academy across Spa Creek.

"Pretty nice that your mom got this place," Pick said, enjoying the view while trying to ignore the puppy love taking place behind his back. He was happy that his eccentric Tejano roommate had found somebody who made him smile, but he just didn't want to spend every weekend liberty feeling like the third wheel.

At least I can hang out with Brad. He's still single.

He listened to them whispering to each other in the kitchen, then heard Hannah break away and walk across the living room to join him at the sliding glass door. "You know you're welcome to come here anytime."

Pick looked over his shoulder and saw her smiling up at him, just as she had done a year ago on I-Day. "Thanks, Hannah."

They stared at each other until it became awkward.

"Pick, I—"

"You guys gonna make me drink alone or what?" Javi called from the kitchen.

"I'm sorry," Hannah whispered, then spun away to fetch her boyfriend another beer.

Sorry for what? It's not like I told you how I felt.

"I think I'm just gonna head back," Pick said, then turned away from the view and headed for the front door.

Javi moved to block his way. "Hey, hermano, you sure?"

"Yeah, I need to unpack and head over to the pool for a team meeting anyway."

"Gracias," Javi mouthed silently with a wink. "Muchas gracias."

"De nada," Pick said, then left the condo.

[THREE]

Bancroft Hall

U.S. Naval Academy

Annapolis, Maryland

1705 19 August 2014

Pick had jogged back to the Yard at a leisurely pace, trying not to think about what was going on back in Mrs. Rosen's condo in Eastport. Javi's wink and silent thank-you had made it perfectly clear what his roommate hoped would happen once Pick left and the couple had some privacy.

But Pick didn't think Hannah was that type of girl.

At least, I hope she's not.

By the time he walked through the doors leading into Bancroft Hall's fourth wing, he was only five minutes late. But muster and evening meal formation were still almost an hour away, so he doubted his absence had even been noticed. He took his time walking up the youngster ladder to his room on the fourth deck and kicked open the door to find his best friend unpacking his things.

"Where you been?" Bradley Trosclair asked.

"With Javi in Eastport."

Brad stopped folding his laundry and glanced at his watch before turning to look at him with a raised eyebrow. "With Javi? In Eastport?"

"Uh-huh."

"Cutting it a little close, don't you think?"

Pick shrugged and walked over to his seabag still sitting on the floor next to his bunk. "Not as close as Javi."

"Where is he?"

"With Hannah."

"From Savannah?"

Pick nodded but didn't say anything. The last thing he wanted to do was give Brad any reason to think he was less than pleased with their roommate's decision to pursue the only girl Pick had shown an interest in. Then again, he had nobody to blame but himself.

"Well, isn't that interesting," Brad said, turning back to resume folding his laundry.

The first fifteen minutes passed in silence as the two midshipmen unpacked their belongings and organized their closets and confidential lockers as they had been trained as plebes. It would take some time for them to get used to the idea that they wouldn't be surprised by an upperclassman barging in their room for an impromptu inspection. But they still needed to present a neat and tidy appearance.

The next fifteen minutes was filled with mindless chatter, sharing stories of their summer training experiences. Most were from PROTRAMID, or Professional Training of Midshipmen, the four-week program that gave new youngsters a one-week glimpse into each of the communities they could expect to be commissioned into following graduation—surface warfare, submarines, aviation, and Marine Corps. For most, it was an opportunity to explore their options. For Pick, it was a confirmation of his.

There was no question he planned on seeking a commission in the Marine Corps after graduation. But Pick thought his decision to pursue a career in infantry instead of aviation would stun a lot of people—General P.K. McCoy most of all.

"Really?" Brad asked. "I thought we would go to Pensacola together."

"I had a great time during the aviation week," Pick said. "I mean, it was great being home in San Diego and going for backseat rides in the T-34. But it's just not what I want to do."

Brad had finished packing and was sitting in his chair with his feet propped up on his desk and his hands behind his head. "What's your dad think of that?"

"I don't know," Pick confessed.

Brad kicked his feet off the desk and leaned forward in his chair. "Wait a second. Are you saying you haven't said anything about this to your dad yet?"

Pick had chickened out on telling Hannah how he felt about her last year and was chickening out now by not telling his dad he didn't want to follow in his footsteps and become a Marine fighter pilot. "I don't think he understands what it's like living in somebody else's shadow."

"You won't know until you talk to him, will you?"

Pick neatly placed the last folded T-shirt into his locker and sat in his own chair, turning to look at his best friend. "My grandpa enlisted in the Marine Corps and became a mustang officer. My dad was the three-star Deputy Commandant for Aviation. I'm pretty sure he surpassed his—"

Suddenly, their door flew open and a voice they both immediately recognized cut him off. "Killer!"

Pick started to jump to his feet but remembered he was no longer a plebe and remained defiantly seated. "What do you want, Randy?"

The newly minted Midshipman First Class Randy Richardson stood in their doorway and patted down his uniform with masking tape to remove stray pieces of lint. "Well, aren't you a little surly for a fresh youngster. Or have you forgotten that I still outrank you?"

"No, we haven't forgotten," Brad said. "You only point it out every chance you get."

Randy brushed away the subtle dig. "Yeah, well, anyway, I came for two reasons. First, Captain Hanes wants to see you in his office—"

"Me?" Brad asked.

"No, numb nuts," Randy said, then stopped pat-pat-patting his uniform and pointed at Pick. "Him."

"What's he want?" Pick asked.

Randy shrugged. "Guess you'll have to ask him yourself. One of the things I learned down at Quantico this summer was that when a superior officer gives you an order, you don't question it."

"I'll remember that the next time a superior officer gives me an order," Pick said, purposely reminding Randy that he clearly didn't view him as a superior officer.

"Does that mean you still plan on trying to become a Marine?" Brad asked.

"I'm not *trying* to become a Marine," Randy replied. "I'm *going* to become one."

"What's the second reason?" Pick asked.

The firstie looked from Brad back to Pick. "I wanted to share another thing I learned down at Quantico this summer."

"What's that?"

"I learned that your dad isn't the only Killer McCoy."

Pick felt his stomach drop. It was bad enough that the upperclassman had spent the first half of his plebe year calling him Ace to openly mock him for being the son of a renowned fighter pilot. But it had gone from bad to worse when Randy discovered that his father's call sign in the Marine Corps had been Killer.

"What are you talking about?" Brad asked.

Randy grinned. "I heard a little story about a certain Marine corporal in Shanghai by the name of Kenneth R. McCoy."

Oh, shit.

[FOUR]

Pick's mind was on what Randy had said as he walked through the hall and made his way to Captain John W. Hanes's office. He was less concerned with why the Marine infantry officer wanted to see him than he was with the fact that somebody had told Randy Richardson of his grandfather's exploits in Shanghai that had led to a less-than-flattering nickname.

When Pick reached the office, he looked through the open door at the lanky officer sporting a high-and-tight haircut and tapping on his keyboard. He knocked on the door before announcing, “Midshipman McCoy reporting as ordered, sir.”

Hanes didn’t look up immediately, but still acknowledged Pick’s presence. “Close the door and have a seat, McCoy.”

“Aye, aye, sir.”

Pick walked into the office and tugged on the door to break it free from its stop, then let it close as he walked across the room and sat in one of the two chairs in front of the company officer’s desk.

When Hanes finished typing out whatever email or report he was working on, he pushed his keyboard away and shifted in his seat to face Pick. “Where were you this afternoon?”

Pick felt his face flush. There was only one reason he could think of for the Marine captain to ask him that question. Somebody must have seen him with Javi at Mrs. Rosen’s condo.

But who? And why? I was only five minutes late.

Pick didn’t know what to say. So, he resorted to employing a tactic intended to buy time and allow his brain to come up with a reasonable answer that would allow him to remain faithful to the Academy’s Honor Concept.

He acted confused.

“Sir?”

“It’s a pretty easy question to answer, McCoy. Where were you this afternoon?”

If Pick was going down, he wasn’t going to take anybody else with him. “I went to Eastport, sir.”

“With who?”

So much for not taking anybody down with me.

“My roommate, sir.”

“Which one?”

The phone on his desk rang, and Captain Hanes lifted a finger to prevent him from answering before scooping the handset off the cradle and bringing it to his ear. "Eighteenth Company Officer Captain Hanes speaking."

Saved by the bell.

"Yes, sir, I have him here with me . . . No, sir, I don't have any details yet . . . Yes, sir, I will call you right back." Hanes ended the call by placing the handset back onto the cradle and again turning to face Pick.

They stared at each other in silence for several seconds before the Marine officer broke the spell. "Well?"

Pick sighed, then settled on telling the unabashed truth. "Javier Santiago, sir. We went for a run off the Yard and ended up in Eastport."

Captain Hanes nodded. "Where exactly did you go in Eastport?"

Who the hell told him where we went? And why is he asking these questions?

"We went to the Tecumseh Condominiums, sir."

The Marine officer pursed his lips and glanced down at his desk blotter. "I expected better from the former Deputy Commandant's son. You're aware of the restriction that midshipmen are not allowed to have their own lodging off the Yard, are you not?"

"Yes, sir, I am."

"Who does the condo belong to?"

Pick had given up his roommate pretty easily, but he reasoned that Javi had only brought it on himself. But rolling over on Hannah wasn't something he was prepared to do.

So, he redirected.

"Sir, I didn't know where we were going when he left the Yard. When we reached the condo, I knew we weren't supposed to be there, and I stayed only five minutes before leaving and coming back to my room." He swallowed. "What's this about?"

Captain Hanes pointed at the phone. "That was Lieutenant Commander Jeffery Carroll, the Nineteenth Company officer."

Pick swallowed. "Yes, sir?"

"Do you know Midshipman Third Class Hannah Rosen?"

He hesitated again. "Yes, sir."

"She is accusing your roommate, Javier Santiago, of sexual assault."

Pick's fear of spending time on restriction for violating Academy regulations evaporated in a blink. In its place, he felt a burning anger and desire to commit violence on the person he'd once considered his friend. It was a completely foreign emotion, but one he was surprisingly comfortable with.

Maybe Killer *suits me after all.*

VI

[ONE]

Intensive Care Unit

Sentara Virginia Beach General Hospital

1060 First Colonial Road

Virginia Beach, Virginia

2100 29 March 2026

Randy Richardson sat in the only chair in the room with his forearms resting on his knees as he stared at the ground in front of him. He had just finished telling Pick and Miller his version of what had taken place earlier that day at the Virginia Beach oceanfront, but Pick was still trying to wrap his mind around seeing his former nemesis in Castillo's hospital room.

"You said you're his son?" Pick asked, standing in front of Randy and looking down at him.

Randy harrumphed. "His *bastard* son."

Miller had been standing silently next to Pick for some time with a look of concern on his face. When he finally spoke, his voice rolled like a peal of thunder. "You're Righteous Randolph's son, aren't you?"

Randy's head whipped up in surprise. "How do you know that name?"

Miller turned away and walked to the window that looked out onto the hallway. The hospital's intensive care unit was buzzing with activity and had been since they arrived. But Pick could tell Miller's mind was racing even faster, and he didn't yet know why.

"Dick? How do you know that name?" Pick asked.

"Randolph J. Richardson III," Miller said. "United States Military Academy, class of 1990."

"That's right," Randy said. "Do you know him?"

Again, Miller didn't answer directly and turned to look at an unconscious Charley Castillo lying in the hospital bed. "Same class as him."

"Yeah, I knew that already," Randy said.

"And the same class as me."

Pick held up a hand and stared directly at Miller. "Wait, so you're telling me that you and Castillo were West Point classmates with his father?"

Miller nodded.

"Did you know him?" Randy asked.

"Oh, yeah," Miller said. "Cadet Private Castillo punched Cadet First Sergeant Richardson in the face but claimed the broken nose was caused by a book falling off a shelf. When I confirmed Castillo's version of the story, Richardson brought us both before a Court of Honor for violating the honor code—a cadet will not lie, cheat, or steal, nor tolerate those who do."

"Jesus," Pick said. "Why'd Castillo punch him?"

"Because Righteous Randolph turned him in for sneaking away to New York City for the weekend while on academic restriction. Charley admitted his guilt when confronted by his tactical officer, and he was busted."

"So, it was payback," Pick concluded.

"Something like that."

Pick looked at Randy, who shook his head. "It's not the same thing, McCoy."

"What's not the same?" Miller asked.

"Just that a Midshipman Lieutenant junior grade Randolph J. Richardson IV once did something eerily similar to a Midshipman Third Class McCoy," Pick said.

Miller chuckled. "Did you punch him?"

"No."

"But he wanted to punch somebody," Randy said.

"Who?" Miller asked.

"Somebody I haven't thought about in a very long time," Pick said, then quickly changed the subject. "But we're not here to have a mini-reunion, and I couldn't care less that you acted like Righteous Randolph when we were midshipmen. Why are you here now, Randy?"

Randy looked like he was going to take offense at being compared to his West Pointer father but instead took a deep breath and looked at Castillo. "He called me yesterday and asked to meet for lunch."

"Why?" Pick asked.

Randy shrugged. "I don't know. I've known him my whole life but only learned he was my real dad when I was fourteen. He had a habit of disappearing for a while—years, even—then popping back in like he wanted to have a relationship with me. I agreed to meet him but planned on letting him off the hook. I might be his son biologically, but I have nothing in common with him and don't want anything from him."

"Is that why you went to the Naval Academy?" Miller asked. "To distance yourself from him?"

"To distance myself from *both* of my fathers."

And yet you ended up acting just like Righteous Randolph when we were midshipmen, and you're here visiting Charley Castillo in the hospital. Fate really is a funny, fickle thing.

"But why are you here at the hospital, Randy?" Pick asked.

"I might hate the guy and want nothing to do with him, but he's still my biological father. More important, he's a hero. What the news is saying about him is true, but it doesn't even come close to what he really did. Like him or not, he deserves to have somebody care for him."

"That's why we're here," Miller said.

Pick said nothing.

"Where's Svetlana?" Randy asked.

Pick looked from Randy to Miller. "Who?"

"His wife," Miller replied.

Pick felt like he had just been punched in the gut. "Castillo's married?"

"Was," the former Special Forces officer said. "Charley won't talk about her anymore, just that he lost her in childbirth."

Apparently, the punch was a one-two combo. "He's got a kid?"

Miller walked to Castillo's bedside and rested a hand on his friend's arm. "No. The kid didn't make it."

"You know I'm right here," Randy said, seemingly upset that they were ignoring his relationship to the unconscious man in the hospital bed. But he quickly moved on. "I didn't know any of that."

"Yeah, well, Charley's not the kind of guy to tell everyone his business," Miller said.

"What about Abuela?"

"Who's Abuela?" Pick asked.

Randy made a clucking sound to express his disgust. "Jesus, McCoy. Why are *you* here?"

Pick bit his tongue, though he desperately wanted to wipe the smug look off Randy's face.

Because the President of the United States ordered me to come here and find out what happened so we can stop something like this from happening again. Because until Charley Castillo is back on his feet, I am the one and only Presidential Agent.

"*Abuela* is Spanish for grandmother," Miller said. "Randy here is referring to Doña Alicia, who is probably either on their ranch in Uvalde or volunteering with the Daughters of the Republic of Texas in San Antonio."

"Should we call her?" Pick asked.

Before Miller could answer, Pick's phone vibrated in his pocket. He held up a hand to pause their conversation before fishing it out and answering.

"McCoy," he said.

"It's Junior."

"Learn anything yet?"

Pick could hear a lot of commotion in the background and figured the spook was still on the scene, trying to uncover who was behind the attack.

"Yeah, actually. You see Castillo yet?"

Pick turned to look at the still form lying in the bed and felt his anger bubbling. He needed somebody to blame—a person he could target. "Yeah, we're here with him now. Tell me what you've learned."

"These guys weren't professionals, but they sure acted like them. Not much in the way of pocket litter we can use to positively identify them, but it looks like they're from one of the 'Stans—Afghanistan, Kyrgyzstan, Pakistan, Tajikistan—"

"I get it," Pick said, cutting him off.

"Yeah, well, anyway, the FBI here is running their prints and photographs through biometric screening to see if any return a hit on the terrorist watch list. But even if not, it's looking more and more like this was the act of a foreign terrorist organization."

"Yeah, but which one?" Pick mused.

"Not sure on that," Junior replied. "But they did find something interesting in one of the hotel rooms rented by the gunmen. Most of the rooms were sanitized completely and they left absolutely nothing for investigators to comb through, but one . . ."

Pick wasn't sure if Junior was drawing it out to be annoying, but he was running out of patience. "Spit it out already."

"Fine. Behind the empty wastebasket in one room, investigators found what looks like a hotel room key inside a sleeve with a handwritten room number on the outside."

"What hotel?"

"It says 'Menger' on the key, but there isn't a hotel with that name in Virginia Beach," Junior said.

"Menger?"

"Yeah, but—"

Miller crossed the room and gripped Pick's arm. "Did you just say Menger?"

"Yeah, why?"

"You ever hear of the Rough Riders?"

"That volunteer unit that Roosevelt commanded in the Spanish–American War?" Pick asked, though admittedly his knowledge of Army history was lacking compared to what he knew about the Marine Corps.

"Teddy Roosevelt was second-in-command under Leonard Wood, but that's not the point," Miller said, then snatched the phone from Pick's hand. "Junior, get that key and bring it with you to Oceana."

"What the hell's going on?" Pick asked.

Miller ended the call and tossed the phone back to Pick. "The Menger Hotel bar was one of the Rough Riders' more notorious gathering places."

"And?"

"And it's located on the Alamo Plaza in San Antonio."

Pick knew he was missing something. "The Alamo?"

"Oh, shit!" Randy said, jumping to his feet. "Abuela!"

[TWO]

Randy followed Pick and Miller from the room and raced through the ICU to the waiting Suburban in front of the hospital. When they exited through the automatic double doors, Pick wheeled on Randy.

"Where do you think you're going?"

"Same place you are," Randy said, then moved to step around Pick and follow Miller into the Suburban's rear seat.

Pick grabbed his arm. "We're not midshipmen anymore, Randy."

"No, we're not." Randy jerked his arm free but stepped closer, seething at being stopped from going with them to the naval air station. "I'm a lieutenant commander in the Navy—"

"Yeah, I thought you wanted to be a Marine. What happened?"

"You know damn well what happened. And if you ever put your hands on me again, I'll bring you up on charges for assault."

Pick was no longer an eighteen-year-old plebe who could be bullied. He was a combat-seasoned Marine Raider and knew he could knock out the Navy officer with one punch. It wouldn't have been the first time a Marine and sailor tussled.

But he knew that wouldn't fix anything.

"Look, Randy—"

"Commander," Randy corrected.

Pick couldn't bring himself to give Randy the respect he thought he deserved. But he wanted to keep the peace. "*Lieutenant* Commander Richardson," he said, purposely choosing not to shorten his rank. "You don't know everything."

"Then tell me," Randy said.

Pick glanced around and caught Miller's eye just as the former Green Beret tapped on his watch to remind him that the clock was ticking. But Randy's patience seemed to have already expired.

"Are you still in the Marines?"

Pick sighed but nodded.

"What's your rank?"

Pick laughed at this. "Jesus, Randy—"

"Commander," Randy corrected again.

Pick's anger flared hot, but he wanted to put this behind them once and for all. "I'm a captain—"

Randy's eyes widened. "Oh, so I *am* a superior officer—"

Pick had had enough. "In my world, rank means two things—jack and shit. You're given a job to do, and you do it. The respect you receive is the respect you've earned. And you haven't earned a damn thing yet, *Randy*."

They stood nose to nose and stared at each other for several seconds, neither willing to be the first to back down. Then Miller's voice bellowed from the Suburban's open rear door.

"Would you girls kiss and make up already so we can go?"

Randy glanced at Miller, then back to Pick. "Just what the hell's going on, McCoy?"

Pick clenched his jaw as he questioned just how much he should tell the naval officer. Randy might have been an asshole midshipman, but the Navy apparently trusted him enough to make him a lieutenant commander. And that probably meant he had a security clearance and knew how to keep his mouth shut.

"Well?"

"Let's go!" Miller yelled.

Pick shot Miller a dirty look before turning back to Randy. "When

I said you didn't know everything, I meant that I'm involved in something that only a few people know about."

Randy seemed to relax. "How many?"

"Well, you met Dick Miller already. The two others on my team are at the oceanfront and will meet up with us at Oceana."

"And that's it?"

"Aside from who I take my orders from? Yeah, Randy, that's it."

"Who do you take your orders from?"

Pick pointed over Randy's shoulder at the hospital. "Until he was shot, I took my orders from Colonel Charley Castillo."

"But he's retired . . ."

"Like I said, there's a lot you don't know. But with him laid up in bed and recovering from being shot, the responsibility has fallen to me."

"The responsibility to do what?" Randy pressed. "What *the hell* is going on?"

"What do you *really* know about Castillo?"

"I know that my dad lied to me and told me he had been kicked out of the Army."

"You know he retired."

Randy nodded. "I was there at his retirement parade and saw him receive another Distinguished Service Medal."

"Why do you think they gave it to him?"

"They read a citation, but I'm sure it was all bullshit. I was told to never ask what he did in the Army, because he wouldn't be able to talk about it. Apparently, he was some kind of intelligence officer and one of the best General McNab had ever known."

I guess that's close enough to the truth.

"But that was long before I even went to Annapolis," Randy quickly added.

Pick nodded. "Let's just say they brought him out of retirement."

"To do what?"

"Did you hear about the secretary of state's kidnapping?"

"Yeah, everybody at the command was—" Randy abruptly stopped talking, as if he realized he was about to say more than he was supposed to.

But Pick had noticed. "What command?"

The lieutenant commander shook his head and waved him off. "Forget about it. What about the secretary of state?"

There was something about the way Randy deflected his question that made Pick think he knew exactly what command Randy was attached to. Almost immediately, he recalled standing next to Castillo in front of a Joint Light Tactical Vehicle as eight Navy SEALs from a Joint Special Operations Command Task Force in Djibouti materialized out of nowhere.

"Castillo was brought out of retirement to locate the secretary of state and coordinate his rescue," Pick said. "And I was recalled from my Raider team in Iraq to be his second-in-command for that operation."

Randy's mouth fell open in a look of stunned disbelief. "Wait a second . . . What was your call sign for that operation?"

"Mako Three."

"Holy shit. That was you?"

Pick nodded.

[THREE]

Naval Air Station Oceana

Tomcat Boulevard

Virginia Beach, Virginia

2230 29 March 2026

After realizing that both Pick and Randy had been involved in the operation to rescue Secretary of State Frank Malone, the two men broke away from the hospital's entrance and climbed into the Suburban for the short drive to the naval air station. Randy rode shotgun while Pick sat in the backseat next to Dick Miller, whose knee bounced continuously as if to spur the government SUV into going faster.

Aided by Randy's credentials, they breezed through the naval air station's main gate and rolled past a row of aircraft on display—the F-14 Tomcat and F/A-18 Hornet the most prominent—on their way to the air operations building. Randy shifted in his seat to face Pick.

"So, is this some kind of Department of Defense task force or something?"

"Something like that," Pick replied, still struggling to accept his role of being the guy in charge. He half expected Castillo to jump out and chastise him for not understanding the meaning of the words *clandestine* and *covert.*

"You're really not going to tell me?"

But he couldn't do it alone. That might have worked for somebody like Charley Castillo. But Pick's father had raised him to believe he shouldn't do it on his own, often commenting that "even the Lone Ranger had Tonto." Of course, the elder McCoy had probably intended to instill in Pick the importance of being a good wingman in preparation for his inevitable career as a Marine fighter pilot.

Randy deserves to know the truth.

Pick reached into his pocket and removed the identification card he had been given upon visiting the White House for the first time. He leaned forward and handed it to Randy. "This is my official title."

"Special assistant to the Director of National Intelligence?"

"Officially," Pick said, then removed the billfold Deputy Director Joel Isaacson had given him and passed it up as well. "This is another one."

Randy took the Secret Service credentials and furrowed his brow. "Supervisory special agent?"

Pick nodded.

"And you're also a Marine captain?"

Again, Pick nodded.

"Wait, you said you used to take orders from Castillo," Randy said, trying to piece it all together. "Who do you take your orders from now?"

Before Pick could answer, his phone vibrated in his pocket again, and he held up a hand to let Randy know he would answer his question after taking the call. "Speak of the devil," he muttered, then swiped across the screen to answer.

"How can I help you, Director Fleiss?"

Randy's eyebrow rose.

"Captain McCoy, was I unclear about my expectation that I receive constant updates on the progress of your investigation?"

Pick glanced at his Critical Mechanics SOF Mk-1 dive watch. A little over six hours had elapsed since Fleiss had given Pick those orders, but he suspected that the Director of National Intelligence was unaccustomed to waiting. "No, sir—"

Another voice spoke into the phone and cut him off. "McCoy, this is President Cohen."

"Madam President," Pick said, straightening his posture in the backseat as if she could see him.

Randy's eyebrow rose even higher.

"I know the situation is fluid, but I would appreciate an update on what you've learned so far."

"Yes, ma'am," Pick said. "We arrived at Naval Air Station Oceana approximately two hours ago and immediately drove to Sentara Virginia Beach General Hospital to check on Castillo."

"How is he?" President Cohen asked.

"It's still too early to tell. He's undergone surgery to stabilize him but will require more in the coming days. He's in stable condition and being sedated for the time being."

"Go on."

"Two of my people proceeded to the oceanfront and met with local law enforcement and the FBI to begin piecing together the clues."

"Anything promising?"

"Nothing concrete," Pick said. "But we are operating under the assumption that the perpetrators of the attack are from somewhere in Central Asia—"

The President cut him off. "Like Tajikistan?"

"Possibly, ma'am. But we don't have enough information to go on yet." Pick thought about her question for a second before asking, "Why do you mention Tajikistan?"

This time, it was Marty Fleiss who answered. "The attack on the Crocus City Hall music venue in Krasnogorsk, Moscow Oblast, Russia, was carried out by a group of extremists from Tajikistan. We had received information on the possibility of such an attack weeks before and warned the Kremlin."

Pick hardly thought that was conclusive evidence that the same organization could have been behind the Virginia Beach shooting.

"Other than their apparent ethnicity, we have nothing to base such a conclusion on," he added, making it clear he was unwilling to make assumptions that could prove disastrous.

"Understood, Captain McCoy," President Cohen said. "What *do* you have?"

"Only a room key for a hotel we think is in San Antonio."

"Texas?"

Is there another one?

"Yes, ma'am. We're not even sure it's related, but a few here were worried that Castillo's grandmother might be in danger—"

"Why would his grandmother be in danger?"

Pick knew her question wasn't meant for him, and he listened in as the President and Director Fleiss discussed this latest thread.

"Doña Alicia lives on the Castillo ranch in Uvalde, Texas."

"That's pretty far from San Antonio."

"But she volunteers almost daily with the Daughters of the Republic of Texas in San Antonio."

"So, do we think she's the target?" the President asked. "Or just that she might be caught in a potential crossfire?"

Pick remained silent, waiting for his cue to speak again.

"That question is for you, Captain McCoy," Fleiss said.

There's my cue.

"We're not entirely sure of that, either, Madam President. But the hotel is located on the Alamo Plaza, and a few here think there could be a connection."

"Who are the few?"

Pick glanced over at Miller sitting in the seat next to him. "One of our pilots on the flight down from Reagan—a man by the name of Richard Miller—"

"I know Dick," President Cohen said. "Good man. Who else?"

"A Navy lieutenant commander by the name of Randy Richardson."

"Who's that?"

Pick glanced up and made eye contact with Randy. "Castillo's son."

His proclamation was met with silence.

"Ma'am, are you still there?"

"Captain McCoy, I'm going to direct the local FBI field office to find Doña Alicia. When you get there, I want you to ensure her safety before anything else. Then I want you to look for any evidence of a connection between the attack in Virginia Beach and a potential plot in San Antonio."

"You want me to fly to San Antonio?" Pick asked.

"Is that going to be a problem?"

"No, Madam President."

"Report back as soon as she's safe."

"Yes, Madam—"

The phone went dead.

Pick stared at the phone in disbelief for a second before lowering it and looking up at Randy. He almost laughed at the incredulous expression on the lieutenant commander's face.

"The President?" Randy asked.

Pick nodded.

"Of the United States?"

"Yes, Randy. That was Natalie Cohen, the President of the United States."

The chauffeured Suburban pulled into the parking lot and stopped in front of Oceana's air operations building. But nobody moved to open the doors and get out. Pick and Randy only stared at each other in silence while Miller ping-ponged between the two.

"What *the hell* is going on?" Randy asked. Only this time, it didn't sound like he was asking because he felt entitled to the truth. The question carried a tone that made it clear he wanted to be a part of whatever was happening. He wanted to be on their team.

"Castillo is . . . *was* . . . the Presidential Agent," Pick said at last.

"I've never heard of that," Randy said. "What's a Presidential Agent?"

"I'd never heard of it, either, until they ordered me back from Iraq and drove me to the White House to meet with the President and Director of National Intelligence. But basically, the Presidential Agent exists to cut through the bureaucratic red tape and accomplish what our bloated federal agencies can't."

"Like find the secretary of state?"

Pick nodded. "Among other things."

"Well, I want in."

Pick glanced at Miller, who smiled and shook his head, then back to Randy. "There can be only one."

"What is this? Highlander?"

"I'm just saying that for almost twenty years, Charley Castillo was *the* Presidential Agent. And now that he's been shot and is out of commission, the President has chosen me to replace him." Pick glanced at his watch again, more out of habit than any feeling that he was late for something. After all, one of the Gulfstream's two pilots was sitting next to him in the Suburban. They weren't leaving without him.

Randy shifted even farther in his seat. "I'm not saying I want to be you. I'm saying I want to help you find out who did this to Charley. And I want to make sure the same thing doesn't happen to Abuela."

Pick looked at Miller again.

"It's your call, kid. You're the man now," Miller said, then opened the door and climbed out.

Pick wasn't sure how Randy would fit into the team—in terms of both personality and skill set—but he had learned long ago that turning down help when it was offered was the worst kind of stupid. "Okay, we can figure out the details on the way."

"You serious?"

Pick opened the door to get out. "Yeah, Randy. Now let's go before I change my mind."

[FOUR]

Pick stood on the darkened ramp next to Randy and watched Dick Miller preparing the Coast Guard C-37A for flight. Though it was almost midnight, the night sky was filled with fighter jets returning to the air station to roost.

"I've got to admit, I'm a little jealous of those flyboys," Pick said.

Randy's arms were folded across his chest, and he turned to give Pick a queer look. "Second-guessing your decision not to follow your old man into the cockpit?"

Pick shook his head, as much to deny Randy's accusation that he secretly wanted to be a jet jockey as to rid his mind of thoughts that bordered on just that. "Not really. But you've gotta admit it looks fun, right?"

Randy laughed. "Oh, yeah, it's fun all right."

Pick looked over at Randy and couldn't help but notice the crooked smile on his face. "You never told me what you did in the Navy."

Randy nodded in the direction of a Super Hornet that touched down on the runway and rolled for half a beat before its pilot selected afterburner and coaxed the fighter back into the sky. "Well . . . that."

"That . . . meaning?"

"Meaning that I was trained to fly fighters," Randy said.

"Then what are you doing hanging around SEALs?"

Randy was about to answer when the doors to the air operations building opened, followed by a commotion that drew their attention away from the flight line. Pick turned to look over his shoulder at Junior and Ani, who were already bickering as they made their way across the darkened tarmac to the waiting Gulfstream.

"I told you it was a bad idea to release the pilot for the night," Junior said.

Ani threw her hands into the air. "For the umpteenth time, how was I supposed to know they'd want to fly somewhere else? We just got here."

"You're supposed to use your brain—"

Ani stepped in front of Junior and poked him in the chest. "This is *your* area of expertise. Not mine. So, don't you—"

Pick stuck his thumb and middle finger into his mouth and let loose a shrill whistle that brought them up short. Even Miller stopped his preflight inspection and looked in Pick's direction.

"Would one of you mind telling me what the problem is?"

Ani wheeled away from Junior to plead her case. "It's all my fault."

"What is?"

"While you were visiting Castillo in the hospital, the Coast Guard pilot asked if we would be RON or planned on making another stop."

Pick furrowed his brow. "RON?"

"Remaining overnight," Randy said from over his shoulder.

Pick nodded in thanks before returning his attention to Ani. "So, you released him?"

Ani nodded sheepishly.

"I told her it was a bad idea," Junior said, but Pick held up a hand to stop him from saying more.

"Can't we recall him?"

"No," Junior answered for her. "We can't."

"Well, why the hell not? We were all recalled short notice, weren't we?"

"Because he won't be legal for another . . ." Junior looked at his watch. "Ten hours, twenty minutes, and thirty-two seconds. Give or take."

Pick just stared at the spook.

Randy cleared his throat. "I think what he's trying to say is that the pilot enjoyed a nightcap and won't be able to get behind the controls of this here jet for another ten hours, twenty minutes, and . . ."

"Twenty seconds," Junior offered. "Give or take."

Miller had heard their conversation and ambled over. "Did I just hear we're short a pilot?"

"Looks that way," Pick said.

"I can get us rooms on base for the night while I coordinate for another qualified Gulfstream pilot to replace the Coastie who got us here," Junior offered. "That's the best I can do."

So much for being a one-man logistics wizard.

"I think I have a better idea," Randy said.

"Who's this guy?" Junior asked.

So much had taken place over the last few hours that Pick had forgotten to introduce them to the newest member of their team. "This is Lieutenant Commander Randy Richardson," Pick said. "He'll be joining our merry band for the foreseeable future."

Junior was unimpressed. "So, what's your idea?"

Instead of answering, he looked at Pick. "You asked what I was doing hanging around SEALs?"

Pick hesitantly allowed a glimmer of hope. "Don't tell me it's flying them around in Gulfstreams."

Randy nodded. "Among other things."

"Great," Miller said. "You can be my co-pilot. Grab your shit and let's go."

Once again, Randy seemed perplexed by the cavalier nature of their outfit and the notion that they could just take the multimillion-dollar jet because they wanted to. "But this is a Coast Guard aircraft . . ."

Junior and Ani were already following Miller toward the open boarding ladder, but Pick took pity on Randy. Even though he came from the world of special operations, it took some getting used to to accept the amount of leeway they were given to accomplish their mission. Instead of answering Randy directly, Pick pulled out his phone and tapped on the number for the most recent incoming call.

"What is it, McCoy?" DNI Marty Fleiss asked.

"Sir, we've run into a bit of a snag and need the secretary of homeland security's blessing to allow a Navy pilot to fly this Coast Guard C-37A."

"Is he qualified?"

Pick looked at Randy, who was staring at him in slack-jawed wonder. "Yes, sir. He assures me he is."

"Then I'll make the call, but don't wait for me to get back to you."

"Thank you, sir. We'll be wheels-up within the hour."

VII

[ONE]

San Antonio International Airport

San Antonio, Texas

0330 30 March 2026

Despite his assurances to Marty Fleiss, their departure from Naval Air Station Oceana had taken a little longer than expected. Pick was fast asleep before the Coast Guard C-37A taxied to the runway and took off with Dick Miller and Randy Richardson at the controls.

"We're here, boss."

Pick opened his eyes and looked around. "Where?"

"San Antone," Junior replied.

Pick sat up and kicked his feet off the divan. He vaguely remembered moving there from one of the reclining executive-style chairs to stretch out and get comfortable. But the rest of the flight was a blur.

"We're in San Antonio already?"

Junior nodded. "You were out cold."

Pick rubbed his eyes to erase the lingering effects of sleep and sniffed under his arms. He had definitely smelled worse. But he could remember when Junior had suggested he take a shower at the safe house in Khartoum.

"You don't smell half as bad," Junior said, as if reading Pick's mind, then gestured through the window at two blacked-out Chevy Tahoe

SUVs idling in front of the fixed base operator. "Besides, they're waiting on us."

"Then let's get to it."

By the time Pick exited the Gulfstream, Junior, Ani, Dick, and Randy had transferred their bags from the jet's cargo hold to the waiting Tahoes. To their credit, the FBI special agents hadn't seemed too put out by having to meet the Coast Guard jet in the middle of the night, and they hadn't asked many questions.

I guess when the request comes from the President . . .

Almost two hours after touching down at the international airport, their caravan reached downtown San Antonio and raced along the quiet streets toward the Alamo Plaza. Pick stared through the tinted windows at the sleepy town and wondered if all hell was about to break loose.

Up front, the Tahoe's radio squawked, and the special agent riding shotgun lifted the handset to his mouth to respond. Both the radio's volume and the agent's voice were too low for Pick to make out, but he thought he detected a trace of something in the conversation.

Frustration? Fear?

The agent turned and faced Pick. "Sir, we still haven't been able to locate Mrs. Castillo."

"Where have you—"

"She's not at the ranch?" Randy asked, cutting Pick off.

The agent turned to look at the other passenger. "No, sir. We sent agents to her house in Uvalde, but nobody was there."

Pick looked over at Randy. "Do you know where she might be?"

As the caravan came to a stop in front of the Menger Hotel, Randy nodded. "I think I might. She keeps an office at the Daughters of the Republic of Texas library."

"Where? At the Alamo?" Pick asked.

The agent riding shotgun answered. "No. It was there until the Daughters ceased being the custodians and handed control over to the Texas General Land Office."

Pick was surprised he felt relieved. He didn't even know Doña Alicia, but he was thankful Castillo's grandmother wouldn't be near the Alamo Plaza if the perpetrators of the Virginia Beach attack had planned something similar for San Antonio.

"Where's it now?" Pick asked.

"In the Bexar County Archive building," the agent replied. "A half-mile away."

Still a little too close for comfort.

Pick looked over his shoulder at the trailing Tahoe just as its doors opened and Dick, Junior, and Ani climbed out. It looked as if they were prepared for battle, reminding Pick of what was at stake.

He turned back to Randy. "Can you get her to safety?"

He nodded. "If she's there."

"We can take you," the special agent said.

"Okay, let me know when you have her. I'm going to meet with hotel security and plan our next move."

"You got it, boss," Randy said.

Pick opened the door and stepped out into the valet's drive.

As he approached the rest of the team, he couldn't help thinking about the oddity of Randy Richardson calling him "boss." He could still remember their first interaction on I-Day at the Naval Academy, and the dynamic of their relationship hadn't changed much in the years that followed.

Until now.

The Tahoe he had arrived in sped off into the night, attracting the notice of the others.

"Where's Randy off to?" Ani asked.

"The Daughters of the Republic of Texas library. Apparently, Doña Alicia has an office there."

"You think she's there this early in the morning?" Junior asked, clearly skeptical.

"She's not at home on her ranch in Uvalde," Pick replied. "And the feds haven't been able to find her yet. Randy thinks that's the best bet."

Ani cleared her throat. "Is he really Castillo's son?"

Pick shrugged. "It sure looks like it. Hopefully, he finds her and can keep her away while we figure out if there's anything to worry about here."

"I've been thinking about that," Junior said. "We've been operating under the assumption that the attack in Virginia Beach was carried out by terrorists who only wanted to stoke fear and promote a sense of insecurity."

"That seems like the textbook definition," Ani said.

"But what if there was an actual target?"

Pick knew what he was driving at. In the decades following September 11th, terrorism had become the default justification for any act of violence that didn't fit neatly into another category. Humans innately needed to make sense of the senseless, and Junior was trying to get them to look beyond their assumptions.

"And the other victims were only intended to serve as a smoke screen and disguise the identity of who they were really after?" Pick asked.

Junior nodded. "It's a possibility, right?"

"Seems pretty far-fetched, but sure."

"So, who was the target?" Ani asked.

Pick knew it was a rhetorical question, but the trio fell silent as they thought about the possibilities. They didn't yet have a list of victims in the Virginia Beach shooting, but Pick knew Junior was working on that. "It could be anybody," he muttered, more to himself than anything.

But Junior had picked up on it. "If the Virginia Beach attack was isolated, then it *could* be anybody. But if we compare it to an attack here—"

"*If* there is an attack here," Pick quickly added.

Junior waved him off. "Maybe we can find a connection between some of the Virginia Beach victims and San Antonio."

"So, you want to wait to see if there's another mass shooting, just so we can find a link?" Ani asked in a tone that made it clear what she thought of that idea.

"No, that's not what I'm saying at all. What I am saying is that we start looking *now* to give us a list of potential targets."

"Are we ignoring the obvious?" Ani asked.

Pick narrowed his eyes. "What?"

"That Castillo is in the hospital and we're here because of his grandmother?"

"Are you saying you think Castillo was the target?"

Ani bit her lip as if second-guessing her assessment, but Junior spoke up. "No, I think she's onto something. Maybe we should see about posting some guards at the hospital."

"That's a good idea," Pick said, disappointed that he hadn't thought of it first.

But Miller came to his rescue. "I'll take care of that. I have a few contacts from the old days who live in the area and are less than thrilled with the boredom of retirement. They'd be more than happy to sit on Charley until this is over."

Pick imagined the brotherhood of the Green Berets was a lot like that of the Marine Raiders, and he knew he could rely on Miller to get it done. "Thanks, Dick."

As Miller disappeared inside the hotel to coordinate protection for Castillo, Pick turned back to Junior. "You really think they could've been after him?"

"Lord knows Castillo pissed off a lot of people over the years, so it wouldn't be a stretch to think he has more than a few enemies who would want to take him out."

Pick didn't want to admit it, but the spook had a point. They couldn't discount the possibility that the attack in Virginia Beach was merely intended to disguise a hit on the Presidential Agent. But for that to be true, they needed to find evidence of a plot in San Antonio.

"Okay, let's get inside and talk to hotel security," Pick said. "They should be able to tell us who made the reservation and checked into the room."

"Assuming they used real identification," Ani said.

"It's someplace to start," Junior said.

Not for the first time, Pick wondered what kind of intelligence and tools the spook had at his disposal.

[TWO]

An hour later, the trio exited the office of the hotel's security manager and returned to the lobby. Though it was still early, bleary-eyed guests were beginning to filter in. The security manager had been less than forthcoming with information until Pick pulled out his Secret Service credentials. After that, he changed his tune and was more than happy to tell Pick anything he wanted to know.

"He said they specifically requested this room," Pick said, holding the room key in his hand. "Why? What's so special about it?"

Junior held up a copy of the hotel's layout that the security manager had given him. "It's on the top floor near the northwest corner with a commanding view of Alamo Plaza."

Pick stared at the key in the paper sleeve with the room's number scrawled on it, then looked up at Ani and saw that she was doing the same.

"Should we go have a look?" Ani asked.

"Have a look at what?" another voice asked.

Pick looked up at Dick Miller, who had silently joined their group while they debated their next move.

"Did you take care of Castillo?"

Miller nodded. "I've got some of the best on their way there now."

"Thanks, Dick."

"Don't mention it. Now, what are we having a look at?"

If there was one thing Pick had learned in the Marine Corps, it was that even a bad decision was better than no decision at all. And like it or not, he was the Presidential Agent, and it was his call to make.

"We were just about to do a little snooping," he replied.

"Then what are we waiting for?"

Junior snatched the key out of Pick's hands and turned for the elevator without waiting for the others. Ani hesitated half a second before following. Pick was less than eager to break into the hotel room, and he shared a brief glance with Miller before deciding to round out the fire team as tail-end Charlie.

"Think it's occupied?" Miller asked.

"I don't know."

With any luck, they'd stumble on a group of jihadists sleeping off a bender from a final night of enjoying earthly pleasures. Pick suspected any terrorists they might encounter—*if we encounter any at all*—wouldn't be any different from the ones he had engaged in Afghanistan, Iraq, or the Sudan. Each believed their debauchery on Earth would be forgiven upon their entry into Paradise, where they would be rewarded for their martyrdom with eternal companionship with a houri—an ethereal maiden woman with beautiful eyes.

"Only one way of finding out," Miller said.

[THREE]

The group rode the elevator up to the fourth floor in silence, spilling out into the alcove the moment the doors opened with a faint metallic *ding*. Pick stepped into the hall and looked both ways, seeing only a lone housekeeper who had probably just arrived and was preparing to start her day. He brushed against the butt of his pistol carried appendix-style and satisfied himself that it was there and ready to go to work if needed. But none of the others seemed overly concerned by the possibility of walking into an ambush.

As the others stepped around Pick to make their way to the room, he reluctantly followed. He might have brought up the rear, but he knew it was still his show to run. "So . . . what are we going to do? Knock?"

Junior looked over his shoulder at him. "Got a better idea?"

"Are you serious?" Miller asked. "Why don't we just announce that we're from the government and here to help?"

"He's right," Pick said, thinking back to Castillo's constant warnings. "I don't think announcing ourselves is the right move. We have the room key, so why don't we just use it?"

This suggestion brought Junior to a halt. "Because there's a good chance that whoever's inside has booby-trapped the door to prevent somebody from doing exactly what you're proposing. If we can convince them to come to the door, they'll at least have to disarm any countermeasures put in place before opening it."

Pick stepped aside for the young Hispanic woman who was pushing a housekeeping cart toward the service elevator, more than a little embarrassed he hadn't considered that possibility. "Okay, you're right. But they still need to open the door."

"Buen día," the housekeeper said politely, smiling with her eyes downcast as she hurried past.

"I might have another idea," Junior said, snapping his fingers. His eyes shifted between the housekeeper and Ani, but his attention on the Hispanic woman hadn't gone unnoticed.

Ani shook her head. "No way."

"Come on, Ani. You're the only one who can pull this off."

"It's way too early," she said.

Pick was about to ask what the spook had in mind when he finally put it together on his own. "It's actually a good idea, Ani."

"No way," she said again, scowling at Junior. "You just want me to put on that cute little outfit to satisfy your sexual fantasies."

Junior feigned insult. "I would never stoop to something like that—"

"You forget I know you," Ani said.

But Pick had made up his mind. "Junior's right, Ani. You're the only one who can get away with it. We need you to pretend to be a housekeeper to get whoever's inside to unlock the door so we can catch them by surprise."

"Didn't you hear me say it's too early? They'll know I'm not a housekeeper."

"Got a better idea?"

Ani's face flushed with anger, but she had stopped arguing against the suggestion. Pick believed men and women were on equal footing when it came to intellectual endeavors, but he hadn't yet come to accept that a man could adequately pass as a woman physically. Sometimes one needed to be pragmatic—and a little sexist—to be successful in subterfuge.

But the vibrating cellphone in his pocket delayed Pick from putting that theory to the test. He pulled it out to answer.

"Yeah?"

"She wasn't in her office," Randy said.

"Any idea where she is?" Pick asked, motioning for the others to give him a moment.

"The security guard at the library said she sometimes spends her mornings at the Alamo before it opens to the public."

Pick felt his stomach drop. "When's that?"

"In a few hours. I'm on my way there now."

"I'm not sure how much time we have," Pick said.

"Why? What's happened?"

"Call it Raider intuition."

"Did you find something in the room?"

Pick gestured the others onward. He could tell by their body language that they felt it, too. "We were just about to make entry. You still with the feds?"

"Yeah, but I get the feeling they're getting tired of playing babysitter—"

"Tough shit," Pick said, cutting him off.

"Okay, we're just turning onto Bonham and will be there in—"

The sound of breaking glass behind the closed door for room 4082 drowned out the rest of what Randy was saying. But the sound might as well have been a starter's pistol for the way it made Pick's heart bolt. "Something's happening, Randy. Get to Abuela. Now!"

"What—"

Pick hung up on him and shoved the phone back into his pocket while simultaneously drawing the concealed pistol. "Go, go, go!"

The others had heard the glass breaking as well and were already stacking up alongside the door. Junior held the room key in front of him but shot a questioning glance at Pick over his shoulder. "It could still be rigged . . ."

Pick knew it was a risk. If the door turned out to be booby-trapped, then it meant they were right, and its occupants were preparing for an attack.

"Open it," Pick ordered.

They might be blown to smithereens, but maybe it would prevent another deadly attack from taking place, and they would save countless lives. But if it wasn't rigged, then the worst-case scenario was that they were about to embarrass themselves by barging in on an unsuspecting guest. Of the two, Pick would take embarrassment over an imminent terrorist attack any day.

Junior skidded to a halt in front of the door and glanced at Pick one last time for confirmation.

"Do it."

I sure hope we don't get blown to smithereens.

Junior pressed the key card against the magnetic lock and heard it disengage with a quiet chirp. He pressed down on the handle, took a deep breath, and . . .

"Here goes nothing."

[FOUR]

Pick held his breath as the door swung inward, but his pistol came up in a smooth arc as he registered two simultaneous thoughts.

I'm still alive. And *Who's the clean-shaven dark-haired man holding what looks like an M4A1 carbine with an M203 under-barrel grenade launcher?*

Pick didn't hesitate and settled the RMR red dot on the back of the man's head and pressed back on the trigger. The gun barked, and a 9-millimeter hollow-point slammed into his target, turning the air behind him crimson. The man dropped the American-made rifle and collapsed in a heap.

"Damn, Killer," Junior said, entering the room only half a step behind him.

But Pick was in Raider mode and quickly stepped left while sweeping his pistol across the room to look for another target. "Clear left."

"Clear right," Junior replied.

Keeping his pistol up, Pick crossed the room and knelt over the dropped rifle. He gave it a quick once-over and opened the grenade launcher's breech to eject a 40-millimeter high-explosive grenade. "This is military-grade hardware," he said.

While Pick focused on the weapon, Junior had turned his attention to the potential shooter, patting him down to look for pocket litter or anything else that might identify him. Neither man said it, but Pick knew they were both hoping they hadn't just shot a friendly.

"Why would he have a loaded grenade launcher?" Ani asked, almost as if in response to Pick's fear that he had just murdered a law enforcement officer.

But he was thinking about the question from a different angle. Pick stood and looked through the broken glass and out onto the Alamo Plaza. "The M203 has an effective range of about three hundred and fifty meters—more than enough to reach any corner of the plaza from here."

"See anything?" Miller asked, crowding over him to look through the window at the faint outline of the Alamo across the street.

Pick scanned the plaza, but when he saw nothing in the early dawn's dim light, he glanced down at the spook, who was still searching the body. Still, the shooter wouldn't have broken the window while holding a loaded grenade launcher if he hadn't planned on using it. "Not a damn thing. You got anything yet, Junior?"

The spook shook his head. "He's clean. What do you want us to do, boss?"

The question instantly reminded Pick that Randy was on his way to find Abuela somewhere in the plaza, and he turned again to look down on the scene below. The Alamo was in the middle of a lengthy renovation project, with construction fencing surrounding much of the grounds, but Pick spotted Randy and two special agents disappearing through the south-facing Mission Gate and Lunette.

He dug into his pocket for his cellphone, hoping he wasn't too late.

"Boss?"

Pick dialed the number for the last incoming call and turned to the others while he waited for it to connect. "Miller, I need you to get down to the plaza and coordinate with the Alamo Rangers if the FBI hasn't already and get some black-and-whites out here ASAP. I think something's about to go down."

"Alamo Rangers?"

"They're like modern-day defenders of the Alamo," Pick said.

"On it." Dick darted from the room.

Pick turned to Junior. "Please tell me you can get your hands on something with a little more *oomph* than my pistol here."

The spook looked down at the rifle the gunman had dropped. "What's wrong with that one?"

Pick shook his head. "This is standard-government-issue crap."

"Which makes me wonder how he got it," Ani mused.

"That's a question for another time. It'll do in a pinch, but I need to get my hands on something I can trust."

Junior nodded with understanding. "On a whim, I had a weapons case loaded on the bird before we left Reagan. It's not much, but—"

"What's in it?"

"Like I said, not much. But we've got four TX4 personal defense weapons from Lone Star Armory."

Pick whistled softly. "They make good guns."

If there was one thing the military had produced in abundance during the quarter century after September 11th, it was a cadre of talented individuals who could modify the crap hardware Uncle Sam had provided to them. He and almost every other Marine Raider had taken their stock M4 carbines and handed them over to their unit armorer to change out the barrels, bolt carrier groups, triggers, and anything else they could think of to make their weapons more lethal.

Lone Star Armory catered to guys who didn't think good enough was good enough.

Guys like Pick.

"We've also got four pistols and enough ammo to take on a small army."

Pick glanced down at the Alamo again. "I don't think we have enough time to get the case from the plane and—"

"Oh, no," Junior said, cutting him off. "I loaded it into the FBI Tahoe before we left the airport."

Picked whipped his head back to the spook. "Good, let's go."

Ani held up a hand. "What about me? What do I do?"

Pick was accustomed to leading experienced Marine special operators who were naturally drawn to the fight. Despite how well Ani had performed in the Sudan, he had to remind himself that she was more comfortable operating in the shadows and unaccustomed to being on the front lines. But that didn't mean she couldn't be useful.

He pointed at the discarded rifle. "Get that serial number and find out where it came from. Then take it with you to the valet and get the Tahoe ready for a hot extract."

"A . . . hot extract?"

But Pick ignored her hesitation. "Once we secure Abuela, we'll make our way back to you. If we can't get to you, our primary exfil point will be on the north end where the Plaza meets Houston Street."

"Got it," she said, still sounding unsure of herself.

"There's a set of encrypted earbuds in the gun case," Junior added. "I'll leave you with a set so you can get up on the net."

Ani nodded.

"You can do this, Ani. Driving in Cairo was probably a lot more dangerous."

She shot him a dubious look.

"You can do this," Pick repeated.

Junior grabbed Ani by the arm and propelled her to the door. "Come on, let's go get our guns."

[FIVE]

Alamo Plaza

San Antonio, Texas

0655 30 March 2026

Several minutes later, Pick stepped out of the elevator and into the lobby, where Junior waited for him, outfitted in a chest rig with several spare magazines, and carrying a short-barreled suppressed TX4, with a spare slung across his back.

Pick was about to ask where his kit was when Junior dropped a duffel bag at his feet. The Raider in him needed no more encouragement than that, and he unzipped the duffel and pulled out an identical set of gear. Preparing for war had become routine for Pick, and he quickly donned the chest rig and removed the matching LSA TX4 personal defense weapons.

"Good to go?" Pick asked.

Junior extended his hand, holding out a set of earbuds for Pick.

As soon as he put them in, he heard a chime in his ear, followed by Ani's voice. It sounded like she was standing right behind him and speaking directly into his ear in a conversational tone. "I'm in the Tahoe. What's your status?"

"We're outside the Menger Bar and getting some pretty strange looks from people," Junior said.

Pick studied the sparse lobby traffic, but he wasn't looking at faces. He was looking at hands. "I sure hope Miller and the feds gave the Alamo Rangers our description and told them we're on their team."

Moving as if they had been training together for years instead of only a week, Pick and Junior swept through the automatic doors and out into the valet driveway. They nodded at Ani in the Tahoe, then jogged into the space separating the Menger Hotel from Alamo Plaza. The renovation project had turned what used to be a street on the hotel's north side into a pedestrian-only access that funneled visitors into the gate where he had seen Randy disappear.

"I've got a police scanner app up and running on my phone," Ani said.

"Any sign that the feds put the word out?"

"Not so far. There have only been . . ."

The way she trailed off sent a chill down his spine. But Pick forged onward and turned left for the Mission Gate.

Ani's voice returned a second later. "Just got the first report of armed men in the Menger Hotel."

"Has to be us," Junior said.

"Anything from the FBI or Alamo Rangers?" Pick asked, knowing that besides the two special agents who had gone in with Randy, the Alamo Rangers provided round-the-clock security for the historic site and would be first to respond. If there was going to be a police response, it would come from them.

"Not yet."

Junior didn't take that news as a good sign. "We still have to account for them, even if we didn't have law enforcement converging on our position from every direction."

Almost as if in response to his assessment, a chorus of faint police sirens filtered through the normal and mundane sounds of city life.

"Several units responding," Ani said, confirming what Pick already knew.

"We need to be quick about this," Junior added.

Pick opened his mouth to respond, but the words never came out. To his left, he saw movement darting behind a stately live oak adorning the southern edge of the plaza. “Heads up,” Pick said. “I’ve got two possible bad guys converging on the Mission Gate.”

From the corner of his eye, Pick saw Junior pivoting to aim his TX4 in that direction. “Got ’em.”

Acting on instinct, Pick and Junior floated apart to make it more difficult for potential threats to target them simultaneously. Pick hugged the hotel on the south side of the pedestrian walkway, and Junior moved along the sidewalk bordering the Alamo on the north.

“I only see two,” Pick said.

“Same.”

“There have to be more. Keep your eyes peeled.”

In the background the police sirens multiplied and grew in intensity as black-and-white San Antonio police cruisers converged on the scene. But even their shrill wailing seemed to vanish in an instant when Pick heard the distinctive *whump* of a 40-millimeter grenade being propelled from a launcher at 250 feet per second.

“Incoming!” Pick screamed.

VIII

[ONE]

Alamo Plaza

San Antonio, Texas

0710 30 March 2026

The grenade detonated with an earsplitting concussion that sent Pick and Junior to their knees. But they quickly realized the blast was on the opposite side of the plaza, and they jumped to their feet to resume their advance on the shooters they had seen earlier.

"That didn't come from the Menger," Junior said.

"I think you're right. It sounded like it came from over my right shoulder."

"Hearing reports of an active-shooter situation at the Crockett Hotel," Ani said, confirming their suspicion that the grenade had likely come from the hotel catty-corner to the Menger.

"Junior, watch our six."

"On it." From the corner of his eye, Pick saw the spook pivot and sweep the pedestrian walkway behind them with the barrel of his personal defense weapon. "We're clear."

Pick darted forward several steps, then quickly dropped to the ground, instinctively reciting a mantra that had been ingrained into him from an early age—*I'm up. They see me. I'm down.* Before attending Assessment and Selection at Stone Bay, and even before going through the Infantry Officer Course at Quantico, his Marine instructors at Annapolis had drilled it into him.

He turned and aimed his TX4 to the rear. "Covering."

"Moving."

Junior jumped up and spun toward the Mission Gate, sprinting forward until he had passed Pick, then flopped to the ground. Mirroring Pick's actions, he once again took up the job of scanning in the direction of the Crockett Hotel.

"Covering."

Pick jumped to his feet. "Moving."

"More reports of active shooters coming from the Federal Building," Ani said, adding another piece of information to help them paint a more complete picture of the tactical situation.

I'm up. They see me. I'm down.

"Where's the Federal Building?" Pick asked, just as he dropped to the ground again.

"North side of the plaza, between Alamo Street and Avenue E."

"Covering."

Junior hopped up and continued bounding forward. "Moving."

In his mind, Pick could see the layout of the entire Alamo Plaza. But with all the construction taking place during its renovation, the temporary fencing made it almost impossible for him to get a clear line of sight to the most likely avenues of approach for gunmen intending to incite chaos through violence. But Randy and two special agents were somewhere inside looking for Castillo's abuela, and he wasn't about to let them be caught in the middle of it.

"Co—"

Junior's statement was cut short as he unleashed a short burst from his TX4. It took all of Pick's willpower not to turn and add his own gun to the fight, but he knew his area of responsibility was the sector to their rear. It wouldn't do them any good if he allowed gunmen to catch them by surprise and cut them down from behind.

"Got one," Junior said, then quickly added, "Covering."

Pick jumped up and spun around to see a black-clad figure lying prone in the middle of the pedestrian walkway—obviously the bad guy Junior had engaged. A discarded M4A1 carbine rested less than three feet from his body, but it didn't appear to be outfitted with the underslung M203 grenade launcher like the one Ani had taken from the hotel room.

Or the one that had fired from the Crockett Hotel.

"Moving," he said, then quickly added, "Shooters appear to be armed with U.S. government–issued weapons."

"I haven't heard back from my contacts yet," Ani said, surprising Pick again with her astute grasp of the situation and providing him with only the information he needed in the moment. "But be advised that law enforcement is arriving on the northeast corner of the plaza at this time."

Again, Pick cataloged this away. The last thing he wanted to do was find himself rushing toward friendlies and mistakenly shooting one of them.

Or be shot himself.

He flopped to the ground and twisted around once more. "Covering."

"Moving."

Pick was breathing heavy, though it was caused more by the surge of adrenaline from knowing combat was imminent than from their leapfrogging sprint toward the Alamo. Still, he focused on slowing his breathing and remaining calm while scanning his sector for threats.

After two seconds, two men dressed in black and carrying carbines appeared in a dead sprint from around the corner where Bonham disappeared to the northeast. Pick didn't hesitate and centered his

EOTech's reticle on the closest of the two gunmen, then squeezed the trigger.

The LSA TX4 bucked in his arms, then cycled smoothly as Pick shifted his aim to the second gunman and fired again. The *crack crack* of gunfire was overlapped by a much quieter *thwap thwap* as two rounds of 5.56-millimeter full metal jacket impacted the shooters and knocked them both off their feet. His shots had been true, but he hadn't been aiming for their heads and instead opted for center mass and a much higher probability of impact in their upper thoracic cavities.

"Contact rear," he said, letting Junior know he had engaged the enemy and that they weren't yet down.

"Two bad guys just entered the Mission Gate," Junior said.

Pick watched the two shooters he had targeted writhing in pain on the pedestrian walkway, willing one of them to get up and present him with an easy target. But both seemed content with moaning in agony while remaining flat on the earth.

Maybe they'll live. God knows we need the intel.

"Ani, get in touch with the FBI and direct them to the corner of Bonham and Crockett, where two bad guys are down but still alive."

"On it."

"Moving," Junior said, reminding Pick that they had been in one place for too long already.

"Right behind you," Pick said. Then he jumped to his feet and followed the spook into the plaza. At this point, it was more important for him to support Junior's advance than it was to cover their rear. Besides, any additional shooters who might have had plans to surprise them from that direction probably saw their compatriots dropped with two well-placed shots and were second-guessing their dedication to committing jihad.

As Pick and Junior slipped underneath the sweeping branches of oak and pecan trees lining the plaza, both men sighted in on the funnel-like gate. The replica was constructed with fake hewed timbers and a built-up earthen embankment, giving the impression that the bulwark was holding back hordes of Mexican troops. A notch was cut into either side where two six-pound cannons were anchored to aid in the mission's defense. But all Pick cared about was finding the gunmen who had disappeared inside.

Whump!

"Incoming!" Pick yelled again, flinging himself away from Junior and into a concrete planter. He hit hard, barely a second before the grenade detonated, again on the north side of the plaza.

Whump! Whump!

"Where's it coming from?" Junior shouted. He had taken cover against another planter but was under no illusions that the pecan tree's branches would protect him from a high-explosive round dropping in from above.

Ani's calm voice answered, "Sounds like it might still be the Crockett."

From his vantage point, Pick couldn't see every window that faced the Alamo Plaza. But he didn't have to. On the south end of the hotel—just underneath and to the right of a large sign proclaiming CROCKETT HOTEL—he saw a window that had been broken out and was filled with yet another figure dressed in black.

"Tally one, sixth floor, three south from the gutter," he said.

Junior craned his neck to spot the shooter. "I got him."

Pick pushed himself up onto his knees and rested the barrel of his TX4 on top of the planter, sighting in on the window. The EOTech wasn't the ideal optic for long-distance shooting, but this was far from a long-distance shot. "I'll cover you. On my mark, get to the Mission Gate."

"Ready."

Pick took several deep breaths to slow his heart rate. "Three, two—"

A sharp staccato of multiple carbines cycling on full auto from inside the Alamo's walls stopped him from completing his countdown.

"Go!"

Junior jumped up and started sprinting for the Mission Gate, and Pick pressed back on the trigger. He watched his bullet impact just beneath the hotel room window, causing the gunman to startle and let loose with a burst from his carbine. But he hadn't been aiming, and his rounds thunked harmlessly into the ground.

But Pick *was* aiming. Using Kentucky windage, he adjusted his aim point on the shooter, and less than a second after his first round impacted the side of the hotel, another round sailed through the window and caught the shooter in the neck.

"Got the shooter at the Crockett," he said.

"More law enforcement responding there," Ani said.

Pick jumped to his feet and followed Junior through the Mission Gate to reach the hallowed grounds. "Copy. Any word from Miller or the FBI?"

"Nothing yet."

Pick cursed under his breath but continued his rush into the gate while preparing for a close-in engagement. The body of an Alamo Ranger slumped against one of the six-pounders, and Pick paused long enough to feel for a pulse.

Nothing.

Pick gritted his teeth in frustration when he noticed that the Ranger had a gun in his hand and a subdued Marine Corps Eagle, Globe, and Anchor pinned to his uniform. The black-clad body of a dead gunman rested just inside the Lunette.

At least you went down fighting. Semper Fi, Marine.

Gunfire continued unabated from the Alamo's grounds, but the tall buildings surrounding the plaza reflected back the sound from multiple angles, making it almost impossible to pinpoint where it was coming from. Pick jumped up and ran into the Lunette, stepping over the slain gunman as he wheeled right.

"Is it coming from the Church?" Pick asked.

"I think it's the courtyard," Junior replied.

Just to the left of the Church—the building most people thought of as the Alamo—a wall enclosed the Convento and Cavalry Courtyards, both adjacent to the Long Barrack. If they ran to the sound of the guns, they would be cornering themselves without a means of escape. That was never a good tactical move.

Pick's cellphone vibrated, and he pulled it from his pocket and saw a text message from Randy.

FEDS ARE DOWN. I HAVE ABUELA. WE'RE HUNKERED DOWN IN THE LONG BARRACK. HURRY.

[TWO]

Pick hugged the right wall of the Lunette exhibit—opposite bronze replicas of the mission as it had appeared during various periods of its existence—and sighted along the top of his personal defense weapon at the Alamo Church. It was a short but exposed distance with a small patch of grass directly in front, fenced off by a single chain. "On your six," Pick said, letting Junior know he was approaching from behind.

"I can't see where they're shooting from, but they're definitely in the courtyard."

Pick dropped to a crouch and raised his TX4 to sight through the EOTech. "I can't, either, but Randy said they got his babysitters."

"What?"

"He has Abuela inside the Long Barrack. We need to get to them and fortify that position until more law enforcement arrives to secure the scene."

Junior glanced over at him. "That's fitting."

"What is?"

"He's referring to the Battle of the Alamo," Ani said. "Several members of the garrison withdrew to the Long Barrack to make their last stand against Santa Anna's soldiers." She paused. "I copied what you said about his babysitters, Pick. I'll let the FBI know they've got agents down."

"Thanks, Ani. We're gonna hit Long Barrack and make that our last stand against whoever these guys are," Pick replied. "You ready, Junior?"

"Ready."

Pick jumped up and darted across the open clearing, aiming for the gap in the wall left of the Church leading into the Convento Courtyard. Massive oak trees towered above the wall and shaded the courtyard's interior, hiding potential shooters from view. Movement off to his left caught Pick's attention, and he swung the TX4 in that direction.

His breath caught when he spotted an older woman in period attire, crouching next to a planter underneath a large pecan tree in the center of the plaza. Scanning to either side, he saw the bodies of two additional Rangers lying where two hundred Texans had defended the mission during a thirteen-day siege. He ignored the rising body count and waved at the woman to get her attention.

"Go that way!" he shouted, gesturing in the direction of the Mission Gate.

She started to move but stopped abruptly when gunfire erupted from the courtyard entrance. Rounds stitched the ground on either side of Pick, and he spun back to face the courtyard entrance while working the trigger to pepper the stone wall protecting the shooter.

"Contact front," Junior yelled, also putting rounds into the same wall.

Pick's bolt locked back to the rear.

"Reloading," he yelled, instinctively extending his trigger finger to eject the spent magazine while reaching up with his left hand for a spare from the pouch on his chest rig. He looked over at the older woman in period dress who appeared frozen by fear.

"Go! Run!" he yelled, the tenor of his voice spurring her into action as he slid a fresh magazine into his TX4 and pressed the bolt catch with his thumb to chamber another round.

Junior's gun fell silent. "Reloading."

Pick once more shouldered his personal defense weapon and aimed it at the courtyard entrance, then advanced to the left of the grassy patch in a crouched walk with a smooth heel-toe gait. He centered his reticle on the center of the gap in the wall, waiting for another target to appear. When he heard Junior's bolt slide forward, he glanced over his right shoulder and saw the spook moving quickly to catch up, rounding the grassy area to the right while also aiming his TX4 at the opening.

As Pick approached the wall to the left of the gate, he aimed into the courtyard and gradually cleared more of the space behind the wall on the right. Junior mirrored him to clear the area to the left. By the time they collapsed on the opening in the wall, they were relatively certain that whoever had fired on them had either changed positions and withdrawn to safety or pressed themselves against the wall on the opposite side.

Pick made eye contact with Junior on the right side of the gate. "I'm first in," he said.

Junior nodded in agreement, and Pick initiated the action with a very pronounced nod. He darted forward and slipped into the courtyard, knowing with absolute certainty that Junior would follow right behind him. He pivoted right, looking over a mangled wrought-iron gate at a man who was roughly his age and dressed entirely in black. It took a fraction of a second for Pick to recognize that the man also held an M4A1 carbine at low-ready, nearly identical to the ones he had seen wielded by the other shooters.

How many are there?

Pick squeezed the trigger without hesitation and sent a round into the man's skull, dropping him straight to the ground. "Clear right."

Pick heard only Junior's soft footfalls and measured breathing as he entered the courtyard and pivoted in the other direction. "Now we know what happened to the feds . . . Clear left."

Pick turned in Junior's direction and saw the fallen bodies of the two FBI special agents who had met them at the San Antonio International Airport. Both had their service pistols drawn. And both had been stitched from head to toe with bullets. Pick swallowed to clear away the lump in his throat. "Move to the barrack."

"Moving."

With Pick covering their rear, the two moved along the walkway under wide oak branches to the arched entrance of the barrack's breezeway. Wood beams stretched across the ceiling and a window was centered in the rubble masonry on the southern wall, but Pick was focused on the solid wood door that was the only thing preventing them from getting to Abuela inside.

"Blue! Blue! Blue!" Junior yelled, moments before barreling into the door.

But he bounced back a few inches.

"Try pulling," Pick said.

Junior cursed under his breath but took Pick's suggestion. The moment he had the door open, both men stumbled into the barrack.

"Took you long enough," a voice said from the shadows.

Pick regained his balance and spun in his direction just as Randy stepped out from behind a curtain to his left.

"Are you okay?"

"Those agents sacrificed themselves to get us to safety. But we're fine. I just don't know how I'm going to get Abuela to safety."

Just then, a trim woman with stark gray hair stepped into the dim lighting put off by the room's chandeliers and pushed Randy aside. She was cradling a shotgun like she knew how to use it. "I do not need to get to safety. I need one of those pendejos to try coming through that door so I can pump double-aught buckshot into them."

"Doña Alicia, I presume?"

"You presume correctly, young man," she said, rising to her full stature. "Are you the person responsible for involving my dear great-grandson in this?"

Pick glanced at Randy, who only shrugged.

"No, ma'am. He actually outranks me."

"Is that so?"

"Captain McCoy, ma'am. United States Marine Corps."

Randy cleared his throat and gestured to the weapon slung across Junior's back. "Is that for me?"

Junior unslung the spare TX4 and handed it over. "Yeah, but just make sure you point the pointy end at the bad guy."

"I think I know how to use it," Randy said, taking the personal defense weapon and extending the buttstock before canting it to the side and partially pulling back the charging handle to verify its condition. "I'm just thankful I didn't have to break into storage and use David Crockett's rifle to defend this place."

"You would never desecrate the Alamo like that," Doña Alicia said.

She's just like Castillo.

"Help is on the way, ma'am," Pick said.

She grunted. "Somehow, I don't think that provides the comfort you think it does."

[THREE]

Pick looked down on the older woman but somehow felt shorter. "Yes, ma'am, but if you wouldn't mind, please take cover behind—"

Doña Alicia cut him off. "Son, I am not a defenseless woman."

"Clearly not, ma'am. I didn't mean to—"

"I am the descendant of Manuel Martinez. Do you know who that is?"

Pick didn't, but he knew they didn't have time to squabble over history. He could tell by the fire in her eyes that she wouldn't be swayed by his persuasive logic to take cover while the men defended their position against attack. "No, ma'am."

"He fell alongside Guillermo de Castillo—the ancestor of my late dear Fernando—here, on these sacred grounds." She tucked the shotgun's buttstock up into her shoulder. "And if they want my shotgun, they are more than welcome to come and take it."

She racked the fore grip to chamber a round.

They sure do make them different here in Texas.

"Abuela—"

"Enough, Randolph," she snapped, cutting him off.

She's not just like Castillo. He's *just like* her.

"A better use of our time would be to fortify our defenses and prepare for them," Doña Alicia said. "Because, make no mistake, they *are* coming."

Pick was so struck by the dichotomy of Abuela's diminutive physical stature and her commanding presence that he simply stood there like he was just a butterbar second lieutenant. But he recognized the validity of her suggestion, snapped out of his shocked introspection, and swung into action.

"Randy, set up in that next room and cover the north entrances," he said, gesturing to an anteroom that separated the makeshift theater where they stood and the museum's exhibits at the opposite end.

"Got it."

Pick said a silent prayer of thanks that Randy hadn't tried throwing his rank around or pushed back like the Castillo matriarch. After the naval aviator had scampered off to set up his defensive position, Pick turned to Junior.

"I want you to set up here and cover this entrance," he said, then pointed across the room. "I'll be just over there to provide overlapping coverage."

"You got it, boss."

At last, Pick turned to Abuela. "Doña Alicia, if you wouldn't mind . . ."

He saw the expression on her face harden, and he swallowed. She terrified him more than any grizzled MARSOC gunnery sergeant ever had.

"You can take up position wherever you see fit," Pick concluded.

She gave him a slight smile and nodded approvingly. "Let them come."

Somehow, I think she means it.

As Abuela turned and stalked to the door leading into the space where Randy had set up, Pick shook his head in amazement. He had thought he was the brave one by traversing an open plaza under fire to save her. But she was the last person who needed saving. Knowing she was a descendant of Texan nobility was one thing. Seeing her embody the spirit of those who had fallen on that very ground was another thing altogether.

"God help anybody who crosses that woman," he muttered.

[FOUR]

As a Marine Raider, Pick was unaccustomed to hiding behind cover and waiting for the enemy to attack. Raiders were specialists in many things, but the defense of a fixed position was not one of them. Sure, he had been trained in all types of military operations during The Basic School in Quantico, Virginia, but it had been far more common for his instructors to shout "Take that hill!"—not "Defend this hill!"

Junior's quiet voice carried clearly over the encrypted earpiece and broke the silence. "Castillo's ma-maw is something else, ain't she?"

Pick glanced at the older woman and chewed on the inside of his cheek before answering. "You can say that again."

Junior didn't. "What's the latest, Ani?"

"Police have cordoned off the entire plaza for one block in every direction. The Texas Department of Public Safety has a Special Response Team en route, and the FBI has mobilized SWAT from the local field office to coordinate a response with the remaining Alamo Rangers."

"Super," Pick said. Several of his former Raider teammates had gone to work for the Lone Star State after leaving the Marine Corps, and he knew that each SRT was made up of officers from the Highway Patrol, the Criminal Investigations Division, and the Texas Rangers. They were bona fide operators and straight-up meat-eaters.

If it didn't become a dick-measuring contest between them and FBI SWAT, they would make quick work of the remaining bad guys.

And they would be smack-dab in the middle of it.

"Do they know we're inside?"

"Not yet," Ani replied. "I'm still at the hotel but will keep trying. Figured you'd want me to be closer."

"Good call," Pick agreed. "Have you heard from Miller?"

"Radio silence," Ani replied. "So, you need to assume that when they give the SWAT team the green light, they're not going to know you're friendly."

"Don't they know you're a supervisory special agent with the Secret Service?" Junior asked, openly mocking Pick's recent commission.

"Tell you what," Pick said. "I'll give you my credentials, and you can run outside waving them above your head and see if that's enough to keep them from shooting you."

"You really think they'll shoot first and ask questions later?"

Pick glanced up at the rustic walls and ceiling of the Long Barrack. "I saw the bodies of at least three Rangers and two FBI special agents outside. This is Texas. You're damn right I think they will."

Through the thick stone walls, Pick heard the muted *whump* of another grenade being employed.

"Incoming!" he shouted, then pinched his eyes shut to protect them while opening his mouth to aid in equalizing the pressure from a concussive blast.

Suddenly the grenade detonated and the building trembled.

"That was close," Junior said.

"Agreed."

"They're coming!" Randy yelled.

Pick took a deep breath. He had been in many firefights before—both as a Marine and as Castillo's understudy—but he had never had to rely on a naval aviator and his great-grandmother to cover their flank. "All right, maintain your fields of fire and conserve your ammo. This is our last stand, folks!"

"You're like the second coming of Chesty Puller," Junior quipped.

"Shut—"

A loud crash at the north end cut off his retort, and he glanced over his shoulder to see a cloud of smoke filling the room from where a door used to be. Randy leaned around the wall he was using for cover and fired three rounds before pulling back. Pick wanted to rush toward the sound of gunfire, but he knew there was a chance that the blast had only been a diversion to draw them away from the real point of entry.

Maintain your field of fire.

He turned back to the door that was his responsibility and ignored the burgeoning firefight that was taking place behind him. He couldn't be in both places at once, and he just had to trust that Randy knew how to handle a long gun and that Abuela would make Manuel Martinez proud if any attackers made it into the theater. And based on the rapid suppressed gunfire from the aviator's TX4, he had a feeling his faith had been well placed.

As the gunfire intensified, Pick and Junior withdrew deeper into the theater but kept their guns trained on the solid wood door. But, by all accounts, it looked like the main thrust of the attack appeared to be focused in Randy's sector.

"Reloading!" Randy yelled.

Pick shot Junior a questioning glance.

"Go," the spook said.

Pick wheeled around and advanced into the anteroom, aiming his personal defense weapon into the darkness while methodically working the trigger at an even pace to keep the advancing gunmen from gaining a foothold inside the barracks. Out of the corner of his eye, he saw Randy slipping a fresh magazine into his TX4 and slapping the bolt catch to chamber another round.

"We need to advance," Pick said, continuing through into the next room. "We can't let them reach cover inside, or we're done for."

"I'm with you," Randy replied.

The two took turns firing into the darkness at the far end of the room, aiming at the most likely places for shooters to take cover. If they could successfully repel this initial assault, they could barricade the north entrance and consolidate their efforts on defending a single point of entry. With the manning and firepower they had at their disposal, it was their best chance of holding out long enough for the cavalry to arrive.

"Reloading," Pick called out, then fired two more rounds before his bolt locked back to the rear. He quickly dropped to a crouch and ejected the spent magazine.

As he reached for his final spare, an explosion rocked the building and sent him sprawling to the ground. Unlike when he had heard the incoming grenade, this one had taken him by surprise, and his ears rang from the blast.

Pick shook his head and completed the emergency reload, chambering a round to ready his weapon. He was operating on stem power and relying on muscle memory to carry him through the fog, but that was why they ran countless React to Contact drills during The Basic School, the Infantry Officer Course, and the MARSOC Individual Training Course.

Through the ringing in his ears, Pick heard Randy's TX4 firing at a much faster cadence than before. He shook his head again and saw the naval aviator continuing his advance on the north entrance. He turned to look over his right shoulder and saw a gaping hole where the wood and glass door used to be. His breath caught when the exposed daylight was suddenly blotted out by the figure of a man dressed in black.

And he was aiming right at Pick.

[FIVE]

BOOM!

The double-aught buckshot caught the gunman square in the face and exploded his head like a baseball bat to a jack-o'-lantern on Halloween night. Pick stared in open-mouthed amazement at Abuela racking another shell into her Mossberg 590 with a stoic expression plastered on her weathered face.

"Are you okay, Captain McCoy?" she asked, though her eyes never left the gaping hole where the door used to be.

He pushed himself to his feet and steadied himself before nodding. "Gracias."

"De nada."

Pick's ears were still ringing, though it sounded like somebody had stuffed them with cotton. He couldn't be sure, but he thought the gunfire had lessened somewhat. He looked left and saw that Randy had taken up position on the southern wall. But he wasn't shooting.

When he looked through the anteroom and into the theater, he saw that Junior was also not shooting.

"What's going on, Junior?"

"You good, boss?"

Before he could answer, he heard a deep baritone voice call out to him, amplified as if by a megaphone. "Killer McCoy!"

Thanks a lot, Dick.

Doña Alicia glanced over at him, but the barrel of her shotgun never wavered. "Killer?"

"It's a long story, ma'am."

"Sounds like a bad Western."

"Something like that."

The megaphone sounded again. "This is the San Antonio Police Department. We have the building surrounded."

"Now it really sounds like it," Abuela muttered.

"Throw down your weapons, Killer. We're coming in."

Abuela watched him carefully. When he nodded, she put the shotgun on safe and pulled the forearm rearward to remove the chambered ammunition, then placed it carefully on the ground at her feet.

"Do as he says, everyone," Pick ordered.

He dropped his magazine and yanked back on the charging handle while engaging the bolt catch. Then he placed it on the ground next to him with the ejection port skyward, allowing anybody who happened upon it to see that it wasn't loaded. He glanced left and right and noticed that both Randy and Junior had done the same.

"Ma'am, are you able to kneel?"

She scowled at him. "Why would I kneel?"

"Because when the police make entry, we don't want them to mistake us for the bad guys."

She stared at him for several seconds before finally nodding that she understood the wisdom of what he was asking them to do. "If you don't mind helping me," she said, holding out her hand.

Pick took it and supported her as she slowly lowered onto one knee first, then the other. When she was settled, Pick knelt next to her and placed his hands on top of his head, interlacing his fingers. She saw what he was doing and followed suit. After glancing in both directions to make sure Randy and Junior were presenting a nonthreatening posture, he called out to the police officer.

"All right, our weapons are down. Come on in."

IX

[ONE]

The Oval Office

The White House

1600 Pennsylvania Avenue NW

Washington, D.C.

1105 30 March 2026

President Natalie Cohen stood with her arms folded across her chest, staring at the Rose Garden through the window behind the *Resolute* desk, and felt the beginnings of a migraine settling in behind her tired eyes. She was the most powerful woman on Earth with unfettered access to the most robust intelligence community on the planet. But she had relegated herself to waiting not-so-patiently for Captain Pickering K. McCoy Jr. to deem her worthy enough of an update.

"He's just like Castillo," she muttered.

The door behind her flew open, and Cohen turned to see a disheveled Marty Fleiss, her Director of National Intelligence, rushing into the room with a look that could have been either constipation or consternation plastered on his face.

"Madam President," he said, both a greeting and entreaty.

"What's got your panties in a wad, Marty? It's not even noon—"

"Have you seen the news?"

She felt a chill roll down her spine as gooseflesh broke out on her arms. There were few reasons why Fleiss would dare barge into the

Oval Office without at least giving her a heads-up. And she knew all of them would do little to tamp down her growing headache. She uncrossed her arms and stooped to reach for the remote control that was resting on the credenza.

"Don't bother," he said. "It's not good."

She dropped her hands to her sides, the miniature TV forgotten. "What happened?"

"There was another terrorist attack this morning."

"Where?"

Fleiss opened his mouth to answer, but quickly snapped it shut and swallowed.

"Dammit, Marty. Just spill it."

"San Antonio," he said.

Cohen's mouth fell open, and she rolled her chair back to sit down. What had been just the hint of a migraine flared hot, and she propped her elbows up on the *Resolute* desk to knead the tension from her temples. "So, the kid was right."

"Appears so."

"When did this happen?"

"A couple hours ago, Madam President," Fleiss said.

"Hours? Why haven't we heard from McCoy? What's he have to say for himself?"

She knew the question sounded accusatory, but she couldn't help it. The reason she had resurrected the Presidential Agent program in the first place was to prevent things like this from even happening. But after Castillo ended up in the hospital following the attack in Virginia Beach, she had hoped that sending McCoy down to San Antonio would prevent a repeat and ensure the safety of Castillo's grandmother.

"I can't get him on the phone," Fleiss said.

She whipped her head up and glared at him. "Well, why the hell not?"

Again, Fleiss hesitated before answering. "Because the San Antonio police took him into custody following a shootout at the Alamo."

"I thought he was working with the local FBI field office?"

"He was," Marty said. "Apparently, the two agents who were assigned to him were killed during the attack."

Cohen closed her eyes, but she refused to allow her mind to sweep her away into the depths of the worst-case scenario. She had done that when initial reports had labeled Castillo as a gunman in the Virginia Beach shooting, and she wasn't about to do it again.

"Well, who *can* you get in touch with?"

Fleiss only stared at her.

"Jesus, Marty!"

[TWO]

Public Safety Headquarters

San Antonio Police Department

315 S. Santa Rosa Avenue

San Antonio, Texas

1015 30 March 2026

Pick didn't blame the police for taking him into custody. Even after Dick Miller had alerted them that a supervisory special agent of the Secret Service was inside Long Barrack, they were hesitant to place him in the "good guy" column until they knew what the hell was going on. And with the bodies of slain Alamo Rangers, FBI special agents, and unnamed gunmen scattering the plaza, there was more than enough chaos to prevent that from happening anytime soon.

But they had still treated him with enough respect that he thought they were at least leaning that way. Pick sat alone in a soundproof secure interview room, hands clasped atop a simple steel-and-wood table placed in the middle. He could have thrown a fit that they had left him cuffed or railed against their treatment of him, but this didn't even register on his scale of discomfort. This wasn't his first time being interviewed by the police.

He heard the electronic lock disengage and the door behind him swing open.

"Special Agent McCoy," a man's voice said.

Pick turned to study the detective and noticed the creased lines in his forehead that probably hadn't been there when he woke up that morning. "Please, call me Pick."

"Okay, Pick." The detective closed the door behind him and waited for the lock to engage before crossing to the table and looking down at McCoy. "My name is Detective Riley Stone, and I could really use some answers right now."

"Okay . . ."

"For starters, what's a Secret Service agent doing at the Alamo?"

Pick watched him carefully but kept his mouth shut. It wasn't that he didn't trust Stone, but he knew the police were looking for somebody to pin this on. And who better than an outsider they found heavily armed after a shootout at one of the most sacred sites in the entire state of Texas? Until he knew which way the winds were blowing their investigation, Pick was content to remain silent.

Stone sighed. "Nothing?"

"I wish I had something to give you," Pick replied honestly.

"How about start with why you're in San Antonio."

Pick leaned back into the uncomfortable chair and held out his cuffed hands—a subtle reminder that he wasn't there of his own free will.

"Are you requesting an attorney?"

"Should I? Are you charging me with something?"

Detective Stone pulled out an opposing chair and sat across from Pick. They locked eyes for several seconds before Stone opened the folder he had placed on the table between them. "There are plenty of crimes we can put on you—"

"In that case, I think I want an attorney," Pick said. He hadn't yet had an opportunity to play the ultimate get-out-of-jail-free card by exposing his relationship to the President. But he wasn't sure he wanted to. Until he knew who had perpetrated the attack, he couldn't afford to trust the detective or risk exposing his mandate.

"Texas Penal Code 42.12, discharging a firearm in a city," Stone continued. "A very serious offense. Or, 46.05, prohibited weapons, subsection one, paragraph A, a short-barreled firearm not registered in the National Firearms Registration and Transfer Record—"

"I can see where this is going," Pick said, cutting him off.

Stone changed tack. "Okay, then. Where did you get your Secret Service credentials?"

Pick shrugged. "Call Deputy Director Joel Isaacson. He'll verify my bona fides."

The detective closed the folder and leaned forward. "Look, Pick. I woke up this morning thinking I'd be investigating petty theft or misdemeanor drug crimes on the River Walk—not a mass shooting at the Alamo that cost the lives of several peace officers."

Pick suddenly turned somber. "How many?"

"Three Alamo Rangers and two FBI special agents."

"I'm sorry," Pick said. "How many civilians?"

"Just one. Thankfully, it was before the Alamo opened to visitors."

This could have been much, much worse.

The electronic lock on the door sounded again, and the door swung open. Detective Stone looked up, unfazed by the interruption, and rose slowly from the chair. "Will you excuse me?"

Pick nodded, though he knew he didn't really have a choice.

The detective exited the secure interview room and once again left Pick alone with his thoughts. Pick was relieved to hear that only one civilian had lost their life in the attack; it could have been much worse. But it was still one too many. And unless somebody intervened on his behalf to spring him from jail, he stood no chance of getting to the bottom of things.

The door unlocked and swung open again, and Detective Stone walked in, followed by a heavyset olive-skinned man who appeared to be in his late fifties. Stone walked straight to McCoy with a sour expression on his face and unlocked the handcuffs.

"What's going on?" Pick asked.

Stone gestured to the newcomer. "This is Don Fernando Lopez—"

"I'm told you're friends with the gringo," Don Fernando said.

"Who?"

"My dear cousin, Carlos Guillermo Castillo."

"And who told you that?"

"Our grandmother, Doña Alicia."

Stone watched the exchange with mild interest, not bothering to hide his perturbance that somebody had interceded on Pick's behalf.

"Does this mean I'm free to go?"

Stone cleared his throat. "Doña Alicia is a well-respected member of the community and has the mayor's ear. She asked to have you remanded into her custody. Against my objections, the chief agreed."

"Wait, remanded?" Pick asked, confused that Abuela had that kind of pull.

"It means you're coming with me," Don Fernando said.

"Where?"

"Back to the ranch."

Pick just stared at the large Hispanic man. "The ranch . . ."

Don Fernando nodded. "I'd advise you not to say anything else until we get there. Abuela can be very persuasive, but even her good standing isn't without its limits. You're lucky she vouched for you and corroborated other eyewitness accounts that you engaged the shooters and helped civilians get to safety."

Stone cleared his throat. "Don't go far, McCoy."

Guess we're not on a first-name basis anymore.

"We're going to have a lot more questions for you."

"Where am I gonna go?"

[THREE]

Detective Stone was silent as he led Pick through the precinct's halls to collect his belongings. It was painfully obvious the peace officer wasn't keen on the idea of allowing Pick to walk with Fernando through the front doors, no matter what kind of pull Abuela had with the mayor or what the chief of police had to say.

But Pick couldn't help needling him just a bit. "What about my guns?"

The back of Stone's neck turned crimson, and Pick suppressed a grin. He knew the detective wanted to find the people responsible for the deadly attack on the Alamo, but he resented being treated like a criminal.

"You can come back for them after the crime laboratory—"

Pick gripped Stone's arm and pulled him to a stop. "Look, Stone,

I know you're only doing your job. But the sooner you accept that I'm one of the good guys, the sooner we can start working together to find out who was behind this and bring them to justice."

The detective's face flashed sudden anger, and he looked down at Pick's hand holding him in place. Pick released his grip and held up both hands in a placating gesture.

"Several good men lost their lives today—"

"And more would have died if we hadn't intervened," Pick said.

Fernando cleared his throat. "Gringo . . ."

Pick glanced over his shoulder at Castillo's cousin and nodded. It was enough of a reminder that it was best not to look a gift horse in the mouth and to take the win. They could convince the San Antonio police that they belonged in the good guys column later. Once they were away and safely on the Castillo ranch.

"Right," Pick said. "Well, thanks for the hospitality."

"Guess you'll want these back," Stone said, handing Pick his Secret Service credentials. "Special Agent McCoy."

After exiting the public safety headquarters, Fernando ushered Pick into the back of a blacked-out Tahoe waiting curbside in front of the building. Pick climbed into the backseat next to Miller and behind Junior riding shotgun in the front passenger seat.

"Nice of the FBI to loan us wheels," Pick said. "Where's Randy?"

Fernando stuck his head in the doorway. "He's riding with us in the Escalade."

Pick looked through the forward windshield and saw a Cadillac SUV idling and waiting for Fernando.

"We'll follow you," Ani said.

Fernando nodded, then turned back to Pick. "Abuela's going to have some very tough questions for you, amigo."

Fernando slammed the door shut, then peeled away for the lead SUV.

"Well, I don't think that went how you expected," Miller said.

Pick turned and glared at the former Special Forces officer. "I thought you were supposed to give law enforcement a heads-up that we were there."

"And tell them what, exactly? That a special emissary of the President of the United States was running around San Antonio armed for war?"

Ani shifted the Tahoe into gear and pulled away from the curb.

"That would have been preferable to being cuffed and holed up in an interrogation room for hours," Pick fired back.

"Which is preferable to being mistaken for a terrorist and shot on sight," Miller countered.

The two stared at each other for several seconds before Pick finally saw the truth in what Miller was saying. He had done exactly what Pick had asked of him and done it in a way that preserved his cover. He was just upset with himself for not preventing another attack and that more people had died. That wasn't Miller's fault, either, and he shouldn't have taken it out on him.

"You're right," Pick said. "I'm sorry."

"You're welcome."

"I guess I should thank Doña Alicia, too."

Junior turned around in the front seat. "Don Fernando was right. Abuela's going to have some very tough questions for you when we get to the ranch."

"Like what?"

"For starters, why didn't she know that her grandson was in the hospital?"

Pick closed his eyes and groaned. "Who told her?"

"Her great-grandson," Miller answered.

"Which will lead to her second question: Why did you drag Randy into this?"

Pick opened his eyes and shook his head. "Drag him into this? He practically *begged* to be on the team—"

Junior cut him off. "If you think that's a suitable defense against Doña Alicia's scorn, then you might want to come up with a better answer."

Castillo had been hard on Pick during the operation to rescue Secretary of State Frank Malone. But he had focused only on the operational side of things, constantly reminding Pick to keep his body count low while emphasizing the word *clandestine* in their clandestine operations. But as the Tahoe turned a corner and accelerated to keep pace with the Escalade, he couldn't help but wish the former Presidential Agent had put more of an emphasis on the time-consuming task of satisfying his family's demands.

His son. His grandmother. His cousin. Who else?

"I think this one's for you, boss," Junior said, handing his phone to Pick.

With a deep breath to steady himself for whoever was on the other end, Pick accepted the phone and brought it to his ear. "Hello?"

"Captain McCoy, this is Director Fleiss. I have the President with me."

Pick suppressed a groan. "Yes, sir. How can I help you?"

President Cohen's voice replaced the DNI's. "Just what the hell happened down there, McCoy?"

Pick bristled at the question. "Madam President, the investigation is still ongoing, but our early assessment is that we were right."

"Excuse me?"

"We were right," Pick repeated. "Terrorists with ties to the perpetrators of the attack in Virginia Beach launched a similar attack earlier this morning, here in San Antonio."

"Isn't that why we sent you down there? To stop it?"

Pick glanced up and saw Ani looking at him in the rearview mirror. He didn't have to look to know that the others were also listening to his half of the conversation and evaluating how he responded to the President's queries. But if the President had chosen Pick as Castillo's replacement because she thought she could bully him and easily bend him to her will, then she was about to be sorely disappointed.

"Actually, it was my idea to come down here—"

Fleiss's voice cut him off. "Watch it, McCoy."

But Pick had had enough. "If we could have stopped the attack from happening, don't you think we would have? We acted on the intelligence we collected in Virginia Beach and found a terrorist preparing to launch grenades into the plaza from an elevated position—"

"Now, listen here, McCoy—"

Pick's voice rose. "No, you listen, General. You picked a Marine for this job, so don't be surprised when a Marine does Marine shit. I dropped that terrorist and immediately deployed my team from the Menger Hotel into the plaza to confront the threat head-on. We took incoming small arms and indirect fire but managed to take out five of the terrorists before collapsing on the Alamo to make our final stand. Two FBI special agents lost their lives protecting Doña Alicia and three Alamo Rangers heroically lost their lives during the engagement. So, I don't appreciate being lectured by you about—"

"Captain McCoy," President Cohen said softly.

Pick's heart was racing, and he could barely keep the disdain from his voice. "What?"

"This would have been much worse without you—"

"And my team," he corrected, still seething.

"And your team," the President added. "I know you understand the significance of two terrorist attacks taking place on American soil in as many days. We simply cannot allow this threat to go unchecked."

The tone of her voice poked a hole in his righteous indignation. "I couldn't agree more, Madam President."

"Marty, would you please read the document we prepared earlier?"

Director Fleiss's voice returned. "Of course, Madam President."

He cleared his throat.

"'Top Secret—Presidential.

"'The White House, Washington, D.C. March 30, 2026.

"'Presidential Finding.

"'It has been found that the attempted murder of U.S. Army Colonel C.G. Castillo (retired); the attempted murder of his son, U.S. Navy Lieutenant Commander Randolph J. Richardson IV; and the attempted murder of his grandmother Doña Alicia Castillo indicate beyond any reasonable doubt the existence of a continuing plot or plots by terrorists, or terrorist organizations, to cause serious damage to the interests of the United States and its citizens, and that this situation cannot be tolerated.

"'It is further found that the efforts and actions taken and to be taken by several branches of the United States government to detect and apprehend those individuals who committed the terrorist acts previously described, and to prevent similar such acts in the future, are being and will be hampered and rendered less effective by strict adherence to applicable laws and regulations.

"'It is therefore found that clandestine . . .'"

There's that word again.

"'. . . and covert action under the sole supervision of the President is necessary.

"'It is directed and ordered that there be immediately established a clandestine and covert organization with the mission of determining the identity of the terrorists involved in the attempted murders and to render them harmless. And to perform such other covert and clandestine activities as the President may elect to assign.

"'For purposes of concealment, the aforementioned clandestine and covert organization will be known as the Office of Organizational Analysis, within the Office of the Director of National Intelligence. Funding will initially be from discretional funds of the Office of the President. The manning of the organization will be decided by the President, acting on the advice of the chief, Office of Organizational Analysis.

"'Captain P.K. McCoy Jr., U.S. Marine Corps, is herewith appointed chief, Office of Organizational Analysis, with immediate effect.'"

Director Fleiss fell silent.

"Do you have any questions, Captain McCoy?" President Cohen asked.

Only about a million.

Pick cleared his throat. "Ma'am, when you brought me in to help find Secretary of State Malone, I was under the impression that such an organization already existed."

"It did, once upon a time," she replied. "When I was secretary of state, the President used an Army major assigned to the Department of Homeland Security to find a missing Boeing 727 that terrorists intended to fly into the Liberty Bell in Philadelphia."

Pick glanced at Dick Miller, who had told him as much earlier.

"Later, the President formalized his relationship with then-Major C.G. Castillo through a Presidential Finding that established the Office of Organizational Analysis. Less than six months later, the program was officially shut down.

"When I brought him out of retirement to find the secretary of state, I did not foresee a lasting relationship. But Director Fleiss has convinced me that the circumstances surrounding these two events demand a formal structure that gives you access to the tools you need to succeed. To be clear, I do not blame you for what happened in San Antonio, Pick. It was my fault—and my fault alone—for not giving you the resources you needed to bring these bastards to justice."

Pick was dumbfounded. What he had first thought was a phone call to critique his handling of the situation at the Alamo had turned into one in which the President took the blame. Even when he agreed to stay on as interim Presidential Agent, he had never expected to be named chief of a clandestine organization.

He could think of only one thing to say. "Thank you, Madam President."

"Keep in touch and let us know how we can help you."

"Yes, Madam President."

The call ended.

Junior turned around and saw the shocked look on Pick's face. "What did she say?"

"She called me Pick."

[FOUR]

Haciende San Jorge

Near Uvalde, Texas

1230 30 March 2026

Despite having just been handed what amounted to a blank check from the President of the United States, Pick felt relatively calm as they traveled west from San Antonio. But all that changed as they neared Uvalde and Don Fernando's Cadillac Escalade exited Highway 90 and drove north on an unpaved road onto the Castillo ranch. Pick thought it was almost ironic that he had been less concerned with confronting armed terrorists than he was with seeing Doña Alicia again.

"You ready, boss?" Junior asked from the front seat.

Pick just glared at the spook as Ani brought the Tahoe to a stop. "You're not helping."

Junior grinned, then reached for the door handle and jumped out. Pick looked over at Dick Miller, who had been surprisingly quiet for most of the ride. Castillo's West Point classmate just shook his head and followed Junior out into the Texas sun.

"You got any words of advice for me?" Pick asked Ani.

"Just be your normal charming self," she replied.

But Pick wasn't sure how much of her comment was sarcasm. He waited until the others had exited the Escalade, then opened the door and climbed out with a resigned sigh. Randy gave Pick a subtle shrug and followed his great-grandmother and second cousin toward the house.

"Welcome to our home, gringo," Don Fernando said, guiding Abuela past the Suburban and up the front steps onto the wide porch of a sprawling, red-roofed, Spanish-style house. It was the largest building on the property, and Pick thought it was probably the centerpiece of the Castillo family enclave.

"I told you not to call him that," Doña Alicia said, elbowing her grandson in the ribs.

"No, Abuela, you told me not to call Carlos that." Don Fernando looked over his shoulder and grinned at Pick. "But this man isn't part of the family, and I can call him whatever I want."

"Not in my house," she fired back.

"We're not in—"

"Fernando!"

He dipped his head respectfully. "Sí, Abuela."

Doña Alicia lowered herself into a sturdy wood rocking chair and dismissed Fernando with a flick of her wrist. "Now go get some refreshments for our guests and let me speak in private with Captain McCoy for a few minutes."

"Sí, Abuela."

Pick stepped up onto the porch when Fernando disappeared through the front door into the casón, followed by Dick Miller, Junior, and Ani. Only Randy remained outside, glancing between his great-grandmother and the man she wanted to have a private chat with.

"You, too, Randy," Doña Alicia said. "Go inside."

"Yes, ma'am," he replied, hesitating for a moment before opening the door to join the others.

When they were alone, the Castillo matriarch gestured for Pick to have a seat next to her. He calmly walked across the porch and lowered himself into the rocking chair, content with letting the silence hang in the air until she was ready to say whatever it was she wanted to say. But it wasn't long before Doña Alicia demonstrated that her patience far exceeded that of a Marine Raider.

Pick cleared his throat. "I'm sorry about Charley—"

"None of that now," she said. "Carlos takes after his father—my late son, Jorge. I doubt there was anything you could have said or done that would have kept him from getting into trouble. He's always been hell-bent on finding it."

Pick breathed a sigh of relief. It was clear she didn't blame him for what had happened to Castillo in Virginia Beach. But it wasn't clear why she wanted to speak with him alone. "Is there something I can help you with, ma'am?"

"I only met you this morning, Captain McCoy. But you have already caused a snag in the fabric of my tight-knit family."

"Ma'am, I assure you—"

Her chair stopped rocking. "May I finish, please?"

Pick bowed his head in apology and gestured for her to continue.

"As I'm sure you have already surmised, I have been around for a long time. Carlos came to us when he was twelve years old, well after my son, Jorge Alejandro Castillo, was killed in action in Vietnam. He never admitted it, but Carlos felt compelled to escape from underneath the weight of his father's legacy. No matter how much my late husband and I doted on him, he never forgot that he was a bastard."

With as much time as they had spent together over the last ten days, Pick was surprised by how little he actually knew about Colonel Carlos Guillermo Castillo, U.S. Army, retired. But he could certainly relate to the compulsive need to be free from his father's shadow.

"Do you know why he was in Virginia Beach, Captain McCoy?"

Pick shook his head. "No, ma'am."

Doña Alicia cocked her head to the side as if to look at the others through the front door. "That boy in there is no different than Carlos."

He had seen no children when he arrived. "Ma'am?"

"Randy. Carlos's son."

Pick suddenly understood. It was hard for him to think of Randy as "that boy," especially since he currently outranked Pick and had been a second class midshipman when Pick was a plebe. "Yes, ma'am."

"Carlos went to West Point because he was the son of a Medal of Honor recipient."

That was news to Pick.

"It was only natural that he become a helicopter pilot, like his father. So, he did. He flew the Apache during Operation Desert Storm and earned the Distinguished Flying Cross on the first night."

Pick was stunned. "I thought he was Special Forces."

Doña Alicia laughed. "Now you understand the lengths to which my grandson went in order to distance himself from his father."

"Yes, ma'am, I understand completely. My own father was a Marine Corps ace in Vietnam and retired as a lieutenant general. As the son of the Deputy Commandant for Aviation, it was a foregone conclusion to some that I would follow in his footsteps and become a fighter pilot, too."

"Randy told me," she said.

"I guess I'm not much different, either."

Abuela nodded. "Do you understand now why Carlos was in Virginia Beach?"

Pick furrowed his brow. Doña Alicia had painted a pretty clear picture of the man Charley Castillo had become, but that didn't mean he was following her logic. "No, ma'am. I'm afraid I don't."

Her chair started rocking again. "My Carlos always saw himself as the bastard son of Jorge Castillo, and he did not want Randy to suffer the same fate. He went to Virginia Beach because he wanted to have a relationship with that boy."

The door opened before Pick could respond, and Randy stepped out holding a longneck bottle of Shiner Bock in each hand. “Cerveza, Abuela?”

“Sí, mi cielo,” she said, reaching for one of the beers. “Gracias.”

Randy held the other one in Pick’s direction. “Beer?”

Well, why the hell not?

He took the bottle and nodded. “Thank you.”

“De nada.”

Randy opened the door to return inside the house, but Doña Alicia took hold of his hand to keep him there. “You may stay. We’re talking about you, after all.”

“About me? Why?”

“I was just explaining to Captain McCoy how he and your father are very much alike,” she said. “And why I don’t think it’s a coincidence he is with you here in Texas now.”

Pick took a sip of his beer while hanging on her every word.

“Like I said, Carlos was always hell-bent on finding trouble on his own. But after Bruce McNab and that other gentleman showed up in a helicopter to whisk him away, I knew that trouble had come to find him.”

Pick thought it sounded eerily like something Ani had said earlier that morning. “Wait. Are you saying you think these attacks are targeting your family?”

“That’s pretty obvious, wouldn’t you say?”

Randy glanced over at Pick before speaking. “Abuela, maybe we should wait until the police—”

“I’ve already spoken with the mayor,” she said, cutting him off. “He has assured me that the chief of police will provide routine updates regarding their investigation into this morning’s attack. But I think we all know who those pendejos were after.”

Pick knew it was likely, but he was hesitant to agree with her without at least circumstantial evidence. The President of the United States hadn't just issued a finding to name him chief of the Office of Organizational Analysis because she wanted him to go off half-cocked and lead his team on a wild-goose chase.

"Doña Alicia, if you wouldn't mind putting the chief of police in touch with me when he calls, I would be happy to coordinate our efforts with their investigation."

She grunted. "Randy told me you wouldn't mind talking with the police."

"Abuela!"

Ice flooded Pick's veins as he glared at Randy. "What did you tell her?"

"Just the truth."

Summer 2014

[ONE]

Bancroft Hall

U.S. Naval Academy

Annapolis, Maryland

1630 22 August 2014

The truth was that Midshipman Third Class P.K. McCoy Jr. felt an odd sense of acceptance as he walked through the hall to Captain Hanes's office. It had been only three days since his company officer had questioned him to validate or disprove the claims that his roommate had sexually assaulted a fellow midshipman. But Pick felt no sense of remorse for throwing Javier under the bus.

The bastard deserves to be tied to the bulwark and flogged.

Pick reached the office and knocked on the closed door before pushing it open a crack and announcing his presence. "Sir, Midshipman Third Class McCoy reporting as ordered, sir."

"Enter," Captain Hanes said.

Pick pushed open the door and saw the Marine infantry officer come to his feet from behind his desk, smoothing out his pristine Service Charlie uniform. "Midshipman McCoy, this is Special Agent Ashlee Warren of the Naval Criminal Investigative Service."

Pick turned to the petite blond woman in a navy-blue pantsuit as she rose to her feet and held out her credentials for him to examine. "Thank you for coming, Midshipman."

Pick studied her identification, but he didn't know the first thing about law enforcement credentials or how to spot a forgery. "Yes, ma'am."

"McCoy, did you take my advice and talk with your father about this?"

"No, sir."

Captain Hanes flexed his jaw muscles and briefly glanced at the NCIS special agent. "Would you like an attorney present during this interview?"

Pick knew it was probably the smart thing to do, considering he had violated midshipmen regulations by spending time in Mrs. Rosen's condo. But he had nothing to hide and didn't want to give the appearance of being less than cooperative. "No, sir."

"Would you like me present?"

It was his company officer's Hail Mary attempt at providing Pick with some form of top cover in the event Lieutenant General P.K. McCoy discovered that his son had been questioned by authorities regarding a very serious matter.

"No, sir."

"Very well." Captain Hanes turned to Special Agent Warren. "When you're done, you may find me roaming this deck, where I will be conducting company room inspections."

"Thank you, Captain."

Without another word, the Marine officer stepped around his desk and placed a firm hand on Pick's shoulder. He gave it a squeeze, then left his office and closed the door behind him.

Special Agent Warren tucked her credentials into her blazer and lowered herself back into her chair. "Would you care to have a seat, Midshipman?"

"Thank you, ma'am."

Pick hesitated only briefly while deciding between the company officer's chair and the one next to the NCIS special agent. Having decided, he walked around Captain Hanes's desk and took a seat in the large executive-style faux-leather chair.

"Do you know why you're here?"

Pick swallowed, remembering when Captain Hanes had informed him that Hannah had accused his roommate, Javier Santiago, of sexually assaulting her. "Yes, ma'am."

"You understand, then, that I am here to ask you questions regarding an alleged crime that took place on 19 August, specifically in violation of Articles 80 and 120 of the Uniformed Code of Military Justice?"

Pick nodded. "If by Article 120 you mean sexual assault, and Article 80 the attempt of, then yes. I understand."

The special agent opened a notepad and scribbled something. "I must inform you that I am not here to gather any information regarding alleged violations of the Midshipmen Regulations Manual, but your statements to me are not to be considered privileged information. The Commandant of Midshipmen may later elect to bring charges against you for any violations admitted to during the course of our interview. Do you understand?"

"Yes, ma'am. I understand."

"And do you still wish to proceed without an attorney present?"

"Yes, ma'am, I do."

When Pick returned to his room in fourth wing almost an hour later, he was seething. Special Agent Warren had been explicit in her telling of Javi's despicable behavior, and Pick had to grip the chair's armrests to keep from bolting from the room.

Flogged isn't bad enough. Javi needs to be keelhauled.

"Well?" Brad asked. "How'd it go?"

Pick dropped into his chair with both hands balled into fists. He looked over at the books piled high on the third desk in their room and wondered how he could have been close with Javi without knowing what he was capable of. The more he thought about it, the more he wanted to put his hands on his former roommate and choke the life out of him.

"I need to blow off some steam." Pick spread his fingers wide as if to shoo away the thoughts of violence running through his head, then jumped to his feet and started unbuttoning his short-sleeved dark uniform shirt.

Brad sat up in his bed. "Want some company?"

"No, thanks."

Pick knew it hadn't been an empty offer and that Brad genuinely wanted to do something to help. But he had so many thoughts and emotions rolling around that he needed to process before he could share his turmoil with somebody else—even his best friend. And since childhood, the only way he knew how to do that was to physically punish his body.

"You sure?"

Pick opened his confidential locker and hung up his uniform shirt, then kicked off his black leather shoes and slipped out of his uniform pants. He had decided against heading over to Scott Natatorium for a few laps and instead reached for his PT gear and running shoes.

"Yeah, I'm sure," Pick said, slipping on the mesh Navy blue shorts and blue-rimmed T-shirt. He dropped into his chair again and slipped on his running shoes. "I'm going out for a run."

Brad flopped back on his bed. "In that case, I'm gonna take a nap."

After tying his laces, Pick lunged from his chair like a sprinter and avoided the temptation to slam his fist into Javi's locker on his way out. It seemed that no matter where he looked, he saw only the face of someone he had considered a friend just days before. But that *friend* had betrayed him. Worse, he had sexually assaulted the girl Pick was only just beginning to realize how much he cared for.

He fled their room amid a torrent of emotions and turned down the wide hallway for the stairwell that would lead him to the fresh air he desperately needed. He knew there were a number of people he could confide in—Brad being only one—but he needed to be alone to sort through his murderous thoughts more than anything else. To do that, he needed to run until he was drenched in sweat and his legs burned with exhaustion.

"Hey, Pick—"

He ignored the voice. He knew it was only one of his classmates who probably wanted the scuttlebutt on the investigation. Keeping something like the presence of an NCIS special agent on campus from the rest of the brigade was difficult. But keeping it a secret from the company was impossible.

Pick didn't care.

He reached the stairs just as he felt the walls closing in around him, and he started down. Slowly at first, but picking up steam with each deck he passed. Pick had made it through his plebe year without feeling like he was trapped on the Yard, but a simple one-hour conversation with a lady special agent had made him feel like Bancroft Hall was a prison. He needed to escape. To breathe. To run. To feel something other than a roiling anger he knew he couldn't control.

After descending four flights of stairs, Pick was almost sprinting for the double doors that led out onto what was known as Red Beach. Some upper-class midshipmen claimed that the nickname stemmed from the code names given to the three beaches on Betio Island in the

Gilbert Islands during the Battle of Tarawa Atoll—an origin Pick appreciated due to his fondness for all things Marine Corps. But still others claimed it was only because of the color of the tiles used to construct the plazas surrounding Bancroft Hall. And because midshipmen used to sunbathe there in decades past.

But Pick found that hard to believe.

Normally, Pick would have spent a few minutes stretching on Red Beach before beginning his run. But he needed to drown out the noise before doing anything else, and he skipped that part of his normal routine. He bounded down the steps and turned left onto Calvert Road, passing the Superintendent's house, thankful he had managed to avoid Vice Admiral Bull Hawkins since his father had introduced them on I-Day.

Within minutes, Pick had found his stride and was comfortably running at a sub-six-minute pace. Six minutes per mile was how fast he needed to run for three miles to achieve a perfect score on the Marine Corps Physical Fitness Test, and he had been training himself to do that since he was fourteen. But running it now, he kept pushing himself harder.

I should have stayed with Hannah.

Faster. Pick wanted his body to hurt more than his heart.

I shouldn't have left her alone with him.

He rounded the corner onto Boundary Road, then quickly turned right onto Garden Road and ran back toward the Naval Academy Chapel on a route he and many other midshipmen often used during their daily runs. But he kept his eyes on the road in front of him and listened to the sound of his shoes pounding the pavement in time with his measured breathing, refusing to look up at the chapel dome that had always been a comforting landmark to him.

I let her down. This is my fault.

Turning left onto Truxtun Road, Pick ran behind the chapel and administration building that had been recently renamed in honor of Admiral Charles R. Larson—a graduate from the Class of 1958—who served as Superintendent from 1983 to 1986, and again from 1994 to 1998. It was Larson's influence that had led to the establishment of the Naval Academy's Character Development Division to reassert the traditional high standards of moral and ethical conduct required of midshipmen.

Moral and ethical?

Pick leaned forward and pushed himself harder, trying to drown out the silent accusation that he had let Hannah down. Intellectually, he knew that Javi was to blame for his actions. Rationally, he knew that his former roommate was the one who had demonstrated a lack of morals or ethics. Logically, he knew that one hundred percent of the guilt could be placed only at the feet of Javier Santiago.

But emotionally, Pick couldn't absolve himself.

He was running well under five and a half minutes per mile by the time he passed the gatehouses on either side of Gate 3 at Maryland Avenue. Although the gate was no longer used and generally closed to both inbound and outbound traffic, Pick recalled hearing that the pedestrian access was known as Bilger's Gate because it had once been used by departing midshipmen who had failed out or resigned. Subsequently, midshipmen in good standing refused to use the pedestrian gate to avoid invoking bad karma.

Bad karma? What could be worse than what Javi did to Hannah?

Pick was already sweating, mostly due to the humidity of late August in Annapolis rather than a lack of physical fitness. But it wasn't nearly enough. He pushed himself even harder, breezing past the Naval Academy Club and around the houses lining Worden Field. Pick ran over the bridge crossing College Creek, then turned onto

Ramsay Road and circled the Naval Academy Cemetery to reach Hospital Point.

Officially known as Forrest Sherman Field, the large grassy area rested under the shadow of the Naval Academy Bridge and was one of the few places on the Yard where Pick could escape and not feel like the walls were closing in around him. He sprinted past the intramural fields along the seawall before skidding to a halt at the northeast corner, panting and out of breath.

With his hands on his hips, Pick turned to look out over the Severn River as the weight of his emotions crashed through his well-preserved facade. He had done a commendable job holding it together for several days, but the strain of the run and the stress of knowing what Hannah had gone through finally stripped away his composure. Almost instantly, his labored breathing became mournful sobs, and he dropped to his knees with his chin to his chest.

"I'm sorry, Hannah. I'm so sorry."

Then he heard a faint voice call out to him. "It's not your fault, Pick from San Diego."

[TWO]

Pick whipped his head around and saw Hannah sitting on the ground with her back against a fenced-off utilities area. She gave him a mirthless grin, then dipped her head in apparent embarrassment.

Pick pushed himself to his feet and slowly made his way over to her. He hesitated for a moment, then lowered himself to the ground next to her. "I'm sorry, Hannah."

"Yeah, I heard you the first time," she said, her tone sharper than she'd probably intended.

"I'm sorry," Pick said again.

Hannah whipped her head around and glared at him. "Just stop fucking apologizing already!"

Her eyes were red and rimmed with fresh tears, but Pick was more stunned by the sudden burst of anger that was entirely out of character. It wasn't like her to cuss at all, but her voice had a tremor as if it had been carried across an undercurrent of hatred and vitriol—something Pick had never thought Hannah capable of.

He held up his hands in a placating gesture, not trusting himself to speak without saying the wrong thing. He hadn't run to the farthest and most isolated corner of the Naval Academy to intrude on Hannah's escape or force her to talk about things she would just as soon forget. But he also couldn't bring himself to abandon her and leave her alone.

Pick leaned his head back against the fencing and looked up as a steady flow of cars crossed the Naval Academy Bridge, bound for the Eastern Shore. He had finally succeeded in quieting his thoughts during the final sprint along the seawall, but now that he was still and sitting next to Hannah, a new stream of consciousness and internal debate settled over him.

Maybe if I had told her how I felt about her, none of this would have happened.

Well, that's pretty vain, Pick, to assume she felt the same.

But she's always been nice to me. She did call me her favorite man—

No, she called Javi that.

But he's not her favorite anymore.

Then tell her how you feel.

Now?

"Why didn't you ever ask me out?" Hannah asked, her voice quiet and barely audible over the wind and *thump-thump-thump*ing of the cars crossing the bridge above them.

Pick swallowed against the dryness in his mouth and turned his head slightly to look at her. She met his gaze for the briefest of moments, then turned away. He thought it looked like her skin had flushed crimson, but he wasn't sure how to interpret that. Aside from Cate, his high school sweetheart, Pick didn't really have any experience in dealing with women. And he had fumbled things so poorly with Cate that he wasn't sure that experience even counted.

"Did you want me to?"

Hannah whipped her head around and glared at him. "You are so dense, Pick from San Diego."

"Hannah, I—"

"I had the biggest crush on you."

Pick's heart bolted, but the resident skeptic spoke up to keep his enthusiasm in check.

She said "had," Pick.

"I . . ." He trailed off.

Just tell her you have the biggest crush on her, too.

That would be a big mistake, Pick. She doesn't need you hitting on her after what she's been through.

She needs to know you're in her corner.

And being here next to her isn't enough?

"Aren't you going to say something?"

"Hannah, I've had the biggest crush on you since I-Day," he said in a rush. It felt like an immense weight had been lifted off his shoulders; a secret that he had harbored for more than a year had finally seen the light of day.

But she acted like she already knew. "So, why didn't you ask me out?"

This time, it was Pick who blushed. He really didn't have a good reason to offer, so he settled on the truth. "Because I was afraid you'd say no."

"I would have said yes," she replied, more candid than he expected. "I think everybody knows how I feel about you."

Even Javi?

"Even Javi," she said, answering his unspoken question. "Which is why things went horribly wrong—"

"No, Hannah. What Javi did isn't your fault."

"I didn't say it was my fault," she fired back. "You really can be so dense, Pick."

"I'm sorry—"

"And, for fuck's sake, stop apologizing."

Pick opened his mouth to apologize again but quickly snapped it shut. Hannah had never shied away from sharing what was on her mind before. But this was different. Pick had no doubt the incident at the Tecumseh Condominiums would stay with her for years, but it was almost as if she had gone through something horrific and emerged on the other side even stronger than before.

"After you left, he asked about you."

Pick raised an eyebrow but remained silent.

"I think he knew he wasn't the roommate I really wanted."

"Could have fooled me," Pick said before he could stop himself.

She shot him an angry look, and he almost apologized for saying something so crass and insensitive but resisted.

Oh, look, you can *keep your mouth shut.*

"Javi and I first started hanging out because of you."

"I'm sorry?"

Why are you being such an asshole? She's been through hell and doesn't need your bruised male ego making this any harder than it needs to be.

"I think maybe I wanted to feel closer to you over the summer and hoped that if I earned Javi's trust he would tell me that you had pined over me all year. But I think Javi knew that, and he used his relationship with you to keep me close while waging a campaign to keep us apart. He started dropping little comments here and there to make me think you weren't interested, that he was the roommate I really wanted."

Pick wanted to be upset with Hannah for letting Javi have such an influence over her. He wanted to be upset with Javi for going behind his back and chasing the girl he knew Pick wanted. But there was really only one person he could be upset with. At least in this, Pick knew it was his cowardice that had allowed the conditions for his roommate to go after her.

"Did you know that both of us grew up sailing?"

Pick nodded. Javi had graduated from the Admiral Farragut Academy, a top-ranked boarding school in St. Petersburg, Florida, where he had been on their sailing team.

"It felt like a natural progression to go from talking about you to bonding over our love of boats. Of course, I know now he had only been grooming me and manipulating me to get what he wanted." Hannah paused and looked away as if to collect her thoughts. "Javier Santiago is a cold and calculating person."

"I think he's far worse than that," Pick offered.

She gave a wry chuckle and turned back. "You're right. He's a monster."

An uneasy silence settled between them, and Pick was hesitant to break it. But he felt like Hannah wanted to tell him what had taken place after he left. "You said he asked about me?"

She nodded. "He said I 'lit up' when I saw you—in a way I never did for him."

Again, Pick's heart bolted. But, knowing what she had gone through, he tamped his excitement.

"I told him that I still had feelings for you and that it didn't seem right to let him think otherwise. He didn't say anything at first and only started drinking more. I was fine with him having one or two drinks, but he really stared downing them."

Pick had seen Javi drink heavily before and knew what kind of drunk he was.

"Then the comments started," she said. "Looking back, I can see what he was trying to do. He was trying to rewind our courtship to the beginning when he had succeeded in making me think you weren't interested in me."

But I was. And am.

"But it wasn't going the way he hoped. I had seen it in your eyes, too, and knew I was right. No matter what he said about you, I knew he was lying. His manipulation tactics weren't working anymore, and that made him mad."

Pick cleared his throat. "What did he do?"

"He pulled me into him, but I pushed him back. He tried kissing me, but I turned away. Finally, he pulled me onto the sofa with him and . . ."

Pick held his breath.

"But I fought him off. The harder he tried, the harder I fought. I suddenly realized that everything he had told me was a lie. Javi wasn't the person he wanted me to think he was. He's not the person everyone else thinks he is."

"No, he's not," Pick said, clenching his fists again. "He's a monster."

Hannah reached over and placed a calming hand on Pick's arm. "He is. And he hurt me. But I didn't let him break me."

Pick clenched his jaw, seething at the thought of Javi—or anybody—hurting Hannah. "I won't let that happen again."

"I know you won't, Pick from San Diego."

Despite the torrent of emotions roiling inside him, he gave her a warm smile to let her know he would be there for her. She smiled back, then leaned in close and kissed him softly on the lips. And with that kiss, every negative thought evaporated into the humid Annapolis air.

[THREE]

Bancroft Hall

U.S. Naval Academy

Annapolis, Maryland

1745 22 August 2014

Despite everything that had happened since returning from summer training, Pick was riding a high as he and Hannah walked side by side and made their way back across the Yard to Bancroft Hall. They walked through the double doors into fourth wing and climbed the stairs in silence until reaching the third deck, where they said their goodbyes and parted ways. Pick watched her disappear, then spun and practically skipped through the hall to his room. His sudden entrance surprised Brad, who was still lying supine on his rack.

"Why are you so damn happy?" the New Orleans native asked.

Pick leaned into the shower and started the water running before kicking off his running shoes and pulling his sweat-soaked T-shirt over his head. "Let's just say I got more out of that run than I was hoping for."

Brad propped himself up on his elbows and looked down at Pick with a queer expression on his face. "Does that mean you're going to stop moping around?"

"I kissed Hannah," Pick blurted.

"Wait . . . what?"

Pick knew he should have played it cool and probably kept it quiet for at least a little while longer. But he hadn't been this excited about anything since he received that phone call from Coach Luis asking him to come for an official visit over Easter weekend his junior year in high school.

"Well, technically she kissed me. But yeah."

Brad's surprised expression vanished and was replaced with a mischievous grin. "So, you finally got the balls to tell her, huh?"

Pick supposed he should have been offended by the insinuation that he had been too scared to tell Hannah how he felt. But Brad was right. He *had* been too scared. "She didn't really give me a choice."

Brad swung his legs over the side of his rack as steam from the shower began filling their room and fogged up the mirror over the sink. "Are you saying she used some Jedi mind trick to pull you over to the dark side?"

Dating a fellow midshipman was known as "going over to the dark side," and it was a common euphemism within the brigade that wasn't altogether flattering. Pick shot him a dirty look, but the truth was, he didn't really care what Brad or anybody else thought. He liked Hannah, and she liked him. That was all that mattered.

"Whatever, man. Don't kill my mood."

Brad laughed. "Oh, I'm not. I wasn't looking forward to rooming with you and your sour mood for the whole year, so this is great news. Just know that I'm going to bust your balls every chance I get."

Pick stripped out of his shorts and climbed into the shower, pulling the curtain closed and letting the hot water loosen his sore muscles as he lathered up. "Yeah, I knew you were going to hold this over my head all year," he shouted over the running water.

"Hold what over your head?" a voice asked.

Pick inched the shower curtain back and stuck his head out to see who had spoken. When he saw Randy Richardson dressed in civilian clothes, he groaned. "None of your business, Randy."

"What do you want?" Brad asked.

"Just checking on my troops," he said.

Pick yanked the shower curtain closed again and reached for the shampoo bottle. "Another thing you learned at Quantico this summer?"

"Yeah, in between riveting stories of one Private First Class Killer McCoy."

Pick was in too good of a mood to let Randy's obsession with Pick's family tree bring him down. Fortunately, it sounded like Brad wasn't in the mood to let the first class midshipman ruin their Friday evening, either.

"Did they also teach you how to dress for liberty? Jesus, Randy . . . don't tell me you expect to get laid looking like that?"

"That's another thing you'll learn—"

Brad's voice was louder. "Get the fuck out, Randy! Nobody cares what you have to say."

Pick rinsed the shampoo from his head, smiling at his roommate for saying exactly what they had all wanted to say when they were plebes. He half expected to hear an indignant rebuttal from the uppity upperclassman, but when Brad's eviction went unchallenged, he stuck his head out again and saw the door swinging shut.

"The coast is clear," Brad said.

Pick shut the water off and reached for his towel to dry off. Each room in Bancroft Hall had a shower and sink that were shared by its occupants, but the toilets were located in communal heads—the naval term for bathrooms—on each deck. Pick wrapped his towel around his waist and stepped out into the three-person room that was now shared by only two, shaking his head at Randy's audacity.

"What's the deal with that guy, anyway?" Pick asked.

"He's probably got daddy issues."

Don't we all?

XI

[ONE]

Haciende San Jorge

Near Uvalde, Texas

1400 30 March 2026

By the time Pick finished telling Abuela his version of past events, the others had grown tired of being camped out inside the house and slowly filtered out onto the front porch. Doña Alicia rocked in her chair slowly and sipped from her longneck while Pick shared the details of something he would have much rather forgotten.

"I understand now why the President chose you," Abuela said. "You're just like my Carlos."

The screen door swung open and Don Fernando walked out carrying two fresh beers. "You mean he's a dumb gringo?"

Abuela snapped her head in his direction. "Fernando!"

"What?" he asked, feigning innocence. "It's a fair statement, given that you just bailed him out of jail."

"I didn't bail him out."

Pick could tell by the sparkle in Fernando's eyes that he was enjoying the banter, despite the dark cloud of knowing that his cousin was in the hospital recovering from multiple gunshot wounds. Pick knew Castillo was an interesting character, but he hadn't expected his family to comprise similar ilk.

"You're not worried about him?" Pick asked.

Fernando turned serious. "Of course I'm worried."

"Fernando and Carlos are like brothers," Abuela added.

Fernando nodded. "But if you knew even half the grief he's caused me over the years, you'd know he's like the proverbial gato with nine lives."

"How many lives does he have left?" Pick asked.

Doña Alicia apparently felt the conversation had taken an unexpected turn that no longer required her presence, because she leaned forward in her chair and slowly stood. She rested a hand on Pick's arm for a moment and gave him a sad look. "The President chose the right person to replace my Carlos. The sooner you believe that, the sooner you can find whoever did this to him and bring them to justice."

With a final squeeze of his arm, she turned for the door and paused just long enough to snatch a fresh beer out of Fernando's hand. She put it to her lips, tipped it back, and walked inside.

After the screen door slammed shut, Fernando turned to Dick Miller, who had been observing their discussion in silence. "What do you think, Dick? Next to me, you've known Charley the longest. Is Captain McCoy here up to the task?"

The former Army aviator sized Pick up and down. Then he slowly nodded. "I believe he is."

"Okay, so what are we going to do?"

Pick shot Fernando a look. "'We'?"

"You don't think I'm going to sit here and babysit Abuela—"

Doña Alicia's voice called out through the screen door. "I don't need you to babysit me, Fernando."

"See?"

Pick was grateful for the Castillo family's connections, which had helped get him out of a jam with the San Antonio Police Department. But he didn't see how bringing a civilian into their operation would help them get any closer to finding the people responsible for the two attacks.

"Fernando, I really appreciate what you've done for me. But I think it's best if you let us handle it from here. My team—"

"Needs me," he said, finishing Pick's statement.

But Pick wasn't shaken by the interruption. "My team is more than capable of finding the people responsible for putting your cousin in the hospital."

Fernando clamped his mouth shut as his nostrils flared with indignation. He slowly turned and looked at the others circling Pick on the front porch. From Ani and Junior to Dick and Randy, it was clear Fernando didn't agree that Pick had assembled the right team to carry out the President's orders.

"Okay, gringo . . ."

Fernando trailed off as if waiting for Abuela's shout of chastisement.

"Where do *you* go from here?"

I haven't the foggiest idea.

And that was the rub. Pick was more than confident that if he had a target to go after, he could plan and execute a direct action mission to take out the bad guys before they had a chance to carry out another attack. But he was insecure in his ability to generate the intelligence needed to get him there. It was something Castillo had tried teaching him during their operation to rescue the secretary of state and probably would have been the focus of his continued mentorship, had he not found himself in the middle of a gunfight in Virginia Beach.

"Well?"

Pick had always believed that a leader needed to demonstrate confidence and competence, but he also knew that sometimes making a bad decision was better than making no decision at all. This was uncharted territory for him, and he decided to tell the truth.

"I don't really know. But I think we have enough clues to at least get us going in the right direction."

"Like what?" Fernando asked, already acting like he was part of the team.

"All the shooters—including the ones in San Antonio—appeared to be of Eurasian descent," Junior said, recognizing the need to lay the facts out on the table for everyone's benefit.

"That's only about seventy percent of the world's population," Fernando countered.

"How many are from Tajikistan?"

Charley's cousin shrugged. "Ten million?"

"Ten-point-seven," Junior said. "And according to my sources in the FBI, two of the Virginia Beach shooters were on the terrorist watch list and confirmed through biometric screening. Dollars to donuts, at least some of the shooters in San Antonio will turn up on that same list."

"How come I didn't know that?" Pick asked, surprised that Junior was just getting around to telling him.

"Because you were in the clink, boss," Junior replied with a wry smile.

"But you—"

"Wait a second," Ani said, cutting him off. "As much as I hate to admit it, I think Junior is onto something."

The spook gave a surprised but flashy bow. "Thank you."

"I don't think any of us are surprised these guys turned up on the watch list," Pick said.

"That's not what I mean." Ani turned to Junior, who was still gloating. "You said these guys are from Tajikistan. Do we know what organizations they're affiliated with?"

"Probably ISIS–K," the spook replied.

Fernando frowned. "Who?"

"The Islamic State–Khorasan Province. They operate primarily out of Afghanistan and Pakistan, but it's been hard to track their movement since the last administration pulled American troops from the region."

"Makes sense," Ani said. "I've got somebody running down the serial numbers for the weapons we recovered at the Alamo, but my contacts in the Army agree that they probably came from a stockpile of weapons we left behind in Afghanistan."

"Okay, but how would they get into the country?" Pick asked. "Even with weak border security, I find it hard to believe a group of this size—especially with this kind of firepower—could make it into the country without being detected."

"I'm not surprised," Junior said. "But I'll ask my contacts in the FBI if there are any ongoing investigations. If there weren't before, the presence of known terrorists in Virginia Beach will have surely set something in motion."

Pick chewed on his lip. "Does anybody not think ISIS–K is behind these attacks?"

Nobody spoke up, but Pick could tell each was evaluating the facts and trying to poke holes in the assumption.

"Whether they're from Tajikistan or elsewhere, we believe the weapons used in both the Virginia Beach and San Antonio shootings came from American weapons we left behind in Afghanistan during the withdrawal." He looked at Ani. "When will we know for sure?"

She glanced at her watch. "Probably by the close of business today."

"Junior, do you have any contacts with Customs and Border Protection?"

He furrowed his brow in thought, then nodded. "I might have one or two."

"Find out where a force of this size might have crossed the border."

"If we're assuming they came into the country through the southern border, that's almost two thousand miles long. Could be anywhere."

Pick nodded. "Yeah, but if they did, there's a hole that needs to be plugged. Like yesterday."

Randy had been quietly leaning against the railing as he listened to the others discussing their investigation. But when he cleared his throat, Pick gestured to him. "Got something to add, Randy?"

"I was just thinking that whoever is behind these attacks seems more structured and organized than you're giving them credit for."

"How do you mean?" Pick asked.

"I mean, these attacks were carried out by two sizable and well-armed forces—one of which had to travel what, fifteen hundred miles from the border to Virginia Beach?"

Pick shrugged. He didn't know the exact number, but he knew what Randy was driving at. "Probably something like that. What's your point?"

Randy pushed himself off the railing and lowered his arms, which had been folded across his chest. "My point is that somebody had to help them. They didn't travel with all this military hardware from Tajikistan—or wherever—to Mexico, cross the Rio Grande into Texas, and make their way halfway across the country without somebody arranging the logistics ahead of time. This was well planned, well funded, and well beyond the capabilities of most junior officers in the Navy."

"Like a logistics specialist?" Ani asked.

Pick saw what Randy was getting at. "Yeah, somebody like Junior."

The spook shook his head. "There's nobody like me."

Dick Miller spoke quietly, but his voice carried across the front porch. "Yeah, there is."

Junior looked offended. "Who?"

"Aleksandr Pevsner."

[TWO]

"Who's that?" Pick asked.

Don Fernando looked surprised. "You mean the anointed one doesn't know?"

Pick shot him a dirty look. If there was any question how Castillo's cousin felt about him, that rhetorical question left little doubt. "How do I get in touch with Alex—"

"*Aleksandr* Pevsner," Fernando corrected.

Dick Miller nodded approvingly, and it seemed like the idea was gaining momentum. Pick wasn't sure that bringing another person from Castillo's past onto the team was the answer they were searching for. But he admitted he was short on ideas and might as well entertain this one.

"At the risk of repeating myself," Pick said. "Who is *Aleksandr* Pevsner? And how do I get in touch with him?"

Miller, who had been silent during much of the conversation, was the first to speak up. "Remember that Boeing 727 that went missing in Africa?"

Pick remembered. It was just another shining moment in Castillo's past that underscored how woefully unprepared Pick was to step into his shoes as the Presidential Agent—no matter what President Cohen or Director Fleiss thought. "You're talking about the one those crazies planned to crash into the Liberty Bell in Philadelphia?"

Miller nodded. "They called themselves the Holy Legion of Muhammad. At the time, I was diplomatically accredited to the Republic of Angola as the assistant military attaché. But in reality, I was on loan to the CIA and covertly acting as the station chief in Luanda. Quite by accident, I was at Quatro de Fevereiro Aeroporto Internacional when the Boeing 727 took off."

"You actually *saw* it take off?"

Miller nodded. "I did. And I immediately notified Langley—"

"And a few others," Don Fernando added.

Miller waved away the accusation. "Yes, yes . . . It shouldn't have surprised anybody that I also forwarded my concerns to a few contacts in the Army. I was, after all, an Army major and the assistant military attaché."

"Who did you forward your concerns to?"

"The G-3 staff of the XVIII Airborne Corps and the Special Activities Section, J-5 (Special Operations), at Central Command."

"What did you tell them?" Pick asked.

"At first, I only told them about the 727 going missing. But when I learned from my sources at Policia Nacional that Sergei Nostroff was known to have been in Luanda during the week prior, I drew my own conclusions and made sure everyone knew what I was thinking."

Pick was beginning to understand the importance of having a network of sources beyond what the CIA, DIA, and other three-letter agencies within the intelligence community could furnish him with. "First, who's Sergei Nostroff? And second, what conclusions did you draw?"

Junior raised his hand. "And third, what does any of this have to do with some guy you think compares to me?"

Miller didn't seem put off by Junior's tongue-in-cheek question and answered matter-of-factly. "Sergei Nostroff was a Russian national and known associate of Vasily Respin, who was reported to own at least three Boeing 727 aircraft. I had concluded that the missing aircraft in Luanda had been flown to Sharjah, United Arab Emirates, where Respin kept his fleet."

"What about my question?" Junior asked.

Pick was shaking his head. "And how the hell is this Respin person connected to Pevsner?"

"They're the same person, gringo," Don Fernando said.

"The same person," Pick repeated.

Miller nodded.

"And he's what? A source?"

"He's closer to family, but we can get into that later," Miller said. "The point is, he has lived most of his life on the wrong side of the law but trusts Charley. Most important, Charley trusts him."

That made no sense. "So, why do you think he had something to do with this?"

"I don't. But if anybody knows who helped those shooters cross the border and make it to their targets, it's Aleksandr Pevsner. He didn't have anything to do with the theft of the Boeing 727 like I had originally concluded. But his intelligence gave us the information we needed to track it down in Costa Rica and—"

Pick held up a hand. "Okay, I get it. You think we need to find out what Pevsner knows."

"I think he's our best bet," Fernando said.

"So, how do you find him?"

Castillo's cousin laughed. "Oh, I don't. That's for the anointed one to do."

Growing frustrated, Pick reminded himself to keep calm. "Okay, how do *I* find him?"

"The last I heard, he was in Pilar, Argentina," Miller offered.

Fernando shook his head. "Charley told me he had slowly divested himself of his Argentine interests over the years. It was a good thing, too. The new president came into office with promises to slash the size of the government and rein in the corruption that had allowed the country to become a major hub for money laundering in South America. Even though Pevsner considers himself *retired*, he is still very wealthy and fears that a right-wing government might seize his money and throw him in prison for past transgressions."

"So, where is he?" Pick asked.

Instead of answering, Fernando looked at Ani and Junior. "Do either of you have any sources inside the SVR?"

Ani looked surprised. "The SVR?"

"The Sluzhba Vneshney Razvedki, the Russian Foreign Intelligence Service."

"I know what the SVR is, but why?"

"Because if there is one man Vladimir Vladimirovich Putin wants to keep tabs on, it's the man he entrusted to fly his gold and surplus arms out of Russia following the collapse of the Soviet Union," Fernando said.

"*His* gold? As in Putin's?" Pick asked.

Fernando nodded. "Who better to trust than a colonel in both the Soviet Air Force and the SVR?"

"And you think—wherever he is—the SVR is keeping tabs on him?"

"Got any better ideas?"

Junior cleared his throat. "I might be able to help."

[THREE]

They were still hours away from sunset, but Fernando invited the others inside to relax while Junior went to work scouring his network of assets. Pick had long since learned to simply accept what Junior said at face value. If he said he could make something happen, he would.

But as the minutes turned into hours, he slowly began to question the spook's abilities. Junior had proven himself more than capable on numerous occasions when his unique skill set was needed. But finding a former Russian intelligence officer who didn't want to be found might have proven too difficult for even him. Still, Pick had no other options, and he was thankful for a few hours of rest.

At last, Junior walked through the screen door and joined the others in the main sitting room.

"Well?" Ani asked.

He gave a little shake of his head. "I gave it my best shot, but none of my sources even knew who I was talking about."

"So, that's it?" Pick asked. "We're stuck?"

"And we wasted all this time for nothing," Ani said, obviously perturbed that Junior had kept them sidelined during his wild-goose chase.

Before he could respond, the phone in his hand began ringing. The spook turned it over and looked at the caller ID, his eyes registering surprise.

"One of your contacts?" Pick asked.

Junior nodded. "But not one I was expecting. I'll be right back."

The spook spun away and exited through the screen door again while Pick and the others shared looks of cautious optimism. It wouldn't have been a surprise for Junior to snatch victory from the jaws of defeat in the eleventh hour. But without a lead they could run down, they were stuck sitting in Abuela's living room and hoping for a miracle.

After several minutes of silence, Junior returned and again gave a little shake of his head. "That was one of my sources with the FBI."

"Do they know how to find Pevsner?" Pick asked hopefully.

"I'm afraid not. But they did provide me with a list of the victims from the Virginia Beach shooting."

Following that morning's excitement at the Alamo, Pick had almost forgotten they'd planned on comparing the names of the victims in Virginia Beach with those in San Antonio to look for an obvious link. They still didn't have the names of the three Alamo Rangers and two FBI special agents, or the one civilian who had been killed that morning. But now they at least had the first half of the puzzle. "Anybody jump out at you?"

Junior shook his head. "Other than Castillo? No."

Pick hadn't really been expecting a miracle, but that didn't mean he wasn't hoping for some divine intervention. "Okay, so we're back to trying to find Aleksandr Pevsner. Is that about right?"

None of the others offered an alternative solution.

"And nobody has a suggestion for how to go about finding him?"

Again, the group remained silent.

Guess this is why I get paid the big bucks.

Hours later, Pick returned to the front porch and sat in a rocking chair to watch the sun setting on Castillo's land. He loathed sitting still when he knew there was work yet to be done, but until Junior came through with a location for Aleksandr Pevsner . . .

"I might have an idea," Miller said.

Pick turned and saw the former Special Forces officer leaning against the side of the house. "How long have you been standing there?"

"Long enough to know you feel lost and need a little guidance." Miller pushed off the wall and sat in the rocking chair next to Pick. "What's on your mind?"

"We don't know who the terrorists are, how they got in the country, or who's funding them. We don't know why they chose Virginia Beach and San Antonio as targets or where they're going to attack next. We have the largest intelligence community in the world and have absolutely nothing to go on."

"Done whining?"

Pick shot Miller a dirty look.

"That was precisely why the Office of Organizational Analysis was established in the first place," Miller said. "The President was frustrated at the complete and total dysfunction of the intelligence community and wanted someone from the outside—someone more than capable, who didn't mind ruffling a few feathers or stepping on toes—to accomplish what his directors at the individual agencies thought impossible."

"Yeah, someone like Charley Castillo," Pick said.

"And now you," Miller concluded.

More than ever, Pick felt his inadequacies compared to Castillo. He was a damn good Marine, but he wasn't cut out for navigating the political minefield laid by countless government agencies that wanted credit for stopping terrorists. "How am I supposed to break through the cumbersome bureaucracy?"

Miller laughed. "The same way Charley did."

"And how's that?"

"By ruffling feathers and stepping on toes."

Pick glared at him. "You said you have an idea?"

"What do you know about Karl Wilhelm von und zu Gossinger?"

Pick closed his eyes and leaned his head back against the rocking chair. "Why don't you just tell me what I should know about him and save us both the time?"

"Okay, boss. Karl Wilhelm von und zu Gossinger is the only son of Erika von und zu Gossinger, a wealthy German woman whose family owned three newspapers—including the *Tages Zeitung*—the Gossingerbrau Brewery, and a good bit of land."

"What does this have to do with anything we're trying to do here, Dick?"

The former Army officer smiled. "The man you know as Carlos Guillermo Castillo was born as Karl Wilhelm von und zu Gossinger."

Pick opened his eyes. "When did he change his name?"

"He didn't. He still has a German passport under that name and sometimes uses it as a cover."

Maybe if I had another name, I'd be more useful to the President.

"I don't see how any of this helps."

"As Karl Wilhelm von und zu Gossinger, he is the owner and Washington correspondent of the Gossinger GmbH newspapers. Or he was. I don't think he has written an article for them in some time."

"You're losing me . . ."

Miller pursed his lips for a moment before continuing. "When Charley came to Angola to investigate the disappearance of the 727, he did so as a reporter for the *Tages Zeitung*. I told him that the Agency not only ignored my concerns about Aleksandr Pevsner, but they buried them."

"What did he make of that?"

Miller shrugged. "It was the only lead we had at the time, so Charley—or Karl Wilhelm von und zu Gossinger—decided to stir the pot by writing an article that specifically mentioned the rumor of a Pevsner connection."

"He what?"

"It worked. Otto Görner, his editor at the *Tages Zeitung* and close family friend, received word that Pevsner would grant Karl an interview in Vienna."

Pick held up both hands to stop the onslaught of information. "Wait a second. Are you suggesting that I convince the President to coerce the editor of a major newspaper into allowing me to write an article about these shootings where I mention Aleksandr Pevsner as a person of interest? Just to flush him out?"

"No, I'm not suggesting that at all."

Somewhat reluctantly, Pick was beginning to respect Castillo's audacity. "Good. Because I don't know much about Pevsner, but I'm pretty sure I don't want to cross somebody Putin considers dangerous."

"You're right," Miller said. "You don't. But I don't think you have to go as far as provoking him to get what you want."

Pick thought about it for a moment and recognized the subtle brilliance of what Miller was suggesting. All he needed to do was let Junior and Ani's network of assets know that he was trying to get in touch with Pevsner, and let the former arms dealer come to him.

"So, we make a few quiet inquiries and let the word spread?"

Miller nodded. "Something like that."

"And what? Hope he can figure out where to get in touch with me?"

"Maybe it would be easier if you gave him a place to look."

"Like where?"

"Why not Vienna? It was good enough for Charley's first meeting with him. Why not yours?"

Pick looked at his watch. It was too late to put anything in motion that would result in a meeting in the next twenty-four hours. "Okay. Let's gather the others and run this idea by them before we do anything else. I want to make sure we're considering the potential consequences from every angle."

"And then what?"

Pick stood. "And then I need to brief the President."

[FOUR]

The Treaty Room

The White House

1600 Pennsylvania Avenue NW

Washington, D.C.

2030 30 March 2026

Natalie Cohen's decades of experience working for several administrations had given her enough insight to know that the President wasn't confined to working only during normal business hours. If anything, the office came with more work than could be accomplished in even a twelve-hour day, and she had no preconceived notion that she would likely ever see a nine-to-five schedule during her term. But that didn't mean she wanted to be chained to the *Resolute* desk in the Oval Office twenty-four hours a day.

As such, she was rigid in maintaining a strict twelve-hour schedule during which she could be found in the West Wing. From six in the morning until six every night, President Natalie Cohen made herself available to her staff to conduct the normal day-to-day business of running the most powerful nation on Earth. But when the clock struck 6:00 p.m., she left the Oval Office, bid her staff a good evening, and retired to the Executive Residence on the second floor of the White House.

Once there, she dressed in a pair of jeans and a faded GW sweatshirt and sat down at her desk in the Treaty Room to resume an uphill battle against a never-ending deluge of reports and briefings. But before she donned her reading glasses and got to work underneath an electrified Victorian crystal gasolier installed during the administration of George W. Bush, she took a moment to appreciate the weight of her responsibility as President of the United States and her role in preserving the republic.

The Treaty Room had hosted some of the country's most notable moments in history and demanded her respect. It was in that room where William McKinley had signed the peace treaty with Spain to conclude the Spanish–American War in 1898. It was there where John F. Kennedy had signed the Nuclear Test Ban Treaty in 1963. It was where George W. Bush had addressed the nation in the wake of the September 11th terrorist attacks and announced the war in Afghanistan.

And it was where Natalie Cohen spent every evening to ensure that she honored their legacies.

With a heavy sigh, she reached for her glasses and slipped them onto her face before picking up the single sheet placed neatly atop a stack of folders containing her evening's reading material. She saw immediately that it was a summary of her week's schedule, something her staff prepared for her each and every Monday. It was a reminder that the last week was now in the past and she still had work to do.

"Another week down," she muttered. "Only two hundred to go . . ."

She scanned the document and didn't notice anything that demanded special attention, with the exception of a public appearance in Annapolis, Maryland, the upcoming Friday. It was something she had been looking forward to, and the edge of her mouth curled up in a faint smile as she made a mental note to go over the details with her chief of staff. Then she pushed the schedule aside and picked up the first folder.

A quiet ringing broke her concentration before she finished reading the first paragraph.

Biting back her frustration, she set the folder down and picked up the phone. "Yes?"

"Madam President, I have Director Fleiss for you."

She pushed the glasses up onto her head and leaned back in her chair. "Put him through."

There was a *click* on the line followed by a brief moment of silence before Marty's voice broke in. "Madam President, I apologize for disturbing you after hours."

"It's all right, Marty. You know my day is never done."

"Yes, ma'am. I would have waited until tomorrow, but figured you'd want to get the latest update from Captain McCoy straight from the horse's mouth."

"Has he contacted you?"

"He's on the other line, and I can patch him through right now."

This ought to be interesting.

"Go ahead."

"Yes, ma'am. Just a moment." There was another *click* followed by a stretch of silence. Then, "Madam President?"

"Still here, Marty."

"I have Captain McCoy on the line."

Natalie leaned forward and rested both elbows on her desk as she looked up at a large oil painting on the opposite wall. The George P. A. Healy work of art—known as *The Peacemakers*—depicted Abraham Lincoln in a strategy session with Generals Ulysses S. Grant and William Tecumseh Sherman and Admiral David Dixon Porter aboard the steamer *River Queen* during the final days of the American Civil War. It had resided in the Treaty Room until Barack Obama moved it into the Oval Office dining room.

One of her first orders of business had been to move it back.

"Do you have an update for me, Captain McCoy?"

"Yes, Madam President. I apologize for disturbing you, but I wanted to make you aware of my plan to contact a former Russian intelligence officer."

"For what purpose?"

"To gain insight into the terrorists' means and methods."

Natalie's back stiffened. "Do you think the Russians had something to do with this?"

"No, ma'am," Pick said. "I was led to believe that this person is something of an expert in black-market logistics and might be able to shed some light on how the terrorists were able to infiltrate our borders."

The voice of her Director of National Intelligence broke in. "Who is this person?"

"Aleksandr Pevsner."

"Do we know him?" Fleiss asked.

"I know him," Natalie said.

"Madam President?"

In a flash, she was transported back in time to when she had served as secretary of state and first heard the name. "Aleksandr Pevsner was a thorn in the Agency's side until Charley Castillo convinced him to help us find a missing Boeing 727."

"Yes, ma'am," Pick said. "We think he might be willing to help with this as well."

"Where will you attempt to make contact with him?"

"At the Hotel Sacher in Vienna," Pick said.

Marty sounded surprised. "Vienna?"

"Yes, sir. It was where he first met Colonel Castillo, and we're hoping it appeals to his sense of nostalgia."

"Aleksandr Pevsner isn't an overly sentimental person, Captain McCoy," Natalie said. "Please be careful and keep us informed once you make contact."

"Yes, Madam President."

"That will be all, Marty. Thank you for keeping me in the loop."

"Yes, Madam President."

Natalie Cohen ended the call and leaned back in her chair, again studying the imposing figure of Abraham Lincoln commanding the attention of his top military leaders. George W. Bush had once commented that the painting reminded him of Lincoln's clarity of purpose, and Natalie couldn't help but wonder what either former President would think of her sending a Marine Corps captain to Austria to meet with a former Russian intelligence officer and arms dealer.

"For a necessary and noble cause," she said, remembering the rest of what Bush had said about Lincoln.

XII

[ONE]

Flughafen Wien

Schwechat, Austria

1230 1 April 2026

Pick was wide awake by the time the Austrian Airbus A320neo touched down on Runway 29 at Vienna International Airport. Both his lack of fatigue and relative punctuality were somewhat remarkable considering he had left San Antonio almost sixteen hours earlier, with brief layovers at Houston's George Bush Intercontinental Airport and London's Heathrow Airport. The journey was made only marginally better by flying the first and shortest of the three legs aboard the Coast Guard C-37A Gulfstream V with Dick Miller and Randy at the controls.

But flying coach on the remaining two legs had erased any notion that being appointed chief, Office of Organizational Analysis, entitled him to such creature comforts as business-class accommodations on a trans-Atlantic flight. Still, Pick managed to smile at the blond flight attendant, decked out in red, on his way off the plane.

"Willkommen in Wien," she said.

"Danke," Pick replied.

Carrying only a backpack, Pick walked up the jet bridge and through an automatic sliding door into a long hallway with floor-to-ceiling windows on one side. He followed his fellow passengers through the Customs and Immigration queue, then exited into the main terminal, where he took a few moments to look around and gather his bearings. The airport itself felt like every other European airport he had ever passed through—clean, modern, and bustling with energy regardless of the time—though he knew it had originally been built as a military airport before being taken over by the British during their postwar occupation.

After spotting signs that directed arriving passengers to ground transportation, Pick turned right and walked down a long, sloping ramp to the Bahnhof Flughafen Wien, where he had several options to choose from to travel the twenty kilometers into the city. Trying his best not to look like every other American tourist, Pick waited in line behind a ticket vending machine for the CAT, or City Airport Train, and splurged for a one-way ticket on the express line, which would take him to Wien Mitte in only fifteen minutes.

By the time the bright green double-decker train pulled into the station, Pick had shaken off any lingering fatigue and was completely engaged in the operation. He had flown into Austria under his true name and was aware that if anybody wanted to speak with him, he would be easy to find. But that was the point. Even so, Castillo had imparted to him a need for constant vigilance, and Pick found himself watching his fellow passengers closely as they boarded the train and took their seats.

Fifteen minutes later, when the doors opened again, Pick took his time and fell in with the flow of traffic exiting the train and let the current carry him through the station and out onto an open-air plaza. It was a clear, cold day, and Pick inhaled the fresh air—the first such breath since leaving Houston, when he had been confined to planes and trains for the better part of a full day. It was for this reason he was reluctant to hail a taxi and instead opted to make the one-and-a-half-kilometer trek to his hotel on foot. Looking around, Pick saw tall, modern buildings flanking the plaza on all sides, but it was impossible to miss the Stephansdom Südturm—the South Tower of St. Stephen's Cathedral—towering over the city to his right. It was one of Vienna's main landmarks, and he turned in its direction, orienting himself to the city as he began walking along Landstraßer Hauptstraße.

After crossing the Wienfluss, Pick left the sidewalk for one of the walking paths entering the Stadtpark, a large municipal green space spanning 65,000 square meters from Vienna's first to its third districts. Groves of ginkgo, honey locust, and pyramid poplar ringed the park to isolate it from the clamor of normal city life. But with it being just over a week into spring, many of the trees were still bare and provided little protection from the noise.

Even so, it gave Pick an unobstructed view in every direction, and it was his best chance for detecting surveillance.

A gentle breeze swept through the park, and Pick turned up the collar on his lightweight Kühl cotton canvas jacket. He followed the walking path along the park's perimeter bordering the river, casually stopping every few minutes to sit on one of the many benches scattered throughout the park while looking for someone who might have followed him. He wasn't sure what he would do if he detected surveillance. After all, he was alone and had nobody he could call for backup.

No Junior. No Ani.

His meandering walk through the park took him past statues of famous Viennese artists, writers, and composers and ultimately dumped him back into the city on Johannesgasse directly in front of an opulent Italian Renaissance–style building known as the Kursalon. Leaving the concert hall and park behind, Pick turned for the Schubertring and the wide tree-lined walking path for the remaining four blocks to his hotel.

The Bristol, a high-end baroque hotel, sat directly across the street from the Wiener Staatsoper—the Vienna State Opera—and was a short walk from the cathedral Pick had used as his landmark to orient himself in the city. Billed as a fashionable residence of the elite, the Hotel Bristol first opened its doors in 1892 and was not unlike the kind of place a wealthy former Russian intelligence officer and arms dealer might choose when visiting the city.

If only Pick could count on Pevsner visiting the city.

In many ways, the building itself reminded Pick of Bancroft Hall, where he had lived for four years while attending the Academy. Although notably different in architectural styles, both the massive dormitory and luxurious hotel were adorned with copper roofs that had developed a beautiful green patina. Turning in off Kärntner Ring—one section of Vienna's "Ring Street" that circled its first district, or Innere Stadt—Pick walked through a revolving door and into a brightly lit room with marble floors and a stately antique grandfather clock standing watch next to an equally observant concierge. The uniformed man nodded at Pick in polite greeting.

Pick nodded back, then walked through a set of double doors and into the lobby, where leather armchairs were arrayed on either side of a fireplace opposite the reception desk to his right. The room was vacant except for the young woman who stood silently behind the desk and waited for him to approach.

Pick smiled as he walked up to her. "Sprechen Sie Englisch?"

"Yes, sir," the woman replied, her hands clasped at her lower back.

"I have a reservation," Pick said.

The Fräulein's eyes briefly took in his appearance, a subtle reminder that he had waded into uncomfortable and somewhat foreign territory. Pick was far more accustomed to wearing a perahan tunban in the tribal regions of Afghanistan or a dishdasha and keffiyeh in Iraq than he was to wearing a custom-tailored three-piece wool suit. But like any good Marine Raider, he knew that if he wanted to blend in and be accepted, he needed to fit in and dress like the locals. Finding something suitable to wear was at the top of his list after checking into his room.

"What is your name, sir?"

"McCoy," he answered.

The woman smiled politely and tapped on the keyboard in front of her to pull up his reservation. Her eyes narrowed slightly, and her lip quivered as if she was trying to keep herself from biting it. But then she looked up from her computer screen. "Can you give me one moment, please?"

"Is there a problem?"

She smiled. "No. No problem. One moment, if you please."

Without waiting for Pick's concurrence, she turned and walked through a door he assumed led to an office. He leaned against the counter and surveyed the lobby, noting the other doors open to the hotel's restaurant and the oldest American bar in Vienna. He had no reason to think there was a problem with his reservation, but that little voice in the back of his head he had taken to calling "Raider intuition" was starting to grow more vocal.

A moment later, the door opened and an older, slightly less attractive woman appeared.

"Herr McCoy?"

"Yes," Pick replied.

"Your room is not quite ready yet," she said, her accent thick and forced. "Would you mind waiting in the lounge? We will come for you when your room is ready."

She gestured to her right—Pick's left—and he saw a handful of guests enjoying a casual drink in the cozy salon atmosphere of the Bristol Lounge. He could tell by the stern expression on her face that no amount of persuading would convince her to find suitable accommodations in a room that was ready, so he just nodded.

"Of course," he said.

"Danke schön."

[TWO]

Bristol Lounge

Hotel Bristol

Kärntner Ring 1

Vienna, Austria

1730 1 April 2026

After a long day of traveling, all Pick wanted to do was check into his room and take a shower. But by the time the minute hand on his Critical Mechanics dive watch had completed its first lap, he had drained his third glass of sparkling water while watching the lounge slowly fill with patrons who wanted to enjoy an early evening cocktail. And Pick was quickly becoming one of them.

He motioned for a waiter to bring him a drink menu and was surprised when the man delivered a hefty tome that began with a two-hundred-and-eighty-five-euro cocktail made with Louis XIII de Rémy Martin Grande Champagne Cognac and ended with an assortment of nonalcoholic drinks. The first was too rich for Pick's meager Marine Corps salary, but he needed something a little stronger than Vöslauer sparkling mineral water to sustain him until he could venture out to the Hotel Sacher Wien and hopefully meet somebody who could lead him to Aleksandr Pevsner.

"I'll have a Hope and Tonic," he told the waiter.

"Sehr gut."

The waiter took the menu and disappeared, leaving Pick alone to study the room's baroque design with honey-colored wood paneling rising nearly all the way to the stark white ornamental ceiling. While most of the lounge was furnished with elegant dark wood tables draped in white cloth runners, Pick relaxed in one of the dark upholstered armchairs arranged in front of the fireplace. The room itself was a juxtaposition of a light and airy design style blended with the cozy comfort of a warm hearth.

The lounge wasn't crowded by any means, but Pick noticed at least three different groups clustered in various locations around the spacious room, none of whom appeared to be connected with a former Russian arms dealer. Not that he had expected it, but Pick had learned in a short time that things weren't always as they seemed and that his role as Presidential Agent required him to expect the unexpected. He studied each group while invoking the soft skills of observation Castillo had attempted to impart on him during their brief stint working together.

First, Pick focused on a group of four stylishly dressed patrons sitting underneath a crystal chandelier near a tall window flanked by flowing, light-colored draperies. He watched them eating and drinking and immediately dismissed them as threats, believing them to be local Viennese enjoying an early dinner before taking in the opera or other event of high society. Their conversation was louder than most—bordering on rude—and made it perfectly clear that they considered their fellow patrons unimportant and unworthy of common courtesy.

Shifting his focus, Pick moved on to a couple in their late twenties dressed in casual evening attire sitting at a table apart from the others. The man had short-cropped dark hair that contrasted with the woman's auburn pixie cut, and the two only nursed their cocktails while sitting across from each other. Although their lips occasionally moved,

Pick got the impression they were only mimicking conversation while focused more on the others than on each other. If they were on a first date, Pick didn't think there would be a second.

Last, in the far corner of the lounge, Pick saw three men crowding around a lone woman with red hair and sharp but beautiful features in her early to mid-fifties. He let his gaze linger on that group the longest, trying to decide if she was being harassed by the apparently intoxicated younger men or simply toying with them. She smiled politely at each in turn but never focused on any one man. And she never made eye contact with Pick.

"Your drink, sir," the waiter said, interrupting Pick's thoughts as he placed the cocktail on a napkin on the table in front of him.

"Danke," Pick replied, reaching for his wallet.

"Courtesy of the lady, sir."

Pick's hand froze, and he glanced up again at the woman who had been surrounded in the corner. She turned to him and locked her eyes on his, tipping her head slightly to acknowledge him with a coquettish smile. Pick took the cocktail, raised it toward her in a silent toast, and stared into her light sky-blue eyes while wondering how to take the gesture. Had she ordered him the drink as a plea for him to rescue her from the surrounding jackals? Or was she the type who couldn't stand not being the focus of every man in the room?

As the waiter disappeared with Pick's empty water glass, he took a sip of the signature cocktail. It was made with Bombay gin, St-Germain elderflower liqueur, fresh lime juice, basil, cucumber, and Fever-Tree Mediterranean tonic. It was both light and refreshing. But the alcohol went straight to his head, and Pick took his time to savor the drink while remaining observant enough to notice the group of four getting up from their table to leave the lounge.

After several minutes of shifting his focus between the awkward couple and the damsel in distress, Pick placed a cocktail napkin on top of the half-empty glass and rose to use the restroom. He felt a little unsteady on his feet—probably more from the traveling and lack of food than from the alcohol—and he paused to chastise himself for acting like he was on vacation when he should have been focused on finding Aleksandr Pevsner. Now was not the time for him to become lax. Not when so much was at stake.

Pick composed himself, then strolled across the room while avoiding eye contact with the redhead. He was halfway to the hallway where the lounge's bathrooms were located when he noticed the awkward couple watching him with interest. It was the first time since they had sat down that both seemed to be in tune with each other.

I'll need to watch my back with those two.

Pick almost smiled at the thought, thinking that Castillo would have been proud that he was finally thinking like a covert agent instead of a Marine Raider. But there was no question Pick was more comfortable punching somebody in the face than he was stabbing them in the back.

Out of the corner of his eye, Pick saw the dark-haired man excuse himself and get up from the table.

This is going to get interesting.

[THREE]

Pick walked into the restroom and headed straight for the urinal but wasn't all that surprised when the dark-haired man from the awkward first date followed him inside and took up station at the urinal next to his. Pick focused on the wall in front of him to avoid looking at the man, but his senses were on high alert. Something about him seemed off, and Pick quickly relieved himself and zipped up his pants but made no move to leave.

A moment later—just as the dark-haired man was finishing his business—the restroom door swung open and permitted two of the redhead's boisterous suitors. They chattered in excited German that was too fast for Pick to make out, but he was less interested in what they thought their chances were with bedding the older woman than he was in the dark-haired man who had followed him into the bathroom.

"Beer goes right through me," the man said in English, startling Pick with his flawless American accent.

Pick grunted, not wanting to identify himself as a fellow American while hoping to preserve what anonymity he had maintained since arriving in Vienna, which was to say not much.

If the man was offended by Pick's lack of response, it didn't show. He zipped up his pants, flushed the urinal, and turned for the sink to ostensibly wash his hands. But before he had taken a step, the bathroom's silence was broken by the unmistakable sound of a fist slamming into a man's gut followed by the violent exhale of air. Pick's heart lurched, and he spun, preparing to defend himself against a surprise attack.

What he found instead was one of the redhead's suitors with a balled-up fist, standing in front of the doubled-over dark-haired man. The second suitor stood off to the side, blocking anyone from entering or leaving the bathroom, while letting a leather sap dangle in his hand. Pick had seen the men only from a distance and hadn't noticed before how physically imposing they were. But up close, there was no mistaking the clear and present danger.

Pick held up his hands to demonstrate he wasn't a threat to them. "I was just leaving."

The man with the sap shook his head and answered in heavily accented English. "No, Mr. McCoy. You weren't."

It took only a split second for Pick to register that the heavily muscled thug had addressed him by name.

"What did you just say?"

"Our boss would like to speak with you."

Before Pick could respond, the dark-haired man sprung upward and sent a fist sailing through the air at the first man's jaw. The thug sidestepped the punch with little effort and brushed him aside, while his companion swung the lead-filled leather sap and brought it down on the man's skull with a sickening *thwap!*

Pick flinched and took a step backward as the man collapsed to the bathroom's tile floor.

"Do you have a problem with that?"

Pick shook his head. "No. No problem."

But he couldn't help but wonder if this was how Castillo had met Aleksandr Pevsner for the first time.

Pick stepped over the dark-haired man's unconscious form and followed the first thug from the restroom while the one who had swung the sap brought up the rear. Exiting the dark hallway and stepping back into the brightly lit lounge, he was somewhat surprised to discover that the auburn-haired half of the awkward couple was nowhere to be seen. Neither, for that matter, was the redhead who had bought his drink or the other goon who had been harassing her. The lounge was empty, save for a handful of waiters who were staged around the room, waiting patiently for guests to serve.

"Where are we going?" Pick asked.

The thug behind him answered. "Outside."

"Why?"

No answer.

Pick could have pressed for more, but he suspected the two were as short on their vocabulary as they were on manners. It was probably one of the reasons why the redhead had sent him a drink in the first place. She had probably endured enough of their charming personalities and was hoping Pick would invite her to join him.

Real smooth, Pick.

The first thug led them from the lounge and through the lobby into the concierge room. Neither the Fräulein behind the reception desk nor the concierge paid them any mind, making him second-guess his regret at not inviting the redhead for a drink.

If you had, she would have been dragged into this mess, too.

He decided it was probably for the best and followed their leader through the revolving door and out onto Kärntner Ring, where they gestured for him to stand off to the side and wait. Directly in front of them was a covered bus stop and falafel stand separated from the hotel's sidewalk by an access road. To their left, Pick saw a satin-gray Mercedes-Benz AMG S 63 with dark tinted windows rolling slowly toward them. When it stopped directly in front of the Hotel Bristol, Pick's stomach dropped.

The sap-wielding thug reached out and gripped Pick's upper arm, his hand easily wrapping around Pick's bicep. "Wait."

Not that he expected either man would be willing to commit violence in broad daylight on Vienna's streets, but Pick still didn't think it would be a good idea to argue. He nodded silently and watched the other man step forward, open the rear door, and gesture for Pick to climb inside.

"Where are we going?"

The man didn't even bother to look annoyed at Pick's question. "Inside, please."

Pick looked down at the hand gripping his arm, then up at the thug it belonged to. He had a suspicion that even if he refused to climb into the backseat of the luxury sedan, Tweedledee and Tweedledum would only force him inside. Probably headfirst.

"Okay," Pick said.

The man released his grip on Pick's arm.

Wondering what awaited him inside the Mercedes, Pick stepped off the curb, ducked his head, and climbed into the backseat. He had barely managed to bring both feet inside before the door was slammed shut and the driver accelerated away from the curb.

"Who exactly are you, Mr. McCoy?" the redhead asked.

[FOUR]

Maybe it was because Pick had spent the day traveling halfway around the world on three different airplanes. Or maybe it was because the gin concoction he had ordered at the Bristol Lounge had gone straight to his head. Whatever the reason, the shock of seeing the redhead in the back of the Mercedes had left him almost as speechless as her question had. She pursed her lips in perturbance.

"This is the part, Mr. McCoy, where you tell me who you work for."

Pick shook his head in disbelief. "I don't think I will."

The redhead shifted casually in her seat, and Pick glanced down to see a pistol in her hand aimed at his midsection. It wasn't the first time somebody had pointed a gun at him, but the juxtaposition of her demure looks with an overt threat of violence made it seem somehow more ominous. With considerable effort, he reacted to the danger only by clasping his hands in his lap and staring calmly into her sky-blue eyes.

"You have thirty minutes to change your mind," the woman said.

Then what?

Pick glanced through the window over her shoulder and noticed the "Steffl"—how locals referred to the South Tower of St. Stephen's Cathedral—in the distance on the left side of the car. Orienting himself to the landmark, he quickly realized that they had reversed course and were traveling east on Vienna's Ring Road, circling its historic first district. He gave her a brief smile, looked into her emotionless eyes, then glanced over his shoulder at the scenery passing in a blur through the window on his side of the sedan.

And there's the Kursalon.

Seeing the concert hall at the south end of Stadtpark gave him all the confirmation he needed to know at least the direction they were driving. Vienna was a large city, and Pick didn't have the luxury of being able to consult a map to know for certain, but he thought they were moving closer to the Danube River and its former arm, the Donaukanal, which cut a passage through the city itself. Where they would end up in thirty minutes was still a question Pick wanted answered.

"Where are you taking me?" Pick asked, turning to study the redhead again.

Her eyes narrowed with something close to humor, but she didn't answer. Instead, she leaned back into the plush rear seat and visibly relaxed while speaking to the driver in a language Pick wasn't familiar with. Though he wasn't certain, he thought it sounded like Russian, and he didn't understand a single word that passed between them.

Except for the name Aleksandr.

The driver grunted in reply, and the Mercedes continued rolling through the Viennese streets as if they had all the time in the world. Even though the redhead had made it clear he had only thirty minutes.

"Do you know Aleksandr Pevsner?" Pick asked.

She said nothing.

"Are you taking me to him?"

She waggled the barrel of the gun from side to side. "You've got balls, Mr. McCoy. I'll give you that."

When the sedan reached the Donaukanal, the driver turned left and accelerated on the wide road. Pick looked across the channel at Leopoldstadt, Vienna's second district, which resided on the island between the channel and the Danube.

"Well, you're not taking me to the Russian embassy, that's for sure," he said.

The redhead cocked her head to the side. "Why would you say that?"

Pick glanced over his left shoulder and through the rear window, taking the opportunity to look for other vehicles that might be tailing them. It didn't take him long to spot an equally expensive Mercedes G-Class SUV in the lane behind them. But he didn't want her to know he had seen it, and he gestured over his shoulder with his thumb. "Because it's that way. South of Wien Mitte."

She pursed her lips in a tight smile. "You seem to know a great deal about Vienna. Have you ever been here before, Mr. McCoy?"

He shook his head.

"Or should I call you *Captain* McCoy?"

Pick's heart hammered in his chest, and his body coiled as if prepared to fight. He knew that if it came down to it, he could probably overpower the redhead and disarm her before she got a shot off. But the driver and SUV full of thugs behind them would be a significantly more challenging obstacle to overcome. It took considerable effort for Pick not to appear surprised that she had discovered more about him than just his name.

"You seem to know a good deal about me, but I don't know the first thing about you. Other than that I have you to thank for my drink."

She tipped her head to acknowledge the comment. "We make it a habit of knowing who comes looking for our friends. But I must admit you were not known to us before you arrived from . . . Langley?"

Pick gave her a wry smile. "I'm sorry to disappoint you, but I'm not from the Central Intelligence Agency."

She made a clucking sound with her mouth, both acknowledging his denial and making it perfectly clear she didn't believe him.

"I'm not with the CIA, the DIA, or any other three-letter agency."

"So, you expect me to believe you're just a Marine?"

This time it was Pick who made a dismissive sound. "*Just* a Marine? Oh, no. No, no. There's no such thing as *just* a Marine."

"Then who do you work for?"

Not that Pick had any intention of telling her that he worked directly for the President of the United States, but he figured the identity of his employer gave him some leverage he could exert over his captor. He glanced down at his watch and saw that ten minutes had already elapsed.

"Tell you what," he said. "I'll tell you who I work for if you tell me your name."

The redhead tilted her chin up slightly, as if considering the proposal. Pick hadn't really expected her to answer, but he figured it was worth a shot. If things turned violent, she would be the first to die. And Pick didn't want to kill her without knowing who she was first.

"Svetlana Alekseeva," she said.

XIII

[ONE]

Cobenzlgasse

Vienna, Austria

1820 1 April 2026

At the north end of the city, near where the Donaukanal rejoined the Danube, their mute driver exited the main thoroughfare and steered the Mercedes luxury sedan to the west. After a few short minutes, he turned again, and the throaty engine growled up the narrow street and echoed off quaint cottages lining both sides. It didn't take long until Pick felt like they had left the city for the countryside and were nearing their destination.

Pick needed to keep Svetlana talking.

"Where are we going?" Pick asked.

But Svetlana shook her head, making it clear she had given him far more than she thought he was entitled to. "No more questions, Captain McCoy. A deal is a deal. Now, who do you work for?"

He glanced over his shoulder at the G-Class SUV following them and knew he was running out of time. He had flown to Vienna in the hopes of finding somebody who could lead him to Aleksandr Pevsner and the answers he needed. Though it might not have happened the way he hoped or expected, he thought that was exactly what this was. It was time to lay all his cards out on the table.

"Would you believe me if I told you I work directly for the President of the United States?"

Her laugh was melodic and fitting for a lady. "Do you take me for an idiot?"

Pick couldn't help himself, and he let his eyes wander up and down her body. "No, actually. I think you are as intelligent as you are beautiful, and I am in way over my head."

He thought he saw just the faintest hint of color rising up her neck, but he doubted Svetlana was the type of woman who could be swayed by mere flattery. As if to prove him correct, she gave him a sad smile and shouted a command at the driver, who quickly pulled off to the side of the road.

"End of the line, Captain McCoy."

Pick watched the driver open his door and step out from behind the wheel, then stalk around the front of the car.

"Wait a second . . ."

Svetlana reached up and pressed the button to unlock the doors just as her brutish driver—the third man who had been "harassing" her in the Bristol Lounge—reached the rear door. Pick reached up and stabbed at the button to lock it again.

"I'm telling you the truth," he said, trying like hell to keep the fear from his voice or sounding like he was pleading with her.

Svetlana's eyes glazed over for just a moment, as if recalling some long-forgotten memory. Then she lifted the gun and pointed it at him again. "There was only one man I knew who worked directly for the President," she said. "And you're not him."

Like a bolt of lightning, Pick suddenly remembered something.

Svetlana?

His voice was little more than a whisper when he spoke. "His name was Charley Castillo."

If Pick's earlier comment had given her cheeks a rose-colored hue, his latest statement drained them of color just as fast. She stabbed at the door's unlock button, and her driver yanked it open and wrapped a meaty hand around Pick's neck. One moment he was sitting in the back of a luxury German sedan. The next he was flat on his back and staring up into the blue Austrian sky.

Pick looked up at the Russian thug leaning over him, then saw Svetlana's face as she emerged from the car, dangling the pistol in front of her. "Who did you say?"

If he was right, this was his only chance of salvation. If he was wrong, it didn't really matter anymore.

"Charley Castillo," he croaked. "Otherwise known as Carlos Guillermo Castillo. Or Karl Wilhelm von und zu Gossinger, if you prefer."

If anything, his answer only made Svetlana more upset, and she leaned in close and pressed the barrel against his forehead. "Why did you say 'was'?"

Pick stared into her sky-blue eyes and saw an emotion he hadn't expected to see there: fear.

"Because the President appointed me to replace him," Pick said.

Svetlana took a long, slow breath in through her nose and exhaled through pursed lips before replying. "I want you to think very carefully about how you answer this next question, Captain McCoy. It might very well be the last thing you ever say. Do you understand?"

Pick nodded slowly.

"Is Charley Castillo still alive?"

Pick nodded again. "Yes, he is."

Svetlana's shoulders slumped with apparent relief. She lowered the pistol and issued another command to her driver in Russian. One moment he was staring up at the blue Austrian sky. The next he was on his feet and staring at a beautiful Russian woman's sky-blue eyes.

"You're his Svetlana, aren't you?"

She shook her head. "Once upon a time, maybe."

"I thought you were dead."

"Is that what he said?"

Pick could sense that she had, for the moment, at least, decided not to kill him. And he was reluctant to say something that might upset their tepid truce. But he also sensed that she wasn't likely to forgive him for lying to her and that she was more than adept at sniffing out a lie.

"He never talked about you," Pick answered honestly.

"Then how did you hear my name?"

"From Randy, when we—"

He abruptly stopped talking, fearing that he was saying too much. But she had caught his gaffe and latched on to it like a dog with a bone.

"Randy . . ."

"His son," Pick said.

Her face soured and she instinctively wrapped an arm around her midsection. "I know who Randy is."

"Of course. I'm sorry."

"What were you about to say, Captain McCoy?"

He hesitated, but only briefly. "I was about to say that Randy told me about you when we visited Charley in the hospital."

Svetlana's back stiffened suddenly. "The hospital? What happened to him?"

"He was shot. Several times."

[TWO]

Cobenzl

Vienna, Austria

1900 1 April 2026

Svetlana had said nothing after learning that Castillo was in the hospital with multiple gunshot wounds. She remained silent after climbing back into the car and watched the sun set while the Mercedes sedan wended its way up the snaking road. The sun had completely disappeared under the horizon by the time the Russian driver parked the car and Svetlana opened the door with a curt "Come with me."

The sky had a faint red glow to the west as Pick followed her from the parking lot and onto an observation deck overlooking the city. Without the sun's warming rays, the air took on a chill that cut through his thin Kühl jacket and caused him to shiver involuntarily. He was hesitant to break their silent truce, so he followed two paces behind as they reached the railing and looked out over the sprawling city beneath them.

"It's beautiful, isn't it?" Svetlana asked, the collar on her wool coat pulled high to shield her from the wind.

"It is," Pick agreed.

"Is Charley okay?" she asked, turning to cast her sky-blue eyes in his direction.

Pick nodded. "He's stable but not out of the woods yet."

He thought he saw her shoulders sag with relief, but then she turned and leaned her back against the railing to face him. "So, President Cohen has chosen you to replace him. Why?"

Pick smiled and shook his head. "Honestly, I don't know. I'm nothing like Charley and don't think I'm cut out for this. I think she made a big mistake in choosing me."

"Then why are you here?"

Pick broke eye contact with her and looked out over the city as more and more lights flickered on. Darkness was settling over the Cobenzl, making him feel even more alone. He had flown halfway around the world to meet a former Russian arms dealer and ended up being abducted by a woman he had thought was dead.

Instead of answering, Pick asked the question that had been rattling around in his brain. "How are you here?"

"You mean, how am I alive?"

Pick nodded.

"What did Randy say?"

"Nothing," he replied honestly. "It was Dick Miller who said that Charley had lost you in childbirth."

Svetlana again wrapped an arm protectively around her belly. "We lost our child, that much is true."

There was so much emotion wrapped up in that simple statement. Pick couldn't fathom the pain a parent must endure after losing a child, but he imagined it had created an insurmountable strain on their relationship. "And your marriage suffered because of it?"

She dropped her hands to her sides and shot him an incredulous look. "Our marriage?"

"Did he blame you for it? Is that what happened?"

In an instant, her relaxed posture became rigid, and she pushed away from the railing. "I blamed myself, and Charley did everything in his power to reassure me. *Everything.*"

Her sudden defense of the man Pick knew only as a harsh taskmaster left him momentarily speechless. Then he understood. "So, it was you who ended things."

Her eyes flashed sudden anger, and Pick immediately regretted his choice of words.

"It's not what you think," Svetlana said in a low, crisp voice. "I *love* Charley more than anything. That is the reason I left."

She said love, *not* loved.

It shouldn't have surprised Pick that he knew even less than he thought he had about Castillo. But he was still trying to wrap his brain around the fact that he was standing on a scenic overlook at the edge of the Vienna Woods with the man's wife.

"I don't understand," he said. "If you loved him, why leave?"

"Do you know how we met, Captain McCoy?"

Pick shook his head.

"We met on a train about three hundred kilometers west of here, near Braunau am Inn. I was a lieutenant colonel in the Sluzhba Vneshney Razvedki, do you know what that is?"

"The Russian Foreign Intelligence Service," Pick replied.

She gave him a tight smile of approval. "At the time, I was the rezident in Copenhagen, and my brother, Colonel Dmitri Berezovsky, was the SVR rezident in Berlin. We believed Charley worked for the Central Intelligence Agency and could help us escape 'purification' at the hands of Vladimir Putin. We offered to defect to him."

"How long ago was this?"

She waved away the question as if shooing a fly. "Another lifetime ago."

"So, you defected, fell in love with the man who helped you flee from Putin, and decided to start a family," Pick concluded. "Is that about right?"

"Something like that."

"And the child didn't survive, so you left him."

Again, her eyes flashed anger. "There is nothing either of us wanted more than to have a child and start a family together. My leaving had nothing at all to do with losing our child. It had everything to do with my complete devotion to Charley."

Svetlana no longer had the pistol in her hand, but Pick still felt like she had a weapon pointed at him. He wisely kept his mouth shut.

"After our defection, I lived with Charley in Texas while my brother lived with our cousin in San Carlos de Bariloche, Río Negro Province, Argentina."

Pick wasn't sure he was going to like the answer, but he asked anyway. "Who's your cousin?"

"Aleksandr Pevsner."

Of course.

"Charley and I were spending most of our time at the Double-Bar-C—"

"The what?"

"The ranch he inherited outside Midland."

Pick gave a little shake of his head. "I thought the Castillo ranch was in Uvalde . . ."

"One of them. Fernando inherited the land in Uvalde, but the ranch outside Midland belonged to Charley. Like I said, we were spending most of our time at the Double-Bar-C, but Doña Alicia wanted us near as the due date drew closer." She paused, and her features softened with a sadness that was impossible to hide. "We buried our baby on that land. And Charley didn't want to leave."

"So, why did you?"

"Because Dmitri learned that Putin had dispatched men to kill Charley—"

Pick's mouth fell open in shock. "What?"

"But that he would consider granting leniency if his 'wayward children' returned to Mother Russia."

Pick couldn't believe what he was hearing. "And you believed him?"

Svetlana laughed. "Of course I didn't believe him. Vladimir Vladimirovich is not a man to be trusted. But I had just lost my child, and I wasn't about to lose my husband, too. As long as Charley remained on his cousin's ranch in Uvalde, he was inviting Putin's assassins to the Castillo doorstep. It was up to me to do something."

"What?"

Svetlana looked like she had been about to answer, then abruptly snapped her mouth shut and turned away to survey the city once more. "That is a story for another day," she answered, putting a definitive end to Pick's inquiries. "Now tell me why you are here. And leave nothing out."

Not that Pick had aims at deceiving her, but he took his role as chief, Office of Organizational Analysis, seriously, and he briefed her just as he would the President or DNI. He explained how Charley had been shot trying to stop a terrorist attack in Virginia Beach. And how clues there led them to San Antonio, where they intervened in a similar attack on the Alamo. He told Svetlana how they believed that the shooters were affiliated with ISIS–K and had come from Tajikistan, wielding weapons the U.S. military had left behind following their hasty withdrawal from Afghanistan. Most important, he told her that they had hoped to make contact with Aleksandr Pevsner, who might be able to help them discover how the terrorists managed to enter the country.

"Alek doesn't live in Argentina anymore."

"I heard," Pick said. "And I also heard that Putin was keeping a close eye on him."

Svetlana flashed a look at him. "Yes, Putin has certain agents within the SVR watching him."

"Who?"

"Me," she replied. "And my brother."

"You . . ."

She nodded. "Alek lives in Mexico now," Svetlana said.

"Where?"

"Cozumel . . ."

Pick felt a sudden hopeful excitement at the news, even though he had been closer to Pevsner before leaving Texas for Austria. He was road-weary and not looking forward to getting on yet another plane, but he couldn't miss out on the opportunity to learn what the former arms dealer knew about crossing the American southern border undetected.

"But he won't see you," Svetlana concluded.

Just as quick, Pick's hopes were dashed.

[THREE]

"What do you mean, he won't see me?"

Svetlana leaned against the railing again and folded her arms across her chest. Pick recognized the universal gesture many women made to demonstrate that they shouldn't have to explain themselves. But then again, Svetlana wasn't just any woman. "It means he won't see you. What don't you understand about that?"

I walked right into that one.

"What if I tell him Charley needs his help?"

She shook her head. "You won't get close enough to ask."

Pick threw up his hands.

"But he knows me," she added. "He will see me."

The hope that had briefly disappeared suddenly swelled anew. "Will you go see him for me?"

"No," she replied flatly. "But I will go with you to see him. I will explain to him who you are and what you are trying to do. I can't promise he will grant you an audience. Or, if he does, that he will have the answers you seek. But I will try."

Pick was so overcome with gratitude that he lunged forward and wrapped his muscular arms around Svetlana's petite frame. She stiffened in his embrace, apparently unsure how to comport herself in the awkward situation.

"Thank you," he said with breathless relief.

"Please release me," Svetlana replied.

As if suddenly realizing that he was hugging the absolutely wrong person, Pick let go and took a hurried step back. Not only had Svetlana arranged for his abduction from the Hotel Bristol, but she was an officer in Russia's Foreign Intelligence Service and Charley Castillo's wife. His momentary lapse in composure could result in any number of bad things happening to him.

"Sorry."

Svetlana gave him a curt nod. "Do that again and you will wish I had allowed Bogdan to use your kidneys as a punching bag."

Pick remembered the sound of her thug's fist slamming into the American's stomach in the restroom at the Hotel Bristol and didn't have to try too hard to imagine what it might feel like. He had been in his fair share of scuffles in the past, but that didn't mean he enjoyed being punched.

"Understood."

"Let's go," she said, shoving off from the railing and making for the parking lot. "I'm sure you're tired from your day of travel and will want to get some sleep before we take the early Austrian Air flight to London. We can connect from there to Houston, where we can catch a flight to Cozumel."

Tomorrow?

"How early?" Pick asked, falling in behind the Russian spy.

Svetlana shrugged. "Before seven a.m. Make sure you book us in business class."

He faltered half a step. He didn't even have a budget and was already wondering how he was going to justify the expense to his boss.

Pick woke up in his hotel room early the next morning and spent far too much time trying to figure out how to work the coffee machine. The infernal contraption was overly complicated and involved filling reservoirs, inserting capsules, and manipulating buttons and levers in the correct order to make it start brewing—an ordeal that was definitely not as simple as the Mr. Coffee single-serve coffeemaker on his kitchen counter back home.

"Damn Austrians," he muttered.

But Pick's mood shifted when the hot and frothy liquid began filling the glass mug he had set under the spigot. He waited until the machine announced that its brew cycle had completed with a *hiss* of steam, then lifted the mug and carried it across the room to a chair set in front of the floor-to-ceiling window. Pick sat down and took in his view of the Vienna State Opera House as he brought the cup to his lips.

For as much trouble as the coffee had been to brew, he had to admit it was quite good. But he was just a simple jarhead who needed only a thick cup of joe to get his day started. And the darker, the better.

He glanced at his watch and did the mental gymnastics to figure out what time it was back in Texas. He had placed a panicked call to Junior before collapsing into his bed the night before, and he hoped the logistics wizard had come through for him in a big way.

"Hey, boss," Junior said on answering.

"Did you have any luck?"

"Well, I'm sure you know all about the rules and regulations put in place by the U.S. General Services Administration to prevent fraud, waste, and abuse when it comes to spending taxpayer dollars on travel."

The dull ache in Pick's lower back was more than ample evidence that he was aware business-class travel wasn't authorized for somebody of his position in the government. Lowly Marine captains simply did not rate that kind of luxury.

"Yeah, Junior, I'm aware," Pick said, choosing his words carefully to avoid coming across like a complete asshole who hadn't yet finished his first cup of coffee. "And I told you that I'm going to be paying for it myself."

"It's not going to be cheap," the spook countered.

Pick sighed. He had gone out of his way to distance himself from the obscene amount of wealth he had inherited, thanks to his great-grandfather, who had founded American Personal Pharmaceutical—the multibillion-dollar publicly traded company that competed with Johnson & Johnson. But if Uncle Sam wasn't willing to foot the bill to secure Svetlana's help, then his uncle John Talbot Sage would.

"How expensive?"

"Almost seven thousand dollars."

Pick closed his eyes and breathed in the steam rising from his mug. "Did you reach my uncle John?"

"Sure did. He was more than happy to pay the bill and offered to wire additional funds into a discretionary account for future needs," Junior said. "Boss, you didn't tell me you had that kind of money lying around."

"I don't," he replied.

My family does.

"Yeah, well, anyway . . . I couldn't get you on the first flight to London like you suggested. But I booked you and your lady friend . . . Who's *Susanna Barlow*, anyway?"

"I'll tell you later."

Junior didn't press him. "I booked you both on the seven a.m. Austrian Air flight to Frankfurt. There, you'll connect with a Lufthansa flight that arrives in Houston at one-thirty-five p.m."

"And the flight to Cozumel?"

"I'm working on it, boss."

Pick thanked him for setting everything up, then ended the call before finishing his cup of coffee. The last thing he wanted to do was get on another flight less than twenty-four hours after arriving in Vienna, but duty called. Pharmaceuticals might have been the Sage family business, but being a Marine was the McCoy family profession. And Pick McCoy was a Marine, through and through.

Glancing at his watch again, Pick knew it was time to stop delaying the inevitable. He rose from the chair and made his way into the bathroom, where he turned on the shower and let the room fill with steam. He took his time and savored the hot water. But for a Marine, that only meant he left the water running long enough to lather up and scrub each inch of his muscular body.

After he had finished showering, dressing, and packing up his meager belongings, he checked the time again and saw that he had just enough time for another cup of coffee before heading downstairs to begin making his way to the airport. The coffee machine seemed much simpler to operate the second time around, and his mood was already improving, despite the prospect of being trapped inside crowded airports and airplanes for the next fourteen hours.

At least this time I'll be in business class.

With a Russian spy sitting next to me.

Pick had almost finished his second cup of coffee when his phone rang again. He answered it without looking at the caller ID. "Hello?"

"Do you have a ride to the airport, Captain McCoy?"

He recognized Svetlana's voice immediately.

"I was just planning on taking the CAT."

"Come downstairs. I'll be there in ten minutes. Bogdan will drive us to the airport."

Pick admitted that the idea of sitting in the back of the Mercedes Benz S-Class sedan for the twenty-kilometer drive was far more appealing than riding the train. Even if Svetlana made him uneasy.

"I couldn't get us tickets on the flight to London—"

Svetlana cut him off. "I know. We're flying to Frankfurt and then on Lufthansa to Houston."

"How . . ." Pick trailed off.

"I *am* an intelligence officer, Captain McCoy," she said. "Nine minutes now."

After she hung up, Pick gathered his things and headed for the door. If there was one thing Svetlana had made perfectly clear, it was that she wasn't the kind of woman who tolerated tardiness. If she was arriving in nine minutes, he would be standing on the curb in five.

[FOUR]

Terminal D

George Bush Intercontinental Airport

Houston, Texas

1445 2 April 2026

After clearing Customs and Immigration, Pick and Svetlana walked through the automatic double doors and stepped out into the mild but humid Houston air. Not surprisingly, Pick felt much more rested after the ten-and-a-half-hour flight in business class aboard the Lufthansa Boeing 747. Although he hadn't slept, he didn't feel like his back was on the verge of locking up on him, either.

"How are we getting to Cozumel?" Svetlana asked, her sky-blue eyes scanning the curb for their transportation.

Pick glanced left and saw a dark Suburban driven by Junior pull over and come to a stop in front of them. "This is our ride," he said, not answering her original question.

As an officer and a gentleman was wont to do, Pick opened the rear door for Svetlana and waited until she was comfortably seated before carrying her suitcase to the open hatch at the rear of the SUV. He placed both her suitcase and his backpack inside, closed the hatch, then walked around to the opposite side and climbed into the rear seat behind Junior.

"What am I? Just your chauffeur now?" Junior asked.

"Junior, this is Susanna Barlow," Pick said, using the cover identity on Svetlana's Argentine passport. "Susanna, this gentleman here is John Smith, also known as Roy Jones and Jeremy Rogers."

"What's in a name, anyway?" Svetlana asked, apparently accepting that their driver wanted to keep his true name a secret.

"But we just call him Junior," Pick concluded.

"Pleased to meet you, Junior," Svetlana said.

"Likewise," Junior replied.

The spook put the Suburban in gear and pulled away from the curb, deftly maneuvering the large SUV into traffic. Within minutes, they were speeding westward and passing the circular airport Marriott hotel placed prominently between the airport's B and C Terminals.

"Where are we going?" Pick asked.

"Signature Aviation," Junior answered, making eye contact with Pick in the rearview mirror.

Pick knew that if their destination was Signature, that probably meant Dick and Randy had flown the Coast Guard C-37A Gulfstream in from San Antonio and intended on using it to shuttle them down to Cozumel. He wasn't sure how Svetlana would feel about getting on board a U.S. government airplane—or, for that matter, what Director Fleiss or President Cohen would think about it—but he figured it was too late to do anything about it now. Signature Aviation was located at the southwest corner of the airfield and only a ten-minute drive from the terminal.

But Svetlana's curiosity wasn't as easily sated. "Are we chartering a plane to Cozumel?"

Junior again locked eyes with Pick before answering. "We have a gassed-up Gulfstream on standby with a flight plan already filed."

Apparently satisfied, Svetlana nodded and leaned back in her seat while watching airliners lift off and climb into the sky through her window. Ten minutes later, Junior turned off Chanute Road and into the parking lot for Signature Aviation. But instead of pulling into one of the parking spots, he rolled the Suburban up to a closed gate next to the fixed base operator's building. He waited patiently for the gate to open and permit them access to the flight line.

When it did, Pick leaned to the side and looked through the windshield at a gleaming white unmarked Gulfstream V sitting alone on the ramp. Its auxiliary power unit was already running to provide electricity and conditioned cabin air to the idle business jet.

"Where's the other bird?" Pick asked.

Junior flashed him another glance in the mirror. "Director Fleiss thought you might want something a little lower-profile for your 'jaunt' down to Mexico."

"That's low-profile?" Svetlana asked.

"My thoughts exactly," Pick added, though he knew what Junior was getting at. If they arrived at Cozumel International Airport in an orange-and-white business jet with United States Coast Guard cheatline markings, it would be impossible to keep their presence a secret.

Junior pulled alongside the business jet and came to a stop in front of the lowered air stairs. Pick climbed out, then walked around to open Svetlana's door for her. The redhead stepped out and followed him around to the rear of the Suburban, where Junior had already collected their belongings and was making his way toward the plane.

Svetlana nodded at the spook's back as he scampered up the stairs with their luggage. "Is he going with us?"

"Apparently he is," Pick replied.

"Who else?"

Pick shook his head. "Honestly, I'm not sure. I'm guessing Ani Shaheen, Dick Miller, and—"

"Randy?"

Svetlana's voice registered genuine surprise, and Pick looked up to see Lieutenant Commander Randy Richardson standing in the Gulfstream's open doorway. His mouth hung open in surprise. "Sweaty?"

Before Pick could question the odd nickname, Castillo's bastard son bounded down the stairs and sprinted across the ramp to hug the woman who had just flown halfway around the world under the name Susanna Barlow. To Pick's surprise, she didn't stand there awkwardly or threaten to have one of her goons rough Randy up. Instead, she returned the Navy pilot's embrace as she would a long-lost family member.

"What are you doing here?" Svetlana asked after breaking free from his embrace.

"I'm here to help find the people who put Charley in the hospital."

Her eyes clouded over with instant sadness and regret, but she quickly masked it. "Are you coming with us to Cozumel?"

Randy nodded. "I'm flying the plane."

Svetlana looked at Pick, who just shrugged.

"Well, let's get going, then," Svetlana said, immediately taking charge. "Cousin Alek will be pleased to see you."

But will he be pleased to see me?

XIV

[ONE]

Aboard Gulfstream V

24.75 degrees North Latitude

89.65 degrees West Longitude

Over the Gulf of Mexico

1610 2 April 2026

If Pick had thought the Coast Guard C-37A Gulfstream was well appointed, he was blown away by the plane Director Fleiss had sent to replace it. The GV's interior cabin was both spacious and bright, with seating for thirteen, configured in a four-place club arrangement, two-place club, divan in the mid-cabin, and four-place conference seating in the aft section. It was there, in the aft, where Pick sat in a rear-facing seat across from Junior and Ani while Svetlana napped on the divan.

"Why didn't you tell me you were bringing Castillo's wife with you?" Junior asked.

Pick glanced over his left shoulder at the stretched-out redhead to make sure she hadn't overheard the question.

"Because she's not here as Castillo's wife," Pick answered.

"Then why *is* she here?" Ani asked.

They were only an hour into the two-hour flight and barely halfway across the Gulf of Mexico. But Pick had known they wouldn't reach Mexican airspace before they forced him to answer that very simple question. "Because she's an officer in Russia's Foreign Intelligence Service—"

"She's with the SVR?" Junior blurted, a little louder than he'd probably intended.

Pick glanced over at Svetlana again. "Keep your voice down. But yes."

Not one to normally agree with Junior, Ani didn't bother hiding what she thought of it. "And you thought it was a good idea to bring her aboard an airplane owned and operated by the Central Intelligence Agency?"

Pick spoke in little more than a whisper, but because of the Gulfsream's legendary lack of cabin noise, he knew both Junior and Ani could hear him. "First of all, I had no idea we would be making this leg of the journey aboard an airplane owned by the Central Intelligence Agency. Second, the last I checked, it's not being operated by the Agency. It's on loan to the Office of Organizational Analysis and being piloted by a retired Army aviator and an active-duty Navy lieutenant commander."

He knew it was little more than semantics, but Pick was quickly learning that details like that mattered.

"You know what I mean," Ani said.

Svetlana's voice carried over their whispers. "You know I can hear you, right?"

Pick glowered at Junior and Ani before responding. "Sorry. We thought you were sleeping."

She didn't respond immediately, but twisted so that she was lying on her side with her head resting on a throw pillow. "It's amazing what you can learn when people think you're asleep."

I'll have to remember that.

"I was just about to explain why you wanted to come along, but maybe you'd like to tell them yourself."

Svetlana fixed him with her sky-blue eyes. "Because the man you're going to see is notoriously reclusive, and you wouldn't stand a chance of getting close to him without an introduction from somebody he trusts."

"And he trusts you?" Junior asked.

She nodded slightly. "Yes, he does. I've been assigned as part of his protective detail for over a decade."

"Does he know you're an SVR officer?"

Svetlana laughed. "Of course he knows. At one time in his life, Aleksandr was a colonel in both the Soviet Air Force and the SVR. He was in charge of Aeroflot's operations worldwide, which gave him the necessary skills he needed to succeed later in his life."

"As an arms dealer, you mean," Junior said.

Svetlana rose from the divan and moved to join them in the conference seats. She lowered herself into the leather chair next to Pick. "That was only part of the role he played following the collapse of the USSR. But yes, as an arms dealer."

"Doesn't he suspect that Vladimir Putin is only using the SVR to keep tabs on him?"

She shook her head. "He *knows* the SVR is only there to keep tabs on him."

"But he still trusts you?" Ani asked.

"He should. We're cousins."

"Cousins?"

She nodded as the Gulfstream jostled with a bit of unexpected turbulence, and Pick turned to look through the large window at the dark blue waters of the Gulf of Mexico 40,000 feet beneath them. Then he leaned forward and rested both forearms on the table. "Svetlana agreed to travel with me to Cozumel to make an introduction to her cousin. But that's as far as it goes. Nobody needs to know she's helping us."

"Not even Director Fleiss?" Junior asked, obviously uncomfortable with the idea of keeping it secret from the Director of National Intelligence. "After all, we're flying on a plane he loaned to us."

"After the threat has been neutralized, I'll include in my report to the President that an unnamed officer of the SVR assisted us in the effort." Pick turned to Svetlana. "Is that acceptable?"

She nodded.

"But until then, we'll do everything in our power to preserve her cover. Is that understood?"

Junior and Ani traded glances before nodding their concurrence.

"Good. So, when we land, how do you want to handle this, Svetlana?"

She gestured at the AirCell flush-mount SIP handset set into the bulkhead. "Can I make a call from here?"

Pick had no idea, so he nodded at Junior in hopes that the spook could answer the question.

"I think so," Junior replied.

Svetlana reached across Pick and snatched the handset from the wall, stretching the retractable cord and pulling the phone to her. She punched in a series of numbers from memory, then pressed the green SND button and lifted the phone to her ear.

Pick glanced across the table and noticed that both Junior and Ani were focused on Svetlana, undoubtedly wondering who she was calling.

"Cousin Alek, it's me," she said. "Can you be a dear and send a driver to retrieve me from the Cozumel International Airport?"

Pick could hardly believe that the man he hoped had the answers he needed was on the other end of the phone. He held his breath as he waited for Svetlana to conclude her call.

"We should be landing in an hour," Svetlana said. "I'm bringing visitors . . . It's a surprise, dear cousin."

When Svetlana pressed the red END button, Pick traded glances with Junior.

[TWO]

Hotel Meliá Cozumel

Cozumel, Mexico

1710 2 April 2026

The Meliá Cozumel resort was located ten minutes north of the international airport near the Cozumel Country Club, a facility that had boasted first-class golf, courtesy of Nicklaus Design, until it was closed several years earlier to make room for condominiums. Pick sat in the rear behind the Mercedes G-Class SUV's driver and next to Randy, who sat behind Svetlana. He stared through the window at the passing scenery of mangroves, marshlands, and tropical rainforest.

"When we arrive, you'll let me do all the talking," Svetlana said, turning to ensure he understood.

"Of course," Pick replied.

The driver slowed and turned up a narrow drive flanked by palm trees on both sides and came to a stop in front of the hotel's front doors. The doors slid open and two very large men dressed in lightweight suits walked out and studied the SUV with eyes hidden behind dark sunglasses. Svetlana opened her door and climbed out, speaking briefly with the first man, who then nodded and reached for Randy's door.

"You ready?" Pick asked.

"Guess we'll find out."

When the door opened, Randy extricated himself from the luxury SUV and stood tall in front of the hulking figure, who gestured for him to raise his arms. He did so, and Pevsner's security guard patted him down, looking for weapons or surveillance devices he might have smuggled onto the property. Pick wasn't keen on the idea of being searched, but Svetlana had prepared them for this.

A moment later, the second guard circled the SUV and opened Pick's door. Pick exited the Mercedes and raised his arms without having to be told in order to endure the same thorough pat-down, believing that it was just the price of admission for receiving an audience with Aleksandr Pevsner.

Satisfied that neither newcomer was carrying anything that could potentially be harmful to their charge, the first man led them through the hotel's front doors and into the lobby. A tasteful blue neon sign behind the hotel's registration desks cast a peaceful glow on the polished tile floors, but Pick barely had time to appreciate the modern furnishings before they were whisked outside once more, this time to the rear of the property and onto the expansive pool deck.

Svetlana walked next to the first guard, clearly comfortable navigating her way across the grounds, while Pick and Randy followed, walking side by side. A glance over Pick's shoulder confirmed that the second guard had brought up the rear and was keeping a close eye on the two newcomers.

"They clearly don't trust us," Pick muttered sotto voce.

Randy grunted in reply, then quickly elbowed Pick in the ribs and gestured across the pool. Across the glistening crystal-clear water, two tanned women—one blonde, one brunette—wore brightly colored bikinis and were stretched out on adjacent chaise longues, enjoying the late-afternoon sun.

"Easy, Tiger."

But Randy didn't seem the least bit deterred. "This is looking less and less like a hardship assignment."

Pick shook his head. "What part of flying to Cozumel in a GV was a hardship for you?"

"Uh, the actual flying part. Not all of us got to take a nap in the back."

Their conversation was momentarily suspended when Svetlana and the first security guard descended a short flight of steps from the patio and turned left toward a row of large thatch palapa umbrellas arrayed along the pool's edge. But despite his warning to Randy, Pick couldn't take his eyes off the sunbathing women, either.

"Who's ogling now?" Randy said with a smirk.

"You're never going to convince me that flying a plane is actual work," Pick said, ignoring the Navy pilot's chastisement in favor of their earlier banter.

To their surprise, the brunette woman rose from the chaise lounge as Svetlana approached and held out her arms in greeting. Pick almost stumbled when the two women embraced, but his heart hammered with eager anticipation when the brunette flashed a look in his direction. Svetlana turned to follow the woman's gaze, smiled at Pick, then said something neither could hear.

"Who do you suppose she is?" Pick asked.

"I saw her first," Randy replied.

"Move," the guard behind them commanded.

Somewhat reluctantly, Pick and Randy continued onward, fearful that they were about to be dressed down for their unabashed staring.

It was worth it.

Pick's eyes traced the brunette's elegant curves and observed her toned and tanned figure with appreciation. It was obvious the woman took care of herself and didn't mind men staring at her. She gave Pick a lecherous look as he walked up and caught the tail end of her question to Svetlana.

". . . the one you were telling me about, Auntie Susanna?"

Auntie?

Svetlana turned to Pick to complete the introduction. "Captain McCoy, this is my niece, Sophie Barlow."

"Your niece?" Pick couldn't help sounding surprised, but he still managed to collect himself enough to take the woman's outstretched hand. "Pleased to meet you, Sophie."

"Sophie is my brother's daughter," Svetlana added.

"Tom," Pick said, remembering the name her brother, former SVR Colonel Dmitri Berezovsky, had adopted following their defection.

"That's right," Sophie said. "Do you know him?"

"I'm afraid I haven't had the pleasure of meeting him yet," Pick said, taking care to maintain eye contact with her. The last thing he needed was for Svetlana to catch him leering at her niece.

"Where is your father?" Svetlana asked.

Sophie gestured over her shoulder to one of the cabanas a short distance away. "He's with Cousin Alek, hiding from the sun."

Pick turned with Svetlana and looked through the open linen curtains of a platformed daybed underneath a thatched roof. Less than fifty feet away sat two men dressed in linen pants and brightly colored short-sleeved shirts. Both had full heads of thick, dark hair and were graying at the temples. Pick was so focused on the two men staring back at him that he didn't notice the blonde getting up from the chaise lounge and crossing to greet Svetlana.

"Poppa said you had business in Vienna," the blonde said.

Svetlana kissed the woman on both cheeks. "Yes, Elena, I've only just returned. It was a very quick trip."

While the women spoke to each other, Pick took the opportunity to admire Elena's figure as well. Aside from also having a toned and tanned body, her appearance was just as striking as Sophie's. The women looked to be near the same age and could have been sisters.

His thoughts were interrupted by Randy, who sidled up next to Pick and was doing a less-than-admirable job of hiding his interest in the women. "And who are these lovely ladies?"

Svetlana turned and grinned at Randy. "I'm sorry, where are my manners?"

The bikini-clad women leaned against each other and smiled at Randy, clearly enjoying being the center of attention. He smiled back, completely oblivious of the two men watching him from the shade barely two dozen feet away.

"Randy, this is Sophie," Svetlana said, gesturing to the brunette, who smiled and gave him a playful wink. "My brother's daughter and your cousin."

Randy's smile faltered as one of the two women suddenly became off-limits.

"And this is Elena," she continued, introducing the blonde. "Aleksandr's daughter and, I guess, your second cousin."

Pick's smile grew wider as Randy's disappeared.

Svetlana put an arm around Randy. "And this is Charley's son, Randy."

Sophie and Elena smiled at Randy's attempt to compose himself. "It was nice to meet you ladies."

"Come, gentlemen," Svetlana said. "We shouldn't keep Cousin Alek waiting."

With Randy's humiliation complete, she spun on her heel and began walking along the concrete path, cutting through the grass to the cabana where two agents of Russia's Sluzhba Vneshney Razvedki drank margaritas in the shade.

Pick locked eyes with Sophie and smiled. "It was nice meeting you both."

When Sophie remained silent, Elena spoke up. "When you're done with Poppa, you should come lay out by the pool with us. There are still a few good hours of sunlight left, and nothing cures jetlag like a tan."

Pick finally looked away from Sophie and stared at the azure waters beyond the thatch palapa umbrellas spread out across the beach. He could think of nothing he would rather do than spend a few hours relaxing in the sun with two beautiful women.

"Captain McCoy," Svetlana called out.

He groaned. "I'm coming."

"You'd better go," Sophie said. "Auntie Susanna's temper is quite legendary."

Pick instantly recalled her pointing a pistol at him and the ominous threat she had delivered after he gave her an ill-advised hug on the Cobenzl. "I'd better."

As he turned to leave, Sophie reached out and gripped his wrist. "Wait . . ."

Pick's heart lurched at the unexpected touch.

"You never told us your *first* name, Captain."

"Pick," he said. "Pick McCoy."

Sophie smiled. "It was nice meeting you, Pick McCoy."

[THREE]

Pick was still riding high from Sophie's touch when he caught up with Randy and Svetlana as they neared the table. Neither man seated there made any effort to get to their feet. And both gave Svetlana only a cursory glance before staring down the two strangers she had brought with her.

"What *surprises* have you brought me, dear cousin?" the larger of the two men asked.

He must be the infamous Aleksandr Pevsner.

Svetlana turned and gestured for Randy to approach. "Cousin Alek, this is Charley Castillo's son, Randy."

"Charley Castillo . . ." Pevsner removed his sunglasses and leaned forward, casting his large and extraordinarily bright blue eyes on Randy. "That's a name I haven't heard in quite some time."

"Pleased to meet you, sir," Randy said, standing tall in front of the seated Russians.

"I was led to believe Castillo was unmarried before wedding my dear cousin *Susanna*," he said, emphasizing Svetlana's adopted name.

"He was," Randy replied. "I was the product of an impetuous union between Charley and my mother."

"Son of a bitch!" Pevsner exclaimed.

"Actually, sir, I'm a bastard," Randy replied, deadpan. "My mother is a lovely woman."

"And who *is* your mother?"

"Bethany Wilson."

Pick was frozen with rapt fascination as the former Russian intelligence officer deftly pulled the information from Randy. He had known none of this, only that Charley Castillo had been his father and that they had been together the day of the Virginia Beach shooting.

"Wilson," Pevsner repeated. "Are you related to General Harold F. Wilson, by chance?"

"He's my grandfather, sir."

Pevsner nodded as if unsurprised by that fact, but again Pick was stunned to learn that Randy was not only the son of a West Point graduate—biological *and* adopted—but the grandson of a general officer. That he'd rebelled against the family and rejected the Army in favor of Annapolis only made his stock go up in Pick's mind.

"Are you also aware of your grandfather's connection to Charley Castillo?"

Randy cocked his head to the side as if confused by the question. "Connection, sir?"

Pevsner exchanged glances with Tom Barlow, who raised an eyebrow with curiosity. "If you're not already aware, I believe it's probably best if I allow Castillo to fill in those gaps in your family's history. Where is Charley, anyway?"

Svetlana fielded that question. "That's the reason we're here, dear cousin."

Tom Barlow leaned forward and pointed at Pick. "You mean, that's the reason *he's* here."

Svetlana nodded and gestured for Pick to step forward. "This is Captain Pick McCoy. He's the man who traveled to Vienna looking for you, Alek."

As if the oddity of having Castillo's bastard son standing in front of him had worn off, Pevsner fixed his gaze on Pick. "Is this true? You traveled to Vienna looking for me?"

"Yes, sir," Pick replied.

"Why?"

"Because four days ago, Charley Castillo was gunned down by terrorists in Virginia Beach while trying to stop an attack."

"It wasn't me," Pevsner said. "I've been toiling in exile."

Pick looked around at the thatch-roofed cabanas and palapa umbrellas, then let his eyes settle on several empty glasses ringed with salt on the table in front of the two Russian men. "I can see that."

Pevsner's eyes darkened and his voice dropped into a low growl. "I have killed men for less."

Pick raised his hands in mock surrender. "I meant no insult, sir. I only meant that you are obviously a man of considerable influence to be granted exile in such a beautiful place, a man with a wealth of knowledge that can be of use to powerful people. That makes you powerful."

"Then speak plainly. Why did you travel to Vienna looking for me? Why are you here? And . . ." His eyes shifted to Svetlana. "Why has my dear cousin chosen to bring you to me?"

Pick glanced at Svetlana and tried reading her blank expression. He couldn't help but wonder what the President or Director Fleiss would think of him divulging the details of his operation with current and former members of Russia's Foreign Intelligence Service.

"Our investigation into the terrorists who put Charley Castillo in the hospital—"

"So, he's alive?" Pevsner asked.

"He's alive," Pick confirmed. "Our investigation led us to San Antonio the following day, where we stumbled upon a similar attack taking place. In both instances, the terrorists were using U.S. military weapons we believe were left behind when our government pulled out of Afghanistan."

"Do you know the identities of the terrorists? What group or groups they're affiliated with?"

Pick shook his head. "Not entirely. Two of the terrorists involved in the Virginia Beach shooting were on a watch list and came from Tajikistan. We suspect that others—including the ones in San Antonio—also came from Tajikistan."

Pevsner nodded with understanding. "ISIS–K."

"That's our theory as well," Pick said.

"I'm sure you're aware of my reputation as one who arranges for the sale of weapons on the black market. But I can assure you I had no part in this. If the weapons were, as you said, surplus U.S. military hardware, then it's likely the terrorists didn't need my help in procuring them."

"We believe that as well."

"And I'm sure my dear cousin has informed you that I have been exiled here in paradise as a courtesy granted by the Russian Federation."

Svetlana had not, in fact, given Pick any details of Aleksandr Pevsner's exile, but he didn't see the need to argue that fact. So, he nodded.

"As you might also be aware, the animals of the Islamic State–Khorasan Province have been tied to the attack on the Crocus City Hall music venue in Krasnogorsk. In this case, I think it's safe to say that our two countries are fighting a common enemy."

"It was my hope you felt that way," Pick said.

Pevsner gestured around him. "But I don't have much I can offer you. I'm 'out of the game,' as they say."

"But probably not so far out that you don't have contacts here in Mexico that can help find what I'm looking for."

Pevsner looked surprised. "Here in Mexico?"

After Pick finished explaining how he thought the terrorists had entered the United States through the southern border, Pevsner invited him to sit at the table while he conferred with Tom in private. Randy had taken the seat next to him but angled it to more easily keep an eye on the two women—his cousin and second cousin—sunning themselves by the pool.

"I don't think you want either Pevsner *or* Barlow catching you looking at their daughters, regardless of whether you're related or not," Pick said.

Svetlana sat in a chair at the head of the table on Randy's opposite side. "And related only by marriage."

But Randy didn't seem to mind their rebukes. "Is there any harm in looking?"

Pick chuckled. "Having impure thoughts about a relative? Uh, yeah. This goes way past the Hatfields and McCoys."

"You don't know they're impure," Randy protested. "For all you know—"

"Silence," Svetlana hissed.

Before Pick or Randy could question the command, Aleksandr Pevsner and Tom Barlow returned to the table. Barlow glanced in the direction of his daughter, then at Pick. "Were you looking at my Sophie?"

Pick's stomach dropped. "No, sir . . ."

"I'll cut your eyes out if you do," he replied, then pointed at Randy. "She's your cousin. You may look."

Randy flashed Pick a triumphant smile before Pevsner dropped into his seat with a sigh. "I made some calls to my contacts here in Mexico, limited as they are."

Pevsner paused when a waitress arrived to deliver a tray of margaritas, setting one on the table in front of each of them. After she had collected the empty glasses that had accumulated there and retreated to the bar, the retired arms dealer continued.

"You understand that a smuggler's livelihood hinges on his ability to move goods freely within his network?"

Pick nodded.

"And that if any of his networks were to be disrupted, he would immediately remember a conversation he had with his Russian friend, Aleksandr?"

Again, Pick nodded.

"And that, upon recalling said conversation, he would surmise that his Russian friend had betrayed him and order the deaths of Aleksandr and every member of his family?"

Pick swallowed. He understood exactly what Pevsner was driving at. He had the information Pick needed to find those responsible, but he was unwilling to share what he had learned without assurances. Pevsner had not lived as long as he had in an unscrupulous world without abiding by a rigid code of ethics. And top among that code was the sanctity and safety of his family.

As much as Pick hated the idea of leaving a weakness in their border defenses unfortified, it was more important to learn who was behind these attacks and if any more were imminent.

"You have my word, as an officer, a gentleman, and a duly appointed representative of the United States government, that nothing you tell me will be used to disrupt the flow of goods across the border."

Randy shot Pick a sideways glance.

"Your word means nothing to me," Pevsner said.

"I have nothing else to offer."

"You might, once you hear my contact's demands." Pevsner picked up his margarita and lifted it in toast. "¡Salud!"

[FOUR]

Pick watched Pevsner casually take a sip of his margarita, but he was already calculating the cost he would be willing to pay to get the information he needed. "What demands?"

The Russian let out an exaggerated sigh as he lowered the glass back to the table. "They use really good tequila here. Are you sure you don't want to try your drink?"

"What demands?" Pick repeated.

The amused smirk on Pevsner's face vanished. "You remind me of my good friend Charley. Even before he married my cousin, I welcomed him into my home. I introduced him to my wife and my children. I accepted him into my family."

Pick felt himself relax.

"And he never missed an opportunity to insult me," Pevsner said. "Now, drink!"

Pick locked eyes with the Russian for several seconds, then reluctantly picked up the margarita in front of him and tipped it back. He drained the glass in one long pull and slammed it onto the table.

Pevsner shook his head. "Just like Charley."

"Then you know I'll do whatever it takes to stop another terrorist attack from happening. I was led to believe you might be able to point me in the right direction. But tell me now if I'm just wasting my time."

Pevsner looked at Randy. "Is he always like this?"

"You have no idea," Randy said, taking a sip of his margarita. "I've known him since he was a plebe at the Naval Academy. Caused me more trouble than I care to recall."

Pick was growing frustrated and didn't bother trying to hide it. "Look, in the last two days, I've flown from San Antonio to Vienna to Houston to Cozumel. I don't even want to add up the number of miles I've accumulated trying to reach you. Am I just wasting my time, Alek?"

The smirk returned, but it carried more vitriol than humor. "What do you know of the balance of power here in Mexico, Señor McCoy?"

Pick looked over both shoulders and noticed that the armed men who had patted him down when he arrived were staged at strategic locations to preserve their privacy. "I was led to believe you were a man of significant power, Señor Pevsner."

"Me? Oh, no, no. I am merely a facilitator and connect parties when their needs align."

"And when it financially benefits you," Pick said, not bothering to hide the accusation.

"Touché."

"What is it about the balance of power you think I should know?"

Pevsner picked up his glass and took another sip before answering. "In the 1970s, the infamous Guadalajara Cartel was established to meet the increasing demand for marijuana and opiates north of the border. But the 1980s saw an increase in law enforcement crackdowns, which allowed several other cartels to rise to power, including the Sinaloa, Tijuana, and Juárez cartels."

"I'm assuming there will be a point to this history lesson," Pick said.

"Yes, yes." Pevsner set down his glass. "You're just like Charley."

Pick gestured for him to continue.

"In the 1990s, as these cartels vied for control, a brutal and bloody rivalry forced the Mexican government to intercede. Their efforts to combat drug trafficking intensified after President Felipe Calderón's military-led war on drugs in 2006."

"And I'm sure you capitalized on the chaos."

Pevsner shrugged. "What can I say? I trade in the currency of relationships and information. The more uncertain the criminal landscape, the more value I can provide. I make no apologies for playing both sides. My priority is my family."

Pick glanced over his shoulder at Pevsner's daughter sunning herself. "And now?"

"And now, cartels like Sinaloa and Jalisco New Generation Cartel dominate that landscape. They engage in drug trafficking, extortion, and other criminal activities." Pevsner paused and took another sip of his margarita. "But they're not the only ones."

Pick was starting to understand where the history lesson was leading. "Who else?"

"The contact I spoke with is highly placed in Cártel del Noreste. Do you know of them?"

Pick didn't. He was well versed in the tribes of Afghanistan and Iraq but knew next to nothing about Mexican drug cartels. "What do I need to know?"

"In the late 1990s, a man named Osiel Cárdenas Guillén took control of the Gulf Cartel and enlisted the help of Arturo Guzmán Decena, a retired army lieutenant, to build a militant arm that would protect him from rival cartels and the Mexican Army. Decena, known by his Federal Judicial Police radio code Z-1, lured deserters from the elite Grupo Aeromóvil de Fuerzas Especiales to fill roles in this arm. They became known as Los Zetas."

"I've heard of them," Pick admitted.

Pevsner nodded. "Of course you have. Barely a decade later, Los Zetas broke away from the Gulf Cartel and surpassed even the Sinaloa cartel in terms of geographical areas they controlled. They were violent and brutal and became Mexico's largest and most expansive drug cartel."

Even though Pick had come to Cozumel to find information on how terrorists from the Islamic State–Khorasan Province managed to sneak into the United States and carry out deadly attacks in both

Virginia Beach and San Antonio, he was beginning to realize how little he actually knew.

"But like the Soviet Union, even the largest and most powerful cartel wasn't immune to fracture. In the following years, separate factions broke away from Los Zetas to challenge them for control. Sangre Nueva Zeta, Zetas Vieja Escuela, Los Talibanes, Grupo Bravo, and—"

"Cártel del Noreste," Pick said.

Pevsner nodded. "My contact in Cártel del Noreste admitted that he helped secure passage across the border near Laredo for the men you're hunting. But, more important, he alleges that he is aware of their next target and would be willing to furnish you with that information."

Pick's heart started beating faster. "In exchange for what?"

Pevsner smiled. "He would like to meet with you personally."

"Me?"

"You, Señor McCoy."

"Where?"

"In Nuevo Laredo."

[ONE]

Cozumel International Airport

Cozumel, Mexico

1930 2 April 2026

The gleaming Gulfstream V business jet was one of four parked on the general aviation ramp adjacent to the terminal at the Cozumel International Airport. In addition to the Agency bird Director Fleiss had procured for their operation, Pick saw a Dassault Falcon—the model with a third engine installed in the tail—a Bombardier Global Express, and another Gulfstream. Pevsner's Mercedes G-Class SUV pulled to a stop in front of the Falcon.

"Wrong jet," Pick said.

"Right jet," the driver replied, his thick Russian accent rolling across the SUV's interior like thunder.

Pick looked over at Svetlana, who had been silent for most of the drive. "What's the meaning of this?"

She turned and fixed him with an emotionless stare. "I'm sorry, but it has already been arranged. You will travel alone to meet with Aleksandr's contact in Nuevo Laredo and listen to what he has to say. Then, when you are satisfied, you will be returned to San Antonio, where the rest of your team will be waiting."

Pick turned to Randy, who gave a subtle shake of his head. Even he didn't like the idea.

"Will you be coming with me?" Pick asked the red-haired SVR officer.

Svetlana shook her head. "I'm afraid I'm needed elsewhere."

Pick was having difficulty reading the expression on her face, but he felt as if he was being set up. It made no sense, since Pevsner could have had him killed at any time since they'd arrived in Mexico. But he still couldn't shake the feeling that his world would change if he boarded the French business jet.

"I don't like it," Randy said.

"We need that information," Pick said. "If he really does know who's behind these attacks and where the next one's going to take place, I can't afford not to go."

"Let's at least talk to the others first—"

"I'm sorry," Svetlana interrupted. "There's no time. You must make your choice now. Either accept Aleksandr's offer of help and board this jet alone or reject him and return to the United States no closer to the answers you seek."

Through the windshield, Pick saw that the Mercedes's arrival had not gone unnoticed. Both Ani and Junior had descended from the Gulfstream's interior and were waiting for him at the bottom of the air stairs. He glanced to his left and saw the Falcon's own stairs beckoning him aboard, teasing him with the secrets that had been promised to him.

All he had to do was trust the word of a former Russian intelligence officer and arms dealer.

Castillo trusted him. Maybe I should, too.

"I'll go," he said, then opened the door and stepped out onto the tarmac.

Randy started to protest, but Pick slammed the door shut on his argument and cut him off. After another fleeting glance at Ani and

Junior waiting for him at the Gulfstream, Pick took a deep breath and began climbing the stairs onto the Falcon.

"You made the right choice, Pick McCoy," a woman's voice said as he ducked inside.

Pick startled and whipped his head to the right. "Sophie?"

The last person Pick expected to see when he boarded the French business jet was the beautiful brunette who had been sunning herself poolside at the Meliá before his meeting with Pevsner. And though she now wore a pair of slacks and a sheer blouse—arguably more suitable attire than what she had been wearing when they first met—Pick still couldn't help his mouth from falling open at the sight of her.

"I have business in Nuevo Laredo and Cousin Alek thought it made sense to have me accompany you," she said, gesturing for him to have a seat in one of the plush leather chairs across from her. "Kill two birds with one stone, so to speak."

With considerable effort, Pick looked away from her deep brown eyes and marveled at how the Dassault Falcon 8X's modern style differed completely from the Gulfstream V's. Both were luxurious in their own way and furnished with supple leather chairs and divans, but the Falcon seemed bright and airy despite its espresso wood trim accents, dark carpeting, and ornately upholstered throw pillows. He sat down in the offered chair, unable to take his eyes off Sophie.

"What kind of business do you have there?" Pick asked, more to fill the awkward silence than to satisfy a genuine curiosity.

"The family kind," she replied.

"By that you mean . . ."

She gave him a playful smile when he met her gaze. "I mean the kind you shouldn't ask questions about."

Before Pick could respond, one of the Dassault's two pilots exited the flight deck and approached Sophie. He was dressed in a pair of dark slacks and a short-sleeved button-down white shirt with four captain's stripes on his epaulettes. "Is everybody on board, Señora Barlow?"

"Sí, Carlos. Gracias."

"Muy bien, señora."

The pilot spun on his heel and disappeared back inside the cockpit as the cabin attendant retracted the boarding ladder and closed the forward entry door, sealing them inside. "How long of a—"

"Oh, good! He's here!"

The sudden appearance of Sophie's blond tanning companion stunned Pick into silence. He watched her saunter up the wide center aisle and plop down in the seat next to Sophie, biting her lip and giving Pick a lecherous smile.

"Behave yourself, Elena," Sophie said.

"I saw him first," the blonde whispered, just loud enough for Pick to overhear.

"Are you in the family business, too?" Pick asked, trying to ignore her statement.

"My whole life," Elena replied. "Sophie and I are closer to sisters than anything else. We have been thick as thieves since we were teenagers, so it only made sense to become business partners as well."

Pick was unsure how to take the blonde's comments, so he only smiled and listened to the Dassault's engines whine as the pilots started them in preparation to taxi. His eyes glassed over with overwhelming fatigue when he realized that a day that had begun in Vienna was about to end in the border city of Nuevo Laredo. It didn't matter if the flight was thirty minutes or three hours; Pick knew he would be sound asleep before they even took off.

"Dulces sueños, Pick McCoy."

He smiled as his eyes closed shut around the image of Sophie Barlow.

Pick opened his eyes when the Dassault Falcon 8X touched down at Quetzalcóatl International Airport in Nuevo Laredo, one hundred and forty miles southwest of San Antonio and only eight miles from the international airport on the U.S. side of the border. He blinked several times before focusing on Sophie, who was sitting in the chair across from him.

"Good morning," she said, not bothering to hide the humor in her voice.

"How long was I out?"

"Only about two hours," she replied. "You must have needed it."

"You have no idea." Pick sat up straight and rubbed his eyes, trying to erase the last vestiges of sleep. "It's been a long day."

"I'm sorry, but it's only going to get longer for you. The captain informed me that a car is already waiting for us at the FBO." Sophie looked at her watch. "But this time of night, the traffic shouldn't be too bad, and it should only take fifteen or twenty minutes to get there."

"Get where?"

"Where El Timón wants me to take you."

It was the first time Pick had heard the name of the person Aleksandr Pevsner claimed had inside knowledge on how the terrorists managed to cross the border with the weaponry they needed to carry out their attacks. He was still skeptical this was the slam dunk he was hoping for, and he still felt like Pevsner was setting him up.

"Are you going with me?"

She smiled. "I have business with him as well."

Surely Pevsner and Barlow wouldn't have knowingly sent their daughters into an ambush.

Pick twisted in his seat and looked through the window at the darkness that blanketed the fifth airport he had been to that day. It looked like any other he had been to and it could just as easily have been a regional airport in North Carolina for how it looked under the blue glow of taxiway lighting. But when the Falcon came to a stop in front of a black GMC Yukon with two armed men standing in front of it, he was reminded just how isolated he was.

The engines began winding down as the forward entry door was opened and the ladder was extended. Sophie stood and joined Elena at the front of the cabin, then turned back to Pick. "Are you ready?"

I sure hope you know what you're doing.

Pick pushed aside his reservations and decided to see how far his faith would carry him.

[TWO]

Holiday Inn Express

FINSA Industrial Park

Nuevo Laredo, Mexico

2230 2 April 2026

Pick sat in the middle seat between Sophie and Elena, both of whom were dressed in relatively conservative business attire, and he had an unobstructed view through the windshield as the driver turned into the parking lot in front of a budget hotel. At first glance, it was a far cry from the Hotel Bristol's exemplification of elegance, but Pick was so tired, he didn't really care.

"This is good. I could really use some quality shut-eye," Pick said, not wanting to think of what time it was back in Vienna.

"Señor?" the armed man in the front passenger seat asked, clearly confused.

Sophie responded in rapid-fire Spanish that was too quick for Pick to understand. Even if he hadn't been as tired as he was, his mastery of the language was limited to what he had learned in hole-in-the-wall taquerias while growing up near San Diego. But whatever she said had obviously been humorous, because both armed men joined the women in laughing at Pick's apparent misfortune.

"I'm assuming I don't want to know what you're laughing about," he said, casting a dubious look at Sophie.

"This is only just the beginning of your journey, Pick McCoy," Sophie said, with humor in her eyes. "You're a long ways away from being able to sleep."

"How far?"

Sophie leaned forward and spoke to the driver in quiet Spanish before responding. "I'd say about six hundred meters, give or take."

The answer confused Pick, but he attributed most of that to his overwhelming fatigue. Still, when the Yukon came to a stop in front of the hotel's main entrance, he wasn't any closer to understanding why they had flown two hours from Cozumel to Nuevo Laredo and driven to a Holiday Inn Express.

"This is where we say goodbye," Sophie said.

"Goodbye?"

"Our business is elsewhere," she replied, opening the door and stepping out to make room for Pick to exit the Yukon.

He hesitated for a moment, then glanced at Elena, who said, "Tell Randy I said hi."

Pick slid across the seat and climbed out of the SUV, trying to read

Sophie's expression for any sign that she had led him into a trap. He felt isolated without weapons or backup and no way of communicating with his team—wherever they were. He stared into Sophie's dark brown eyes for several seconds, then turned to the men who had just exited the hotel and were waiting for him.

"Are you sure about this?" he asked Sophie.

She glanced at the men, then back to Pick. "Are you sure you're willing to do whatever it takes to get the answers you need?"

Pick had met Svetlana only the day before, and his interaction with Aleksandr Pevsner and Sophie's father had been even more brief. But he hadn't gotten the impression they were willing to go to such elaborate lengths to toy with him if they'd just wanted him dead. Russians might be notoriously fond of using poisons, but at their core, they tended to be pragmatic people. If they had wanted him dead, they would have just put a bullet between his eyes.

On the Cobenzl or in Cozumel.

"I have to," Pick said at last.

Sophie smiled, then leaned forward and gave him a chaste kiss on the mouth, leaving the taste of fruit on his lips. "Then go with these men and find what you came for."

He was still entranced by her kiss, but he nodded and turned to leave.

"Pick McCoy," she said.

He stopped and turned back.

"I'll see you again soon."

Pick wished that simple statement could have given him at least a modicum of comfort, but he was still on edge as he followed the men into the lobby of the Holiday Inn Express. Instead of leading him to the reception desk, where he could have rented a room with a moderately comfortable king-size bed for the night, the two men led him across the lobby to a door that was clearly not intended for access by the hotel's guests. Neither seemed to care if anybody watched them enter as they pushed open the door and stepped into the dark room.

But before the door clicked shut behind them, the men wheeled on Pick and slammed him up against a concrete wall. Pick instinctively brought his hands up in a defensive posture and kicked at the closest man, connecting with his hip and pushing him across the cramped room into a metal railing.

The resounding *gong* and man's grunt echoed off the concrete walls, but Pick had already shifted to the second man. He pushed off the wall and darted forward, closing the distance before the man could draw the pistol he had concealed underneath his ill-fitting jacket. He saw the man reach for his weapon, and Pick reacted on instinct, launching at the man the way a linebacker might in the seconds before sacking the quarterback.

But before Pick could wrap his arms around his assailant and knock him off balance, he heard something whistle through the air and connect with the back of his head. His flying attack faltered, and Pick collapsed to the ground just inches from his target. His ears were ringing, and stars danced at the corners of his vision.

The man behind him—the one he had push-kicked into the railing—said something in clipped Spanish, but Pick didn't understand a lick of what he had said. He shook his head and pushed himself to his feet, prepared to battle until his lights were turned out for good. Gritting his teeth, Pick rose into a combative posture.

But before he could resume his assault, a thick hood came down over his head and sealed in his fear.

"Enough," a raspy voice said, close enough that Pick felt the man's breath on his neck. "El Timón wants to see you, so you're coming with us."

"Where?" he asked, trying like hell to keep his nerves in check.

"You'll see."

In for a penny. In for a pound.

[THREE]

It didn't take long for Pick to realize that the room the men had taken him to was little more than an anteroom for access to the hotel's boilers and emergency power equipment. Though the air hummed with energy from the industrial machinery, Pick felt his own energy ebb as the thug behind him secured the hood around his neck with a zip tie and cinched it tight. He coughed and took a ragged breath before an unseen hand wrapped around his upper arm and propelled him forward into the darkness.

"Pisar," the man commanded.

"What?"

"¡Pisar! ¡Pisar!"

"I don't understand," Pick said.

"Step," the second man offered.

Pick lifted his right foot and waggled it in front of him, looking for a tread. But when the first man shoved him from behind, he lost his balance and fell forward. For an instant, it felt like his foot had passed through the floor in front of him, but then it connected with solid ground several inches beneath his left foot. He hadn't been expecting it, but Pick suddenly realized the stairs were leading *down*. Not up.

Having oriented his mind to the invisible staircase in front of him, Pick took a second step that was far more graceful. His third even more so. By his fifth step, he had perfected his technique of shuffling his foot forward to feel for the edge of the tread he was on before dropping it onto the next. After fifteen such steps, his foot shuffled farther forward without finding the edge, and he realized they had reached a landing. That suspicion was confirmed in a tactile way when the hand gripping his arm jerked him to the side and propelled him in a new direction.

"Pisar," the man commanded again.

"Yeah, I got it."

This time, Pick was ready. He stepped down and resumed his methodical shuffle-step gait until reaching the next landing. Each time he did so, he didn't require the perfunctory tug on his arm or command to step.

Pick lost count of how many flights of stairs they had descended and was only vaguely aware of the sound of the hotel's HVAC machinery fading away above them. But even more than the growing distance, the air seemed heavier and thicker, gradually growing warmer and more humid with each flight.

Then, as if they had stepped in front of an air conditioner, they were hit with a sudden blast of cold air, and Pick shivered. Somewhere deep in his subconscious, he knew that each cold zone occurred after three flights of stairs, giving him some unit of measure he could use to track their progress.

How many is that? Three cold zones, so nine flights of stairs? Fifteen steps per flight, so . . .

His fatigued brain couldn't manage the simple math, though he knew it mattered.

How deep are we?

Pick assumed that each flight took them another ten feet underground, but he couldn't fathom why they had descended to a depth of almost one hundred feet. Starved of his vision, Pick's ears took up the slack and began feeding his brain with the information it needed to paint a mental picture of his surroundings.

"Parése," the man said and jerked him to a halt.

"It means *stop*," the second man offered.

"Yeah, I got that much."

Pick's voice sounded hollow, as if its sound couldn't carry and was being deadened by the walls around them. Motionless for the first time in several minutes—*How long did that take us?*—Pick was suddenly aware of his racing heart, as if he had just played an entire four quarters of water polo instead of walking down some stairs. But even though he remembered feeling the same way after chopping up to his room on the fourth deck of Bancroft Hall, he inwardly seethed at being winded by something so simple.

Get a grip, McCoy.

Pick froze when he felt something sharp press against the base of his skull, and he winced at the loud *snap* of the zip tie breaking free from his neck. When the hood was ripped from his head, he snapped his eyes shut to protect them from the dim lighting that felt extraordinarily bright. Slowly, he eased them open and took in his surroundings.

He was speechless.

The man released his grip on Pick's arm and stepped around him to duck through an opening in the earthen wall that was barely three feet high. He scurried forward several feet before clicking on a headlamp and illuminating the dark tunnel. Pick could hardly believe what he was seeing, though he recognized it immediately.

"Where does this go?"

"Gringolandia," the second man said, flashing Pick a toothy smile as he held a Motorola radio close to his ear.

Pick had Fernando to thank for not needing a translation, but he was more curious about the radio. Especially after he heard it break squelch, followed by a soft voice speaking in hushed Spanish.

"Todo claro," he said into the tunnel.

"Bueno."

The light cast from the first man's headlamp began moving deeper into the earth, and Pick just shook his head. It was no mystery that drug cartels employed a multitude of means for carrying their product across the border and into the United States, tunnels being only one. They were most commonly found along the California and Arizona borders, and Customs and Border Protection had uncovered more than two hundred subterranean passages, including forty underneath the highly touted border wall. But in Texas? Pick was no geography expert, but he was almost certain that the Rio Grande separated Nuevo Laredo from the United States.

"Your turn," the second man said.

The glow of the headlamp had moved on, and the maw of the tunnel was pitch-black. Pick shook his head. "No way. What about the river?"

The man's smile grew. "We go under."

"Under," Pick repeated.

He nodded, then thrust a headlamp into Pick's hands and shoved him to the entrance.

Oh, shit.

[FOUR]

Growing up the son of a Vietnam War veteran, Pick had heard stories of the Army's infamous tunnel rats—men short in stature but well endowed in the areas that mattered most. Armed only with flashlights and .45-cal 1911 pistols, these men descended into the pitch-black to face off against an enemy that used their vast tunnel network to avoid detection. With the threat of feces-covered booby traps or poisonous snakes, spiders, and centipedes around every bend, the tunnel rats lived in perpetual fear and oppressive darkness hundreds of feet into the earth.

So, Pick wasn't all that surprised when he ducked into the tunnel and immediately felt an overwhelming sense of claustrophobia. No matter how much he tried distracting himself, he couldn't stop thinking about the weight of the earth pressing down on the tunnel's ceiling, held in place by nothing more than roughly hewed four-by-four beams. But his fear would quickly bubble over into panic if he thought of the rushing waters of the Rio Grande flowing above them.

Just keep moving forward . . .

The tunnel itself was little more than shoulder width, and several times Pick had to angle his body slightly to pass through a narrow section. Though it wasn't so short that he needed to advance on his hands and knees, Pick's lower back screamed in agony at the awkward angle he was forced into by the low ceiling—made even more awkward by the beams sporadically placed every few feet. But he pushed through the pain and focused on his headlamp's weak beam of light, which seemed to be swallowed up by the darkness.

After several minutes of steady progress, Pick's heart bolted when he heard a loud scuffling behind him. He couldn't help but imagine a centipede as long and as thick as his thigh scurrying forward on tiny legs to sink its pincers into him. He almost jumped into the tunnel's ceiling when a heavy hand came down on his lower back.

"Stop!" the voice hissed. "Turn off light."

Pick recognized the voice of the cartel gunman, but that did little to keep his panic in check. "What? Why?"

"Sensors," the man replied, pushing Pick to the ground and reaching over him to toggle his headlamp off.

Almost immediately, Pick was plunged into the most oppressive darkness he had ever experienced. With the weight of the sicario on his back, he found himself on the losing end of a battle to retain his sanity. He squirmed to get out from underneath the gunman, but he was met with resistance that only caused him to spiral even closer to panic.

"Stop! No move," the man whispered.

Get ahold of yourself, McCoy!

His eyes were wide open, but they might as well have been clamped shut for all that he could see. He took a long, slow breath in through his nose and held it despite the pungent scent of damp earth that reeked of decay. He counted slowly to four before exhaling through his mouth, releasing just a fraction of the tension keeping him bound in fear.

Pick stopped resisting and allowed his cartel guide to hold him still.

"Bueno," the man whispered.

Pick took another deep breath, counted to four again, and released even more of his panic. He was far from being calm, but neither was he on the verge of losing control. He didn't know how long they would need to remain motionless in the dark more than a hundred feet underground, but he was resolved to endure however long it took.

Seconds and minutes ticked by with Pick's ears ringing in the silence. After what felt like an eternity, he heard the sicario's Motorola break squelch three times. It was little more than a whisper, but it was apparently the signal they had been waiting for, because the pressure on his back lifted as the man released his hold on Pick.

"Todo claro," he said. "All clear."

Pick reached up to click on his headlamp and immediately regretted it. His pupils had dilated nearly all the way to permit light where none existed, and the sudden brilliance instantly blinded him. He snapped his eyes shut, then let his eyelids flutter slowly as he adjusted to being able to see again.

"All clear," the man repeated. "Move."

Pick pushed himself off the ground and resumed his painful hunched-over posture, then began shuffling forward again. He had no way of knowing how far they had gone or how far they still needed to go. But he was eager to reach the other side, exit the tunnel, and breathe fresh air again. He couldn't fathom making the return trip and secretly admired his cartel guides for their nonchalant attitudes.

I wonder how many times they've been through this tunnel.

That thought reminded Pick that he was there because one of Aleksandr Pevsner's contacts—a man known as El Timón—attested to having firsthand knowledge of how terrorists managed to make it into the United States undetected. And that thought logically made him wonder if he was following in the footsteps of the men behind the shooting in Virginia Beach or the attack on the Alamo.

With his purpose again at the front of his mind, Pick successfully suppressed his fear and drove onward. He no longer thought about the tons of earth and water above him or the risk of being trapped where nobody would ever find him. He no longer worried about whether Pevsner had set him up. He no longer cared if he was—or was not—the right person to replace Charley Castillo as the Presidential Agent.

In that moment, he just was.

He was focused on the mission and nothing else. If this was the price he had to pay to find the men responsible for putting Castillo in the hospital, he wouldn't hesitate. The fear was gone, and in its place was a calm sense of detachment that he was on the right path and getting close to exposing his enemy's secrets.

XVI

[ONE]

0120 3 April 2026

Without even looking at his watch, Pick knew he had been awake for well over twenty-four hours—not counting the nap he had managed to take on the flight from Cozumel—and he felt intoxicated with fatigue. His motivation waned, but his determination and discipline drove him onward through the tunnel.

Then he saw it. It was little more than a glow where there had been none before. It wasn't quite the proverbial light at the end of the tunnel, but it was enough to bolster him and propel him onward.

With each step, it grew brighter. Gradually, Pick realized he no longer needed his headlamp to see in front of him, and he reached up to click it off. It was far from bright, but after spending so much time in nothing but absolute darkness, it was a welcome change.

The closer he got, the more he realized there was nothing but an earthen wall at the end. But the light was coming from somewhere, so he assumed there had to be an opening in the ceiling or a bend he couldn't yet make out. When he had closed to within twenty meters of the end, the first sicario stepped out from a passage to the right.

Pick froze when he recognized the object in the man's hand.

Not another hood.

He felt the familiar sense of panic begin to swell, but he tamped it back and continued onward. After the darkness of the tunnel, the dimness of the hood didn't seem to bother him half as much as it first had. He would gladly don the hood again if it meant he could escape the tunnel and gain the answers he needed.

Pick made eye contact with the man and nodded, letting him know he didn't intend to resist. After several more paces, he came to a stop in front of the sicario and lowered onto his knees. The man draped the thick canvas over his head and secured it once more with a zip tie around his neck. Pick didn't struggle and only waited for the man to grip his arm and guide him to the exit.

"Pisar," the man commanded.

Pick lifted his foot and felt in front of him for a tread, sighing when it connected with something solid. Though he had been expecting it, he was still relieved to discover that the stairs were leading up. Not down.

He allowed himself to be guided up the stairs, turning of his own accord at each landing to continue his ascent. He breathed in the stale air through the hood, eager to reach the surface and again feel fresh air on his skin. With each blast of cool conditioned air every three landings, he felt his energy return and drive him onward.

Wherever the stairs went, he was eager to get there.

Anything was better than being underground.

[TWO]

South Laredo Wastewater Treatment Plant

Laredo, Texas

0145 3 April 2026

When his guide finally jerked on Pick's arm to make him stop, his heart thundered in his chest as much from the anticipation of reaching the end of his journey as from the exertion needed to climb the stairs.

He stood in silence and waited for his guides to cut off the zip tie securing the hood.

But they surprised him by again gripping his arm and guiding him farther. He heard what sounded like a metal latch being manipulated and a door swinging open, its rusted hinges groaning ominously and echoing off the surrounding walls. His guide pushed him closer to the now open door, then placed a hand on his head and forced him to bend over at the waist and duck through the opening.

Pick stepped from the room and felt loose gravel underfoot. Immediately he recognized the sounds of nature in a wide-open space surrounding him and what sounded like rushing water a short distance away. But he also heard the quiet sound of a car's idling engine getting closer as he was guided across the uneven ground.

"I think you can remove his hood now," a new voice said. He sounded like a gringo.

"Sí, El Timón," the man holding his arm said.

"Captain McCoy gave his word to Señor Pevsner that he wouldn't expose our smuggling route to authorities," the man known as El Timón said. "And we both know you don't lie, cheat, or steal. Isn't that right, McCoy?"

He cocked his head at the odd statement but responded anyway. "Yes, sir."

Again, Pick felt the sharp press of wire cutters against the base of his neck as the zip tie was cut away and the hood was ripped from his head. This time, he didn't flinch or snap his eyes shut. He stared directly into the green eyes of a man he had endured much to meet.

"I appreciate your compliance."

Pick studied El Timón's tan skin and dark, perfectly arranged hair with curiosity, unable to help feeling like he had met him somewhere before. He stood tall and carried himself with authority, dressed in a tailored suit that was more appropriate for business dealings in the boardroom or courtroom. Not whatever this was underneath the stars in an open field.

"Where are we?"

"The South Laredo Wastewater Treatment Plant," El Timón said.

Pick looked around and noticed several industrial-looking buildings and tanks of varying shapes and sizes, including the one he had just exited. A glance over his shoulder revealed the seven-story Holiday Inn Express several hundred meters in the distance and a wide easement on the near side of the Rio Grande that he suspected was used for routine sweeps by Customs and Border Protection.

"Don't worry," El Timón said. "Their next patrol won't be along for another thirty minutes, and we'll be long gone well before then."

"Where are we going?"

"To my home, Captain McCoy. My wife has prepared the guest room for your arrival, and I understand you've had a long day and are eager for some sleep."

That was an understatement, but Pick wasn't so tired that he'd failed to miss that the cartel boss had invited him into his home. He didn't know much about Mexican drug cartels, but he didn't think everybody he had business dealings with were shown the same level of hospitality.

Maybe Pevsner's more of an ally than I thought.

"I would be grateful," Pick said, choosing his words carefully.

"Very good. My wife will be pleased to hear that."

El Timón opened the Cadillac Escalade's rear door and gestured for Pick to climb inside. Pick did so and was surprised to discover only a driver who didn't appear the least bit interested in what his boss was up to. After shutting the door behind Pick, his host spoke briefly with the sicarios who had guided him through the tunnel, then walked around the Escalade and climbed into the rear seat on the driver's side.

"We can go now," El Timón said to the driver.

"Very good, sir."

The driver immediately put the Cadillac SUV in gear and pulled away from the storage tank Pick had just exited from only minutes earlier. They made their way slowly along the gravel access road and turned toward a gate on the north side of the plant. Pick stared through the windshield at the ground illuminated by the Cadillac's brilliant headlights, but he was more interested in the man sitting next to him. Pick was more and more certain he had met El Timón somewhere before.

"Is there something you want to say?" his host asked, obviously aware of Pick's hesitant sideways glances.

"I appreciate your hospitality, so I don't want you to take this the wrong way . . ."

El Timón shifted in his seat to face Pick before gesturing for him to continue.

"But have we met before?"

The businessman smiled. "Very good, Captain McCoy. I was afraid you wouldn't recognize me."

Pick stared deep into the man's eyes, still unable to place him. "I'm afraid I still don't. Other than a nagging feeling that we've met before, I can't recall any specifics. I'm sorry."

El Timón waved away the comment as if he didn't mind. "Nothing to be sorry for. Nothing at all. In fact, we only met once. And it was quite brief, if I'm being honest."

Pick remained silent, hoping his host would provide him with additional clues to help solve the mystery. But when it became apparent

El Timón intended on being less than forthcoming with information to ease Pick's anxiety, he gave in to his curiosity. "When did we meet?"

The businessman smiled again—with his eyes this time—and he shook his head. "I'm afraid I'm enjoying this far too much to just give you the answer." He pulled back the sleeve on his suit to examine an expensive-looking watch. "We have about twenty minutes until we arrive. Maybe by then you'll have figured it out for yourself."

Pick wondered how much his fatigue factored into not being able to remember when they had met before, and he doubted that would change over the course of a twenty-minute drive. But he knew he was at his host's mercy, so he only nodded and leaned back against the supple leather seat and closed his eyes.

[THREE]

Hacienda Puerto

Laredo, Texas

0215 3 April 2026

Pick opened his eyes and bolted upright. The Escalade was parked in front of a grand-looking estate with Spanish mission architecture, and Pick was surprised to discover that he was alone. He flinched when his door suddenly opened.

"Welcome to Hacienda Puerto, Captain McCoy," El Timón said. "My home."

"Thank you," Pick replied, still shaking off the cobwebs as he stepped out of the SUV and stared up at the large home.

"I'm afraid my wife has already retired for the evening, but your room is ready if you'd care to follow me." He turned on his heel and started for the front door without waiting to see if his guest followed.

Even though Pick hadn't unearthed El Timón's identity during their twenty-minute drive as his host had suggested, he decided not to press it. He wasn't thinking clearly and needed a few hours of sleep more than anything else. Pick closed the Escalade's door and followed his host inside the mansion.

If anything, the interior of the home was even more majestic than its outside was. The foyer was grander than any Pick had ever seen before and had travertine floors with expensive-looking artwork adorning the walls on both sides. An ornate table sat in the center of the room with a spring bouquet of brightly colored flowers. El Timón led Pick through the foyer and up a curved staircase to the second floor.

"I can give you a full tour of our home tomorrow," Pick's host said over his shoulder. "For now, I think it's probably best that we both get some sleep before we discuss your reason for coming here."

Though it felt like a timer was counting down the minutes and seconds until the next terrorist attack, Pick nodded in agreement. Even one night was more than he wanted to give up, but he didn't have much choice. He was tired. Exhausted. And his host was dead set on waiting until morning to speak.

"This way, Captain McCoy," El Timón said at the top of the stairs, turning right down a hallway.

Pick followed him blindly, listening to the silence echoing through the halls. Only his host's soft footsteps clicking on the tile floors resounded off the walls. They passed several doors on both sides before El Timón opened a door and stepped aside to let Pick enter.

"There's an adjoining bathroom with everything you need."

"Thank you," Pick said, trying hard not to float across the floor and collapse onto the luxuriously appointed bed. It looked softer than anything Pick had ever seen before.

"Breakfast will be ready at seven. But if you're an early riser—and I suspect that you are—you may join me for coffee on the veranda at six."

"Thank you," Pick said again, knowing that 6:00 was only a few short hours away. "Would it be possible to use a phone to contact my team and let them know I'm safe?"

El Timón studied Pick for several seconds before nodding. "Of course. I'm sure you'll need to speak with your superiors."

He has no idea I report directly to the President of the United States.

"But I only ask that you refrain from informing them of your location until we've had a chance to speak." El Timón reached into his pocket and removed a cellphone, then handed it to Pick. "This phone is encrypted and utilizes Voice over Internet Protocol and a virtual private network to route its connection through a myriad of servers arrayed across the globe. It would be fruitless to try tracing the call to determine your location."

Pick had been hoping for that exact thing, but he wasn't about to admit it. He took the phone. "Thank you again for your hospitality."

"I'm very protective of my family, Captain McCoy."

"I understand. Thank you."

His host smiled politely, then closed the door. Pick stood motionless for several seconds while straining to hear if the door had been locked from the outside. When he didn't hear the telltale *click* he had been expecting, he pressed his ear to the door and listened to El Timón's footsteps echoing down the hall. Pick tried the doorknob and found that it turned easily.

Satisfied that he hadn't just been locked in what amounted to a prison cell, Pick powered on the phone and dialed the only number he had memorized that might connect him with his team.

"I can't believe I'm doing this," he muttered.

The phone made several odd beeps and squeaks while it connected from server to server until reaching a cellphone with a phone number only a spook could pull off. When it started ringing, Pick held his breath and waited to see if Junior would pick up.

"Hello?" a tired voice asked.

"Junior, it's Pick."

There was shuffling on the other end as if Junior had been sleeping and was suddenly wide awake. "Boss, where are you?"

Pick walked across the large bedroom and entered the en suite bathroom. Just as his host had said, it was stocked with every toiletry item he might need—soap, shampoo, toothbrush, and toothpaste. "I'll get into that later. I just wanted you to know that I'm safe and with Pevsner's contact right now."

There was a pause. "Are you under duress?"

Pick was exhausted, but he didn't think that counted as duress. "No, I'm good. I'll give you more details tomorrow."

"Boss, it *is* tomorrow."

"Right." Pick thought about crashing for a few hours but couldn't resist the idea of a hot shower to wash away the remnants of the earthen tunnel he had scurried through like a human rodent. "Anything new on the investigation?"

"Yeah, actually, we just got a list of the victims in San Antonio."

Pick didn't bother getting his hopes up. "Anything interesting?"

"Randy said you knew one of the Alamo Rangers."

Pick's heart raced with sudden anxiety that instantly erased his crushing fatigue. "Who?"

"John Hanes?"

The name tickled at the back of Pick's mind. But even though he was instantly awake, he wasn't operating at full mental capacity and was struggling to place the name with a face. "Who's that?" he asked again.

"Randy said he was your company officer or something?"

Suddenly, two images flashed in Pick's mind. The first was of a young Marine Corps infantry captain who had been the 18th Company officer at the Naval Academy during his youngster year. The second was of a slain Alamo Ranger with a subdued Marine Corps Eagle, Globe, and Anchor pinned to his uniform.

"Yeah," Pick said, pausing to clear his throat. "I remember him now."

"Anyway, that's it. Nothing that will help us stop another attack."

"Thanks, Junior. I'll call you tom—" He stopped himself. "I'll call you in the morning."

"If I hear anything else, I'll let you know."

Pick ended the call, then turned on the shower and let the water heat up before stripping off his clothes and stepping under the rainfall showerhead. Pick closed his eyes as the water cascaded down on top of him but couldn't help thinking about the senseless act of violence in San Antonio that had claimed the life of a Marine and three others. He took his time washing himself, letting his anger and frustration replace any lingering fatigue.

The longer he remained in the shower, the more certain he was that he wouldn't be able to rest until those responsible were brought to justice. He had traveled all this way to figure out how the terrorists had entered the country, and he intended to learn more about the man who came to collect him from a storage tank in a wastewater treatment plant. The man wasn't Mexican, of that much Pick was certain. But he was more than likely Hispanic, and reminded Pick of Castillo's cousin Fernando.

So, maybe he's Texican like the Castillos.

Does it matter if he is?

No, but I wonder if Doña Alicia knows him.

Pick shut off the water and reached for a thick cotton towel before stepping from the shower to dry off. He stared at the dulled image of himself in the fogged-up mirror and wondered what he looked like after traveling halfway around the globe from Vienna to end up in a cartel boss's guest quarters. But the shower had rejuvenated him, and he quickly toweled off and slipped back into his filthy clothes.

"There's only one way of finding out who I'm dealing with," Pick said to his reflection.

That's probably not the best idea.

"Always faithful, always forward," he said, echoing the Marine Raiders' values.

[FOUR]

Hacienda Puerto

Laredo, Texas

0250 3 April 2026

Pick turned the cellphone's ringer off, then slipped it into his front pocket before opening the bedroom door, lifting slightly on the doorknob to take tension off the hinges and prevent them from squeaking. When the door was a little more than a foot ajar, he craned his neck through the gap and peered into the dark hallway. He was greeted by the same silence he had heard on his arrival.

Sounds like everyone is asleep.

You can't be certain of that.

Pick opened the door wider and slipped through the crack, then reached behind his back to close it. He stood motionless for several seconds while listening to and cataloging the normal sounds of the house in the dead of night. No footsteps. No ticking of a grandfather clock. No hushed voices or television shows broadcasting in a low volume. It was silent—just the way Pick liked it.

Looking left and right, he decided on making for the stairs and returning to the first floor. He reasoned that a home office could be almost anywhere in a house of that size, so he approached it just as he would when clearing a building with his Raider team. He reached the curved staircase and descended one step at a time, pausing on each tread to listen for a change in the night. No footsteps. No hushed voices. It was still silent.

When he reached the ground floor, he crossed the foyer and entered a room that was arguably larger than his entire town house back in North Topsail Beach, North Carolina. Furnished with elegant sofas and oversized armchairs, it reminded Pick of the Bristol Lounge in Vienna. He pressed through to a hallway on the opposite side of the room, wondering how many cartel cocktail hours had been hosted in that room.

Unlike the hallway on the second floor where his room was located, this one was short and had only two doors—one on either side—and a framed painting of a Texas landscape on the wall at the opposite end. He tried the door on his left, and the handle turned effortlessly, permitting him access to a room that looked like a storage closet or pantry of some kind. He backed out and tried the door on the other side.

Locked.

Pick made a mental note of its location before retreating into the hallway and making his way back across the sitting room and into the foyer.

Orienting himself again to the layout of the house, Pick walked toward the rear and into a grand room with floor-to-ceiling windows that stretched from wall to wall. Though it was still pitch-black outside, his eyes were naturally drawn to ornamental landscape lighting that illuminated an assortment of Texas trees and shrubs. Pick turned left and walked through a large gourmet kitchen with industrial-looking appliances and a built-in coffee machine that had the potential of being even more complicated than the one he had manipulated to start his day.

How long ago was that?

Pick shook away the pointless question and continued through the kitchen and adjoining dining room, mentally placing the locked room on his left. But when he couldn't find another entrance into the room that had been locked, he retreated and crossed to the opposite side of the house and a much longer hallway that was directly beneath the one leading to his room on the second floor. With each step, Pick mentally calculated the dimensions of each room and sketched a crude blueprint in his mind.

Down the hall, he discovered a half-bathroom, a room that had been converted into a home gym, and two additional bedrooms, each with en suite bathrooms. He found a closet, a laundry room, a mudroom, access to the attached garage, and a door leading onto the veranda where he was to take his coffee with El Timón in only a few short hours.

After mapping the entire first floor, he returned to the formal sitting room and the secrets hidden inside a locked room at the end of a short hallway. He probably could have ignored it and returned to the second floor to resume his search, but he didn't like the idea of leaving the ground floor without first completing his search.

Kneeling in front of the door, Pick reached underneath his belt and felt for the concealed pouch where he kept a few items that would come in handy in the event he were ever kidnapped.

Like in Vienna?

Or Nuevo Laredo?

His belt was constructed of double layers of nylon webbing, stitched together for rigidity and to provide a low-profile option for mounting his appendix-style Kydex holster. Though the gun had been discarded long before he'd left for Vienna, he had retained the belt with its basic lockpick kit and handcuff key hidden inside the integrated pouch.

Pick removed the lockpick kit and inserted the tension wrench into the lock's plug while turning it to apply pressure to the pins. Very carefully, he inserted the pick and felt for the binding pin, then lifted it until it set into place. Pick was methodical in moving from pin to pin, angling and shifting his tools until each pin was set and allowed the plug to twist freely. It took him several seconds of trial and error to perfect his technique, but after he had done so, he felt the last pin seat into place, then twisted the knob and pushed open the door.

As he had hoped, the room was El Timón's home office. A vacant tufted leather executive-style swivel chair sat behind a large wooden desk in the middle of the room, with three flat-screen monitors placed on top. A large window framed the desk, letting in soft moonlight that glowed on a bookshelf that was decorated with plaques, framed pictures, and books likely chosen more for their appearance than for their content.

Pick was halfway across the office when the cellphone in his pocket vibrated. He paused, pulled it out, and stared at the phone number on the screen.

202-763-2591

The sneaky one.

Pick answered it. "Hey, Junior—"

"Pick, it's Randy."

"What's going on, Randy?" One of the plaques on the bookshelf caught Pick's eye.

The Admiral Farragut Academy?

"Junior said he told you about Captain Hanes."

"Yeah, he did," Pick replied, turning from the plaque to a framed picture that made him uneasy.

"It got me thinking back to our time in Annapolis, so I went over the list of victims from the Virginia Beach shooting again."

Pick froze. He wasn't sure he liked where this was going.

"Find anything?"

"Does the name Liam McIntyre ring any bells?"

His stomach dropped, and his mouth ran dry. But before he could answer, he sensed a presence in the room and spun to see El Timón standing in the doorway, pointing a gun at him.

"If you wouldn't mind hanging up," the cartel boss said.

"You there?" Randy asked on the other end.

Pick ended the call to cut him off and slowly raised his hands into the air.

XVII

Fall 2014

[ONE]

Northern Judicial Court

Washington Navy Yard

Washington, D.C.

0910 14 October 2014

Midshipman Third Class P.K. McCoy Jr. stood with others in the public gallery as a heavy wooden door opened and permitted five commissioned officers into the courtroom. Once the court's members had taken their places, he and the other visitors sat. Pick was there on official business and wore his Service Dress Blues uniform adorned with a single diagonal gold stripe on his left sleeve and single row of ribbons above his left breast pocket—a far cry from the rank insignia and chest candy worn by the court's members.

The room was silent, and Pick visibly seethed, clenching and unclenching his fists while staring at the back of Javier Santiago's head. He would have given anything for the opportunity to be left alone with his former roommate—even for just a few minutes—certain that his method of justice would be far more fitting than whatever the court doled out. Pick knew the minimum punishment for sexual assault was a mandatory dismissal from the Navy, and that the maximum was confinement for thirty years.

But he was under no illusions that Javi would get anywhere close to that.

"All rise," the bailiff said. "The Northern Judicial Court is now in session, the Honorable Judge McIntyre presiding."

Again, Pick rose to his feet and waited until the military judge—a Navy lieutenant commander—had taken his place on the bench. An odd sense of detachment settled over Pick, as if he were only an actor in a movie, standing or sitting when the script called for it.

"Be seated," Judge McIntyre said, then shifted on the bench while examining whatever documents had been placed before him. He waited until the court's members and visitors were seated before looking up at the prosecution's attorney. "In the case of *United States versus Midshipman Third Class Javier Santiago*, I understand that the accused has entered into a plea agreement."

The Navy judge advocate general wearing the rank insignia of a lieutenant rose to his feet. "Yes, Your Honor. The accused has agreed to plead guilty to aggravated sexual contact in exchange for favorable sentencing."

"Has the victim's legal counsel been advised of this plea agreement?"

A civilian attorney seated next to the lieutenant stood. "Yes, I have, Your Honor."

"And does your client feel that justice will be served by the court accepting this agreement?"

"Yes, Your Honor."

The judge nodded thoughtfully, then turned to address Javi. "Midshipman Santiago, do you understand that you may only enter into a guilty plea for a crime that you committed?"

Pick's ears rang with a sudden rush of blood to his head. He wasn't sure he was ready to listen to Javi actually admit to assaulting his girlfriend, but he leaned forward in his seat and strained to hear anyway. One way or another, his former roommate was going to pay for what he had done to Hannah.

Javi rose to his feet, as did several civilian attorneys that surrounded him on both sides. "Yes, Your Honor."

Judge McIntyre removed the reading glasses he had perched on the end of his nose and glowered down at him. "Midshipman Santiago, out of respect for the victim and her wishes, I am tempted to accept your guilty plea instead of trying you for the original charge of sexual assault. But it is my opinion that any person who has sworn an oath to support and defend the Constitution of the United States is held to a higher standard and thus should not escape the consequences of their actions."

One of Javi's attorneys spoke up. "Your Honor—"

Judge McIntyre raised his hand to silence him. "I'm not done."

"Yes, Your Honor. My apologies."

"Midshipman Santiago, this court takes rape and sexual assault charges seriously, and I find it especially reprehensible that you would assault another who has put on the uniform and sworn the same oath. This country placed its faith in you by granting you an appointment to the United States Naval Academy. You not only violated the trust of Midshipman Rosen, but that of every citizen of this great country."

Pick held his breath.

"For that reason, I will not accept your guilty plea . . ."

A quiet murmur broke out among those assembled in the courtroom, but Pick never took his eyes off the back of Javi's head.

". . . and will instead accept the preliminary hearing officer's recommendation to try you for sexual assault. This court intends to see that you receive an appropriate punishment for your actions. Do you understand?"

Javi's voice quavered slightly when he responded, "Yes, Your Honor."

Judge McIntyre stared Javi down for several seconds, then focused on his lead attorney. "Counselor, are you prepared to provide an adequate defense? Or do you require additional time?"

Javi's attorney didn't sound like he had just received bad news. His voice was strong and confident. "Your Honor, we are prepared to offer our defense. But given the stakes for our client, we would be grateful if the court granted us additional time to prepare."

"Is one week sufficient?"

The lead attorney looked to the others on his team, each nodding their concurrence. "Yes, Your Honor. One week would be more than sufficient."

Judge McIntyre turned to the JAG lieutenant representing the prosecution. "Does the prosecution have any objections?"

The lieutenant stood. "No objections, Your Honor."

"Very well. This court will stand adjourned and reconvene in one week."

The sound of his gavel echoed across the silent courtroom, and Pick flinched when the bailiff called the court to rise. He stood with the others as his mind swam with the implications of the judge's refusal to accept Javi's plea agreement. When he had first walked in, he had expected justice for Hannah. But the prospect of a plea agreement made that seem less likely.

Judge McIntyre had single-handedly restored Pick's faith in the system.

After the judge and court's members exited the courtroom, Pick turned and watched a Hispanic man dressed in an expensive-looking suit leave the seat closest to the bar behind Javi and make for the exit. He noticed Pick's attention, and the two locked eyes.

There was something about the stranger's green eyes that made Pick uneasy.

They were green like Javi's.

XVIII

[ONE]

Hacienda Puerto

Laredo, Texas

0320 3 April 2026

Pick squinted when El Timón reached for the light switch and flicked it on, instantly ending the darkness that had cloaked Pick's snooping. He would have shut his eyes completely, but he couldn't bring himself to take his eyes off the pistol held in his host's hand—he'd learned from experience that bad things happened when you took your eyes off the threat.

Like my dad used to say: "Lose sight, lose the fight."

"What are you doing in my office, Captain McCoy?"

Pick stared into El Timón's green eyes. "I remember where we met."

"I thought you might," he said. "My name is Rafael Santiago. But you may call me Rafi."

"Not El Timón?"

Rafi stared at him. "It means 'the helm' and was given to me partly because of my role on the board and my affinity for sailing."

"What board?"

Rafi lowered the gun and nodded at the plaque Pick had noticed earlier. "I sit on the board at the Admiral Farragut Academy."

Pick watched the gun lower but kept his hands above his head. He had been caught dead to rights and didn't think a brief shared history was enough to keep Rafi from tying up loose ends by putting a bullet between Pick's eyes. He had always known the President made the wrong choice when she appointed him to replace Castillo, but he regretted that he wouldn't be able to stop the terrorists from finishing what they'd started when they gunned down the *real* Presidential Agent in Virginia Beach.

"Lower your hands, Captain McCoy," Rafi said. "I'm not going to shoot you."

Pick's eyes flashed to the gun, still hesitant.

Rafi noticed. "You triggered a silent alarm when you picked the lock, and I didn't know who I was going to find rummaging around in the darkness. But I knew who I was inviting into my home before I agreed to help my friend Aleksandr. Now answer my question: What are you doing in my office?"

Pick lowered his hands. "Looking for something to jog my memory."

"Did you find it?"

Pick nodded to the picture of his former roommate standing tall next to a younger Rafi on I-Day. "Why didn't you just tell me who you were instead of making me fly all the way from Cozumel to Nuevo Laredo?"

Rafi closed the door and gestured with the pistol for Pick to have a seat in one of the two leather armchairs arranged in front of the desk. After Pick sat, Rafael Santiago placed his pistol on the bookshelf and lowered himself onto the opposite chair.

"You told Aleksandr you wanted to learn how the terrorists had entered the United States undetected, correct?"

Pick nodded. He had already guessed that El Timón was an American citizen in the employ of the Cártel del Noreste, and that the tunnel under the Rio Grande had been used to smuggle the terrorists into the country. But he wasn't sure exactly how his former roommate's father fit into the attacks. Had they been aimed at Pick and the people close to him as retribution for his testimony that landed Javi behind bars?

If so, who's next?

"I wanted you to see the tunnel so that you would know I had nothing to hide."

Sure, he had followed in the terrorists' footsteps and scurried through a tunnel like a rat, but it hadn't given Pick any insight as to where the terrorists came from or where they were now. Most important, he wasn't any closer to finding out what their next target was, and it appeared that Rafi was angling for something else.

"Why do I get the feeling that you know more than you're telling me?"

Rafi sighed. "I had hoped to wait until the sun was up before having this conversation."

Pick's anxiety crept higher with the fear that he was to blame for everything, and he braced himself. "This can't wait, Rafi. I'm running out of time to stop another attack from happening, and I need to know whose side you're on. I need to know if you're behind these attacks and an enemy to the United States."

Rafi's face flushed crimson with the implied accusation. "I assure you I'm not."

Pick's grip on his anxiety was weakening, and he took several deep breaths to calm himself before speaking. "I don't know if I can believe you."

"Why? Because Javier Santiago is my son?"

Pick opened his mouth to rebut the argument but snapped it shut when he realized Rafi was right. Rafi had told Aleksandr Pevsner that he would show Pick how the terrorists entered the United States, and he had. He had welcomed Pick into his home and made him feel like a guest and even given him the means to communicate with his team. He had not threatened Pick in any way and was guilty only of siring the man who had sexually assaulted his college sweetheart.

"He's my son, but we're not the same," Rafi added.

Pick heard the sincerity in Rafi's voice and met his gaze. "You're not upset with me for testifying against him?"

"'Midshipmen are persons of integrity: They stand for that which is right. They tell the truth and ensure that the truth is known. They do not lie.'"

Pick recognized the first part of the Naval Academy's Honor Concept, having recited it numerous times to assuage his guilt amid mounting criticism from classmates for his testimony at Javi's court-martial. "Javi was like a brother to me. I would have done anything for him."

"You did the right thing," Rafi said. "I'll admit that it took a long time for me to let go of my anger and accept the truth in that. But you did what I would have done had I been in your shoes."

Pick remained silent.

"He is our only son, and we . . ." He corrected himself. "*I* . . . wasn't hard enough on him as a boy. I let him get away with little things, believing that he only needed time to mature. When he got older, I sent him to the Admiral Farragut Academy, hoping that if I could get him away from the negative influences he was surrounded by here in Laredo—"

"Because of your business dealings with the cartel?"

Rafi didn't seem to mind the interruption. "Yes, because of my business dealings with the cartel. I had hoped that boarding school would accelerate his maturity and help him grow into a man I could be proud of."

Pick thought it ironic that somebody who smuggled drugs and people across the border for a living cared about the kind of man his son was to become. But he kept his thoughts to himself.

"When Javi told me he was applying to the Naval Academy, I thought we had succeeded. I thought he had turned a corner." He gestured to the framed picture that Pick had been looking at. "I was so proud of him when he took his oath of office and became a member of the Brigade of Midshipmen."

Pick studied Rafi for signs that he wasn't being truthful and found none. But he still didn't see how it factored into the mission the President had given him. "I'm sorry, but what does any of this have to do with smuggling terrorists into the United States?"

Rafi's jaw muscles flexed with frustration, though Pick wasn't sure whether it was aimed at him or at his prodigal son. "What I'm trying to tell you, Captain McCoy, is that until recently I wasn't aware that my tunnel had been used to smuggle terrorists into the United States. When I learned that it had, I made inquiries with my leadership in the Cártel del Noreste, who assured me that they were also unaware."

"And you believe them?"

Rafi shrugged. "As much as I can believe anybody in this business. But yes, I don't think they are behind these attacks. It serves no purpose and would only encourage the United States to take action against us—your presence here is proof enough of that."

Reluctantly, Pick had to agree with him. If the cartels wanted to keep their ratlines open to continue smuggling product across the border, it wouldn't make sense to give the American government a reason to come down on them. But Pick was still suspicious of Rafi's motives.

"So, who's behind the attacks?"

Rafi looked embarrassed. "This is why I wanted to wait until morning—"

"We don't have time," Pick said, cutting him off. "Who's behind these attacks, Rafi?"

"I can't be certain—"

"Who?"

"Javi."

[TWO]

Pick only stared at the cartel boss as he let the name sink in.

"But that's not possible," Pick said, shaking his head in disbelief. "He's in prison."

"Not anymore."

"How? He was sentenced to thirty years . . ."

But Pick knew Javi was the perfect narcissist who had manipulated Pick into thinking they were friends. He had manipulated Hannah into believing Pick wasn't interested in her. And he had manipulated the prosecution into offering a plea agreement that would have resulted in a lesser sentence. If not for—

"Judge McIntyre," he blurted.

"Excuse me?"

Ignoring Rafi's puzzled expression, Pick reached into his pocket for the cellphone Rafi had given him and quickly dialed the "sneaky one."

The call was answered after one ring.

"What's going on?" Randy asked.

"What was the name you mentioned before we got cut off?"

If Randy was confused by Pick's brusqueness, he didn't let it show. "Liam McIntyre. He was the—"

"Military judge in Javi's court-martial," Pick said for him.

"Yeah, I thought it was an odd coincidence."

Pick's heart started hammering in his chest as if he had already had several cups of coffee. "It's more than just a coincidence, Randy. I need you to get your hands on everything related to that court-martial and make a list of potential targets."

"Targets?" Randy sounded confused.

"I'll explain later, but I have reason to believe that anybody involved in that case is in danger." Pick glanced at Rafi and saw a worried expression on his face. "I'll call you back."

He ended the call and fixed his host with a determined stare. "Start talking."

"I love my son, Captain McCoy."

Pick waved Rafi on, accepting that even a father who was disappointed in his son might still have love for him.

"After the judge sentenced Javi to thirty years in prison, I cut him off and swore not to enable him any longer. Everything I'd feared had come to pass, and Javi had turned his back on the kind of man I'd hoped he would become. I cut off funding to his legal team and believed it was time for Javi to face the consequences of his actions on his own. Like a man."

"But he got thirty years," Pick said. "That means he should still be in prison for another eighteen."

Rafi nodded. "He was paroled early."

"How? Without your legal team supporting him, how did he manage to convince a parole board to grant him an early release?"

Rafi sighed, and Pick again got the feeling he wasn't being completely transparent. "I believe he found somebody else to back him."

"Who?"

Rafi's eyes darted to the framed picture of him with his son on I-Day, and Pick noticed a sadness settle over him. It was understandable, given a father's love, that he might feel disappointment in who Javi had become, but it seemed somehow more pronounced.

"Rafi, we're running out of time," Pick said.

"I've had my suspicions for a while, but I believe that somebody within the Cártel de Jalisco Nueva Generación is trying to make a move on my network."

"The Cártel de Jalisco . . ."

"Nueva Generación," Rafi finished for him. "They're aggressively trying to gain new territory, and the tunnel you traveled through to reach the United States from Nuevo Laredo is an established route. It would give them an advantage they currently don't have."

"And you think they're using Javi to influence you into giving them access?"

Rafi gave a sad laugh. "Captain McCoy—"

"Call me Pick."

"Okay, Pick. I'm afraid you don't understand how Mexican cartels work."

"Then enlighten me."

"If I'm right about this, then they're not planning on using Javi to *influence* me. They're planning on using him to *replace* me."

Pick didn't like the sound of that. "Replace you?"

Rafi nodded. "I believe they offered him financial support and helped secure his early release from prison in exchange for taking over my network and aligning with Cártel de Jalisco Nueva Generación."

Pick had enough to worry about with ISIS–K terrorists from Tajikistan planning even more attacks in the United States without also having to worry about a power struggle between Mexican cartels on the southern border. But as unlikely as it seemed, Rafi was claiming that the two were connected. "Okay, so you think the Cártel de Jalisco . . ."

"Nueva Generación."

"The Cártel de Jalisco Nueva Generación turned Javi against you in exchange for helping him get out of prison." Pick was willing to accept that Javier Santiago was capable of doing something like that, but he still didn't understand how it related to the attacks in Virginia Beach or San Antonio. "But why do you think he's behind these attacks?"

Rafi started wringing his hands. If it was an act, Pick thought it was a convincing one. "Because some of my men came forward and told me that he arranged for the terrorists to use my tunnel to bring them into the United States. I still haven't heard from him since he got out of prison, but he's been in and out of Laredo, doing things behind my back."

"You don't think he's just using his new relationship with the Cártel de Jalisco Nueva Generación to stake his claim on your network?"

Rafi shook his head. "You don't understand my son, either."

Pick probably understood Javi as well as anybody could and knew what he was capable of. He just didn't want to believe it. "You think he's using his new relationship to seek revenge."

Rafi nodded. "Yes, I do."

"So, who's next?"

The elder Santiago met Pick's gaze but said nothing. That was all the confirmation Pick needed, and his stomach dropped.

"It's Hannah, isn't it?"

"I believe so, yes."

"And you brought me here so that I would stop him."

Rafi's green eyes bore into Pick with an intensity that disturbed him. "I need you to do what I couldn't."

Pick believed the legal system had worked the way it was intended to and that Javi had been justly punished. But even though he and Hannah had split up before graduation and hadn't spoken much since, he still wanted an opportunity to be alone with his former roommate and to show him how a Marine Raider handles business.

How Killer McCoy handles business.

"I need to stop the terrorists before—"

A piercing alarm echoed through the hacienda and cut him off. He shot Rafi a concerned look, but the older man was already on his feet.

"What is it?"

"Intruders."

[THREE]

Pick saw the fear etched on Rafi's face and knew immediately that they were under attack. If what his host had told him was true, then Javi had sent men to the hacienda to eliminate his father and claim the tunnel as his own. Pick didn't care about the cartel's power struggle, but he wasn't about to cede control of a smuggling route that had been used at least once by terrorists to cross the border and commit atrocities in two separate cities.

"Do you have security?" Pick asked.

"Yes, but they're positioned outside at various locations around my property. If intruders are already inside my house, then we have to assume they took out my men. We're on our own, Captain McCoy."

"It wouldn't be my first time."

Rafi suddenly looked distracted. "My wife . . ."

"Where is she?"

"In our room. Upstairs."

"Do you have any weapons?"

El Timón nodded, then moved around behind his desk and reached underneath to activate a hidden switch. Pick heard a *click* as one segment of the bookshelf—the one with the framed picture of Javi—swung away from the wall. Pick stared into the dark opening, wondering what secrets the older man had hidden inside.

"It's a safe room," he told Pick. "But I have a rack with a few rifles, pistols, and shotguns inside."

"Ammo?"

"As much as you need."

Pick hoped Rafi was right. He believed in the law of superior firepower and was going to need *a lot* of ammo. He glanced at the closed office door, then snatched the pistol off the bookshelf and tossed it to Rafi. "Get to your wife and keep her safe."

"What are you going to do?"

"What a Raider is trained to do," Pick said.

Rafi stared at the pistol in his hands for several seconds as if debating whether he could trust Pick, then turned for the door. He pressed his ear close for a moment, then opened it and darted into the hallway with his pistol stretched out in front of him. Pick watched him disappear, then turned out the light and spun for the safe room to prepare himself for combat.

Without light to illuminate the space, Pick felt around blindly for the weapons rack Rafi had told him was inside. But as his eyes adjusted to the darkness, he began to make out more than just "a few" rifles, pistols, and shotguns.

"Now, this is my kind of room," Pick muttered with a touch of admiration.

The entire back wall was adorned with a pegboard-style rack system that held various rifles, pistols, and shotguns. Pick knew that if he took his time inspecting each weapon, he would probably find several valuable pieces that belonged on display inside a museum instead of hidden in a cramped room behind the bookshelf. But he didn't have that kind of time. He needed to outfit himself with enough firepower to defend the hacienda from whomever Javi had sent to take out his old man.

Okay, I need a long gun first.

Pick looked over the rifles and plucked a suppressed short-barreled AR off the wall, then retracted the charging handle and locked the bolt to the rear. After ensuring that it was empty, he inserted a twenty-round magazine and slapped the bolt catch to chamber a round. With the first green-tipped 5.56x45-millimeter NATO cartridge loaded, he closed the dust cover, verified that the weapon was on safe, then slung it over his shoulder. He knew the rifle would do what he needed it to do, even if it hadn't been crafted with the same artistic precision as the LSA personal defense weapons Junior had provided for them in San Antonio.

Now I need a sidearm.

Just as his eyes had naturally gravitated toward the suppressed carbine decked out with an EOTech holographic sight, Pick's gaze settled on a Staccato HD P4 pistol chambered in 9 millimeter and fitted with a Trijicon RMR HD Optic and SureFire X300U-A weapon-mounted light. He pulled it off the pegboard, locked the slide back to verify its condition, then inserted a fully loaded eighteen-round magazine and released the slide to chamber a round.

Finally, he tucked a paddle-style retention holster into his waistband and slid the pistol into place. Satisfied that he was armed appropriately, he tucked two spare pistol magazines into his back pocket, then slung a satchel over his other shoulder and filled it with four AR magazines.

Pick was ready to engage the enemy.

He was ready for direct action.

Before leaving the safe room, Pick pulled out his cellphone and again dialed the "sneaky one."

Again, Randy answered. "Pick, I've been trying to run down—"

"Listen, Randy," Pick said, cutting him off. "I don't have much time. I'm in Laredo at the home of Rafael Santiago—"

"Santiago?" Randy sounded surprised.

"My old roommate's father," Pick said.

"In Laredo? Texas?"

"Yes. And we're under attack."

This time, there was no mistaking Randy's surprise. "Under attack? What the hell's going on?"

Pick's ears twitched at a sudden muffled cry that carried through the walls. He couldn't make out who had shouted, but he recognized the sounds of mortal combat with sudden clarity. "There's no time for that, Randy. Believe it or not, Javi is behind everything."

"Javi?"

"I'll explain later. For now, put all your focus into finding Hannah. We think she's the next target."

And there's no way I'm going to let Javi hurt her again.

"We'll find her, Pick."

Pick was thankful Randy hadn't asked him how.

The lessons from "A Message to Garcia" live on, he thought.

Several gunshots rang out and added to the cacophony of whatever was taking place outside Rafi's home office.

"I gotta go," Pick said, clenching his jaw in determination.

"Pick."

"Yeah?"

"Give 'em hell, Marine."

"Ooh-fucking-rah."

Pick ended the call and slipped the phone into his pocket, then unslung the rifle and brought it up to the low-ready position. He slipped from the safe room and crossed the office to the door Rafi had disappeared through only a few minutes earlier. The clamor of combat seemed to have died down, which only further encouraged Pick to hasten into battle.

With a deep breath to steel his nerves, Pick opened the door and went to war.

[FOUR]

As Pick entered the hall in a crouch, he turned left toward the foyer and immediately wished he were wearing a set of Ground Panoramic Night Vision Goggles like those he had used as a Raider. Featuring four unfilmed white phosphor image intensifier tubes, the GPNVGs provided users with an unprecedented 97-degree field of view. Far more than what he could have seen with older-style dual-tube NVGs.

And far more than he could see now in the darkened hacienda with only his naked eyes.

Pick sensed movement to his right as he stepped from the hall and quickly spun to place the EOTech's holographic reticle center mass on a dark human shape. But he hesitated.

Know your target and what's behind it.

No matter how many firefights he had been in, Pick still heard the voice of his ITC cadre cautioning him before pulling the trigger. But in this case, Pick wasn't being evaluated during Phase 2 of the MARSOC Individual Training Course. He had seen enough of the shadowed figure to recognize that it wasn't Rafi. And that the man was raising a submachine gun in Pick's direction.

He pressed back on the trigger and the suppressed rifle coughed.

Thwap!

Pick immediately followed up his first shot with a second, catching the cartel assassin in the head as his body collapsed to the ground. Without a second thought, he pivoted again to the foyer and continued his advance toward the stairs.

Even as Pick moved silently through the house, his brain scrambled to process an onslaught of new information. Though he hadn't gotten a chance to examine the gunman's weapon up close, he thought it looked like a short-barreled submachine gun with a folding stock—similar to the kind used by Mexican police and other state and municipal security forces. Pick's area of expertise was the Middle East and violent extremist organizations native to that region, but he guessed that Mexico had dirty cops, just like anywhere else in the world.

Or maybe the cartels have other ways of getting their hands on military-grade hardware.

With that thought in mind, Pick reached the curving staircase and aimed his rifle up as he took the first tread. Though he continued collecting empirical data for later analysis, his sole focus was on the sights and sounds filling the darkened hacienda. He needed to neutralize the threat before he did anything else.

At the top of the stairs, he paused when he saw a body slumped against the wall. Again, he recognized that the shape didn't belong to Rafi and probably had been the source of the cry he had heard in the safe room. The elder Santiago had at least made it to the second floor while trying to reach his wife and protect her from the invading cartel sicarios.

Pick stepped over the body and continued down the hallway.

His heart pounded inside his chest like a metronome, steady and solid. He wasn't anxious. He wasn't scared. He was in his element. And he continued taking slow and steady breaths to keep the oxygen flowing to every part of his body—especially his brain.

He'd taken only a handful of steps farther down the hall when the shrill scream of a woman echoed through the house and stopped him dead in his tracks. He spun back toward the staircase, leading with his rifle, and scanned the darkness for more armed shadows while listening to the night. At first, he heard nothing. Then, from downstairs, he heard hushed voices speaking in Spanish.

Dammit, why couldn't Castillo be here?

Without wasting an ounce more of energy lamenting his lingual deficiencies, Pick retraced his steps to the staircase and descended back to the ground floor. The voices had grown louder, and he was almost certain one belonged to a woman.

Is that Señora Santiago?

Pick's footsteps on the travertine floors echoed softly as he moved into the great room at the rear of the house. He moved cautiously but quickly, trading stealth for speed as he raced toward the sounds of hushed voices. He ignored the off-white glow of the ornamental landscape lighting through the floor-to-ceiling windows and instead focused his attention on the darkest of shadows, searching for the outline of another shooter.

Suddenly a dark shape darted across the backyard and blotted out each narrow beam of light, one by one.

Pick whipped the rifle's barrel toward the shadowed figure, just as the windows shattered with incoming gunfire, showering the great room with shards of glass.

Still unable to identify a target and afraid of letting loose a volley of his own without knowing if Rafi's wife would be caught in the crossfire, Pick took his finger off the trigger and dove left toward the gourmet kitchen. He came down hard and slid across the tile floor into an oversized island, grunting with the impact. He glanced over his shoulder at the shattered windows just as a dark shape stepped through the gaping hole, shouldering a compact submachine pistol.

Clear field of fire.

Pick didn't hesitate and aimed his suppressed carbine at the intruder, pressing back on the trigger even before the glowing EOTech reticle had settled on the man. His long gun coughed in rapid succession as Pick fired several rounds at the figure, walking each one incrementally closer.

Thwap!

When his fourth or fifth shot—he couldn't be sure which—found its mark, Pick pressed his advantage and rose into a crouch while swinging the long gun up and aiming it out into the exposed backyard. He spotted two additional gunmen preparing to make entry into the great room through the shattered windows, but they had seen him first.

He ducked back beneath the kitchen island as small-caliber bullets buzzed through the air like a swarm of angry wasps and slammed into the wall behind him. The deluge of gunfire shredded the gourmet kitchen's custom cabinetry and showered him with wooden splinters and shards of plaster. He flinched at the angry onslaught but continued working his trigger, holding the rifle above his head and firing blindly from behind cover.

But the incoming gunfire seemed only to increase in intensity as more and more shooters entered the fight.

How many more are there?

Pick's rifle fell silent as the bolt locked to the rear. He quickly retracted the rifle from above the island while reaching forward with his index finger to press the magazine release and let the empty mag fall free. Before it had clattered to the ground, he reached back for the satchel loaded with spare magazines.

The gunfire drew nearer as his fingers fumbled through the satchel's folds of fabric to find its opening, and Pick grew increasingly anxious. He suddenly longed to be wearing his Tactical Tailor chest rig with ballistic body armor and stacked magazine pouches for easy access. But that wasn't the hand he had been dealt, and there was no use wishing things were different.

With an empty long gun and his free hand frantically trying to come up with a spare magazine, Pick felt more vulnerable than ever before. He caught movement out of the corner of his eye, and amid a sudden ebb in the gunfire, Pick spotted a shadowed figure in the great room to his left.

In a rush, he abandoned his search for spare magazines and released his hold on the empty rifle, then reached back to draw the Staccato pistol from his holster and present it to his target. Using a two-handed grip, Pick activated the weapon light and fired a narrow beam of one thousand lumens at the shooter, momentarily blinding his attacker while he sighted through the Trijicon RMR HD Optic.

Pick pressed back on the trigger and was surprised by the crisp break.

Crack!

His first shot hit the intruder in the shoulder and spun him away. Pick quickly adjusted his aim and fired again.

Crack! Crack!

Unlike the suppressed carbine, the 2011-style pistol cycled with thunderclaps as balls of fire exploded from the barrel. But Pick was at home behind the pistol and easily tracked each round as it impacted his target.

Shoot and move, Pick.

With the voice of his ITC cadre again echoing in his brain, Pick rolled away from the great room and took up shelter on the opposite side of the island. He needed to get his long gun back up and running before other shooters entered the hacienda and overwhelmed him. He released his grip on the pistol with his support hand and again resumed fishing for a spare rifle magazine in the satchel. This time his fingers found the smooth polymer with ease, and he plucked it free.

"Señor McCoy," a voice called out in heavily accented English.

I'm really getting tired of people knowing who I am.

"Yeah?" he shouted back.

With practiced hands, Pick slid the pistol into the holster, then regained his grip on the carbine and guided a fresh magazine into the well.

"We have Señora Santiago," the voice shouted. "And we have you surrounded."

Good.

Pick slapped the bolt catch and chambered a fresh round.

That means I can attack in any direction.

Pick pushed himself off the tile floor and spun toward the rear of the house, thinking only of the woman being held captive by the cartel gunmen. He had never met Javi's mother and had seen his father only that one time in the Washington Navy Yard courtroom. But Pick believed she didn't deserve to be caught up in the mess her son—or husband—had made.

Two gunmen were already inside the great room, aiming their submachine guns in Pick's direction. His sudden surfacing from behind the island startled them, but they recovered quickly and sprayed the gourmet kitchen with gunfire. Pick sighted in on the first shooter and dropped him with two quick rounds to center mass.

Thwap! Thwap!

He pivoted and fired several more at the second shooter but only caught him in the arm and knocked the submachine gun from his grip. As it clattered to the ground, Pick stepped around the island and advanced forward, taking his time to align the holographic reticle on the sicario's head.

Adios, motherfucker.

Click.

Shit!

Pick tossed aside the rifle and let it whip around his body, tethered only by the nylon sling. He reached for the holstered pistol on his hip, accepting that the carbine had malfunctioned and not bothering to waste time diagnosing it. He needed to take out the sicario.

Unfortunately, the sicario had heard the *click* and was already lunging for him.

In that split second, Pick realized he wouldn't be able to bring his pistol to bear before the cartel assassin was upon him. Abandoning his draw, Pick braced himself for hand-to-hand combat, hoping that the other cartel gunmen would hold their fire while Pick grappled with their compatriot.

Crack! Crack!

No such luck.

Apparently, his hope meant nothing. Rounds continued whistling through the darkened kitchen as the muscled sicario collided with Pick and lifted him off his feet. Pick scrambled to wrap his attacker in a bear hug before coming down hard on his back. The blow knocked the wind out of him, and he smacked his head against the unforgiving travertine floors. Instantly, stars ringed his vision and his ears rang from the concussive impact. But he was still alive.

You're still in the fight, Pick.

Rounds continued pouring into the kitchen, and Pick rolled away from the windows to distance himself from the hail of gunfire while trying to gain the upper hand by maneuvering into the mount position. But any hope that the sicario was unskilled in martial arts was dashed to pieces when his attacker effectively blocked Pick's escape and began raining punches down onto him.

He reacted to the sudden violence by covering his head and neck to prevent a knockout blow while scrambling to improve his position. He again attempted to wrap his attacker in a bear hug and stop the fists from hammering into him like pistons, but he was rewarded with a sharp knee to his kidneys and a renewed flurry of follow-on punches to his head and neck. Pick grunted with each hit but avoided focusing on the damage being done to his body.

Do something!

Despite the ringing in his ears and the swarm of angry 9-millimeter wasps splitting the air overhead, Pick still managed to register the sounds of angry voices shouting to be heard over the clamor. He didn't know who they belonged to and didn't know whether he should be elated or despondent that people were shouting. His sole focus was on the man straddling him who smelled of body odor and stale cigarette smoke.

The man who showed no signs of running out of steam.

With sudden clarity, Pick remembered plebe boxing at the Naval Academy. Without any formal martial arts experience, Midshipman McCoy had come out swinging with no notion of restraint and completely drained himself before the bell had signaled the end of the first round. He had been too gassed to put up a defense in the second and hadn't lasted long enough for the bell to save him. It was the one and only time Pick had been knocked out, and he silently prayed for his attacker to make the same mistake.

But in the real world, there would be no bell. He needed to survive the onslaught and conserve his energy while waiting for the right time to exploit his attacker's mistakes.

If he ever makes any.

As the haymakers began to slow, Pick sensed the time was drawing near. Though his entire body ached from the cumulative effects of dozens of strikes, Pick noticed that they were starting to weaken. It was a subtle ebb in the torrent of punches, but it was exactly what Pick had been waiting for.

He quickly dropped his guard and reached for his pistol again, just as his attacker twisted with a fist aimed at his jaw. Pick dropped his chin into his shoulder and absorbed the blow on his cheekbone, feeling his skin split open under the man's knuckles. But it wasn't a knockout punch.

And Pick wasn't a plebe.

With every ounce of strength he had held in reserve, Pick shoved his forearm into the sicario's neck to stunt his attack while wrapping his fingers around the handgun's stippled grip. The man recognized what Pick was attempting to do and grunted with frustration, but his initial attack had sapped him of his strength.

"Should've paced yourself," Pick whispered.

He completed the draw, tilted the pistol's barrel up into the sicario's stomach, and squeezed the trigger with the fervor of a man who had been on the cusp of defeat. Pick felt the man's body twitch and jerk as it absorbed each round of 9-millimeter parabellum. But he continued squeezing the trigger until the slide had locked back to the rear and the trigger broke with a *click*.

In the sudden ensuing silence, Pick realized that the remaining cartel gunmen had also stopped shooting. He pushed the lifeless sicario off him and reached back for a spare pistol magazine in his back pocket, but froze when a brilliant beam of light shone directly into his face.

"Drop the gun!"

XIX

[ONE]

The White House Situation Room

The White House

1600 Pennsylvania Avenue NW

Washington, D.C.

0610 3 April 2026

President Natalie Cohen took her place at the head of the table and gestured for those already gathered there to sit. She hadn't been looking forward to this meeting but knew she could put it off no longer. Her predecessors might have believed in the President's right to unilaterally issue proclamations—whether it came to matters of national security or not—but she didn't share the same opinion.

And yet, here you are.

"Thank you, everyone, for coming," Natalie said, while arranging the folders in front of her into a neat stack. "Before we begin with the morning's agenda, I need to clear the air."

She saw several members squirming uncomfortably in their seats, but only her Director of National Intelligence, Marty Fleiss, appeared unfazed. She knew that was because he had already voiced his objections over the matter she was about to discuss and had nothing further to say on the topic.

"When I ran for President, I vowed to be the candidate of transparency and cooperation. As secretary of state, I witnessed my predecessors skirt their Constitutional obligations for oversight in favor of expediency. And I swore I would not do the same thing once elected President."

Marty turned to look at her, and they locked eyes.

"Unfortunately, I have done just that," she said.

There were no impassioned outbursts or even hushed murmurs. Whether those gathered around the conference room table agreed with her decision or not, they understood their roles in the administration and would wait to collect all the facts before offering their opinions.

"In 2005, the President issued a Finding to establish what became known as the Office of Organizational Analysis. This Finding formalized the appointment of an Army Special Forces major as its chief."

Benjamin Drake, her stocky secretary of defense, cleared his throat.

Natalie fixed her gaze on him but reminded herself that the purpose of the meeting was to ensure that she didn't fall into the trap of believing she was above the law. "Yes, Ben? You have something you'd like to say?"

The retired Marine Corps four-star general cleared his throat again and shifted in his seat to face her. "I'm sorry, Madam President, but did you say an Army *major* was appointed as its chief?"

She nodded. "Yes, I did."

"I know you never served . . ." The comment hung in the air for a beat, long enough for her to bristle at the notion that her lifetime of service somehow hadn't counted because it wasn't in uniform. "But the chain of command exists for a reason. Giving an Army major the kind of authority warranted under the title of *Chief* is both reckless and contrary to good order and discipline."

Natalie's neck flushed with the accusation, but she kept her emotions in check. It was exactly this kind of pushback she expected in her administration.

Even from pompous assholes like Ben.

"I completely agree," she said, smiling at the surprised look on his face. "And so did my predecessor. The OOA was initially placed under the purview of the secretary of homeland security—"

"Matt Hall?" the current secretary asked.

"Yes, Thomas."

"Makes sense," Secretary Drake said. "Didn't they serve together in Vietnam?"

Thomas Kincaid nodded. "I believe they did—"

"Gentlemen." Secretary of State Frank Malone's voice boomed over their sidebar discussion. At six-foot-four and two hundred and forty-five pounds, the fifty-nine-year-old Malone was an imposing figure. "Your President has something she would like to say."

Secretaries Benjamin Drake and Thomas Kincaid fell silent.

Natalie looked at Frank and nodded her thanks before continuing. "The Office of Organizational Analysis eventually came to fall under the Director of National Intelligence before it was shut down—rightfully—because of a lack of oversight."

Secretary Drake grunted with apparent satisfaction.

"But I have resurrected it."

His grunt ended in what sounded like a choke. "Excuse me?"

Natalie reached over and placed her hand on Secretary Malone's forearm. "When Frank was kidnapped in Cairo two weeks ago, I brought the Presidential Agent out of retirement."

She kept her eyes locked on her secretary of defense, avoiding the almost overwhelming temptation to look at Frank Malone. As far as the secretary of state knew, the Navy's JSOC task force had orchestrated his rescue.

"Is that what we're calling this major? The *Presidential Agent*?"

Natalie could tell from his indignant tone what he thought about a lowly major being given that kind of authority. "Actually, no. Four days ago, I issued a Presidential Finding that appointed a Marine Corps captain as chief, Office of Organizational Analysis, within the Office of the Director of National Intelligence. He reports directly to Marty, who reports directly to me."

The secretary of defense did not appear pleased with that arrangement. "A Marine Corps captain . . ."

"His name is P.K. McCoy Jr.," Marty said, picking up where Natalie left off.

"Killer McCoy's son?" Benjamin sounded surprised.

Marty nodded at Secretary Drake.

"Who's Killer McCoy?" Thomas asked.

"General Pick 'Killer' McCoy," the secretary of defense answered with some reverence. "He retired as the Deputy Commandant for Aviation. A fighter ace in Vietnam and legend in the Marine Corps fighter community."

"It sounds like you know him," Thomas said.

"I do." Secretary Drake looked embarrassed as he turned to face Natalie. "And if this captain is anything like his old man, you couldn't have appointed a better person, Madam President."

She nodded her thanks, knowing that the compliment didn't mean he relished the idea of having a junior member of the military in a position only two steps removed from the President. "As I was saying, I believe in transparency and cooperation and do not intend for Captain McCoy to run an organization without oversight."

Secretary Drake lifted a hesitant finger. "What about the Army major?"

"He retired as a colonel," Marty offered.

"That's my point," the secretary continued. "If you want oversight, maybe we could offer this colonel—"

"Castillo," Marty said. "His name is Carlos Guillermo Castillo."

"Maybe we could offer Colonel Castillo a Senior Executive Service position to provide oversight for the Office of Organizational Analysis."

Natalie had been considering that exact thing before the attack in Virginia Beach. So far, Captain McCoy had performed remarkably well under pressure—both in the operation to rescue Frank Malone and in the most recent terrorist attack in San Antonio—but she knew he was out of his league. He still needed somebody to provide him with guidance and help navigating the treacherous swamp that was the District of Columbia.

"That's a great idea, Ben," she said. "But unfortunately, we'll need to table that discussion for another time. Five days ago, Colonel Castillo was critically injured attempting to stop the terrorist attack in Virginia Beach."

Again, she saw Frank Malone flash a look in her direction, and she ignored it.

"Was he the target of the attack?" Ben asked, more astutely than she would have expected.

"Unknown," Marty replied. "Discovering the organization or organizations behind the attacks and their motives is the sole purpose of the Presidential Finding."

"What's his prognosis?"

"He's currently in intensive care," Natalie said.

"So, you've given Captain McCoy carte blanche to discover who's behind the attacks," Ben concluded.

She nodded.

Marty spoke up. "Like the President said, Captain McCoy reports directly to me, and I report directly to her. He's on a short leash, Ben."

"I'd still feel better—"

"Your objection has been noted, Mr. Secretary."

Natalie grimaced. This was not at all how she had hoped for her morning to start. She knew that as a retired four-star general and former commander of the Special Operations Command, Marty was more than capable of standing up to the secretary of defense. But transparency wasn't the only attribute she aspired to promote within her administration.

"Gentlemen," she said, her tone conveying that the time for discussion had ended. "The purpose of this meeting was to make you aware of my decision to reinstate the Office of Organizational Analysis. The manner in which it will be run and how best to provide the necessary oversight is a topic for discussion at a later time. Currently, Captain McCoy is following a lead with a former asset of the Central Intelligence Agency who might be able to shed some light on how these terrorists entered the country. We believe that the attacks in Virginia Beach and San Antonio—"

"They were related?" Secretary Kincaid asked.

Natalie held up her hand to forestall further interruptions. "We believe that the attacks in Virginia Beach and San Antonio are part of a greater plot, and time is of the essence to determine when and where the terrorists will attack again. *That* is what's important right now, not who gets to keep Captain McCoy under their thumb. Do I make myself clear?"

"Yes, Madam President," Secretary Kincaid replied.

She shot a look at the secretary of defense. "Ben?"

"Yes, Madam President."

"Very well. Then let's get down to business—"

Before she could open the first folder sitting in front of her, the conference room door opened, and the senior director for the White House Situation Room entered. Natalie remained still, with both palms flat on the table in front of her, as he leaned down and whispered in her ear.

"You have a call from Captain McCoy, Madam President."

Natalie jumped to her feet and headed for the door.

"Marty, Ben, will you please join me?"

Without further explanation, President Cohen left the conference room and walked into the adjacent huddle room, where a phone was placed in the middle of a much smaller circular table. She leaned over it, anxiously waiting until both her Director of National Intelligence and secretary of defense had joined her.

When the door clicked shut, she stabbed at the blinking light on the phone to put the call on speaker.

"This is the President, Captain McCoy."

"Good morning, Madam President," Pick replied.

"You're on speaker with Director Fleiss and Secretary Drake," she added.

"Good to hear from you, son," Marty said. "How's Cozumel?"

Natalie saw Secretary Drake flash an odd look at Marty, and she couldn't help but grin. She was certain the retired Marine Corps general was wondering what kind of leads had taken the captain and the fledgling Office of Organizational Analysis to a Mexican island in the Caribbean.

"Actually, I'm back in Texas now," Pick said.

"Maybe you should start from the beginning, McCoy."

"Is that General Drake?"

"It is," the secretary of defense said. "How's your dad?"

"With respect, Mr. Secretary, we have more important matters to discuss," Pick responded, much to Natalie's amusement. "But he's fine."

Maybe it was something ingrained in the type of men who pursued careers in special operations, but Natalie could have seen Castillo saying something very similar. "What do you have for us, Captain McCoy?"

There was a brief pause on the other end, and for a moment Natalie thought the call might have been dropped.

But then he spoke. "I met with Aleksandr Pevsner in Cozumel who introduced me to a business associate with ties to Cártel del Noreste."

"Bunch of thugs," Ben muttered.

Natalie flashed him a dirty look, and he clamped his mouth shut.

"They flew me to Nuevo Laredo and showed me the entrance to a tunnel into the United States."

Marty cleared his throat. "Captain McCoy, this is Director Fleiss. Correct me if I'm wrong, but doesn't the Rio Grande flow along that part of the border?"

"Yes, sir, it does."

"And do you really think such a tunnel exists?"

"Yes, sir, I do."

Secretary Drake stabbed at the phone to place it on mute. "This is *exactly* why we need somebody with more seniority heading up this . . . this . . ." He grew flustered. "Whatever *this* is."

Natalie reached for the phone and took it off mute. "Why do you believe that, Captain McCoy?"

"Because I entered the tunnel in Mexico and exited in Texas."

She could tell Secretary Drake was about to protest, so she held up her hand as a subtle reminder for him to bite his tongue. "Go on, Pick."

"The man who met me there stated that the tunnel belonged to Cártel del Noreste, but that they had no previous knowledge of its use to transport terrorists across the border undetected."

"And you believe this man?" Marty asked.

"Yes, sir, I do."

"Does he know who's behind these attacks?"

"Yes, sir," Pick said, then hesitated before continuing. "He believes that a man by the name of Javier Santiago has sided with Cártel de Jalisco Nueva Generación to take over the tunnel and associated smuggling network."

Natalie made eye contact with Marty and mouthed, *Who's Javier Santiago?*

He shrugged. "Son, we've never heard that name before. Is he a Mexican citizen?"

"No, sir. He's American," Pick replied.

"How can you be so sure?" Secretary Drake asked, still not believing that a lowly captain could have such a firm grasp on the situation.

"Because he was my roommate at the Naval Academy."

[TWO]

Hacienda Puerto

Laredo, Texas

0620 3 April 2026

"Your roommate? What the hell's going on, McCoy?"

Pick pulled the phone away from his ear as the secretary's voice boomed across the line. He had known General Drake his entire life and wasn't all that surprised by the outburst.

"Mr. Secretary, I'm afraid I don't have all the answers for you,"

Pick replied, then glanced over his shoulder through what remained of the panoramic floor-to-ceiling windows, to where law enforcement officers from a multitude of agencies had swarmed the gourmet kitchen. He was thankful the local police showed up when they had, but it was quickly becoming a zoo.

"Isn't that your job?" Secretary Drake asked.

"With respect," President Cohen said, "I thought I made it perfectly clear that I'm the only one with the authority to tell Captain McCoy what his job is."

Pick grinned at the President's testy response.

"Yes, Madam President. My apologies."

"But the secretary's right . . ."

His smile vanished.

"Your appointment as chief, Office of Organizational Analysis, gave you all the necessary authorities and resources to ensure you have the answers to our questions."

"Yes, Madam President," Pick said, aware that his response sounded even more sheepish than the secretary's.

"Going forward, I expect you to provide Director Fleiss with routine updates. No more surprises, Captain McCoy. Is that clear?"

He thought an illicit midnight tunnel crossing and early-morning gunfight between rival cartels were two very good excuses. But he couldn't tell her that. "Crystal, Madam President."

There was a brief pause on the other end before the President's voice came through again. "Now would be an excellent time to start."

Pick took a moment to survey the darkness enveloping the estate before beginning. "Initially, we believed the attacks were somehow connected to Castillo—possibly in response to actions he had taken while serving as Presidential Agent. Though nothing directly connected the attack in San Antonio to Doña Alicia, it was too significant to dismiss as a simple coincidence."

"Do you have evidence that contradicts that theory?" Marty Fleiss asked.

"Not exactly, sir. While that theory could still prove correct, I believe the evidence suggests an alternative motive."

"Which is?"

"Revenge," Pick said.

Secretary Drake didn't bother trying to hide his skepticism. "For?"

"When I was at the Naval Academy, my roommate sexually assaulted a fellow midshipman. I testified against him at his court-martial, and the judge sentenced him to thirty years in prison."

"This was what, ten years ago?"

"Twelve," Pick corrected. "But he was released early."

Pick didn't know President Cohen all that well, but he could imagine she was shooting daggers with her eyes into the secretary of defense for allowing someone like Javi to be released from prison early.

"I'll look into it, Madam President," Secretary Drake said, all but confirming Pick's suspicions.

"Why do you think these attacks are related to that case?" Director Fleiss asked.

"Aside from the fact that his own father told me that just before cartel sicarios raided his Laredo home, we've linked a few of the victims in each shooting to this case."

"Wait just a second," Secretary Drake said. "Cartel sicarios?"

To Pick, that wasn't the important part of what he had just said. But he patiently responded to the query. "Yes, Mr. Secretary. Apparently, I landed in the middle of some type of power struggle between rival cartels that spilled over onto American soil."

And something about it doesn't seem quite right.

"What happened?"

"I found myself in a gunfight until local police showed up and scared off the attackers."

But their sudden retreat and Rafi's disappearance seem a little too convenient, Pick thought.

"What about the victims?" President Cohen asked, steering their discussion back to the matter at hand. "Who did you link to that case?"

Pick shook off his unease before responding. "Liam McIntyre, the presiding judge in Javier Santiago's court-martial, was killed in the Virginia Beach attack. And our company officer at the time, a Marine infantry officer, was one of the Alamo Rangers who responded to the attack in San Antonio. He was killed in the firefight."

"Who else might be on a list of potential targets?" Director Fleiss asked.

Pick didn't need to consult the list he had asked Randy to come up with to know who was at the top. "Obviously, I'm on there."

"Does he know where you are?"

Pick glanced over his shoulder again just as an FBI special agent stepped through the shattered window frame and into the backyard. "You mean, does he know I'm at his parents' house? No. I don't think so."

But that didn't seem to be what the DNI had in mind. "A little over two weeks ago you were in Iraq with your Raider team. Does he know you're back in the United States?"

Pick thought about it for a moment and realized that he hadn't even told his parents he was back. Things had happened so fast. The pace at which he had been recalled from Iraq and rushed into action to rescue the secretary of state hadn't left him with much time to reconnect with friends and family. He had visited Coach Luis at the Naval Academy only because of its proximity to Washington, D.C.

"No, sir. As far as I know, few people know where I am. Those who do are on my team and trying to stop the next attack."

"Who else?" President Cohen asked.

Pick stopped his pacing when the FBI special agent halted directly in front of him with a phone in his hand. He knew the agent wanted a word and held up a hand to indicate that he would be with him shortly.

"Hannah," Pick muttered.

Secretary Drake didn't sound amused. "Speak up, Captain."

"The midshipman he sexually assaulted," Pick explained. "Hannah Rosen."

"Where is she now?" the President asked.

"I don't know," Pick replied.

Even after ending their romantic relationship, Pick and Hannah had had every intention of remaining close friends. But as relationships forged in the military often do, they lost touch over the years.

"Special Agent McCoy?"

Pick shot the FBI special agent a dirty look and covered up the handset. "I'm on the phone."

"This is important—"

"What's your name?"

"Special Agent Mark Robbins. I'm the—"

"I don't really care, Mark," Pick said, cutting him off. "I'm on the phone with the President right now."

Pick could tell the FBI special agent didn't believe him, but he didn't care. He took his hand off the phone and held it up to his ear again. "I apologize for the interruption, Madam President," he said, just loud enough for Robbins to hear.

"Did he just call you Special Agent?" Secretary Drake asked.

Pick sighed. "It's a long story, Mr. Secretary."

The President didn't seem interested. "What's your next move, Captain McCoy?"

"I need to find Hannah," he said.

For the first time in days, it was the only thing that made sense.

[THREE]

After Pick ended the call, he pocketed the phone and turned back to Special Agent Robbins, who had a look of annoyance on his face—clearly not used to being dismissed like a rookie on his first assignment. But Pick had more important things to worry about than whether he had upset the FBI agent.

"Was that really the President?"

Pick nodded. "It was."

If anything, Robbins's scowl only seemed to deepen. "We have officers from the Laredo Police Department and deputies from the Webb County Sheriff's Office inside the house. Rangers from Company D are on their way here from Weslaco." He tapped on his windbreaker's gold-printed FBI letters over his left breast. "And I'm here because the Federal Bureau of Investigation wants to know what happened. But I guess I'm just a little fuzzy on how the Secret Service fits into all this."

Pick was a little fuzzy on how the police managed to conveniently show up just as he was about to be overrun. But he was more worried that Rafi had disappeared during the gunfight. He knew he had the authority to brief Robbins on the Presidential Finding, but until he understood what was really going on, he wanted to keep the details of his mission close to the vest. So, he kept his answer vague.

"The President sent me."

The FBI agent's eyes narrowed. "Did she also send you to San Antonio?"

Pick shouldn't have been surprised. He had used the Secret Service credentials that Deputy Director Joel Isaacson had given him to soften the blow of being smack-dab in the middle of a shootout at Texas's most revered landmark. He should have expected the police to run his name and discover he had been there, too.

"In a manner of speaking," Pick replied.

"Cut the crap, McCoy," Robbins fired back. "You've been leaving behind a trail of dead bodies everywhere."

The comment struck a nerve. It was eerily similar to something Castillo had said to him almost two weeks earlier in Cairo—reminding him that he was never too far from escaping the stigma his grandfather had earned as a private first class in Shanghai.

Killer McCoy.

"Okay, Robbins. What I'm about to tell you is classified Top Secret Presidential." McCoy paused long enough for the balding G-man to nod his understanding before continuing. "Last Sunday, terrorists affiliated with the Islamic State–Khorasan Province opened fire on the Virginia Beach oceanfront, killing over thirty and wounding twice that. During our investigation—"

"Whose? The Secret Service?"

Pick shot him a dirty look but plowed on. "We discovered a connection to a plot in San Antonio. By the time we arrived, the attack was already underway."

Robbins didn't seem appeased. "And you just *happened* to be armed with custom-made personal defense weapons from Lone Star Armory? That's military-grade stuff."

Pick didn't have the heart to tell him that "military-grade" was actually of far lesser quality than the weaponry Junior had procured for them. He also chose to ignore the unspoken accusation that "Killer" McCoy was prone to leaving a trail of dead bodies everywhere he went, and forged on with his explanation. "I was in San Antonio because the President issued a Finding ordering me to determine the identity of the terrorists involved and to render them harmless. My investigation led me there."

"And two FBI special agents and three Alamo Rangers paid the price."

Pick locked eyes with the federal agent and took several breaths to calm himself before continuing. "Did you know them?"

"I didn't have to know them to care—"

"I did," Pick said. "One of the Alamo Rangers, at least."

Robbins snapped his mouth shut.

"So, before you lecture me on the loss of life, you should know that my sole focus is on finding those responsible and bringing them to justice."

Robbins glanced back at the house, where deputies and officers were combing the crime scene for evidence, then lowered his chin to his chest and sighed. "Special Agent McCoy—"

"Call me Pick."

Robbins looked up. "Okay, Pick. I've been in South Texas for a long time and have seen a thing or two."

"I'm sure you have."

The FBI special agent pointed at the house. "This looks a lot like a cartel hit to me, not another terrorist attack."

"I think you're right about that," Pick said.

"Then I'm sure you can understand my confusion at finding you in the home of a prominent local businessman after cartel gunmen decided to use it for target practice."

Pick knew Robbins was one of the good guys who was only trying to do his job. "I'm afraid I can't give you any more information than I already have."

"You don't have any ideas what happened to Mr. Santiago? Or who could have wanted him dead?"

His son? Cártel de Jalisco Nueva Generación? Take your pick.

"No, I don't."

"And no idea who's to blame for the terrorist attacks?"

Other than Javi and ISIS–K?

"Not a clue," Pick said.

Robbins hung his head again. "You're not being very helpful."

Pick looked past the special agent and into the house, again wondering what happened to Rafi and his wife. For the moment, it seemed that Javi's plan to forcibly take over his father's network and deliver it to the *Cártel de Jalisco Nueva Generación* had succeeded. That left only his plan of going after Hannah unresolved. And Pick was going to do everything in his power to see that it remained that way.

"Is there anything else I can do for you, Special Agent Robbins?"

The federal agent shook his head and plucked a business card from his coat pocket just as Pick's phone started vibrating with an incoming call. "If you come across anything in your investigation that might be helpful to us . . ."

Robbins trailed off as Pick accepted the business card and stole a glance at the caller ID.

Sneaky one.

"I'll be sure to give you a call," Pick said.

Robbins took the hint, nodded, and turned back for the house. Pick waited until the special agent was out of earshot before answering the phone.

"Talk to me."

"We found her," Randy said.

[ONE]

Signature Aviation

Laredo International Airport

4805 Maher Avenue

Laredo, Texas

0715 3 April 2026

Pick McCoy stood on the flight line and listened to the wind whipping across the tarmac as he watched the growing glow on the eastern horizon. It was eerily quiet and felt a bit like the calm before the storm. Randy had told Pick they were loading up on the Agency's Gulfstream V in San Antonio and would be wheels-up within the hour to pick him up in Laredo before heading east. They had found Hannah, and he needed to get to her.

"Of all the places," Pick muttered.

He shouldn't have been all that surprised that Hannah had been selected for a flag aide position. Or even that she had been assigned to the Superintendent's staff at the U.S. Naval Academy. She had always been a gregarious and model midshipman, so it was no wonder she had continued that trend as an officer.

But he still hadn't expected things to come full circle.

Pick's eyes twitched up to the deep blue sky when his ears caught the high-pitched whine of a business jet on approach to the airport. He glanced at his Critical Mechanics SOF Mk-1 dive watch with some satisfaction.

Right on time.

He spotted the Gulfstream's navigation lights and followed it through the sky as it descended from the north and touched down on the inboard parallel runway. The luxury business jet rolled to the end, where it momentarily disappeared behind a row of hangars on the south end of the large parking apron.

Pick glanced over his shoulder, toward where a ground crew from the fixed base operator had already taken up position to receive the Gulfstream. If what Randy had told him was true, they probably didn't need to take on gas and would delay only long enough for Pick to climb aboard before returning to the runway and blasting off for the thirteen-hundred-mile flight across the eastern United States to the nation's capital.

A few seconds later, the Gulfstream came back into view and turned onto the ramp. The space in front of Signature Aviation was largely vacant, and the ground crew held up lighted wands to guide the business jet into its parking space only feet from where Pick was standing. To his surprise, the engines began spooling down before the entry door opened and the ladder was lowered into place.

Randy appeared a few seconds later, bounding down the steps to greet him.

"Have you gotten in touch with her yet?" Pick asked.

Randy shook his head. "We've made several calls to the Academy but keep getting the runaround. You ready to go?"

Pick nodded. "Why'd you shut down? Thought we were in a hurry."

Randy hooked a thumb over his shoulder and gestured to the jet. "Go on up and make yourself comfortable. We're just going to top off the tanks, and I'll be right back."

Pick knew the Gulfstream's range far exceeded the distance they would need to fly to get to Washington, D.C. "Do we really need the gas?"

"It's poor form to stop in and not fill up," Randy said, slapping Pick on the back as he breezed past on his way to the FBO's office. "Like I said, it shouldn't take long. I need to go pay for the gas, but Junior's waiting to talk to you."

Pick didn't like the sound of that.

"Did Svetlana come?"

Randy shook his head. "She flew to Virginia Beach to be with Charley."

Pick had been hoping to talk to her about the business Sophie and Elena had with the Cártel del Noreste, but that could wait until later. He was itching to get into the air, and he bounded up the steps as a fuel truck pulled up to the business jet and came to a stop.

Hannah was in danger, and he couldn't get to her fast enough.

Why won't she answer the damn phone?

After climbing aboard, Pick poked his head into the cockpit and greeted Dick Miller, who was busy filing their flight plan to Ronald Reagan Washington National Airport in Virginia. There were other airports in the area that could have accommodated the Agency's Gulfstream V—including Baltimore/Washington International—but the business jet was based at Reagan, and that seemed the most logical choice.

Especially if he'd had any success in convincing the DNI to transport them from the commercial airport to Maryland's state capital by helicopter.

"Any word yet on the chopper?" Pick asked.

U.S. Army Major H. Richard Miller Jr. (retired) glanced up at Pick and shook his head. "Might want to talk to Junior about that one."

"Why does everyone keep saying that?"

The six-foot-two black native of Philadelphia shrugged and returned to what he was doing on the iPad. Pick backed out of the cockpit and turned toward the rear of the plane, nearly bumping into Junior.

"Hiya, boss," the spook said.

The look on his face was characteristically blank.

That is one person I never want to play poker with.

"Why do I keep getting the feeling you're about to give me some bad news?"

"You know that chopper you wanted to use to get to Annapolis?"

It felt like an invisible hand had wrapped its fingers around Pick's heart and was slowly squeezing. "Yeah?"

"It's a no go."

From the moment the President had chosen Pick to lead the Office of Organizational Analysis, he had known he was only two rungs beneath the President of the United States. On paper, at least. With her weight behind him, it should be a simple matter to remove any obstacles or barriers to success. He pulled out his phone.

"Who are you calling?" Junior asked.

"The President."

Pick dialed the number for the White House switchboard and brought the phone to his ear. Within seconds, a woman's voice answered.

"White House."

"This is Captain P.K. McCoy for the President," he said, surprised at how natural it sounded.

"The President is unavailable, Captain," the operator said. "Would you like me to transfer you to the White House chief of staff?"

Pick clenched his jaw in frustration. "Can you patch me through to the Office of the Director of National Intelligence?"

There was a pause on the other end.

"Are you still there?" he asked.

"Wait one."

The line went silent, and Pick pulled the phone away from his ear to make sure the call hadn't been dropped. The operator had probably put him on hold to consult with her supervisors about whether a lowly Marine Corps captain warranted unfettered access to the Director of National Intelligence—let alone the President.

"Director Fleiss already shot it down," Junior whispered. "The President—"

But Pick held up a finger to stop him, letting the spook know he wasn't interested in excuses.

Moments later, the operator returned with a cheerful, "Director Fleiss, I have Captain P.K. McCoy on the line."

"Thank you," the DNI said. "Captain?"

"Sir, I'm sorry to bother you . . ."

He trailed off as he locked eyes with Junior, still unable to read his expression.

"I'm a bit busy at the moment, Captain. Is there something I can help you with?"

"Yes, sir. We're about to take off from Laredo for Washington Reagan, and we'll need to get to Annapolis as quickly as possible—"

There was an audible sigh on the other end. "I presume your people already told you I said no."

It was a statement, not a question.

"Yes, sir. But this is a matter of—"

"Captain McCoy." Director Fleiss paused to make sure he had Pick's attention before continuing. "By the time you arrive in Washington, the Secret Service will have already shut down the airspace around Annapolis in preparation for the President's visit."

Pick suddenly felt sick to his stomach.

"The President's visit?"

"Your people should have also told you that the President has accepted the Superintendent's invitation to be the reviewing dignitary at the Naval Academy's formal parade."

"When?"

"Today," Fleiss responded.

Pick pinched his eyes shut. "But formal parades are only held on Fridays."

"Today *is* Friday."

With as much as he had been traveling, Pick wasn't surprised he had lost track of time. But he couldn't get over the thought that with Hannah as the most likely next target, her proximity to the Superintendent meant that the admiral might become collateral damage. And with the admiral standing right next to the President when the Brigade of Midshipmen pass in review during the formal parade, the President would be in danger.

"We need to call it off," Pick said.

Director Fleiss seemed stunned by the suggestion. "Why?"

"Because we have reason to believe that Javier Santiago's next target—"

Fleiss cut him off. "Is Hannah Rosen. Yes, you told us that already."

Pick bit his tongue to prevent himself from giving the retired general a scathing rebuke for interrupting him when he clearly didn't understand what was at stake. Instead, he took several deep breaths and said, "Yes, but I haven't yet had the chance to tell you that we learned she's been assigned to the Naval Academy as the Superintendent's flag aide."

"The Naval Academy . . ."

It sounded like the DNI was beginning to understand, but Pick decided to speed the process along. "Right where the President is supposed to be later today."

"How soon can you get up here?"

Now he's getting it.

Pick glanced at his watch, added three and a half hours for the flight time, and accounted for the change in time zones. "We should be able to land at Reagan around twelve-thirty," Pick said. "One, at the latest."

"Okay," Fleiss said. "I'm going to speak with the Secret Service. Get here as fast as you can."

To Pick, the solution seemed simple. "Just have her call it off."

"I've got some calls to make."

"Sir, we still haven't been able to get in touch with Hannah."

The Director of National Intelligence exhaled loudly in frustration. "I'll have the Secret Service run her down. Just get here as fast as you can."

"Sir—"

The phone went dead, and Pick looked up at Junior. This time, his expression was unmistakable.

"You think the President is in danger?"

Pick swallowed back the lump in his throat and nodded.

[TWO]

Aboard Gulfstream V

33.67 degrees North Latitude

86.89 degrees West Longitude

En route to Washington, D.C.

1045 3 April 2026

Randy had been true to his word, and they didn't waste any time on the ground in Laredo before Dick Miller fired up the luxury business jet and took off again. Since learning Castillo had been wounded in Virginia Beach, and especially after the attack on the Alamo in San Antonio, Pick had felt like he was in a perpetual race against the clock. But now that he knew who was behind the attacks and who the most likely next target would be, his unease had ratcheted up a notch.

Pick slammed the phone down in frustration. All his attempts at reaching somebody at the Naval Academy who could put him in touch with Hannah had failed. He was running out of options almost as fast as he was running out of time.

"What are we gonna do if the President doesn't call off her visit?" Ani asked.

Pick really didn't think that was likely. He had been a supervisory special agent of the United States Secret Service for only five days, but he had complete faith and confidence in their ability to keep the President out of harm's way.

"The Secret Service will never allow it," Pick said.

"They'll never allow it if there's a credible threat to the President," Junior corrected.

Ani whipped her head in Junior's direction. "Don't you think the attacks in Virginia Beach and San Antonio are proof enough of a credible threat?"

"Not to the President," he countered. "If everything Pick learned in Laredo is true, then Hannah Rosen is the target. Not the President."

"But what if they're in the same place at the same time?"

Pick leaned back in his plush leather seat and listened to Junior and Ani arguing over the semantics of a potential terrorist attack. Even if the President ended up canceling her visit, that didn't alleviate his obligation to stop Javi before he harmed anyone else.

"For all we know, Hannah's already dead."

Pick's stomach twisted painfully as he scooped up the phone to make another fruitless phone call while shooting daggers with his eyes in Junior's direction.

"Sorry, boss," he said. "I just meant that the President is only in danger if Hannah is there when she is. If we can't convince President Cohen to cancel her visit, maybe we can reach Hannah and convince her to call in sick."

"You don't know Hannah like I do," Pick said, holding his thumb over the phone's keypad. "Besides, we don't know what Javi has planned. He could have already planted an improvised explosive device to be detonated at a specific time or triggered by a specific event. He's already shown he doesn't care how many innocent people he kills. Just as long as he gets his revenge."

"But if he misses her, he misses his opportunity," Ani argued.

"You don't know Javi like I do," Pick said.

He's a monster.

"But you really think he could have already planted something?" she asked. "On the grounds of the United States Naval Academy?"

Pick nodded. "The Academy has over one hundred thousand

visitors every year. What's one more? I know you'd like to think it's a hardened military facility, but that's just not true. And don't forget, Javi spent a year living there and knows how to get on and off the Yard without being caught. If anybody can pull this off, he can."

"There's just one thing that has me bothered," Junior said.

Pick replaced the phone in the cradle mounted on the bulkhead and leaned forward in his seat. "What's that?"

"In both the attacks, in Virginia Beach and San Antonio, he used proxies from Tajikistan. He wasn't physically present for either one and relied on ISIS–K terrorists to carry out the attacks. What makes you think this will be any different?"

That thought had been nagging at Pick, too. Even if they succeeded in arresting the terrorists in Annapolis before the formal parade, it meant they had only delayed the attack. Not prevented it. Hannah would be at risk for as long as Javi was still walking around free.

"Because he's your textbook narcissist," Pick said with more confidence than he actually felt. "He'll want to be there in person to bask in the glory of his masterpiece."

Junior stared back at him without giving away what he thought of Pick's assessment.

"Okay, but we still think he's got something big planned, right?" Ani asked. "After the first two attacks, this one will have to be pretty spectacular to really make a statement. If you think Hannah is his final target, then it's got to make a splash."

It tore Pick up inside to discuss Hannah's looming assassination in such a casual manner. But whether he liked it or not, he needed to face the reality of what they were up against if he wanted to succeed in stopping his former roommate. "Right," he said, his voice little more than a whisper.

"You mentioned IEDs," Ani continued. "Do you think that's something he's capable of?"

"Other than plebe chemistry, they didn't really teach us how to blow things up at the Academy." Pick chewed on the inside of his cheek. "But who knows what he learned while he was in prison."

Or what skills and weapons the terrorists brought with them when they snuck across the border.

"Other than explosives, what else would make a major statement?" Ani asked.

"I'd say taking out the President of the United States would make a pretty big statement," Junior retorted.

"So, maybe she *is* the target."

Pick shook his head. "A happy coincidence, maybe. Or collateral damage Javi could exploit as cover for his true purpose. But I really don't think he gives a shit if the President lives or dies."

Though he probably should, given his new partnership. The Vice President has been even more vocal than President Cohen on the topic of illicit drugs.

"Then I guess we'd better hope we can catch him before it's too late," Ani said.

Not for the first time, Pick wished he had dealt with Javi back when they were midshipmen. He picked up the phone and dialed the Academy's main office.

Again.

[THREE]

Ronald Reagan Washington National Airport

Arlington, Virginia

1250 3 April 2026

A little more than an hour later, they were no closer to finding Hannah when the Agency Gulfstream V flew the river visual from the south and touched down on Runway 1 at Reagan National Airport. As they exited the runway, Pick looked through his window on the right side of the plane at the Washington Monument standing tall across the Potomac.

"Looks like we've got company," Randy said over the business jet's public-address system.

Pick glanced across the aisle at Junior, whose face was pressed against the window on the opposite side of the plane. The spook leaned back and turned to Pick. "Lots of flashing lights out there."

"So much for clandestine," Pick muttered.

After clearing the runway, they taxied south while Pick prepared to make a hasty exit from the business jet. Without a helicopter flying them to Annapolis, he knew they would be at the mercy of fickle beltway traffic. And Pick had spent enough time in the National Capital Region to know that was the one thing he didn't want to put his faith in when the lives of the President and Hannah were at stake.

As they rounded the banjo-looking south terminal, Pick spotted the orange-and-white painted Coast Guard C-37A Gulfstream V his team had borrowed before Director Fleiss had arranged for something less conspicuous. It was parked on the ramp next to Signature Aviation, but Pick didn't think they were too worried about their conspicuousness given the law enforcement activity surrounding their arrival.

"Well, this will be interesting," he muttered.

The jet came to a stop, and Pick jumped up before the twin Rolls-Royce turbofan engines began winding down. He opened the boarding door and lowered the ladder, stunned to see a crowd of men and women in suits surrounding a host of black government SUVs.

Pick recognized only one of them.

"Deputy Director Isaacson," Pick said as he descended the ladder. "I wasn't expecting you here."

"I thought I told you to call me Joel," he said, stretching out his hand to greet Pick.

Pick shook it while scanning the people the Secret Service deputy director had brought with him. "What's with the welcome committee?"

Joel led Pick away from the Gulfstream. "Director Fleiss brought us up to speed on what you think might be going down in Annapolis later today."

"Are you calling off her appearance?"

"That's not our call to make." Joel fixed Pick with a sympathetic look. "I agree with your assessment that the President is in danger—"

"Then why haven't you—"

Joel placed a hand on Pick's shoulder to cut him off. "*If* you're correct about Lieutenant Rosen being the next target."

"Have you found her?"

Joel shook his head. "We have people out looking for her. But right now, we have no intelligence supporting your assessment that she's the next target."

Pick shrugged off the deputy director's hand. "What do you call what I've been doing?"

"An investigation."

Pick again surveyed the waiting SUVs and Secret Service agents who had come to greet them. "Look, Joel, I'm a Marine—a Marine Raider—and I'm not cut out for conducting an investigation of any kind. The President sent me to find the head of the snake and chop it off, and that's what I intend on doing. You can either take the *intelligence* I've given you and do your job or get the hell out of the way so I can do mine."

Joel didn't seem put off by Pick's impassioned argument. To the contrary, he seemed relieved.

"That's why I'm here, Pick."

Suddenly, the flashing lights and waiting SUVs made sense. "You're going to give us an escort?"

"Not exactly . . ."

Before Pick could question what Joel meant, his ears picked up the rhythmic thumping of a helicopter nearing their location. It was a sound he had become intimately familiar with during his time in the Marine Corps, but one he hadn't expected based on his conversation with Director Fleiss. Pick turned and looked over his shoulder at a gloss-black UH-60 Black Hawk helicopter with gold trim approaching from the south.

"Is that for us?"

"When I learned what you were up to, I asked Director Kincaid if he would loan us a Customs and Border Protection Black Hawk from Air and Marine Operations to get you and your people to Annapolis," Joel said, then paused as the Black Hawk flared and settled onto the tarmac. He continued in a shout. "Though it chaps my hide we don't have our own assets."

"Join the club," Pick shouted back.

Joel nodded at the pristine white Gulfstream V behind him. "Not yours, then?"

Pick followed his gaze and watched Junior, Ani, and Randy emerge from the luxury business jet. The first two were carrying large Pelican cases in each hand. "I wish. We managed to convince Director Fleiss this would be more inconspicuous than one decked out in orange-and-white Coast Guard colors."

"Not sure a black-and-gold helicopter is the look you're going for, then."

Pick agreed. But in this case, expediency trumped secrecy. "Don't have much of a choice."

"What's the plan, boss?" Junior asked as he drew near.

Pick pointed at the Black Hawk. "Load up on that."

Junior raised an eyebrow, then sized up Joel in one glance. "Pays to have friends in high places."

"You want me to come, too?" Ani asked.

Pick nodded. "We're going to need everybody we can get to have any chance at all of finding Javi and stopping another attack." He turned back to Joel. "Please tell me you've got the Naval Academy covered."

"In addition to Hawkeye Brewer, I've dispatched—"

Pick cut him off. "Hawkeye who?"

"Hawkeye Brewer."

"Who's that?"

"Not who—what. *Hawkeye* is the designation for the Counter Assault Team assigned to the President," Joel explained. "And *Brewer* is—"

"The President's code name," Pick concluded.

"You got it."

Pick remembered that President Natalie Cohen had gone to Vassar College, but beyond that he wasn't really interested in the etymology of Secret Service code names. "You were saying you dispatched more teams?"

Joel nodded. "We've added a second Counter Assault Team to support the Presidential Protection Division and have special agents not assigned to other protective details canvassing the local area. But we don't really have the manpower to commit much more than that."

Pick could tell Joel agreed that the potential threat warranted having all hands on deck to root out a potential ambush and that he was frustrated by his lack of resources. "Well, you've got us."

"I'm not sure that's going to be enough."

"Maybe I can help."

Both men turned and looked at Randy.

"That is, if you can get me a ride down to Virginia Beach."

Joel clearly didn't understand. "You going to see Castillo?"

Randy locked eyes with Pick, and unspoken volumes passed between them. "I'm going to ask my friends for help."

"I'll call Director Fleiss," Pick announced.

[FOUR]

Forrest Sherman Field

United States Naval Academy

Annapolis, Maryland

1330 3 April 2026

Pick sat on the helicopter's steel deck with his legs dangling from the open door on the port side as the Customs and Border Protection UH-60 Black Hawk flew low over the Severn River on its approach to

Hospital Point. For as chaotic as the last week had been—several weeks, if he was being honest—there was something calming about seeing the Naval Academy from the air. For the midshipmen there, it was just another day as they marched steadily through spring to graduation and commissioning week.

Time, tide, and formation wait for no man.

The pilot maneuvered the helicopter to land on the large, open green space of Forrest Sherman Field, and Pick adjusted the TX4 personal defense weapon slung around his neck to lean forward and spot their welcoming committee. A caravan of black Suburbans with red and blue flashing lights was waiting to receive them on Ramsay Road—the street separating their intended point of landing on the intramural field from the cemetery stretching up the hill.

"Sir, it sounds like there's some action," the pilot said over the intercom.

Pick ducked his head back inside as the pilot turned to look at him. "What do you mean?"

"The Secret Service have identified a location of interest—"

Pick's heart bolted in his chest. "Where? On the Yard?"

"I don't know, sir. I'm only picking up chatter over the command net." The pilot returned his focus to the front just as he raised the Black Hawk's nose and flared the helicopter to stop its forward travel, while simultaneously lowering the collective to bring them back down to Earth. "Just wanted to give you a heads-up."

Pick shot a look across the cabin at Junior and Ani. Both were sitting on a bench seat and cradling the Lone Star Armory TX4 personal defense weapons that had been stored in the Pelican cases transferred from the Gulfstream. Pick still had hope the Secret Service would be able to identify and neutralize the threat before the President even left the White House. But he knew better than to rely on hope as a strategy.

“Thanks for the heads-up,” Pick said to the pilot, then doffed his headset and prepared to fulfill his mandate to locate, close with, and destroy the enemy. He lifted his legs straight out as the Black Hawk’s landing gear settled onto the grass field, then hopped off the edge and dropped into a crouch.

Without waiting, he turned and ran toward the front of the helicopter while keeping his head low. He didn’t bother looking, but he knew Junior and Ani were right behind him. Once clear of the helicopter’s rotor arc, he turned and ran straight at the closest Secret Service Suburban.

Several agents milled about, shielding their eyes from debris as the pilot increased power and lifted off from the intramural field before turning and flying back out over the Severn River. One of the agents stepped away from the caravan to greet him.

“You Captain McCoy?” he shouted over the din.

“That’s me,” Pick said, letting the special agent guide him to the second SUV.

“We’ve got a potential target.” As the helicopter retreated into the distance, he resumed speaking at a normal volume. “Local SWAT and HRT are en route, but I was told to get you there right away.”

Pick readjusted his grip on the TX4 as he thought about stacking up on the objective with shooters from a police SWAT unit and the FBI’s vaunted Hostage Rescue Team. Presidential Agent or not, Pick was a Marine through and through and wanted to be in the fight.

But he still had to think about the bigger picture. “Why do they want me there?”

"They said you're the guy who can identify our target."

Pick nodded. If there was even a chance that Javi was at the location the Secret Service had identified, then he needed to be there. "All right, let's go."

The Secret Service agent held the rear door open for Pick, who had barely settled into the rear seat before the door shut behind him. He looked over his shoulder and saw Junior and Ani climbing into the trail SUV. Once inside, the remaining Secret Service agents returned to their vehicles, including the one who had escorted him to the Suburban. He climbed into the front passenger seat and spoke into a microphone tucked in his sleeve.

"Killer Two Four secure."

Pick couldn't hear their responses, but he assumed the others had echoed their preparedness, because the convoy accelerated as one and started rolling away from the impromptu helicopter landing zone. Once moving, the special agent turned in the front seat to face him.

"It'll take us about ten minutes to get there."

"Where are we going?"

The special agent's eyes flickered, and Pick could tell he was processing information coming across the radio through his earpiece. He lifted his microphone again to respond before answering Pick's question. "Killer is en route. ETA ten mikes."

As the convoy raced along the shore of College Creek, Pick could see police cruisers from the Naval Support Activity Annapolis Police Department blocking traffic. They careened around the corner across from the boathouse and raced north toward Gate 8.

"Where are we going?" Pick asked again.

"We've identified a location in Eastport . . ."

Pick felt his stomach drop. He had a feeling he knew exactly where Hannah was.

"The Tecumseh Condominiums?"

The special agent's eyes grew wide. "Yeah."

"Step on it."

XXI

[ONE]

Tecumseh Condominiums

312 Severn Avenue

Annapolis, Maryland

1345 3 April 2026

Aided by strategically placed roadblocks, the convoy raced through downtown Annapolis and across Spa Creek before turning onto Severn Avenue. The four Chevrolet Suburbans came to a halt a block from the condominiums, where their occupants opened the doors and spilled out onto the already crowded street. From his vantage point at the second vehicle, Pick could see that a Quick Response Team from the Anne Arundel County Police Special Operations Division was already in place.

Junior and Ani joined him at the second vehicle, carrying their TX4 personal defense weapons at the low-ready position. "What is this place?" Ani asked.

"The Tecumseh Condominiums," Pick replied.

Junior eyed him suspiciously. "How'd you know that?"

In his mind, Pick clearly pictured the layout of the property. From the main entry door recessed into the brick wall, to the stairwell leading up four flights to the unit Hannah Rosen's mother had purchased before their youngster year, to the condominium's interior, where Javi had sexually assaulted her.

"I've been here before."

The Secret Service agent who rode shotgun in Pick's vehicle held a hand to his earpiece, then spoke loudly enough for them to hear. "We've identified the unit—"

"E412," Pick said, cutting him off.

Ani's eyes grew wide. "You're starting to scare me, boss."

"Like I said, I've been here before." Pick gestured for the Secret Service agent to come closer before explaining. "I've been inside that unit. It's owned—at least at one time it was—by Paige Rosen, the mother of the woman we believe is being targeted by the terrorists."

The special agent nodded, then spoke into his microphone to relay Pick's intelligence across the command net. He listened for several seconds before replying. "Okay, we've confirmed that it is, in fact, owned by Paige Rosen. Her daughter, Lieutenant Hannah Rosen, has been living in the condo for the last six months."

She's been the Supe's flag aide for that long?

Pick winced. He had been on the Yard only the weekend before, to visit Coach Luis. If he had shown the least bit of interest in what Hannah was doing with her life, he might have been able to keep her safe before any of this even happened.

"Do we think she's inside?" Junior asked.

The Secret Service agent shrugged. "We haven't received visual confirmation, but there's been movement."

"He's got her," Pick said, gritting his teeth against the anger roiling in his gut.

"We don't know that," Junior said, somewhat unconvincingly.

"*I* know it."

"Well, the time for wondering that has passed," the special agent said. "HRT's on the scene and preparing to make entry."

"Not without me they're not." Pick readjusted his TX4's sling and turned to the nondescript black armored vehicle he suspected belonged to the FBI's Hostage Rescue Team.

"Captain McCoy," the special agent said. "You're here in an advisory capacity only."

"The hell I am," Pick replied. "If they're going in, I'm going in with them."

"You don't have the—"

"Authority? Let's call the President and see about that." He paused and turned to Junior and Ani. "I need you two to head back over to the Academy and search the area around Worden Field to make sure we've covered all our bases."

"What's Worden Field?" Ani asked.

"It's where the formal parade will be held in . . ." Pick glanced at his watch. "A little over two hours."

"We're on it," Junior said, then tugged on Ani's sleeve to turn her back to the waiting Suburban.

Before they had left, Pick started walking to what he guessed was the HRT command and control vehicle. Though he carried the credentials of a Secret Service supervisory special agent and was backed by the weight of a Presidential Finding, Pick didn't think either would be required to convince the on-scene commander that he would be a force multiplier. The Hostage Rescue Team had a long history of integrating with the military's special operations forces, and Pick's pedigree as a Marine Raider was all he needed.

He walked up to an agent decked out in military fatigues with POLICE reflective patches on both the front and back of his plate carrier. Nothing about him screamed G-man, but Pick knew HRT guys weren't your typical feds. The operator was studying blueprints of the condominium complex and seemed to be engrossed in operational planning.

"You the guy in charge?" Pick asked.

The man looked over and eyed him with suspicion. "Who's asking?"

"Captain McCoy," Pick said. "I'm here on the President's authority to—"

"I know why you're here, Captain." He turned to face Pick. "The name's Lester Bradley, and I'm the Blue Team senior leader."

Pick had no idea how the Hostage Rescue Team was organized, but "senior leader" sounded like just the person he was looking for. "I was told your boys were about to breach the objective."

Lester nodded. "We've got thermal confirmation of multiple tangos inside the unit."

"And one hostage," Pick added.

Lester eyed him with something close to amusement. "You know our name is *Hostage* Rescue Team for a reason, right?"

Pick bit off a scathing reply. "Fair enough. But how many of them have been inside the unit and know the layout?"

Lester gestured to the blueprints spread out before him in the BearCat's open rear hatch. "I think we've got that covered, too."

Pick glanced up the road and saw the assault team gathering near the recessed entrance. He had been in enough breaching stacks to recognize the team was only moments away from making entry. He again considered playing his Presidential Agent trump card, but decided against it.

"What's your background, Lester?"

It appeared as if his patience had run out. "If you couldn't tell, I'm a bit busy at the moment."

"You're the man who says 'go,' so humor me. Army?"

"Don't insult me," Bradley fired back.

"Ooh-rah," Pick said, satisfied that he had guessed correctly.

"Yeah, I know you're a Marine, McCoy. I know all about you."

"Then you know I'm not about to let your boys breach that building unless I'm in the stack."

Lester shook his head, but his smile was obvious. "You're just like him, you know that?"

The comment took Pick by surprise. "Like who?"

"Castillo," Lester said. "That sonofabitch always got what he wanted."

"You know him?"

"Well enough to know that he'd kick my ass if he ever heard me refer to him as that," Lester said, then pulled up his sleeve and looked at his watch. "Look, if President Cohen picked you to replace him, then that's all the bona fides I need. But you'd better double-time it over there, Captain—we're about to go in."

Pick gestured to his body armor. "Got an extra set lying around?"

Lester reached inside the rear of the armored vehicle and handed him a spare plate carrier. "Don't make me regret this."

"You really a Marine?" Pick asked.

"Retired gunnery sergeant."

"Then you already know I won't."

[TWO]

After outfitting himself with the plate carrier, an Ops-Core high-cut bump helmet, and a ComTac headset, Pick jogged across the street and joined the rear of the stack. He lovingly cradled the same LSA TX4 he had carried with him into battle at the Alamo as Lester's voice came through loud and clear over the headset.

"All right, boys, this joker running up on your six is a shooter—code name Killer."

Pick knew he had Castillo to thank for that, but one of the HRT operators apparently thought it was too grandiose. "*Killer?* Who chose that?"

"Beats me. But somebody in the Secret Service apparently thinks highly of him."

Or Castillo just wanted to make sure I never forgot my roots.

"Still better than his predecessor's code name," Lester added.

Pick saw grins on the HRT operators' faces as they enjoyed a brief moment of levity at the newcomer's expense that made him feel right at home. In his experience, if there was one thing every high-performing team had in common, it was the almost incessant and irrefutable need to give one another shit.

But his curiosity got the better of him. "What was it?"

"Don Juan," Lester replied, deadpan. "Suited him well, too."

Based on Pick's interaction with Castillo during their recent operation to rescue Secretary Malone, he had a hard time seeing the retired Special Forces colonel as a ladies' man. "If you say so."

"All right, Killer, listen up," Lester said, instantly shifting gears. It was another hallmark Pick recognized from his time in special operations. True professionals knew when they could get away with playing grab ass and when it was time to get serious. Lester Bradley had just made it clear it was time to get to work. "You'll remain at the rear of the stack and let my boys lead the way. You're only there to advise and assist my team, so don't go all John Wayne on me."

"Roger that."

"The only reason I'm even allowing you that much is as a courtesy to Don Juan." Lester paused. "So, out of respect for him, don't fuck this up."

Pick understood the uncomfortable position he had put Lester in. As a Raider team leader downrange, Pick had participated in several operations that targeted American citizens who had been accused of aiding and abetting terrorist organizations overseas. Each time, he had been forced to bring along members of the FBI's Hostage Rescue Team to ensure the overzealous Marines didn't ignore the targets' Constitutional rights. And even though they had all been more than competent and proved themselves valuable additions to the team, having them foisted onto him at the last minute always made him uneasy.

And now he had just done the same thing to Lester Bradley.

"I'll play by your rules," Pick said, trying to assuage his concerns. "Let's just get in there and take down the bad guys."

The operator in front of Pick turned and offered his fist to acknowledge the comment. Pick brought his own up and the two bumped knuckles. If there was one thing that drew men to units like the Raiders or HRT, it was the overwhelming desire to protect the good guys and kill the bad guys. They might have worn different uniforms, but they were cut from the same cloth.

"All right," Lester replied. "TL, you've got a green light to execute on your call."

The operator positioned at the rear of the stack on the opposite side of the door squeezed the shoulder of the man in front of him, beginning a chain reaction of nonverbal cues until reaching the point man. He nodded once.

Execute.

Pick had been on breaching teams before and had plenty of experience clearing buildings, but the speed at which the HRT guys made entry into the Tecumseh Condominiums stunned him. As they cleared their areas of responsibility and swept up the stairwell, Pick was left flat-footed while listening to a chorus of "clear" calls coming over the net. But he quickly kicked into operator mode and followed the man in front of him, raising and lowering his personal defense weapon's barrel as he moved, to avoid flagging the others.

"Second floor," the TL said, announcing their progress over the command net.

The men moved swiftly and silently up the stairs, and Pick kept pace while marveling at how fluidly the team moved together. With each step that brought him closer to confronting the enemy who had taken Hannah, he grew more and more confident that Lester's men would succeed in fulfilling the HRT's mandate.

Servare vitas.

To save lives.

"Third floor," the TL said. They were only one floor from reaching their objective.

But even without following the eight men in front of him, Pick would have known exactly where to go. For years he had seen Mrs. Rosen's condo in his dreams. And he had seen it in his nightmares, too. If Hannah was inside . . .

She has to be.

. . . he was going to give everything he had to keep her safe and get her away from the monster they once thought of as a friend.

And then he was going to kill him.

"Fourth floor," the TL announced. "Stacking up to breach."

Before Pick could round the landing and take the last flight of stairs up to join them, a door opened down the hallway and brought him up short. He turned to raise his TX4 and let the reticle settle on the space in front of the door.

"I've got movement," Pick said.

The TL's response was immediate. "Hostile?"

The last thing anybody wanted was for the enemy to sneak up behind them while the entire team was focused on making entry into unit E412.

"Stand by . . ."

The door opened wider, and Pick rested his finger on the trigger, prepared to take out the slack and put down a threat with green-tipped full-metal-jacket rounds at 2,750 feet per second. He saw a shadow fill the doorway, and his heart thundered in his chest as he took long, slow breaths to keep his aim steady.

[THREE]

The shadow materialized into a human shape as a woman stepped out into the hall. She froze when she saw Pick aiming his personal defense weapon at her, then her eyes grew wide, and she quickly disappeared back inside the condo unit, slamming the door shut behind her.

"Friendly," Pick said.

He exhaled slowly and allowed his pent-up tension to evaporate into the air, then lowered his TX4 and spun to continue his ascent to the fourth floor.

"Preparing to make entry," the TL said over the command net.

"No change," Lester replied.

As Pick resumed his place at the rear of the stack, he noticed a thin strip of explosives placed between the door handle and the jamb. In the Marine Corps, breachers often used shotguns to shoot out the hinges, but on heavier doors, they used explosives to defeat the locking mechanism and ensure a positive breach. With Hannah likely being held hostage inside, they weren't going to take any chances.

The TL nodded to the breacher, who responded with "Fire in the hole."

As one, the operators turned their backs to the door as the breacher actuated the detonator. Pick pinched his eyes shut and opened his mouth to prepare for the concussive blast that disintegrated the door's handle a split second later.

"Flash out," another operator said.

Pick kept his eyes shut as the flash-bang grenade sailed into the condo and detonated with a blinding flash of light and a loud bang. A heartbeat later, he sensed the stack moving through the door, and he opened his eyes to follow them inside.

Thip! Thip!

"Got one," an operator said.

"Hall right," another replied.

Thip! Thip! Thip!

"Door left." Another voice. "Got him."

By the time Pick passed through the doorway and entered the condo, the two stacks of operators had exited the entry hallway and cleared both the main-floor bedroom and the kitchen. He stepped over the slain body of a terrorist who was dressed just like the men he had encountered in San Antonio and had a U.S.-made rifle in his lifeless hands.

"Stairs right," another operator said.

Four shooters peeled off and raced up the stairs as the others fanned out in the main room and aimed their rifles up into the loft. Pick moved slowly through the hallway and glanced left into the bedroom, where a second terrorist was splayed out on the bed with an assault rifle on the floor nearby.

Where is she?

Thip! Thip!

"Got another."

Pick left the bedroom and returned to the hallway, but it was clear from the resounding silence that the assault team had already cleared the entire unit.

"Where is she?" Pick asked.

But instead of answering, the TL delivered his situation report to Lester over the command net. "Sector clear. Three EKIA. Negative friendlies."

"Good copy," Bradley replied. "I'm sending in the rest to conduct SSE."

Pick walked through the living room to where the TL stood looking through the sliding glass door at the Naval Academy on the other side of the water. Through the adjacent buildings, he could just make out a flotilla of sailboats leaving Santee Basin at the Academy's sailing center. But the TL didn't seem interested and removed his bump helmet to run a hand through his sandy blond hair, obviously disappointed that they hadn't captured Javi or rescued Hannah. "What'd we miss?"

That simple question carried more weight than Pick expected. Ever since Rafi disappeared during the gunfight in Laredo, he had thought of nothing but what his former roommate might have planned. But it just didn't feel right. "We still got three of them."

"Is that enough?"

"I don't know. Maybe they'll uncover something during sensitive site exploitation, but there's no question he *was* here."

The TL turned to Pick but pointed at the copper dome of the Naval Academy Chapel. "Yeah, and now he's probably over there somewhere."

Pick still wasn't so sure. He looked around the condo, trying to imagine an older Lieutenant Hannah Rosen living there. In his mind, she was still the key to finding Javi. If they could just locate her, then they could find him. And if the President still intended on reviewing the formal parade, it was the only way of keeping her safe.

"We've got people scouring the Yard for him," Pick said. He knew the FBI and Secret Service—not to mention the Department of Defense police officers from Naval Station Annapolis—had every inch of the Naval Academy's grounds covered. But he was thinking only of Junior and Ani, who he had sent to look over the parade field.

"Yeah, and this was our best lead," the TL said. "Our *only* lead."

Pick understood how the man felt. His Raider team had hit several dry holes over the years that left him feeling like a complete failure despite executing each operation flawlessly. But before he could offer words of encouragement to console the team leader, his headset crackled with Lester Bradley's voice.

"Yo, Killer. You on the net?"

Pick bristled at the code name but keyed his push-to-talk to reply. "Yeah, McCoy's up."

"Got a call from your people at the Academy."

Pick reached into his pocket and retrieved his cellphone, not surprised to see that he had missed several calls from Junior while they were clearing the condo. "Got it," he said. "I'll call them back."

"Don't sweat it. It's good news."

Pick locked eyes with the TL, who returned his helmet to his head and adjusted his headset to listen in on the conversation.

"What do you mean?"

"They spotted somebody matching Lieutenant Rosen's description. Looks like she hasn't been kidnapped by the terrorists after all."

Then why were they in her condo?

The TL chimed in. "Are we sure about that?"

"Just relaying what they told me," Lester replied. "They said she was in summer whites and wearing a gold loop on her shoulder."

He's referring to the braided aiguillette of an admiral's aide-de-camp.

"Where?"

"She just parked in front of the Superintendent's house."

Pick had a sickening thought, and the TL's eyes grew wide, as if coming to the same conclusion. "Get law enforcement over there and surround the vehicle now," Pick said. "The terrorists could be using a VBIED."

[FOUR]

Pick brushed past an army of federal agents converging on Mrs. Rosen's condo as he fled for the stairs with the TL and other HRT operators hot on his heels. He hadn't wanted to consider it a possibility, but after taking out several terrorists at the Tecumseh Condominiums, Hannah being spotted in a car in front of the Superintendent's house was a little too convenient to ignore.

"Do you really think they've rigged the car with explosives?" the TL asked.

Pick didn't want to answer that question. He knew that both the FBI and the Secret Service had Explosive Ordnance Disposal teams that could render safe any vehicle-borne improvised explosive device that Javi intended on using to kill Hannah. But the fact that she was still alive lent credence to their fears that he wanted to make a splash with her death.

And nothing would make a bigger splash than the assassination of the President of the United States.

"I don't know," Pick replied. "But we need to keep the President away, just in case."

Lester's voice came over the radio again. "Hawkeye Brewer is moving to intercept."

"We need to get there first," Pick said. "If they think she's a threat to the President, they won't hesitate in dropping her."

"We've still got time," Lester replied. "But hurry."

"We're on it, boss," the TL said from the stairwell behind Pick.

When Pick reached the first floor, he sprinted through the door onto Severn Avenue and turned for the idling BearCat, where Lester Bradley was waiting for them. Pick still wasn't sure how far the retired gunnery sergeant was willing to go, but he didn't want to give the HRT senior team leader a reason to second-guess his decision to help. He jumped into the back of the armored vehicle and made room for the others.

"Last man," one of the shooters said when he had climbed aboard and shut the door.

"Let's move it," another said, obviously just as eager to leave Eastport.

The truck lurched as Lester Bradley put it in gear and pulled away from the curb. After navigating through parked police cars and road-blocks, it quickly gained speed and turned onto 6th Street, heading for the bridge crossing Spa Creek. Pick rose from the bench seat and craned his neck to look through the porthole over his shoulder. He watched buildings whipping by as they descended from the bridge and entered historic downtown Annapolis.

"Relax, Killer," the TL said.

Pick looked down at him. "The name's McCoy."

"Okay. Relax, McCoy. We're all doing the best we can."

He lowered himself back onto the bench, but his knee bounced up and down with nervous energy. He had an uneasy feeling that he was missing something, but he was more concerned with who he might see at the end of the line and didn't know who he would rather see again—

Hannah or Javi. Both would be complicated in their own ways, but he was certain of how only one of them would end.

"I'm sorry," Pick said. "I know you are."

Lester's voice came over the command net. "The Secret Service just announced that Marine One has lifted off from the White House—"

"But it's not secure yet!" Pick shouted.

"They're going to remain in holding over the Chesapeake until we give them the green light," Lester continued.

Pick fished his cellphone out and tapped on Junior's number before tucking it underneath his headset. The spook answered after only two rings.

"We found her, boss."

"Yeah, I know," Pick replied. "We took down three bad guys at the condominiums and are on our way to you now."

"The Secret Service has the whole area blocked off," Junior said.

"Where are you?"

"Ani and I are across the street from the chapel next to some phallus-looking monument."

"That's Herndon," Pick replied.

"Is it true they grease it up and make you climb it?"

"Something like that," he said.

Pick didn't feel like getting into details surrounding the tradition. It was a hallmark of commissioning week when the plebe class climbed Herndon Monument to replace a blue-rimmed Dixie Cup hat that had been placed on top with an upperclassman's combination cover to signify the end of their first year. But they had more important things to worry about.

"I always knew Navy guys were weird," Junior concluded.

"Yeah, well, I'm not arguing that," Pick said. "I'm a Marine. But the President is wheels-up from the White House and on her way. We need to get to Hannah before the Secret Service decides she's a threat."

"Why haven't they called it off yet?"

"I don't know." It seemed like the most logical course of action, but it was probably too late for him to do anything about that now. "So, we just need to focus on finding Javi before it's too late."

"We haven't seen anything suspicious yet, but there are feds crawling all over this place right now. He would be insane to try something at this point."

Insane *is a pretty good description of him.*

"Either way, this doesn't end until Javi is stopped," Pick said. "I was told that the Secret Service is keeping Marine One in a holding pattern out over the Chesapeake until they give the all-clear."

"Where will they land?"

"Probably on Hospital Point—where the CBP Black Hawk delivered us."

"Makes sense," Junior said. "Want us to head over there and poke around?"

Pick felt as if he was being pulled in two separate directions. On the one hand, he believed that the President's presence at the formal parade was only a smoke screen for Javi to exact revenge on Hannah for spending the last twelve years of his life in prison. On the other, he knew there was a chance—no matter how slim—that the President was truly at risk and that nothing else mattered.

Pick was torn between his obligations as the Presidential Agent and as a friend.

"Boss?"

He gritted his teeth as he wrestled with the decision. But in the end, he knew where his priorities were.

"I've got a better idea."

XXII

[ONE]

Gate 3

U.S. Naval Academy

Annapolis, Maryland

1515 3 April 2026

Lester Bradley had driven the BearCat armored vehicle around the traffic circle near Ego Alley, where gridlock on Randall Street forced him to continue on Main toward Church Circle. With Secret Service and FBI agents scouring the Naval Academy's grounds for terrorists, Pick should have expected that every gate would be closed to inbound vehicular traffic. But he was laser-focused on getting to Hannah.

Fortunately, he knew the city like the back of his hand, and he guided Lester away from the crowded Main Street and up the hill toward State Circle, where the Maryland State House was located. After taking the circle a quarter of the way around, they exited on Maryland Avenue, leaving them with a straight shot to the normally closed Gate 3.

"What's the plan here?" Lester asked.

"Get us as close as you can," Pick replied. "We can go the rest of the way on foot."

"And then what? The gate's closed."

"Do you think I went to school here for four years without knowing where to jump the wall?"

"This place sounds like a prison," the TL said.

You're not lying.

The BearCat came to a stop just short of King George Street, where bumper-to-bumper traffic prevented them from crossing over. "Looks like the end of the line, boys," Lester said.

The HRT operators opened the rear doors and piled out onto the brick street. After Pick dropped to the ground, he ran around to the front of the armored vehicle and banged on the driver's door, acknowledging Lester's help in delivering them to the fight. But unlike their takedown at the Tecumseh Condominiums, Pick was no longer relegated to remaining at the rear of the stack, and he led the assault team through traffic on King George Street to the closed pedestrian gate.

Junior and Ani stepped out from behind the guardhouse as they approached.

"What now, boss?" Junior shouted.

Pick didn't stop running, but pointed to his right, in the direction of the Superintendent's house. "Meet us down there, behind the chapel."

"To do what?"

"You'll see," he shouted over his shoulder, rounding the corner onto Hanover Street.

By virtue of it being a dead end and flanked on one side by the Naval Academy's perimeter wall, it was one of the quietest streets in Annapolis. Historic homes lined the street on their right, and cars were parked in spaces along the wall to their left. Pick knew the perimeter was probably monitored by high-tech surveillance equipment that would trigger silent alarms and result in police being dispatched to investigate. But that was the least of his concerns.

As Pick led the eight HRT operators even with the Naval Academy chapel, he spotted the place he was looking for. Two-thirds of the way down the street, the top of the perimeter wall stepped down to account for the change in elevation. Without slowing, he hurled himself at it, using a technique he had perfected on the Marine Corps obstacle course to swing one leg over, then the other. Within seconds, Pick was over the wall and falling onto the Naval Academy grounds.

He came down hard, only inches from a surprised Junior and Ani, and rolled away from the wall to make room behind him. One by one, the other HRT operators followed him over like lemmings. Pick jumped to his feet and scanned the street in both directions before turning and leading the gaggle toward the Superintendent's house.

"Where we going?" Junior asked.

"Going to get Hannah and lock her down inside the house," he said.

"What about the VBIED?" the TL asked.

Pick was fairly certain they had both witnessed the devastating effects of vehicle-borne improvised explosive devices in Iraq and Afghanistan and knew that a government sedan like the kind a flag aide drove could hold enough explosives to still be a threat.

Lester Bradley responded over the command net. "EOD is on the scene now."

"What about the President?" Pick asked. A quick glance at his watch confirmed that they were less than an hour from the formal parade's start time. "Have they waved her off yet?"

"Not yet," Lester said.

Pick growled to himself but focused on making entry into the Supe's house. He had been inside only once before, when Vice Admiral Jim "Bull" Hawkins had welcomed Pick's classmates and their families to a garden party during commissioning week. Of course, being friends with his father, the admiral had given Pick's family a personal tour of the house, which had been home to every superintendent since 1911.

"How are we going to get in?" Junior asked.

The alley nestled between the chapel and the perimeter wall came to an end at the rear of the Superintendent's Residence. The house itself was on their left, but the fenced-off gardens stretched right to Porter Road, known as Captains Row, where several historic homes were located, to provide housing to the Academy's senior officers.

"This way," Pick said, angling left for the driveway. It had been more than a decade since Admiral Hawkins had shown his family into the long dining room at the rear of the house, which boasted concave Girandole mercury-glass mirrors framed by gold-and-crystal-drop candelabra on the walls—both courtesy of Captain James Lawrence, whose brave words during the War of 1812 had lived on as a rallying cry for the Naval Academy.

Don't give up the ship.

"Hey, Killer," Lester said.

But Pick ignored him. They were running out of time, and he wasn't going to stop until Hannah was safe and he was certain that Javi could no longer hurt others. No matter what, he wasn't going to give up. And he suspected Lester Bradley was about to try to talk him out of it.

The HRT senior team leader tried a different tack. "Pick, you there?"

Pick hesitated just as a door at the rear of the house flew open. He skidded to a stop and lifted his personal defense weapon.

"Hey, Pick from San Diego," Lieutenant Hannah Rosen said.

Pick exhaled and lowered his gun, awash with both relief and embarrassment. "Hey, Hannah."

"The admiral sent me out to stop you before the Secret Service did."

"That's what I was trying to tell you," Lester said over the command net. "They spotted you guys climbing over the fence and were waiting for you."

"Thanks for the heads-up," Pick said.

Hannah gave him an awkward smile, then gestured for him to come inside. "We need to talk."

Why do I get the feeling I'm not going to like this?

[TWO]

Superintendent's Residence

U.S. Naval Academy

Annapolis, Maryland

1535 3 April 2026

As Lieutenant Hannah Rosen stepped aside and made room for Pick to enter the Superintendent's house, he heard the bass drum of the Naval Academy Band resonating through the walls. It was a clear sign that it was almost time for the Brigade of Midshipmen to step off from Bancroft Hall and march down Stribling Walk to Worden Field.

And an even clearer sign that they were running out of time.

Before Pick had taken two steps, Hannah broke the uneasy silence between them. "Just what the hell are you doing here, Pick?"

He froze and turned to look at her, still amazed at her ability to make him feel awkward and unsure of himself with a simple question. She stood with her arms folded across her chest, letting him know that she was less than pleased that he had shown up at the admiral's back door with a team of well-armed operators in tow. Pick softened under her intense focus, struck by the thought that the years had been good to Hannah.

She's more beautiful than ever.

"Well?"

Pick shook away his momentary longing. It was clear from both her demeanor and the ribbons on her chest that she had earned every right to wear the aide-de-camp's aiguillette.

"You're in danger," he said, unable to blunt the truth to the only woman he had ever really loved.

"What are you talking about?" She lowered her arms to her sides and stepped closer. "With the President visiting, this is probably the safest place on Earth."

"I don't know how—"

Lester's voice came through over the command net and cut him off. "Killer, EOD has given the all-clear on the vehicle. No signs of explosives."

Pick felt himself relax a little, and Hannah picked up on his change in posture.

"Don't know how what?" Hannah prodded.

He sighed when he realized there was no way around it. He needed to tell her everything and hope that she believed him—at least enough to stay out of sight until he could find Javi and eliminate the threat. To both her *and* the President. "Javi was released from prison."

She stiffened at her attacker's name and took half a step back. "What?"

"I don't have time to go into all the details—"

"Then give me the abridged version," Hannah countered.

They locked eyes, and Pick felt the same way he had on I-Day when she'd first introduced herself. But standing inside the Superintendent's house under the threat of another terrorist attack, her gregarious and easygoing personality was a thing of the past. Hannah Rosen was a naval officer, first and foremost, and no longer needed Pick's protection.

Maybe she never really did.

“The terrorist attack in Virginia Beach appears to have been only a cover for the murder of Liam McIntyre, the presiding judge in Javi’s court-martial,” Pick said.

Hannah didn’t appear convinced. “I thought the news reported that ISIS–K was behind that.”

“The shooters were from Tajikistan, but we think he manipulated them to carry out the attack in his quest for revenge.”

Even as he said it, it didn’t feel right.

“And the one in San Antonio? Are you saying Javi was behind that, too?”

Pick nodded. “Captain John Hanes—”

“Your company officer?”

Again, Pick nodded. “Apparently, after leaving the Marine Corps, he took a job as an Alamo Ranger and was killed while trying to stop the attack.”

The bass drum’s tempo changed, and Pick recognized that their time was almost up. If he couldn’t make her believe that she was the next target on Javi’s list, then he would have to focus on convincing the Secret Service to wave off Marine One. He wasn’t willing to risk the President’s life because of his failure.

“Come on, Pick. You can’t be serious.”

“I *saw* his body,” Pick said.

The expression on her face softened. “You were there?”

“I went there to stop the attack, but I was too late.”

Hannah glanced at her watch before again locking eyes with him. “And now you think Javi’s come for me?”

He held her gaze. “Those men outside? They’re with the FBI’s Hostage Rescue Team, and we just killed three terrorists inside your condo.”

She staggered back as if he had just slapped her. "What? My condo?"

Pick gave her a sad smile. "That's why I'm here, Hannah. I was too late to stop Javi from killing Judge McIntyre and Captain Hanes. But I'm not about to let him hurt you."

"But I'm safe here," Hannah repeated, then looked at her watch again. "Time's up, Pick. I need to get the admiral to Worden Field to review the parade."

She started to turn away, but Pick grabbed her arm to stop her. "Hannah, I—"

She wheeled on him. "I know you think you're doing the right thing, but there are certain things you just don't know, certain things I can't get into."

Pick released her arm but waited for her to explain.

Lester Bradley's voice came over the command net. "Yo, Killer, you on the net?"

He held Hannah's gaze until she turned away. "Yeah, what's going on?"

"We just received word that Commodore has gone missing."

"Commodore?"

Hannah froze.

"Who's that?" Pick asked.

"I don't know," Lester said, sounding just as puzzled. "I don't have my Secret Service decoder ring with me, but it sounds like another high-profile bigwig under their protection is here."

"Who—"

Hannah cut him off. "Midshipman Fourth Class Ethan Cohen."

Pick's mouth fell open as his brain processed the name. "Cohen . . ."

"That's what I couldn't get into," she said. "The President's son is a midshipman."

[THREE]

Pick stared at Hannah, not quite able to process what she had just said. He admitted that he knew very little about President Natalie Cohen's personal life and couldn't ever remember hearing that she had a son—let alone one old enough to be a plebe at the Naval Academy.

"She has a son?"

"Three, actually." Hannah sighed. "Before she became secretary of state, she and her husband had two sons, Daniel and Justin. Both followed their father into banking after graduating from Princeton."

Pick was stunned. "She's married?"

"Was," Hannah corrected. "She quietly divorced Mortimer Cohen at the end of her tenure as secretary of state and discovered she was pregnant with her third not long after."

"Who's the father?"

Hannah shrugged. "That's all I know, Pick. She just wanted to give Ethan the same kind of life his older brothers enjoyed and sent him off to the same preparatory school in St. Petersburg, Florida."

"Wait a second . . ." Pick felt his stomach drop. "What school?"

"The Admiral Farragut Academy," Hannah replied. "Hence his Secret Service code name."

Pick closed his eyes and groaned. "We've been thinking about this all wrong."

"What do you mean?"

"Hannah, you know who went there . . ."

"Yeah, all three of the President's sons. I just said that."

He shook his head. "No, Hannah. *Javier* went there."

And his father was on the board.

"Yeah, but that was well before Ethan even got there. And Javi's been in prison; there's no way they could have crossed paths."

Pick agreed with her on that point. But if there was one thing he had learned during his brief tenure as the Presidential Agent, it was that there was no such thing as a coincidence. "We've been operating under the assumption that you were the next target."

"Why?"

"Because his father told me . . ." Pick trailed off as he wondered if the cartel turf war and Rafi's disappearance were staged to throw him off.

"His father?"

"But what if you're not the target?" His mind was racing, trying to find a plausible explanation. He knew Javier was in Annapolis—the terrorists they had put down at the Tecumseh Condominiums were proof enough of that—and there had to be a reason.

"If I'm not the target, then who is?"

"I don't know," he admitted. Whether the target was President Natalie Cohen, Midshipman Fourth Class Ethan Cohen, or Lieutenant Hannah Rosen, Pick wasn't sure. He just knew he wasn't about to let anything happen to any of them.

Hannah gave Pick a sad smile that reminded him of the one she had given him when they agreed to end their relationship. It was the one look he had hoped to never see again. "What are you going to do about it?"

Pick thought for a moment, then reached into his pocket for his phone and dialed.

"Who are you calling?"

Pick held up a hand when his call was answered. "This is Captain P.K. McCoy for the President," he said.

It didn't take long for Pick to convince the operator to patch him through to Marine One, and he waited somewhat impatiently for the President to answer. When she did, her voice made it clear that she wasn't in the mood to entertain any nonsense and was just as impatient. She wanted to get straight to the point.

"What's the status, Captain? We're running out of time."

"Madam President, I'm with Lieutenant Hannah Rosen at the Superintendent's Residence," he said.

President Cohen sighed with what sounded like relief. "Thank God she's safe. When I heard that HRT couldn't find her after killing three terrorists in her condo, I started to fear the worst."

"The worst might still happen, Madam President."

Natalie Cohen was silent for a moment. "What do you mean?"

Pick chose his words carefully. He didn't want to come across as if he was accusing her of keeping things from him. But he needed her to understand that he was considering every possible angle when it came to the terrorists' motives. "Ma'am, Lieutenant Rosen just informed me that your son is a fourth class midshipman."

"He is," the President replied without hesitation. "But she shouldn't have told you that; she shouldn't have even known that. Secretary Drake assured me that his identity would remain confidential."

"Madam President, with respect to the secretary, I'm sure you can appreciate that he had to notify the Superintendent that your son was being admitted to the plebe class."

"Of course."

"Then I'm also sure you understand the admiral wouldn't be able to keep it a secret from his aide-de-camp."

Natalie Cohen sighed. "I suppose not. I just didn't want Ethan to be treated any differently because of who I am. He already had to live in the shadows of his two older brothers."

Pick was an only child and couldn't appreciate what the younger Cohen brother had to deal with. But he knew what it was like growing up with a Marine Corps legend and Vietnam fighter ace as a father. "I understand, Madam President. I didn't call to pass judgment."

"Why *did* you call, Captain McCoy?"

Pick looked at Hannah, who was listening to his side of the conversation with a little more than idle curiosity.

"I think your son might be in danger."

"My son?"

"I think we may have been wrong all along."

"You said you thought this Javier Santiago person was there to target Lieutenant Rosen," Natalie Cohen countered. "And now you're saying he's not?"

"Ethan attended the Admiral Farragut Academy in St. Petersburg, Florida, correct?"

"All of my sons did," the President replied. "Just like their father. After Daniel and Justin graduated, they went on to Princeton—also just like Mortimer—but Ethan forged his own path."

Forging a different path was something Pick was intimately familiar with. "Yes, ma'am, I understand. But my former roommate, Javier Santiago, also went to the Admiral Farragut Academy before coming to Annapolis. And his father was on the board."

Natalie Cohen inhaled sharply. "But . . ."

"I don't know if they're related, but I can't ignore the coincidence," Pick said. "I'm begging you to call off your visit and order the Secret Service to pull Ethan out of the parade formation and get him here to the Superintendent's Residence before something horrible happens."

Despite knowing that the President was aboard a Sikorsky VH-92

Patriot helicopter in a holding pattern over the Chesapeake Bay, he heard nothing over the phone that even hinted that she was flying. "He's not marching in the parade, Captain McCoy."

Pick's shoulders sagged. "Wait. Where is he?"

"He picked up sailing at the Admiral Farragut Academy and—"

Captain P.K. McCoy Jr. hung up on the President of the United States.

[FOUR]

Ten minutes before the formal parade was scheduled to begin, Pick burst through the rear door onto the rear driveway and surprised Junior and Ani, who were passing the time by talking with the HRT operators. Hannah followed him outside, shouting at him and demanding that he tell her what was going on. But a freezing-cold dagger of fear had pierced Pick's heart and was driving him onward.

"Boss?" Junior said when Pick hesitated in the driveway.

How could I have been so stupid?

"Pick McCoy, you tell me right now what's going on," Hannah shouted.

"He's not marching in the parade," Pick said.

"Who's not?" Ani asked.

But Hannah had caught up with Pick and stood in front of him. "I could have told you that. He's—"

"On the sailing team," Pick said, cutting her off.

"Who are we talking about?" Junior asked, echoing Ani's confusion.

Pick looked at each of them, but his brain was already trying to process the problem. "Midshipman Ethan Cohen," Pick muttered.

Junior's eyes registered surprise. "Cohen?"

"The President's son," Hannah said.

"The President's son?" Ani's shock was quickly replaced with understanding. "So, that's *Commodore*."

As if hearing the Secret Service code name had spurred Lester Bradley into action, his voice came through over the command net. "Hey, Killer, something has the Secret Service all worked up."

In the distance, over the Naval Academy Band's bass drum thumping the cadence for the marching midshipmen, Pick could just begin to make out what sounded like a helicopter approaching. "Is that . . ."

Lester continued. "Hawkeye Brewer is moving to Hospital Point. Sounds like Marine One is making its approach now."

"No," Pick said, as the icy dagger twisted.

Junior and Ani looked at each other when they realized what they were hearing. "What's she doing?"

Pick ignored the question. It was obvious that President Cohen had completely disregarded his warning and was intent on continuing with her reckless plan to review the parade. Even after everything that had happened, after everything Pick had uncovered, she was going to ignore it all and put herself in harm's way.

He turned to Hannah. "I need to get to Santee Basin."

She didn't hesitate. "I'll take you," she said, turning for the nondescript navy-blue sedan parked at the rear of the admiral's residence.

"What's Santee Basin?" Ani asked.

Pick raced around to the sedan's passenger side as Hannah settled in behind the wheel. "I don't have time to explain," he shouted. "But I think the President's son has been the target all along. I don't know what it is, but there has to be a connection between Rafi Santiago and Mortimer Cohen."

"What?" Junior asked.

Pick hesitated before lowering himself into the passenger seat. "I don't know, but we need to find out what it is."

"I'm on it."

"And get in touch with Randy. Tell him that if he's planning on coming through with his friends from Virginia Beach, now would be a pretty damn good time."

"We got it, boss."

Pick dropped into the seat as Hannah started the engine. She had the car in gear and stomped her foot down on the gas before he had even closed the door, let alone buckled his seat belt. Junior, Ani, and the eight HRT operators jumped out of the way as the car lurched from the driveway and turned down the street toward Captains Row.

"Do you really think he's here?" Hannah asked.

Pick glanced over and saw that her knuckles were white from the death grip she had on the steering wheel. "Yeah, I do."

"But why?"

Pick knew it didn't make sense. There was nothing he could say that would make her feel any better after learning that the man who had sexually assaulted her had just been released from prison and aligned himself with ISIS–K terrorists. Whether for revenge or for another reason, there was nothing he could tell her that would make Javi's motives seem anything less than insane.

"I don't know, Hannah. But I need to stop him once and for all."

At the end of Captains Row, Hannah turned right and headed toward the Armel-Leftwich Visitor Center and the Naval Academy's main gate.

"You're going the wrong way," Pick protested.

She shot him a dirty look. "You know I went here, too, right?"

"Yeah, but . . ."

Hannah jerked the wheel left onto King George Street and raced toward the water between parked cars and Lejeune Hall. "Just shut up and hold on."

Hannah had never really been what he thought of as timid, but her assertiveness was completely foreign for the woman he thought he knew. But time had a way of changing them all—for better *and* for worse—and maybe Hannah just wasn't the woman he had once been in love with. She jerked the wheel hard again, shortcutting across the roundabout in front of the visitor center and onto Brownson Road.

Through the windshield, Pick spotted the green-and-white Sikorsky VH-92 Patriot helicopter racing from right to left, low over the Severn River. He knew the replacement to the Sea King was nimbler and carried a more advanced countermeasures system. But knowing that didn't make him feel any better about the President of the United States racing closer to the man who had orchestrated two terrorist attacks on U.S. soil and was preparing to kill the President, her son, or both.

"What is she doing?"

Pick hadn't expected an answer to his question, but Hannah's foot came down harder on the gas pedal in response. They were already racing dangerously close to cars parked along the side of the road, but Pick's entire focus was on reaching the Naval Academy's sailing center and stopping Javi before he caused any further harm.

When they reached the corner of the Wesley Brown Field House, Hannah didn't even bother slowing and raced through the intersection like a missile aimed at the seawall. But before they reached the concrete barrier, her foot came off the gas.

"Oh my God."

Pick glanced up at the remark and saw a smoke trail arcing through the sky.

And it was headed straight for Marine One.

XXIII

[ONE]

Marine One

U.S. Marine Corps VH-92 Patriot

Over the Severn River

Annapolis, Maryland

1555 3 April 2026

President Natalie Cohen knew it wasn't the smartest thing she had ever done when she ordered her pilots to continue inbound to Hospital Point, regardless of the Secret Service's threat assessment. But even more than her role as President of the United States, Natalie felt an intense obligation to fulfill her duties as Ethan's mother. She had long regretted her choices in advancing her political career over spending time with Daniel and Justin, and she vowed she wouldn't make the same mistake with her youngest son.

But regardless of her well-meaning intentions, her maternal instincts were suddenly overshadowed by crippling fear when the Presidential helicopter abruptly banked away from the Naval Academy and plummeted to Earth. Instantly weightless, she felt her stomach leap into her throat, and she gripped the arms of the plush leather chair before instinctively reaching for her seat belt to cinch it down tighter over her trim waist. She hadn't seen or heard anything to indicate that they were in danger, but a fleeting glance through the side window was all she needed to confirm her worst fears.

No . . .

Brilliant flares fanned away from the helicopter in almost every direction, smoking and tumbling through the air to decoy what could only be a—

Surface-to-air missile!

That intrusive thought sent her spiraling toward panic as a concussive blast rocked the helicopter and the Marine pilots reversed direction. Her limited view of the clear blue sky shook from the explosion and was suddenly replaced by the dark and murky waters of the Severn River. But a split second later, she realized that the missile had detonated on the flares and not on Marine One.

Thank God!

The nearly silent interior of Marine One normally provided her with much-needed relaxation, but now it seemed almost claustrophobic in its eerie calmness. If not for the tilting cabin and disorienting g-forces that kept her pinned to her leather seat, she wouldn't even have had the faintest idea they were in any danger.

"What's going on?" she shouted, trying and failing to keep the edge of fear from her voice.

"Just hold on, Madam President," her Secret Service shadow shouted back, reaching up and adjusting her earpiece while listening in to the Secret Service command net.

Fighting against vertigo caused by the helicopter's twisting and turning, Natalie focused on the special agent's face, trying to read her expression for confirmation that they would be okay. She had no idea in which direction they were flying, but the fear for her life had suddenly become supplanted by the fear that she was abandoning Ethan when he needed her most.

Where's my son?

She glanced through the window again and saw the blue-and-gold spinnakers of Navy 44 sloops racing past in a blur. It took her only a moment to recognize that the helicopter was mere feet over the water and heading back out to the Chesapeake Bay.

"Wait . . ." Her stomach churned. "Where are we going?"

The special agent didn't answer her and seemed focused on the radio chatter coming through over her earpiece. "Brewer is feet wet and egressing back to the Bay."

Back to the Bay . . .

"What just happened?" Natalie asked, not wanting to accept what she already knew.

Captain McCoy had been right in fearing that Javier Santiago had his sights set on a target bigger than a simple Navy lieutenant—even one who had put him behind bars. She hadn't wanted to believe it was possible that someone would go to such great lengths to harm her—*or Ethan*—but all the proof she needed was racing by outside her window.

"We were fired on by a man-portable air-defense system," the Secret Service agent replied.

"A what?"

"A surface-to-air missile, ma'am." The agent swallowed as she locked eyes with Natalie. "It appears this was an assassination attempt."

"But . . ." Natalie Cohen trailed off as she pushed aside any lingering thoughts of her own safety and thought only of the safety of her son—the fourth class midshipman whose identity she thought she had managed to keep a secret.

Until Captain McCoy learned the truth.

"We defeated the missile, Madam President," her protective agent said with obvious relief. But her look of relief suddenly evaporated with some news that had just come in over the command net. "Say again your last . . . What's the status of Commodore?"

Natalie met the woman's eyes, and her heart sank. "What is it? What's happened?"

[TWO]

Robert Crown Sailing Center

U.S. Naval Academy

Annapolis, Maryland

1605 3 April 2026

Hannah slammed on the brakes, and they skidded to a stop next to the seawall bordering Santee Basin, drawing suspicious looks from a small gathering of eight midshipmen decked out in khaki shorts and navy-blue polo shirts. Pick jumped from the passenger seat, cradling his LSA TX4 personal defense weapon, and hurdled the waist-high concrete barrier between him and a wood dock where several smaller boats were moored.

As Hannah stepped out of the sedan, her summer white uniform and gold braided aiguillette drew even more attention from the young men.

"Ma'am! Did you see that?" one of them asked, pointing at the Severn River.

She didn't have to ask what he meant. Just beyond the mouth of the basin, the green-and-white helicopter carrying the President of the United States flew low over the surface of the water as it raced south toward the Chesapeake Bay. The missile's smoke trail had faded, but a cloud of blue-hued smoke swirled around Marine One, remnants of the decoy-flare salvo.

"Did you see where it came from?" Hannah asked in response.

Another midshipman stepped forward. "Was that the President, ma'am?"

Pick stood on the seawall and watched as the helicopter disappeared behind the sailing center and made for safer waters, then he turned back to the group of midshipmen. He had seen the sailboats leaving the basin before the parade and didn't understand why they were still on dry land. "Shouldn't you guys be out there on the water?"

The first midshipman—the one Pick assumed was in charge—took in his appearance and decided he was in a position of authority. It might have had something to do with the reflective POLICE patch on the front of the plate carrier he had borrowed from Lester Bradley or his suppressed personal defense weapon from Lone Star Armory, but Pick would take any advantage he could get. Javi had already taken a shot at the President.

"Yes, sir. We were supposed to be—"

"Then why aren't you?" Hannah asked, cutting him off.

The eight midshipmen stopped walking and gathered hesitantly around the Superintendent's aide and a bearded man outfitted for war who none had ever seen before. There was no way they could have known he was a captain in the Marine Corps, and they turned their focus to the Navy lieutenant.

"One of our crew didn't show up," their skipper answered.

Pick felt his stomach twist into knots. "What's his name?"

"Ethan Co—"

The skipper elbowed the midshipman in the ribs. "Just a plebe."

Hannah glanced over her shoulder at Pick. The gnawing fear in his gut had been replaced by anger that oozed from every pore, and he moved closer to the half-circle of midshipmen. "Just a plebe?"

The skipper swallowed. "Yes, sir."

"And you couldn't sail without him?"

The one who had almost given up Ethan Cohen's identity opened his mouth to answer, but the skipper silenced him with a cold look before answering. "We would have, but our boat was already gone."

"Which boat was it?" Hannah asked.

The skipper held Pick's gaze for several seconds before looking down at the lieutenant. "*Defiance.*"

Hannah turned to Pick. "Do you think he has him?"

She didn't have to elaborate. Like Javi, Hannah had been on the offshore sailing team and knew they provided a flotilla of sloops with billowing blue-and-gold spinnakers as a backdrop for guests viewing the parade on Worden Field. They both suspected Javi had commandeered one of the boats to use as a platform for targeting Marine One. But the possibility that he could have Ethan Cohen on board only made the situation more dire.

"Has who?" the skipper asked.

Pick ignored him and stared into Hannah's eyes. "We have to assume so."

"What are you going to do?" she asked with a shudder.

The midshipman in charge was growing increasingly agitated at being ignored by both of them. "*Who* has *who*?"

Pick pressed the push-to-talk on his plate carrier and spoke over the command net. "All stations, all stations, this is Killer. Suspect is believed to have kidnapped Commodore aboard Navy sloop *Defiance.*"

The response was immediate. "Hawkeye Brewer is en route. Say status."

"Killer is moving to intercept."

Hannah nodded at Pick to let him know he was doing the right thing, then turned back to the midshipmen and began issuing orders. As the sound of Marine One's rotors faded away, Pick slung the TX4 across his back and turned for a rigid-hull inflatable boat tied off at the end of the wooden dock.

Killer is moving to intercept.

[THREE]

Pick paused only long enough to untie the mooring lines and toss them aside before leaping onto the rigid-hull inflatable boat. The entirety of his small boat experience had come from his time in the Marine Raiders, but he hoped the sailing coaches who used the RHIB were just as lax with security and had left the keys in the ignition.

As he took his position at the helm, he breathed a sigh of relief when he saw the bright orange flotation key chain dangling from the key. But his relief was only momentary. The oppressive weight of what he was about to do had finally settled over him, and he felt a slight tremor in his hand as he reached for the switch to lower the outboard into the water.

Pick listened to the electric whine as the motor was lowered into the basin's dark waters, but the sound of his heartbeat threatened to drown everything else out. It took several seconds for him to recognize a voice coming in over the command net, a voice that was addressing him by name.

"Pick, this is Mako Six. Do you read?"

Mako?

The last time he had heard the call sign, he and Castillo had joined forces with a team of Navy SEALs from the JSOC task force to rescue Secretary of State Frank Malone. He struggled to place the voice while twisting the key to fire up the outboard motor. It started with a quiet cough and a belch of blue-gray smoke.

"Pick—Pick McCoy—this is Mako Six. Do you read?" The voice had a hint of desperation.

"Mako Six, clear the net," another voice replied. "This is for official Secret Service—"

Pick reached for his push-to-talk switch to cut him off. "Mako Six, this is Pick."

"Pick! It's Randy."

With the RHIB's outboard purring like a kitten trying to hack up a furball, Pick reached for the throttle, shifted out of neutral, and pushed it forward while cranking the wheel to pull away from the dock. He would have normally kept his speed down while navigating the tight confines of the basin, but he knew this was anything but a normal situation. The boat lurched as he shoved the throttle to the stop.

"Randy, Javi took a shot at Marine One and has the President's son aboard a Navy 44."

Randy was silent for a moment, but then replied somberly. "Copy all, Pick. What's your status?"

"I'm driving a RHIB out to make contact—"

"Negative, Killer," another voice said. "Hawkeye Brewer is moving into position."

Randy's reply was immediate. "Who the fuck is Hawkeye Brewer?"

Pick smiled. "I'll explain later. Where are you?"

"You know those friends I told you about?"

Pick had been hoping for some good news. "The ones who use the call sign Mako?"

"Those are the ones," Randy said. "We're on our way right now."

Over the roar of the outboard and the wind battering against Pick, he heard the faint sound of a helicopter's rotor blades coming across during Randy's transmissions. "How far out?"

"ETA ten mikes," Randy replied.

I don't know if we have ten minutes.

"Hurry," Pick said, then hung up and pushed the throttle as far as it would go.

Within seconds, the RHIB had exited the basin into the slow-moving Severn River. He broke the wheel hard to the left and leaned with the boat as he steered directly for the flotilla of sailboats running a racetrack pattern around two buoys to keep their blue-and-gold spinnakers inflated. He was almost surprised to see that they hadn't broken formation and fled for the open waters of the Chesapeake Bay after watching a surface-to-air missile narrowly miss the President's helicopter.

But then he remembered what it was like being a midshipman.

"Okay, where are you, Javi?"

The RHIB skipped across the water's choppy surface, and Pick squinted against the afternoon glare to try spotting the sloop named *Defiance.* It wasn't quite like trying to find a needle in a haystack, but Pick thought that identifying the right boat among a tangled mess of ten identical boats came pretty close.

He aimed the nimble RHIB at the sailboat closest to him. It was reaching on the upwind leg and driving downriver, but it was too far away for Pick to make out. As it passed an orange buoy bobbing on the surface of the water, the helmsman spun the wheel and swung the nose around to let the wind catch the spinnaker and inflate it. He just had time to catch the name on the transom.

Tenacious.

Not him.

Pick shifted his aim for the next boat in line, but he quickly dismissed that one, too, when he recognized that the deck was crawling with sure-footed sailors managing the lines to keep their sloop in position.

"Come on, Javi. Where are you?"

The RHIB skipped across the surface of the water, drawing looks of surprise from the midshipmen manning the boats. But his eyes continued to scan the boats' decks, looking for even the slightest clue that would lead him to his former roommate and the President's son. He passed the next boat in line and craned his neck to read its name.

Warrior.

Dammit!

Pick looked past the white sails and blue-and-gold spinnakers to the boats on the other side of the formation sailing up the river. He couldn't make out their names, but he could clearly see that each one appeared to be manned by an entire crew. And since he and Hannah had spoken with the crew of the *Defiance* on the sailing center's seawall, he knew that the sloop Pick was looking for would be manned by only one person.

Javier Santiago.

He raced by a third sailboat, catching sight of its name along the side of the hull.

Gallant.

The midshipmen at the helm waved him off, obviously perturbed by the presence of an ugly and noisy motorboat that seemed intent on ruining the parade backdrop. But Pick ignored the skipper's warning and jerked the wheel to the right, cutting close behind the *Gallant* and in front of the trailing boat. Looking over his shoulder, he quickly corrected back to the left and drove upriver toward the second buoy in the middle of the circling boats.

But far ahead, beyond the sailboats' racetrack pattern, Pick spotted the blue-and-white hull of a Navy 44 with no spinnaker flying and only the main sail lazily pulling. Pick squinted against the wind and the spray dousing him and thought it looked like the boat was idle and drifting with the current.

"There you are," Pick muttered.

He raced past another sloop on his right-hand side that was approaching the far buoy and preparing to turn back downriver, and he cut the RHIB across its bow. Once on the outside of the formation, Pick steered back to the left and aimed directly at the lone sailboat.

"Killer, break off your pursuit and pull alongside Hospital Point to recover Hawkeye Brewer."

Pick didn't recognize the voice but knew it belonged to the special agent in charge of the Presidential protection detail. But even though he carried the credentials of a Secret Service supervisory special agent, he didn't fall under the detail's chain of command.

"That's a negative," Pick replied. "I have eyes on the target."

"That's an order, Killer."

Pick thought about responding but knew it wouldn't do any good. The person on the other end of the radio only wanted to secure Commodore as fast as possible and saw the rigid-hull inflatable boat as his best opportunity to put the Counter Assault Team into play. But Pick wasn't about to break off and risk letting Javi get away again.

Instead of responding to the SAC's command, Pick depressed the push-to-talk switch to query the cavalry. "Mako Six, what's your status?"

Randy's voice came back immediately. "I can see the chapel dome from here. We're close."

"Mako Six," the SAC said. "Clear the net immediately—"

"Belay that order," Pick said. "Mako Six, be advised that the target is on the closest sailboat to the Naval Academy Bridge. It's the one without a spinnaker, and it appears to be adrift."

"Mako Six copies. What's your status?"

Pick skipped over a wave and steadied the wheel to aim directly at the sailboat's stern. He would have only one chance of making this work. "I'm preparing to make contact," Pick said, adjusting his aim to counter for the current.

"Copy," Randy said.

Pick moved out from behind the console and stood on the starboard side, holding the steering wheel with his left hand while placing his right foot on the gunwale. The deck of the *Defiance* appeared vacant, and Pick suddenly worried that he was too late.

No! I can't let him get away again . . .

As the RHIB raced closer to the forty-four-foot sailboat, Pick braced himself and practiced his tactical breathing to steel his nerves. His timing needed to be perfect.

Now!

Just when it appeared as if the RHIB was going to slam into the sailboat, Pick jerked the wheel hard to the left and pushed off from the gunwale. In one moment, he was racing along the Severn River in the coach's motorboat. In the next, he was sailing through the air like a missile aimed at the sloop's open cockpit.

That's when he saw Javi.

[FOUR]

Javier Santiago looked like a completely different person. He wasn't the lanky nineteen-year-old Pick remembered sharing a room with as a midshipman at the Naval Academy. He had apparently packed on muscle during his time in the slammer, shaved his head, and inked his body with prison tattoos that were just barely visible underneath his navy-blue polo shirt.

Javi's eyes went wide when he turned and saw the bearded man in a plate carrier and helmet flying through the air. But his genuine surprise shifted to something else, something Pick couldn't quite make out.

Pick slammed into his former roommate, and his momentum carried them both across the sloop's open cockpit. For his part, Pick tried angling his body to make as clean a tackle as possible. But Javi almost appeared ready for it and shifted his body—not to counter the hit, but to amplify it. They came down hard on the fiberglass deck and tumbled over flaked lines and block and tackle until slamming into the braided steel lifelines.

"I knew it'd be you," Javi said, trying to regain his breath.

Pick pushed himself off the deck while trying to retain some form of control over his former roommate. He had heard the words but focused the entirety of his attention on controlling Javi's hands. The man he had once considered a friend was nothing more than a target, an enemy combatant who was a clear and present danger to the nation he'd sworn to defend.

Against all enemies, foreign and domestic.

Javi broke free from Pick's wrist lock and angled his body to gain a positional advantage as he came up on a knee. But Pick reached down for Javi's heel and swept it forward, ending his precarious balance and toppling him onto his back. But again, it seemed as if Javi had been expecting it.

"Don't you want to know why I brought you here?"

To torment me?

To make me regret not choking the life out of you twelve years ago?

"Not really," Pick said, taking the opportunity to come up into a squat and put some distance between them. He felt the weight of the TX4 personal defense weapon slung across his back, instantly reminding him that he was still armed.

Javi grinned. "Sure you do."

Pick leaned left and peered through the opening Javi had emerged from, hoping to spot the President's son inside the sailboat's cabin. He knew Javi was only trying to goad him into reacting, so Pick struggled to tamp down his anger and resentment and focused only on the mission. It was the one thing he had absolute control over.

But Javi wasn't about to let Pick gain the upper hand. Even a psychological one.

"How's Hannah?"

Pick's heart bolted with sudden anger, and his eyes flicked up into Javi's face. The look he saw there was one of satisfaction mixed with amusement. It was almost as if Javi had lured Pick there to torment him over perceived past transgressions.

"How was prison?" Pick countered.

Javi's eyes hardened with a brief flash of anger. He took advantage of the distance Pick had put between them and came up onto a knee again, slowly rising into a squat. It was Pick's first opportunity to appreciate the physical transformation his former roommate had undergone during his decade-plus in prison. In many ways, Javi resembled the young, muscled, testosterone-fueled Marines he had led in the Raiders.

"Valuable," Javi replied. "How's the Marine Corps treating you?"

You'll never understand.

Pick glanced through the hatch and into the sailboat's cabin again, and his eyes settled on a pair of deck shoes attached to the motionless legs of a person lying in a pool of blood. His heart bolted and he took a step forward.

Javi moved to block him. "I don't think so, old friend."

Pick looked up at him. "Why are you doing this?"

"Doing what?"

Pick saw the amusement return to his former roommate's face and knew that Javi was enjoying himself. "Why did you side with the Cártel de Jalisco Nueva Generación and promise to deliver your father's smuggling network in exchange for supporting your quest for revenge?"

Javi's facial expressions didn't change. "Is that what you think?"

No. I don't.

Pick again glanced at the deck shoes below in the cabin and feared that he was already too late. If Javi had already killed Ethan Cohen, there was nothing left for him to do but to ensure that his former roommate atoned for his sins in the most violent way possible.

"I think you blamed everybody but yourself for your incarceration. You blamed Captain Hanes for standing aside while NCIS collected all the evidence they needed to put you away, so you had him killed at the Alamo. You blamed Judge McIntyre for refusing to accept a plea agreement that your legal team had maneuvered to put into play, so you had him killed in Virginia Beach."

"Correct on all counts," Javi said. "But you still don't understand."

Pick was tired of playing games with Javi and had already given him enough rope to hang himself with. It didn't really matter how Javi had managed to justify his actions. Pick reached back to unsling the TX4, deciding that it was time to end Javi's charade once and for all.

"Time's up, Javi."

Javi watched Pick swing the gun around and took a hesitant step back toward the front of the boat. He lifted his hands slowly out to his sides, but the look of amusement never left his face. "I didn't come here for Hannah."

He's stalling.

As the sound of an approaching helicopter broke through Pick's laser focus, he slowly raised the personal defense weapon and thumbed the selector off safe. "If you say so, Javi."

Standing behind the steering helm, Javi's smile vanished. "I came for you."

Too late, Pick realized that during the melee, the helm had been bumped, putting the boat into a slow, arcing left turn. In a blur, the gybing boom swung across the deck and connected solidly with Pick's plate carrier, knocking the wind out of him and driving him airborne over the steel lifelines and into the murky water.

XXIV

[ONE]

If there was one place Pick felt completely at home, it was in the water. Having grown up mostly in Southern California, Pick had taken up surfing at a young age and spent most of his summers either at the beach or in the pool playing water polo. His passion for the sport had led him to the Naval Academy, where he'd lettered all four years and been named team captain.

But none of that mattered when he plunged into the Severn River.

The swinging boom had knocked the wind out of him, but thankfully the plate carrier had blunted its impact and prevented any real damage. But that bright side was quickly overshadowed by the weight of the ceramic ballistic plates pulling him to the bottom of the river.

Pick had lost his grip on the LSA TX4 when he hit the water, but his more immediate concern was the very real threat of drowning. Had he been wearing the plate carrier he normally wore while with his Raider team, he would have already grasped the emergency doffing handles on his cummerbund and yanked on the toggles on his shoulder straps to separate the front plate carrier from the rear, freeing him from the deadly anchor.

But he wasn't. And he wasn't sure if the borrowed FBI plate carrier even had an emergency doffing mechanism.

Pick's ears popped as the weighted chest rig carried him deeper into the river. He could have tried an eggbeater kick to keep himself afloat—he had trained himself to tread water while holding weights during water polo conditioning—but it would have sapped him of his strength and left him with nothing in the tank. Instead, he focused on slowing his heart rate while releasing a thin stream of bubbles to relieve the pressure on his taxed lungs.

Methodically, Pick felt across the front of his plate carrier, searching for a loop that would instantly free him. Finding none, he worked his hands down to the cummerbund and ripped one side of Velcro free, then the other. He reached for the shoulder straps and pushed upward, trying to lift the plate carrier off over his head. But it wouldn't clear past the bump helmet and headset.

Dammit, Pick!

A burst of bubbles broke free in a frustrated grunt as he released his grip on the shoulder straps and reached for the chin strap holding the helmet in place. Kneeling on the muddy bottom, ten feet below the receding sailboat, his lungs burned for air, and he fought against the almost overwhelming instinct to take a breath while pinching on either side of the buckle to release the chin strap. It broke apart easily, and he ripped the helmet from his head and flung it to the side before again grasping the plate carrier's shoulder straps.

He started kicking his legs to slow his descent while shoving upward again on the straps to lift the plate carrier over his head. Tossing it to the side, he let go of the weight that had been pulling him down and felt an immediate buoyancy that almost seemed to propel him upward to the surface.

But he had no idea how far he had to swim before he could breathe.

Hold on, Pick!

Just hold on.

After several seconds of panicked swimming, Pick finally broke the surface and gasped for air. His lungs ached with the exertion of not breathing and his legs burned from the lack of oxygen. But with that one inhale of fresh air, Pick felt invigorated and immediately back in the fight.

He was no longer armed, protected by the ballistic plate carrier, or connected to the Secret Service command net. But he was alive and bound and determined to show Javi what it meant to face off against a Raider. And not just any Raider.

It's high time I lived up to my legacy.

Pick looked left and right, orienting himself as he bobbed just above the surface of the water. The sailboat was just beyond his reach to his left, but his eyes were already tracking movement on the starboard bow, where Javi was climbing aboard a rigid-hull inflatable boat. For a moment, Pick thought it was the same one he had borrowed from the Santee Basin, but quickly realized it was not.

It must have already been tied alongside the sloop.

He kept his profile low to the water, knowing that he was a sitting duck if Javi looked back and saw him breaking the surface. But he couldn't just bob like a cork in the water and do nothing.

Especially when he saw the bound and gagged midshipman sitting in the back of the RHIB, staring at Pick with wide and helpless eyes.

Ethan!

Pick lowered his head and began swimming to the boat just as he heard the outboard motor cough and sputter. He lifted his head and saw Javi standing at the center console, looking over his shoulder at Pick with a blend of surprise and humor. He probably hadn't expected

Pick to surface from the depths of the Severn and thought he still had the upper hand.

Pick put his face back into the water and kicked harder, trying to eat up as much distance as possible before his former roommate put the boat in gear and sped off with the President's son. Then he heard the outboard roar to life and felt a rush of water suddenly blasting into him. He looked up and saw the RHIB just feet from his face.

But it was quickly pulling away.

No!

Pick buried his face in the water again and sprinted against the boat's wake. He knew it was futile to try catching up to the motorboat, but it wasn't in his nature to give up. No matter how dire the situation, no matter how hopeless it seemed.

Pick was the grandson of Corporal Kenneth "Killer" McCoy and the son of General P.K. "Killer" McCoy. He was a third-generation Marine, a Marine Raider, and the Presidential Agent.

It's time I accepted who I was born to be.

Then Pick felt something slither along his body, and he quickly clamped his outstretched hand onto the retreating line. Synthetic fibers burned into his skin from the friction as he tried to gain purchase on the rope, but he only squeezed tighter.

Suddenly, his hand came to a stop on a knot, and he felt his body being pulled through the water.

It's time Javi met a real Killer.

[TWO]

If Pick thought he was drowning before, being pulled through the water behind the rigid-hull inflatable boat gave him a new appreciation for the sensation. He coughed and sputtered, twisting his head left and right to try to find clear air to breathe. But through it all, he never lost sight of his goal and reached hand over hand to pull himself closer to the boat.

Javi must have seen Pick clinging to the mooring line, because the boat suddenly swerved erratically and plunged him into the thickest part of the boat's wake. Pick almost lost his grip, but he used the momentary slack in the mooring line to wrap a loop around his hand, creating additional friction to hold him in place. But losing his grip was quickly becoming his secondary concern.

Pick's lungs—already taxed from being dragged to the bottom of the river—were screaming at him once more. He twisted and turned from one shoulder to the next, trying to find a small eddy of air from which to inhale a shallow breath. Without it, he was at risk of blacking out and drowning while only feet from the President's son and the man who had abducted him.

But why?

It was an intrusive thought, a question that bubbled to the surface even as he fought for his life. But something was gnawing at the back of Pick's mind. What was in it for Javi? Why go through all the trouble of orchestrating terrorist attacks across the country, then take a potshot at the President and abduct her son? He just wasn't seeing the whole picture.

Maybe Junior and Ani will find the missing link.

The RHIB reversed directions, and Pick surfaced long enough to gasp in a lungful of air. He skipped across the surface and reeled himself closer before the slack line went taut and submerged him once more. But being closer to the boat, he was able to angle his chest upward against the water and find clear air to breathe.

It was only then that Pick realized Javi's erratic maneuvering wasn't to evade a soggy Marine Raider clinging to the RHIB's mooring line. Hovering just above them was a dark gray Black Hawk helicopter with several bearded operators dangling from the open door and aiming assault rifles down at Javi. A glance over each shoulder confirmed Pick's suspicions that Randy had indeed brought the cavalry.

On either side of them, identical Black Hawks maintained flanking positions to prevent the RHIB from escaping to either shore.

Ting! Ting!

It took Pick a second to recognize the sound over the cacophony of three helicopters in close proximity and the dinghy's noisy outboard. But when the outboard faltered, coughing and sputtering with an associated loss of power, Pick knew that one or both of the SEAL snipers aboard the flanking helicopters had immobilized the rigid-hull inflatable boat.

As the boat coasted to a stop, the mooring line Pick had been clinging to suddenly went slack, and he felt himself submerging in the water once more. He knew this was his chance to close with and destroy the enemy, and he pulled himself hand over hand again until reaching the transom, where the smoking outboard sat impotent and useless.

Pick pulled himself up until his chin was level with the boat's gunwale, but Javi reacted to the boarding attempt by wheeling on him and slashing down with a fixed-blade knife. Pick released his grip on the boat and slid under the surface just as the blade narrowly missed his face and plunged into the side of the boat.

The *inflatable* boat.

Hissss . . .

Pick swam down into the darkness before angling underneath the boat and crossing over to the opposite side. He surfaced slowly, his eyes staring through the brackish water to ensure that Javi hadn't noticed his deception and followed him to the other side. With the coast momentarily clear, Pick kicked hard to the surface and lunged for the gunwale, where he pulled himself up onto the boat's deflating side tube.

The hiss of escaping air had started to gurgle as the helicopter's rotor wash forced water up into the jagged hole created by Javi's temporary loss of composure. It was only a faint sound—barely a whisper compared to the thunderous roar of the swarming helicopters—but it helped disguise Pick's splashes as he kicked once more and propelled himself over the side and into the boat.

As much as he wanted to take a few seconds to catch his breath and relax, the pleading eyes of the President's son spurred him into action. He pushed himself up onto his feet and tried to steady himself against the floundering boat's unpredictable movement. But even that much motion attracted Javi's notice, and Pick's former roommate spun to face him with a surprised sneer.

"You just won't die, will you?"

"You said you came here for me," Pick said. "Now you'll have to deal with me."

Javi glanced up and squinted against the helicopters' rotor wash while twirling the knife in his hand. "And your friends, too, apparently."

"No, Javi. Just me."

His former roommate grinned at him. "Looks like you finally decided to accept what you really are."

It was much the same thought Pick had had only moments earlier, but he wasn't about to admit that to somebody like Javi. "What's that?"

"A killer."

Pick clenched his jaw tight and fought against the torrent of emotions assaulting him. He wasn't just a killer who left a trail of dead bodies in his wake, as Castillo had claimed. He was *Killer* McCoy, a legacy Marine, and the Presidential Agent.

Pick nodded at the President's hog-tied son. "Why not let him go? You've got me."

Javi followed his gaze with feigned disinterest. "He was just business. Dealing with you is personal."

Just business? Whose? ISIS–K? The Cártel de Jalisco Nueva Generación?

"Then let him go, Javi."

Javi shrugged. "Okay, amigo."

Javi bent down and reached for Ethan's bound ankles with the wicked-looking knife. Just as Pick thought he was about to slice through the synthetic rope and free the President's son, he jerked upward on his ankles and toppled him backward over the side of the boat. Pick lurched for Ethan but grasped only air as the plebe disappeared into the Severn with a splash.

"Him or me," Javi taunted.

[THREE]

Pick was frozen with the shock of what had just happened, but he saw several dark shapes dropping out of the surrounding helicopters from the corner of his eye. In an instant, he realized that SEALs had dropped into the river to rescue the hog-tied midshipman, leaving Pick to focus on the threat in front of him.

"You," he growled.

Javi smiled. "I was hoping you'd say that."

Pick lowered his head and lunged for his former roommate, attempting another tackle without the burden of cumbersome body armor. But Javi had been expecting it, and he countered with a lunge of his own, twisting and driving the knife up into Pick's midsection.

Pick saw the glint of steel slicing through the air and brought his forearm down to block the strike, but the blade cut through his flesh as Javi yanked the knife back in frustration. Pick's forearm erupted with icy agony, but he was enraged by the thought of Javi getting away with such death and destruction. At first he had wanted to make Javi pay for what he had done to Hannah. Now he just wanted him dead.

"I expected more from you," Javi said, reversing the grip on the knife with a flourishing twirl, then spinning to deliver a backhanded strike aimed for Pick's head.

But the flashy nature of Javi's martial arts meant that he had telegraphed his intent even before taunting his opponent. Pick bladed his body and used his wounded arm to block the second attack, knowing that a second wound on the same limb would be less harmful than opening a fresh cut on his right and dominant arm.

"I've not yet begun to fight," Pick said, as he parried the strike and quickly retreated before sustaining another cut.

"Did you just quote John Paul Jones?"

Pick wasn't sure he'd heard the question correctly and shook his head. He was starting to feel dizzy and glanced down at his arm to see blood pouring from the cut and dripping onto the sinking boat's deck. Even without consciously being aware of it, Pick knew he was losing a lot of blood and needed to end the fight before it got much worse.

"That's not the one I'd go with," Pick replied, careful not to slur his words and give Javi any reason to think he had already been defeated.

"No?"

Javi thrust the knife at him, but Pick quickly jumped back and chopped downward with both hands to prevent the blade from piercing the soaked shirt covering his chest.

"Which one, then?"

As Javi yanked the knife back, Pick lost his balance and stumbled forward. He went down on one knee and braced himself with his bleeding arm as he looked up into Javi's smiling face. Then, with a burst of energy, he lunged upward and wrapped Javi in a tight bear hug, pressing the side of his face against that of his former roommate as he listened to the knife clatter to the deck.

"Whoever can surprise well," Pick said, "must conquer."

Then, with every ounce of strength he had remaining in his body, Pick twisted and pulled Javi down on top of him, toppling over the deflated gunwale before crashing into the water.

This time, Pick was prepared for the sudden plunge into the river water. He had taken one last gasp of air before his head submerged, but he guessed his former roommate hadn't, based on the way he struggled and fought against him. That thought alone fueled Pick with the energy he needed to keep his arms wrapped tightly around Javi while snaking his legs around him.

A burst of bubbles escaped from Javi as he thrashed from side to side to escape Pick's python-like embrace. Pick twisted and rolled, keeping his head pressed against Javi to prevent him from using his skull as a weapon. He was prepared to drown to end Javi's campaign of terror, but he felt something brush against his opposite cheek and felt as if God himself had intervened and given him the perfect solution.

No dumb bastard ever won a war by going out and dying for his country.

Keeping his left arm clamped around Javi, Pick reached back with his right and grabbed the floating piece of debris he recognized as the mooring line he had used to pull himself aboard the boat. He closed his eyes to picture the submerged battlefield, then looped the line around Javi's neck. He looped it around a second time, then released his hold on his former roommate to grasp the rope with both hands and plant his feet against Javi's chest.

Then, with all the strength Pick had remaining in his body, he simultaneously pulled on the rope and kicked Javi with both feet. He felt the line go taut in his grip as the loops closed around Javi's neck and cut off blood flow to his brain.

He won it by making the other poor dumb bastard die for his country.

With the words of George S. Patton Jr. echoing in his mind, Pick continued to pull on the rope long after Javi stopped struggling to free himself. His ears were filled with the sound of his heartbeat thundering over the swirling water of the Severn River, but he wasn't about to release his grip and give Javi the chance to escape justice yet again. Pick was going to see this through to the end, no matter its cost.

But the sound of his heartbeat began to grow faint, and the adrenaline fueling his rapid heart rate began to ebb, leaving him feeling weak and lethargic. His arm burned, and his lungs ached. His coherent thoughts suddenly became less so, and he realized he was on the verge of blacking out.

Pick gave one last tug on the rope, then released his hold and began to swim for the surface. He looked up and saw rays from the afternoon sun shining into the water before the darkness swallowed them whole. He kicked and propelled himself upward, trying like hell to reach the light before the darkness consumed him, too.

But it was too late.

Pick stopped swimming as his vision closed in and a sense of peace settled over him.

At least I got him.

XXV

[ONE]

Marine One

U.S. Marine Corps VH-92 Patriot

Over Hospital Point

Annapolis, Maryland

1635 3 April 2026

President Natalie Cohen leaned forward in her seat and pressed her face against the window as the Sikorsky VH-92 Patriot descended over the athletic fields of Hospital Point. There were three other helicopters already there, dark gray MH-60M Black Hawks she was told belonged to the elite U.S. Army helicopter unit, the 160th Special Operations Aviation Regiment.

"What's going on?" she asked, probably for the fiftieth time since they had taken evasive action to escape the shoulder-fired surface-to-air missile.

The Secret Service agent who had been by her side during the entire flight listened to the radio chatter over her earpiece, patiently trying to field her boss's questions while gleaning whatever intelligence was being relayed over the command net. "They've recovered Commodore," she said. "He's unharmed."

Natalie leaned back in her seat and closed her eyes with a loud exhale. "Thank God—"

But the special agent continued with her debriefing. "They've pulled Killer from the river as well, but he's wounded and unconscious."

Her eyes shot open, and she leaned forward again. Her afternoon had been a roller coaster of emotions that she couldn't quite rein in. "What happened to him?"

"We're not sure yet."

The helicopter's deck tilted upward slightly as the pilot flared to stop their forward movement and settled Marine One onto Hospital Point's grassy surface. Following protocol, she waited in her seat until the Secret Service detail on the ground gave her protective agent the all-clear signal. But it seemed to be taking too long, and Natalie was growing impatient.

At last, her shadow looked at her and nodded. "It's all clear, Madam President."

Natalie grasped her seat belt's buckle and struggled for several moments to release the mechanism before flinging it to the side. What was supposed to have been a quiet afternoon for a proud mother to secretly watch her youngest son live out his dream of attending the United States Naval Academy had been anything but. It had started out as a potential terrorist attack staged from a condo in nearby Eastport and evolved to a missile attack on Marine One and an attempted assassination of the President of the United States. It was understandable that Natalie was flustered.

By the time she freed herself from her seat, the forward boarding door had been opened and the stairs lowered. But before she even stood to make her way to the exit, a large and muscular man bounded up the steps and turned to her with something akin to relief etched on his face.

"Thank God you're safe, Madam President."

She recognized the deputy director of the Secret Service immediately. "I'm fine, Joel."

"Fine? Somebody tried taking a shot at you—"

"And missed," she said, ending his thought for him but sounding far more confident than she felt.

He hung his head. "This is my fault, ma'am."

Natalie stood and placed both hands on Joel's shoulders. "I'm fine, Joel. But if you plan on keeping me from seeing my son a second longer, I'll expect your resignation on my desk first thing in the morning."

He glanced up and saw the familiar sparkle in her eye that hinted that she was only half-joking. "Yes, Madam President."

He moved aside to let Natalie and her personal shadow descend from Marine One and out onto the open space of Forrest Sherman Field. But she paused before stepping out from the claustrophobic confines of the helicopter and gripped Joel Isaacson's arm.

"I need you to do something for me, Joel."

"Anything, Madam President."

"Find my son and bring him straight to me."

Joel nodded resolutely. "Yes, Madam President."

After he had disappeared, she continued her descent from the helicopter and came face-to-face with a gathering of large and bearded men outfitted for war and wearing a subdued camouflage pattern. Only one of them stood out as clearly not an operator, and she leaned in to her protective agent as she wondered who she had to thank for saving her son.

"Who're they?"

"SEALs from the Navy's JSOC task force in Virginia Beach," the special agent replied. "Apparently, Killer arranged for reinforcements on his own."

He's just like Castillo.

"Who's that one?" Natalie asked as the young man turned and locked eyes with her.

"I'll find out, ma'am."

Natalie stopped and watched her protective shadow crossing the grass while gesturing for the man who was clearly not a SEAL to join her. He hesitated for a moment, then broke away from the group and met with the Secret Service special agent in the open. They spoke quietly for several seconds before the special agent turned and led him back to where Natalie waited.

"Madam President, this is Lieutenant Commander Randy Richardson of the Navy's JSOC task force."

"So, you *are* a SEAL," Natalie said.

"No, ma'am," Randy replied. "I'm actually a naval aviator."

"A *pilot*?"

"Yes, ma'am."

She looked to the dark gray helicopters that were sitting idle. "I thought these were Army helicopters. But thank you for flying those SEALs here to rescue my son."

Randy gave her a strange look, then his eyes widened. "Oh, no, ma'am. I don't think you understand. I didn't fly one of the helicopters. You have Army pilots to thank for that."

"You didn't? Then what are you doing here?"

Randy shook his head. "To be honest, I'm not really sure. It all started about a week ago when I was preparing to meet with my biological father for lunch in Virginia Beach."

Virginia Beach . . .

"Who's your father?" Natalie asked.

Randy seemed reluctant to answer at first. "Well, the man who got my mother pregnant is a retired Army colonel by the name of Charley Castillo."

Natalie reached out and grasped Randy's hands. "Charley's your father?"

Randy shrugged. "Other than taking me flying for the first time with my grandfather in a Cessna, he wasn't much of a father. But maybe I got a little bit of his personality, because I've been helping Pick McCoy find the person responsible."

"McCoy? Where is he?"

Randy's answer—if he gave her one—was drowned out by the one voice that could make her forget that she was the President of the United States.

"Mom!"

[TWO]

When Pick opened his eyes, he was surprised to discover that he was no longer submerged in the Severn River and scrambling to reach the surface. He wasn't resting on the fiberglass deck of a boat or the steel floor of a helicopter. Instead, Pick recognized that he was lying flat on his back in the grass, staring up into the deep blue sky while a myriad of strange faces surrounded him. Most of them had beards and reminded him of the Raiders he had left behind in Iraq.

"He's coming around," one of them yelled. He looked the most like a Viking pillager.

Another—clean-shaven and dressed in a green Navy working uniform—leaned over him and shined a brilliant light into each of his eyes. "Captain McCoy, can you hear me?"

Pick blinked against the light and turned his head to escape the beam's brilliance. "Yeah, I hear you. I just can't see you."

"Do you know where you are?"

His head felt thick, almost as if his thoughts had turned to sludge and were slow in reaching the point where he could understand them. But a dull pain radiating up his arm had triggered a memory that he suspected was more recent than he cared to admit, and he lifted his head to look down at his bandaged arm.

"Where is he?" Pick asked.

"Who?"

"He means Commodore," the pillager replied, squatting low as if to speak with Pick in confidence. "We pulled him from the water. He's wet and scared, but otherwise unharmed."

Pick shook his head and rubbed his tongue across the roof of his mouth. It felt thick and heavy, mimicking the way his brain felt. "No. Not him."

"Who?" the clean-shaven sailor asked again.

"What are you? An owl?" another bearded warrior asked.

Pick saw the sailor look up at the stranger with bewilderment, but the memory of a knife cutting through his arm sliced through the fog enveloping his brain. Suddenly, the entirety of the afternoon's events flashed through his mind, and he remembered everything.

"Javi," Pick croaked, then paused to try swallowing against the dryness in his mouth. "Javier Santiago. Where is he?"

"Who's he?" the sailor asked.

"That the bastard you sent to Davy Jones's locker?" the pillager asked.

Pick's mind had cleared enough to recognize that he hardly considered the bottom of the Severn befitting a metaphor for the oceanic abyss and final resting place of drowned sailors. But he took the man's point. "Did you recover his body?"

At first the squatting Viking said nothing and only looked at his brethren circling them. "Yeah. We got him. You did him good, too."

Pick breathed a sigh of relief but felt nothing for having taken a life. He had long since accepted that there were people in the world who merited remorse, and there were those who didn't.

Javi was one of the latter.

"You look like shit, boss."

This time, Pick needed no help in placing a face to the voice. He turned his head and saw Junior and Ani strolling across the grassy field, flanked by several of the Hostage Rescue Team operators. He pushed himself up onto an elbow, swatting aside the corpsman's attempt to keep him on his back.

"At least Randy showed up with these frogmen when he did," Pick said. "But I'm a little fuzzy on what happened after I blacked out and almost drowned. Anybody care to fill me in?"

Junior waved aside the corpsman and squatted next to Pick. "After Javier pushed Commodore over the side of the boat, a few of our intrepid undersea brothers—"

"You make them sound like mermaids," Ani protested.

"We prefer mermen," the Viking said, then waved at Junior to continue.

The spook nodded his thanks before going on. "Anyway, a few of these *mermen* here dropped from their Black Hawks to rescue the hostage. With you focused on Javier, they were able to get the President's son hoisted back aboard the helicopter and to dry land in no time."

"And they left me there?"

"Maybe they should have," another voice said. Pick turned his head and saw Randy walking up with a smile on his face.

Pick recognized the good-natured jibe. "You righteous piece of—"

"Relax, *Killer*," Randy said, his lip curling up into a smile. "You really are the most stubborn bastard I've ever met."

That's ironic, coming from Castillo's bastard.

Pick had always doubted that the President made the right choice in selecting him to replace Castillo as the Presidential Agent. But after what he had just gone through, maybe he had been too harsh in his self-evaluation.

Randy continued. "And it's a good thing, too."

"Why's that?"

"Because the President said she's going to need you to figure out why Javier Santiago kidnapped her son."

"Because he was doing his father's bidding," Pick said.

"His father?" Randy asked.

"I had it all wrong. Rafi fed me a story about rival cartels and his son's quest for revenge, but it was all bullshit." Pick pushed himself upright, wincing at the sudden flare of pain radiating through his body as he turned to Junior. "Did you find out how they're connected?"

Junior shot a hesitant glance at Ani, who nodded. "Tell him," she said.

"Tell me what?"

The spook hesitated for a moment before answering. "Mortimer Cohen—the President's ex-husband—sits on the Admiral Farragut Academy's board of directors. But he's not the only familiar name."

Pick already knew. "Rafael Santiago."

"That's right," Junior said.

"So, they know each other. But what would motivate Rafi to kidnap the President's son?"

"Mortimer Cohen is a money guy. He graduated from Princeton and worked as an investment banker until his career took a backseat to then–Secretary of State Natalie Cohen. After their divorce, he started a venture capital firm and invested heavily in risky start-ups."

"Let me guess," Pick said. "Was one of them a company out of Laredo?"

The spook nodded. "Rio Bravo Energy."

"What's that?"

"The company Rafael Santiago started to use as a cover for a narcotic-smuggling and human-trafficking operation with ties to Cártel del Noreste. And according to my sources in the FBI, Mortimer recently threatened to pull his funding for Rio Bravo Energy."

"That's a pretty good motive," Pick said.

"It wasn't the first time, either," Ani added.

Pick turned to her. "Why would he do that?"

"We think it's because he was growing nervous about the company's legitimacy."

"You said he had threatened it before. Does that mean he didn't follow through?"

Again, Ani was the one who answered. "We think Rafael Santiago used his position on the school's board of directors to learn that Mortimer's youngest son had accepted an appointment to the Naval Academy and that it was being kept a secret from the public. That's what we like to call leverage."

"Okay, so he threatened to expose him? Harm him?"

Junior shrugged. "We're not sure. But we do know that two weeks ago, Mortimer pulled funding from Rio Bravo Energy and filed an affidavit with the FBI claiming that Rafael Santiago was engaged in illicit activities."

"That's what we like to call motive," Ani added.

If what they were saying was true, then it meant that Pick's suspicions had been right. Everything he had learned on his trip south of the border had been a ploy to convince him that the attacks were nothing more than Javi's personal vendetta against those who had put him behind bars. Worse, it meant that Rafi's disappearance had been orchestrated as part of his overall plot to willingly sacrifice his own son while putting pressure on the President's ex-husband."

"Where's Mortimer now?"

"We don't know," Junior said. "Nobody can locate him."

Randy spoke up. "Which brings us back to what the President said to me not five minutes ago."

"Remind us," Pick said.

"She said—and I quote—'I'm going to need him to figure out why Javier Santiago kidnapped my son.'" Randy paused. "I'm just guessing here, but she's probably going to want you to find out what happened to her ex-husband, too."

There would be time later to figure out whether the President would even want to continue with the Presidential Agent program. As Castillo had been apt to point out, Pick had left a trail of dead bodies in his wake and could use a bit more work on the clandestine side of things. His first time at the helm of the Office of Organizational Analysis hadn't gone as smoothly as anybody had hoped, but better than he had expected.

Pick knew he would likely be summoned to the White House in the coming days to atone for his sins, but that was a problem for future Captain P.K. McCoy Jr. The problem current Captain P.K. McCoy Jr. was facing was what to do about the only woman he had ever truly loved.

As the gathered SEALs broke away to prepare for the return flight to Virginia Beach, Pick saw the Superintendent dressed in his summer whites conferring with the President and her son, Midshipman Fourth Class Ethan Cohen. Lieutenant Hannah Rosen stood off to the side like a dutiful aide-de-camp.

Pick ambled close while cradling his bandaged arm and struggling to come up with the right thing to say. Maybe if he had been the ladies' man Charley Castillo had apparently been during his younger years, he might not have been terrified of facing her again.

"Nervous?" a voice asked from behind him.

Pick turned around and saw Randy shadowing him with a grin on his face. "I'm terrified," he said.

"Just tell her how you feel. You don't have to be smooth or debonair. Just be yourself."

Pick was surprised by the advice and thought it was actually quite good. Based on their interactions as midshipmen, he hadn't expected Randy to be an expert on the opposite sex. "That's it?"

Randy smiled at him, then walked away. Pick watched him making his way back to the Black Hawk helicopters, then turned to see Hannah breaking away from the admiral's side and walking toward him.

Here we go.

She stopped a few feet away and thrust her hand out to him. "My name's Hannah. From Savannah."

He grinned at the memory. "On purpose?"

The corners of her mouth twitched downward as if to hide her smile. "What's your name? Where are you from?"

"Pick McCoy," he said. "And where I'm from doesn't rhyme."

"It doesn't have to."

This time, Hannah didn't bother trying to hide her smile. She stepped forward and wrapped her arms around Pick for a hug that was long overdue.

[THREE]

Sentara Virginia Beach General Hospital

1060 First Colonial Road

Virginia Beach, Virginia

1230 5 April 2026

U.S. Army Colonel C.G. Castillo (retired) groaned as he pressed on the remote control's button to elevate his hospital bed. He felt every bit of his age, clearly not in the same shape he had been when he had taken two short Russian rounds—the 5.45x39—in the ass and the leg while trying to rescue DEA Special Agent Timmons.

You've come a long way, Charley. But maybe it's time to let the young bucks have their turn in the spotlight.

His bed reached the highest setting, and Charley moved his thumb to the button to turn on the television that was mounted high on the wall in the corner of the room. He had avoided watching the news since coming out of anesthesia following his last surgery, but thought it was time he faced the music. He had completely botched his response to the attack on the oceanfront, and he could no longer ignore the facts.

You're not the man you once were.

The door to his private room opened and a nurse appeared, his favorite of all the nurses who had attended to him since he regained consciousness in the hospital. She was short, with long, dark hair and deep brown eyes that seemed to radiate a warmth he suspected was reserved only for the truly deserving patients. In his younger years, he might have even made a pass at her.

But times have changed, Charley, my boy.

"Mr. Castillo?" the nurse asked, hesitantly sticking her head into the room and flashing one of her patented smiles in his direction.

"You can come in," he said.

She hesitated for a moment longer, then pushed open the door and walked in. "Are you comfortable?"

Castillo gestured to the web of wires and tubes connected to or inserted into his body in one fashion or another. "Comfortable enough, I guess," he said. "Unless you can arrange to make two martinis."

She blushed. "I'm on duty and not allowed to drink."

"Oh, no," he said. "They're both for me."

If anything, the coloring in her cheeks deepened with embarrassment. "Is there anything I can get you?" She paused. "Anything other than a martini . . . or two?"

Castillo pointed the remote at the television. "Think you can have them adjust the satellite dish so I can get a clearer picture of what's going on in the world?"

The nurse looked up at the TV set and saw that the picture was indeed distorted by static. But she shrugged. "I'm sorry, but I'm not sure who to call for that . . ."

He took pity on her. She was probably only in her late twenties and not accustomed to the more refined forms of flirtation. In his day, Castillo had been known as something of an aficionado.

But those days are long gone, Charley.

He sighed. "It's okay. At least I can hear what they're saying."

The nurse checked his chart, then walked around his bed to open the curtains and let more light into the room. Castillo squinted, wishing she would just leave him be so he could wallow in self-pity over being past his prime and no longer in the fight. He had thought long and hard about it over the last few days and decided that he would call Natalie Cohen—*President Natalie Cohen,* he reminded himself—and tender his resignation.

Killer McCoy might not be entirely ready to step into the role of Presidential Agent, but he had to be at least as good as Major Charley Castillo had been when the President asked him to find a missing Boeing 727.

"Mr. Castillo?"

He craned his neck to look up at the nurse. "Yes, my dear?"

"I forgot to tell you. You have a visitor."

He had been afraid of that. Ever since the terrorist attack had thwarted his attempts to make amends with his bastard son, he had been expecting Randy to come storming in and demand some form of apology. Of course, he hadn't expected things to turn out the way they had. "You can send him in."

"Him?" The nurse sounded confused. "I'm sorry, but your visitor is a woman."

Abuela.

"I should have known," he muttered. "You can send her in, too."

The nurse excused herself and Castillo took a few moments to smooth out his sheets and make his hospital bed appear almost as neat as the ones he had made as a cadet at West Point. No matter what effort he put into it, Doña Alicia would find faults in it. And she would both excuse and ignore them outright.

Of all the people in his life, she was the only one who had never let him down or let him fall too far from expectation. She put all her faith in him—warranted or not—and never let him feel like a failure. She had been that way since the first moment he met her when she came to das Haus im Wald to relieve his mother from the burden of trying to care for a twelve-year-old while terminally ill.

His Abuela was a true gift from God above, and he felt ashamed that she would have to see him like this.

"Charley?"

The timid voice from the doorway sent chills down his spine. "Who's that?"

The door opened wider, and his heart stopped when he saw a shock of red hair sweep into his hospital room. He almost stabbed repeatedly at the button to administer several doses of pain medication, fearing that he was suffering a dreadfully realistic hallucination brought about by his physical injuries. But as he watched the woman walk into the room and stared into her eyes—as lucid and hypnotic as the day he had met her—he knew the truth.

"Svetlana?"

She took in his appearance, and her brow furrowed with concern. "Oh, my Charley!"

"Svetlana!"

She rushed to his bedside and collapsed on top of him, oblivious to the discomfort she caused. But to be fair, Castillo was oblivious to the same. His heart had stopped beating upon hearing her voice and only resumed its natural cadence when she placed her chest on his.

"Why are you here?" he asked.

It was only the first question of many.

"Because I'm your wife," Svetlana replied. "And a wife belongs with her husband."

Good enough for me.

★ ★ ★

AUTHOR'S NOTE

In the summer of 1990, when my friends and I weren't playing soldiers in the woods around our neighborhood in the Pacific Northwest, we were glued to the television. Instead of watching Nickelodeon or MTV, we tuned in to CNN to watch Saddam Hussein defy the United Nations and invade Kuwait. For me, it was the prologue to a career that spanned almost three decades.

By the time Desert Storm kicked off, I already knew what I wanted to do with my life. In November 1985, *Boys' Life* magazine published an article titled "A Day at the Naval Academy." I was eight years old and more impressed by the size of the "enormous four-winged dining room" than I was with what it really meant to serve in the military. But that article changed my life—even more than the superlative documentary on the United States Navy Fighter Weapons School that came out the following year.

Before Saddam Hussein invaded Kuwait, I already knew that I would attend the U.S. Naval Academy, become a fighter pilot, and go to Top Gun. I went to air shows, toured Navy ships during Seattle's annual Seafair celebration, and read every book about the military that I could get my hands on—both nonfiction and fiction.

Tom Clancy, Dale Brown, Stephen Coonts, Larry Bond, and W.E.B. Griffin. Next to the television in the den at my friend's house was a floor-to-ceiling bookshelf that covered an entire wall. I spent hours perusing the titles of the books there and can still remember being drawn to a green paperback titled *The Berets*.

One by one, I borrowed each novel in the Brotherhood of War series and fell in love with the storytelling of a person who would become one of my favorite authors. By the time I reported to the U.S. Naval Academy, I had moved on to The Corps series, which greatly influenced my decision to join the Semper Fi Society and pursue commissioning as a Marine officer following graduation.

But in the end, I remained true to the goals set by an eight-year-old, and I commissioned as an Ensign before reporting to Pensacola for flight school in the summer of 1999. During my career, I flew combat missions from three different aircraft carriers, graduated from Top Gun, called in air strikes from the ground in Afghanistan, and hunted terrorists in Africa with the Joint Special Operations Command. Over twenty-three years, I traveled the world, served with heroes, and lived out a dream that began with a *Boys' Life* article in 1985.

It would be a gross understatement to say it is an honor to add to the legacy of W.E.B. Griffin. In many ways, it feels like I have been preparing my whole life for this moment.

Jack Stewart